THERE ARE THIRTY WAYS TO MAKE A SCENE

LISA JOELLE

LISAJoelle

 FriesenPress

One Printers Way
Altona, MB R0G 0B0
Canada

www.friesenpress.com

ISBN
978-1-03-917520-4 (Hardcover)
978-1-03-917519-8 (Paperback)
978-1-03-917521-1 (eBook)

1. FICTION, FRIENDSHIP

Distributed to the trade by The Ingram Book Company

To the beautiful group of ladies who attend canvas, past, present, and future: The creativity in me sees the creativity in you and blesses it.

1.

October 14. Sunny 15C°.

Isla's rusted brown hatchback looked out of place on the newly paved street, it's boulevards boasting spindly young trees. These trees would grow alongside the small children who inhabited the newly constructed houses. Isla slowed and u-turned again, looking for a parking spot amongst the rows of mini-vans and sport utility vehicles. She spotted a space behind a sleek black SUV, with shiny aluminum rims and dark tinted glass, a cool vehicle except for the tell-tale sign of suburbia, stick figure decals on the tinted back window: golf dad, yoga mom, ballerina daughter and hockey son.

"I hate the suburbs" said Priya, using the cracked passenger-side view mirror to apply plum lipstick as Isla parked. "I don't care what gender this baby is. Why do we have to spend our free time at a large bleak house with tedious people?"

"Bleak and tedious? Would you like a moment to deal with your negativity?" countered Isla, lingering in the driver seat. "I don't really want to be here either, but Emma is our best friend."

Isla reached into the back and grabbed a small package wrapped in brown paper and tied with a simple piece of string.

"You brought a gift?" asked Priya, dismayed.

1

"You didn't?"

"In the past year and a half, I have bought a shower gift, a bridesmaid dress, a wedding gift, a housewarming gift, and soon, a baby gift. No, it didn't cross my mind to bring a gender reveal gift! And how is Emma going to repay me? Do you think she'll attend a party to raise money to pay for medical school?" said Priya.

"I can picture it now," said Isla. "It will be completely tacky. Off brand chips and boxed wine served in plastic cups, and a giant bucket for cash donations."

"They could've sent an email." Priya dropped her head to the dashboard. "I'm so fucking tired."

"And cranky. This isn't my idea of fun either, but Emma invited us, and I *have* to be here, or I'll hear it from the professor. So thank you for coming with me. Please be nice and don't say '*fuck*' – there will be small children." Isla got out of the car, and they crossed toward the grey two-story house, which looked just like every other house on the block, except for the teal door.

Isla Peters was petite and curvy with long unruly red hair and bright green eyes, her pale skin dotted with freckles. She dressed in bright colours and mixed patterns; today it was green jeans, with an ikat patterned navy tunic and heels –always heels. In contrast to her, Priya Dhaliwal was tall and slim with medium brown skin, her black hair was cut short and asymmetrical. She had on ripped black jeans and a simple white t-shirt, her heavy make-up hiding the fact that she had been up most the night studying.

Best friends since the middle of ninth grade. Both girls had struggled to find their place at a new much larger school. Isla's locker was next to the locker belonging to Justin Green, who at six foot four and still growing, was a popular sports star already. Regularly he would close his locker, turn, and not see Isla, who was much shorter. Then he'd run into her, throwing her into the lockers and continuing on his way. One day in February, he slammed into her without apologising.

"Yes, she is short, but watch where you are going, dumb ass!"

Isla looked to see who was yelling, and there was Priya. Her hands on her hips glaring up at giant Justin Green. Justin looked from Isla to Priya and mumbled an apology. That was the moment Isla knew she had found her person.

"Hello and welcome to Andrew and Emma's! I'm Alicia, the official greeter!" The woman who answered the door was unfamiliar. She was dressed in trendy activewear with her hair pulled tightly into a high ponytail, and her voice had a bouncy, birdlike quality to it. "Let me guess—you must be Isla and Priya? Come in! I've been dying to meet you. Emma speaks so highly of both of you. Her childhood best friends, how precious!" Alicia pressed her hand to her heart and gaped at them. She continued her chirping while Isla and Priya exchanged annoyed looks.

"Thank goodness today is such a gorgeous day! You never know with this time of year, it could be the last warm day before winter. The party is in the yard. Go down through the kitchen and out the garden doors. How silly of me–Isla you're Andrew's sister? You have been here before?"

Isla forced a smile until they were out of sight.

"Living the suburban dream," Priya whispered sarcastically as they walked through the pristine house.

"Don't laugh, this will be us someday."

"Maybe you, but not me."

"We'll see, Ms. Never-Getting-Married," said Isla.

"I think you mean *Dr.* Never-Getting-Married."

Isla laughed as she pushed the garden door open, and gasped as they entered onto the deck. The yard was decorated in pale pinks and blues, bunting was strewn above the deck, and clusters of balloons were equally spaced around the perimeter of the yard. A table was set up with a multi- coloured cake. On the top, a mini chalk board sign asked, *"Boy or Girl?"*

A gang of children chased each other, weaving between the adults, as their mothers yelled out ignored instructions: "Be careful!" "Please don't get that dress dirty!" "No more cookies!"

"Priya! Isla!" came a squeal from across the yard. Emma rushed towards them, her shoulder-length, gold-blond hair catching a glint of the late afternoon sun. Isla stared at how much rounder Emma looked since the last time they had seen her, just two weeks ago.

Isla and Priya made it through ninth grade, the next year they were lucky enough to have lockers separated by only one locker. And it was Emma who had the one between them. Quickly, her organized, steady, calmness in both dramatic and mundane moments turned the inseparable duo into a trio.

"Em!" Isla exclaimed accepting the first hug. "You look—pregnant. I mean amazing."

"I've really popped in the last couple of weeks," Emma said proudly, smoothing her pink maternity dress over her bump so they could admire it.

"You look great," said Priya, accepting a hug as well.

"Thanks. Alicia and I have been doing prenatal yoga. Can you believe she's due only a month after me? She's hardly showing, and it's her third. Anyway, prenatal yoga: A-maz-ing! It's really helped me keep in shape, and plus I feel so in tune with Li—-the baby. Oh shoot, I almost gave away the surprise!" Emma giggled.

"Aunt Nancy!" she called suddenly, waving at the older couple who just entered the yard. "We'll chat later—have a drink and some snacks," she said, pointing at the lavish spread of food before dashing off.

Priya poured herself a glass of punch. "What's the likelihood there's booze in this?"

"Ha," replied Isla, piling a plate full of chips and dip. Glancing around, they tried to figure out what to do next. Priya raised an eyebrow towards the group of young men standing in the corner of the yard.

"Don't get your hopes up. They're all married," said Isla, waving at her older brother, Andrew, who was standing in the middle of the group.

Just then, a heavyset woman in her late fifties came barrelling past them. Today, she was wearing teal pants with a large purple cardigan with tiny, embroidered carrots. She had shoulder length greying dark hair with a streak of pink in front. Though her eccentric appearance didn't always convey her intelligence and ambition, it did however express her contempt for staying in fashion.

"Mom!" called Isla. The woman stopped and turned back to the girls.

"Isla! You're here on time!" exclaimed the woman, grabbing her daughter's cheek and kissing it, turning to Priya and doing the same.

"Hi Dee," replied Priya.

"What are you wearing?" Isla questioned.

"Isn't it hilarious? Carrots!" Dee said, breaking into loud peals of laughter. "I found it at MCC this week. Perfect for fall, don't you think?"

Isla shook her head no. Dee ignored her and continued, "So glad you guys made it! Quite the party huh?"

"Oh yes," said Priya.

"Between you and me, it's ridiculous to spend money on something like this. In our day, we found out what we were having the moment it popped out. Emma said they even have a name picked out. Can you believe it? Isla, I thought you were bringing Michael?" Dee rambled without taking a breath.

"I—uh, he couldn't make it," replied Isla, holding her breath that the subject would be dropped.

"There's Joan! You guys should come say hi — that reminds me, Priya, did you have a chance to read that book on intersectional feminism that I lent you? I would love to hear what you thought, as a woman of colour. Let's talk later, shall we?" she said, rushing away without waiting for an answer.

"The professor is in fine form today," said Isla, scanning the yard for her father.

Priya grabbed her shoulder and looked directly into her eyes. "You haven't told your parents about Michael yet?"

Isla glared back. "No, and now is not the time."

"When are you going to tell them? It's been nearly a month since he dumped you," said Priya.

"It's only been seventeen days, but I don't want to talk about this now. I'd like to make it through the party without crying. I'll tell them at lunch on Sunday."

"Promise me, or I will tell them."

"Fine." Isla huffed. She pointed towards a tall slim man with red hair fading into pale grey, bent over a small flower bed tucked next to a small shed. "Look, there's my dad!"

"Hi, Dad!" Isla called. The older man stood up, startled. He had dirt all over his hands and red creeping into his cheeks.

"Are you weeding?" she asked.

"Well, you see, once the grass starts to creep in and take hold, it becomes very difficult to…umm yes, I was weeding" He picked up a rogue pink napkin as it floated by, wiping most of the dirt off his hands. "How are you guys?"

Priya and Isla shrugged, neither of them willing to offer much. Andrew broke away from his group to join them. He was tall and slim like his dad, but had his mother's brown hair and dark eyes, framed by a fashionable pair of glasses Emma had recently picked out for him. As he was about to greet them, Emma rushed up and grabbed his arm.

"Time for the surprise!" she exclaimed, dragging him back to the deck. The look on his face said *shoot me now*. Isla knew this party was a step away from hell for her introverted brother.

Isla had been thrilled when her brother and best friend got married. They'd been together for so many years, she could hardly remember them being apart. But now Emma and Andrew had crossed over to a new world, full of mortgages and life insurance. She and Priya were left behind, not sure if they even wanted to follow. With a baby on the way, the strings that held them all together had begun to fray.

Emma led Andrew up onto the deck, where Alicia was playing ringmaster, calling everyone to gather for the main event. The cake was front and centre, everyone gathered around, buzzing with anticipation.

"Is this for real?" Priya muttered.

Isla shushed Priya, smiling apologetically to the young mother next to them.

"All right ladies and gentlemen, the moment we've all been waiting for! Time to discover what Emma and Andrew are having," announced Alicia.

"It's a velociraptor" hissed Priya.

Emma and Andrew together picked up the knife, which had pink and blue ribbons tied around it, and sliced into the cake. A professional photographer blitzed around them, capturing the hallowed moment.

"It's a boy!" cried Alicia, and everyone cheered.

Priya rolled her eyes. "I hope he smashes it in her face."

"Alicia's or Emma's?" asked Isla.

"Em's. she deserves it for throwing such a stupid party," said Priya. "How long until we can leave?"

Emma got the crowd's attention. "We are thrilled to be having a boy! His name is…" She paused for dramatic effect. "William Bennet! And we are going to call him Liam."

Receiving the reaction she wanted, she continued, "Thank you all so much for coming! We are so happy to have such wonderful neighbours and friends around us as we enter this new stage of our life." Emma looked lovingly to Andrew who squirmed uncomfortably in the spotlight. "I love my little family so much!"

Immediately, Emma was surrounded by a group of young women, none of whom Isla or Priya recognized. Isla sighed. "Let's go."

Dee caught them sneaking out the gate. "Are you leaving already? You just got here!"

"Pri worked all night, she's tired and grumpy—and it's not really our crowd," Isla said, gesturing to the group of women fawning over Emma.

"They're such nice ladies. Emma's lucky she has made some good friends. I'm sure if you took the time to get to know them, you'd have tons in common with them," Dee encouraged, ever the diplomat.

"She didn't need new friends," Isla protested.

Dee sighed, as they watched the group of women pressing gifts into Emma's hands. Baby blankets, miniature grown-up outfits, and educational toys.

Unimpressed, Isla said, "I'm sure they're all really nice, but I don't think we have anything in common. All Emma cares about these days are babies and decorating her house."

"And we like rum and single men," piped up Priya. Isla jabbed her in the ribs.

"I'll pretend I didn't hear that," said Dee. "Give it time. You three have been friends for so long, I'm sure you'll figure this out."

2.

January 24. Sunny, -28C°.

Each inhale plunged icy air deep into Isla's lungs; each exhale came out as smoke. Each breath slowly stole her inner warmth. Winnipeg was trapped in winter's assault; the wind blew from the north, whipping its way through the cement corridors of downtown. Her destination was only blocks from the famed Portage and Main intersection, coldest in Canada.

She pulled down her wool hat, covering half of her eyes, her shoulders hunched, her body curling into itself, protecting what little warmth remained. Frozen, she arrived at the cement high rise home of Harrison Richard Advertising. Isla was a lower-level bookkeeper, literally – her office was on the lowest floor of HRA.

Instantly hot the moment she entered the elevator, Isla unwrapped the thick scarf from her neck and unzipped her parka. She was envious of everyone else in the elevator who had parking spots in the heated garage below. The spot would cost more than her vehicle was worth, an expense she couldn't justify.

The elevator reached her floor, and she entered through a glass door with the simple HRA logo, square just like everything else at Harrison Richard, each detail of décor precise and meticulously executed. Their clients consisted of lawyers and financial institutions, blue suits, and white shirts. Isla never imagined advertising could be so boring. When her father, one of the blue-suit, white-shirt lawyers, told her about the job, she imagined modern creativity and spirited, democratic discussions. What she hadn't imagined was the cramped storage room she and her officemate shared, or the tediousness of data entry that filled her day. Still, it was better than her past jobs, better than holding a flag for a construction crew, better than serving coffee to the under-caffeinated. What else could a university drop-out do?

"Good morning, Janine" said Isla to her officemate. Isla's was the first desk you came to upon entering the room, so she acted as receptionist, just in case anyone came to visit.

No one did.

The financial department had a distinct hierarchy, and Isla was on the bottom. Her boss, Janine was tucked further back, her desk adjacent to a row of filing cabinets. Not that that was a bad spot to be in — Janine was a benevolent ruler.

"Good morning." Janine responded automatically without looking up, already sitting at her desk, her hands, empty of adornment, steadily clicking away at her computer. Her mousy brown hair with streaks of grey was pulled back in a severe pony-tail, her face bore minimal make-up, and her clothing was dated and ill fitting, aging her prematurely. After a quick glance at the wall clock, she said, "Only two minutes late today."

Because of the bus schedule, Isla was always late. Janine knew it, and neither of them acknowledged it, besides her daily declaration. Janine was one of those people who believed on-time meant five minutes early; for Isla, on-time meant less than fifteen minutes late.

Isla hung up her parka and unpacked her bag, placing her sketchbook next to her keyboard. "I'm going to grab some coffee. Do you want any?"

Janine shook her head, as she did every morning.

On her way to the common area, Isla stopped in to see Greg Teung, who provided technical support for everyone, and occupied the warmest office due to the heat coming off the floor-to-ceiling computer server. Isla pushed the door open and looked around for the small man.

"Damn crickets," muttered a voice from behind the desk.

"Good morning!" Isla said cheerfully, as the cricket chirped again.

Greg banged his head on the desk. He groaned as he emerged, a thick book in one hand, his black hair standing on end. "We're on the twelfth floor and the middle of winter," he said sounding baffled.

"Can I get you a coffee?"

"No," he said, dismissing her with a wave as he sat back at his desk. She was the third person to use coffee as an excuse to warm up in his office that morning.

As Isla left, she heard another chirp. Giggling, she headed for the break room. Besides their offices and a couple of other storage rooms, most of the bottom floor was taken up with the break room. Large floor-to-ceiling windows lined the east wall, showing glimpses of the Red River behind the skyscraper across the street. The room had polished concrete floors, and white walls with large black and white photos. Tables and chairs sat in various configurations and black leather club chairs lined one wall. A small kitchenette was on the other side, stocked with fresh fruit and coffee.

Kelly Morgan was filling four coffee cups. Even though she was a design intern, she dressed like she was the CEO. Fitted suits made of luxurious fabrics, manicured nails, her dark brunette hair hung long down her back — never stringy or frizzy. She wore dark makeup and managed to look chic instead of gothic. Isla was desperately jealous. Design intern sounded a lot more glamorous than bookkeeper-stuck-in-a-storage-room.

Kelly gave Isla a smile in greeting. Isla liked to imagine they were friends, or would be if it were more convenient.

"Queen Suzy must be on a diet," Kelly said, holding up four bright pink artificial sweetener packets.

She was referring to Sue Trembly, head of everything in the small HRA branch. Isla liked Sue, the two times she had been in the same room with her. She was smart, pragmatic, and fair, and she had a certain elegance that some how put you at ease while requiring your best behaviour.

The professor had raised Isla to pay attention to female leadership. Women must work twice as hard for half as much. They *always* deserve respect and deference. Respect for male leadership, on the other hand, needed to be earned, with competence and kindness.

"Have you heard? Some of the partners from Vancouver are coming in this afternoon — some big announcement. Everyone is on edge. Ryan snapped at Angela over her use of the word 'ardent,' and Eric is wearing a suit. Not that I care, but at least it's better than the usual boredom," said Kelly.

Isla smiled and nodded, pretending to understand. To her they were only names learned off the company's website, Ryan Penner graphic designer, Angela Sloan copy writer, Eric Sorenson web design.

"Rumor has it that the Queen is retiring."

"She's way too young to retire!" protested Isla.

"She's older than she looks. The wrinkles on her neck don't lie. Have you seen her husband? He's ancient!" replied Kelly. She finished her line of coffee cups and balanced them on a tray. "I'll see you later."

Isla poured coffee into her handmade mug, her first try at the potter's wheel. It had a wonky wave, and the handle was too small and in an uncomfortable place. But she loved it. She poured cream into the coffee, taking pleasure as it swirled, gradually turning the transparent dark liquid into something opaque and cozy.

Once back at her desk, she spent her morning sorting through bank statements and receipts, her mind on everything but the job at hand. Absentmindedly, she picked up a pencil and started doodling on the paper in front of her.

"You're drawing again," interrupted a voice from behind.

Startled, Isla dropped her pencil, and looked up to see Janine holding out an eraser to her.

Janine sighed out of frustration, "Don't take this the wrong way, but why are you here?"

"Excuse me?" squeaked Isla.

"Why are you a bookkeeper? You obviously don't like your job, and let's be honest – you're not particularly good at it."

Isla, speechless, stared at the papers on her desk. She choked out, "Are you firing me?"

Janine's stern face relaxed into a look of concern. She adjusted her chair and sat down facing Isla. "I'm sorry. That was blunt. Sue asked me to do a six-month evaluation on you this week."

"Evaluation?" asked Isla, her heart sinking. This probably wouldn't end well.

Janine had a clipboard with questions, a pen in hand.

"First question: Has your experience at Harrison Richard Advertising been satisfactory?"

"Yes," Isla said with a false smile.

"Care to elaborate?" asked Janine, clearly not buying it.

"I get to wear nice clothes." Isla regretted her answer immediately. She wasn't going to tell Janine her dream of moving to the art department, a dream that was slowly dying each day in their forgotten basement office.

"Do *you* like this job?" Isla asked, turning the tables.

"I do, very much," replied Janine truthfully. "I get a thrill whenever the numbers reconcile."

Isla's eyes narrowed. It seemed unlikely that numbers could ever produce a thrill in anyone – but Janine looked sincere.

A thrill? Really?

"Why did you choose accounting?" Janine asked, picking up Isla's latest doodle. "You should be designing logos and ad campaigns — why are you down here?"

Feeling cornered, Isla blurted "I didn't choose accounting Michael did."

"Michael did? Who's Michael again?"

The last thing Isla wanted to do was bring her sad personal life up at work, but Janine's voice was kind and her interest seemed genuine. Isla allowed the emotion and words to tumble out, "Michael was my boyfriend. —-I'm here because *he* wanted to be an entrepreneur. *He* thought he had loads of good ideas. And *he* decided it would be best if I quit art school and took a six-month bookkeeping course."

Michael's invented grown-up voice still rang in her head.

"What are you going to do with an arts degree, anyway? Art school is going to muddle your personal style."

She'd listened to him. She'd quit school. Imagine how the professor felt about that.

"We'll be a team! I'll have the business, you can make art and do my books on the side."

"At the time his business plan was shifting weekly," she told Janine. "But I believed in his ideas. I thought he was brilliant and ambitious."

"What happened?"

"Well, Michael's plans didn't exactly work out the way he had hoped. My dad told me about this job, and I applied, thinking it would be temporary until we figured everything out."

"And then?" asked Janine.

"I need to tell you something." He sat in a booth across from her, the bar was packed and loud. There was live music, an electric banjo

14

played at a quick tempo. On their table sat two beers and a plate of nachos. His hand was firm around hers. "I care about you so much Isla, so much, like you don't even know. You are my best friend."

But. Isla saw his lips form the B, his lips so familiar, as familiar as her own.

"But this isn't working any more. You're different now that you have this corporate job. I feel like you don't support my dreams anymore."

All the air was sucked out of the room. Isla couldn't breathe, couldn't speak. She stared at his hand still holding hers. It used to be beautiful, now grotesque. The weight of it trapped her. He'd expected her to fight; that's why they were in public. He was a coward.

Then the final blow.

"I don't think I love you anymore."

"I didn't see it coming," said Isla, her throat clenched up as emotion threatened to spill over.

Janine didn't say anything. Her face was still, her eyes were unfocused as if she too were reliving a different time.

"You gave up your dream and then he stopped loving you. Men are trash," Janine whispered, her words for herself and not Isla. She sat thoughtfully for a moment before continuing. "My ex-husband didn't think I was intelligent enough for university, and I believed him, for years, until he left. My first day at post secondary school was a week after my son's sixth birthday. I was a mature student, I went to school in the mornings, waited tables evenings and weekends, studied during the night while my babies slept in the next room." Janine put the evaluation form back on her desk and reprinted the statement Isla was working on. She took the one Isla had drawn on and replaced it with the clean one. "Don't get stuck here Isla. This is just a stepping-stone. I'll help you reconcile those statements before the meeting."

Later, upstairs, Isla took her time walking through the halls looking at all the artwork on the walls. As she approached the conference room, Kelly grabbed her by the elbow, and cocked her head in the direction of a young man, leaning against the wall typing on his phone, his jaw clenched and unsmiling. He was well dressed, with a slim-cut grey suit showing off his tall athletic frame, his hair wavy on top and short on the sides, recently cut, and his handsome face was clean shaven.

"Yum." Kelly giggled loud enough for him to hear. He didn't look up.

The conference room was standing-room-only by the time they squeezed in, and the stale donuts had been picked over, leaving two empty boxes and half a plain cake donut. They squeezed into a spot by the window.

"Did you see *him*?" Kelly swooned. Before Isla could answer, Sue called everyone to attention. At the front of the room, she was standing next to an older man, dressed comfortably in a sweater and jeans. He had dark hair flecked with grey and a well-groomed beard, and friendly smile that put the room at ease. Isla recognized him from the website as Graham Richards, one of the founding partners from Vancouver. Behind him was the younger man from the hall, still focused on his phone.

"It's nice to be back in sunny Winnipeg," started Graham. The group laughed politely at the obligatory winter weather joke. "We at Harrison Richards value quality, consistency, and diligence. Growth and success in this industry is built on risk takers, those who are willing to step out of their comfort zones and try new things. Sue Tremblay has always exhibited those qualities. That's why when she decided to open this office eleven years ago, we all worked together to make it happen. HRA Winnipeg has grown and flourished under Sue's leadership into this successful company that you are all apart of. But growth and success always come with a flip side. Up until now, Sue has effectively balanced being head of creative as well as managing all the accounts. Now, however, the job has grown too large for just one person — even if that person is as competent and brilliant as Sue."

"He's laying it on thick," whispered Kelly.

"Some changes are coming to HRA Winnipeg. I'd like to introduce you to Knox Harrison." Graham gestured to the younger man who was no longer on his phone. "Knox is HRA's newest partner. He will be taking over the accounts and handling the day-to-day management of the Winnipeg office starting immediately. He has big dreams to grow the business here in Manitoba. With Knox here, Sue will be able to turn her full attention to the creative department."

Knox stepped forward, his face passive, his voice confident. "We have a lot of work to do in the upcoming months. Besides current business, we will be taking steps to become independent from the Vancouver office. We will no longer require approval from them regarding projects; we will also be upgrading our administrative and accounting software, and creating internal systems."

Isla was momentarily distracted by a parade of young children waddling down the sidewalk outside the window, each one dressed in brightly coloured winter-wear, making them appear as wide as they were tall. Each child held onto a loop, each loop was attached to another with a bright yellow rope. The rope kept them in line, sort of. The children were bookended by adults, gender undetermined due to the number of layers required, and they were trying hard to herd the children together.

Isla brought her attention back to the front just as Knox wrapped up his instruction. "Please make sure all your client files are current and on our cloud. I will need access to everything. We hope this will be a smooth transition for all involved."

Kelly and Isla hung back, taking their time before returning to their duties, watching as everyone clamored to meet the new boss.

"I think I'm going to enjoy the new direction HRA is heading in," Kelly said wistfully, smoothing her hair down.

Isla rolled her eyes "He's a bit intense, don't you think?"
Kelly grinned. "I'm up for the challenge."

Knox had learned and forgotten fifteen new names. His day had started eleven hours earlier, with a cab ride to the airport. What had seemed like a good idea in the familiar but stifling office in Vancouver, now felt foolish. Did he really want to start a new life in this small, freezing prairie city?

As he followed Sue and Graham out of the room, he noticed two giggling young women lingering. He was tired, hungry, and eager to set a tone.

Approaching them, he didn't offer his hand. "Sorry to interrupt. I'm Knox Harrison, and you are…?" He first addressed the redhead.

"I am Isla—-Isla Peters," she said, clamming up.

"You say that like you're questioning it." He smirked as she blushed, slightly. "So, Isla Peters—question mark—do you have your files backed up already?"

She shook her head, avoiding eye contact by looking down at her shoes.

"Then I suggest you and your friend quit wasting time and get back to work," he said harshly. He enjoyed the rush that came with power. Now to find some coffee, he thought, as he sauntered out of the room.

3.

February 12. Cloudy and breezy, -14C°.

Priya's thighs burned as she ran down the hallways of the Health Sciences building. She was searching for the rooftop access after being paged to help with an air ambulance call, her heart pumping with adrenaline. Today was the first shift of her ER rotation.

When she finally arrived, the nurses and doctors had already donned their protective gowns, gloves and masks, and a doctor was calling out orders as he glanced out the window looking for the helicopter. Turning back, he noticed Priya.

"Who are you?" he demanded.

"Priya Dhaliwal, doctor – med student, third year." She stammered under his intense gaze.

"I'm Dr. McAlister. Gown up and stay out of the way." He pushed the doors open as the helicopter touched down. The team of doctors and nurses rushed out onto the roof, pushing a gurney.

Left alone, Priya scrambled to find the right gear to put on. A gust of cold wind took away her breath, as she fumbled the blue mask on her face. By the time she was ready, the team was already rushing back inside, towards the elevator. The pace overwhelmed her. Her last rotation had been slow and methodical, and everything had been explained thoroughly before hand.

She shoved her way into the elevator as the doors closed. Directions were yelled, and others responded with quickness and precision. The doors opened and the team nearly knocked her over as they raced down the hallway towards a trauma room. Priya found her feet and caught up, but she couldn't keep up with the information flying across the room.

She gathered that the patient had fallen from a high distance onto a pile of construction rubbish where a piece of rebar had punctured a lung. Priya's head started to swim when she caught sight of the rebar sticking out of his side. She grabbed behind her to find something to steady herself. As her knees weakened, she heard someone yell, "Get her out of here!"

Then she blacked out.

When Priya came to in the room next to the trauma room, she was alone. She looked at her watch; only fifteen minutes had passed since her pager had gone off. She tentatively climbed out of the bed and walked over to the door, peering through the window. She could see the medical team working together, like a choreographed dance. She stared for a long time mesmerized, unable to look away.

The team stabilized the man, and packed him for surgery. Dr. McAlister's eyes met hers as they wheeled the gurney out of the room. She looked away quickly.

Priya went back to the bed and sat on it, unsure of what to do next. Would anyone come check on her? She felt like a failure, and she wanted to run away, but she still had ten hours left in her shift.

After few minutes, the door swung open and a young man sauntered in. He was average height, with thick toned arms and wide shoulders. He balanced two cups of coffee on a stack of charts. Priya recognized his dark eyes immediately. She gazed at his classically handsome face, masking her own emotions to offer him her most dazzling smile.

He sat next to her on the bed handed her a coffee.

"First trauma?" he asked kindly.

"Was it that obvious?" she joked.

"Hyperventilation – it happens to the best of us. You need to learn how to breathe properly during a trauma. When your adrenaline's pumping, it's important to remember to breathe – I almost passed out during my first birth in Labor and Delivery."

Priya smirked. "Well, babies are terrifying."

"No kidding." He grinned at her. "Are you feeling, okay?"

"I'm fine, just a wounded ego."

"I'm sure you'll recover quickly; healthy egos are a prerequisite for med school."

"How's the patient?"

"He was stable last I heard. His co-worker saved his life by stuffing the puncture with towels. It stopped his lung from collapsing. The tricky part will be getting the rebar out. He's in surgery now, out of our hands."

"Wow," Priya said.

"What was your name again?" he asked.

"Priya Dhaliwal, third year."

"Brian McAlister, ER resident," he said, offering her a clean-scrubbed hand. "Do you think you can handle 'three-year-old versus coffee table head laceration,' and then, let's see…" He looked through his stack of charts. "After that I have a possible food poisoning."

Priya nodded "I think I can handle that—"

"Good." Brian drained his coffee cup, and held the door open for her.

"This coffee is shit," she said, hopping off the bed. "Maybe I should take you out for a good cup sometime."

He grinned, taking the cup out of her hand and tossing it in the garbage.

"Sounds like a plan," he said.

Priya grinned back. Her ER rotation was looking up.

4.

March 9. Partly cloudy, -15C°.

As the weeks went on, each day was more difficult than the previous. Isla and Janine struggled with the speed at which new things were being introduced. New systems, new software. Each day a new set of instructions. Often it felt like the new ones contradicted the old. Knox spent a few mornings in their office, perched on a stool, his long legs comfortably resting on the ground. He hovered over their shoulders, making his silent presence known. *Ahem.*

Known, but not helpful.

Yesterday, Isla found Janine crying in the washroom.

"I can't do this," she had sobbed "It doesn't make any sense! The software we used before was so straightforward; this requires so much information and re-entry. We're so behind. I haven't been sleeping because I lay awake at night stressing about what will happen if I can't figure this out. What if I lose my job? What if I can't pay my bills? What if I lose the house? We'll be homeless—"

"Whoa! You're not going to lose your house and you're not going to lose your job. Today, all we need to figure out is today," interrupted Isla. "We are two strong, smart, independent women, and we

22

are going to figure this out together. We can conquer this software and we will not be intimidated by that fascist douche-bag, whose life must be so boring that he has nothing better to do than ruin our day."

Janine laughed, and wiped her face with the back of her hand. "Ok, I feel better now."

"I had my meltdown yesterday when I got home. I sat on my couch, still in my parka, and wept. We will conquer. Victory shall be ours!" Isla punched her fist in the air.

"Victory," said Janine half-heartedly. Isla held her hand up to Janine who gave it a weak high five.

They made it to Friday. Isla had seven minutes left in her break, then two hours before she could leave the hell hole her office had become and go see her new nephew. Andrew had been updating her since Emma was admitted to the maternity ward the night before. William Bennet had been born at 1:19pm, and he was perfect.

Isla returned to her desk as Janine was finishing a phone call. She sounded panicked.

"It's Kody— he got hurt at hockey and he's on the way to the hospital." Janine was normally calm, but now franticly paced back and forth, moving papers from one stack to the next, distracted and afraid. Judging by the pictures on Janine's desk, Kody was the eldest of Janine's kids, maybe sixteen years old. Her daughter Maddie looked to be twelve.

"He got hit hard at hockey practise and was knocked out. I need to go." She waved her hand to the pile of work on her desk. "Do you mind?"

My nephew, thought Isla.

"Yes, of course. Go! I can finish up," said Isla as Janine grabbed her jacket and bag. She paused and awkwardly hugged Isla.

"Thanks so much, Isla. What would I do without you? Just finish the pay roll, the rest can wait until Monday."

Isla surveyed the different piles on their desks. Posting pay roll wasn't hard, but it would take her all afternoon and into the evening.

Emma stared at her baby boy, his paper-thin skin wrinkled and red. He slept, peacefully curled up in her arms. She could not believe this tiny being had been inside her less than eight hours ago. Her body was exhausted, but sleep wouldn't come. She wanted to stare at the face she had just met, but seemed to have known forever.

Bill and Dee had just left. Alicia had been by earlier — she had brought a thermos of organic bone broth *"full of healthy vitamins and good for milk production."* Emma found it revolting. After a few polite sips, she had given up.

"Andy, what time is it?" asked Emma, stiffly shifting in her hospital bed, trying not to disturb the sleeping baby in her arms. "What if they don't come?"

"They'll come, they wouldn't miss this," Andrew replied. He had been awake for nearly forty hours. Adrenaline continued to sustain him. He was a father. He had a son. Everything had changed, and yet he looked out the window and people continued as if nothing significant had happened. He wanted to yell at the woman walking her pug, "I have a son!" but she kept walking by.

"Visiting hours are almost over. What if they don't make it?"

Andrew got up and sat on the edge of Emma's bed. He took her hand. "Babe, they love you. I'm sure they have a good reason. If they don't make it, they'll come to the house tomorrow once we're home." Inwardly he cursed his flaky sister.

"We had a plan—I really thought they'd come," said Emma, tears welling up in her clear blue eyes.

"Try and get some sleep, you're so tired. Everything will be fine, just rest."

There was a quiet knock on the door, and in crept Isla and Priya, both dressed in green Winnipeg Regional Health Authority scrubs, masks, and shoe covers. Priya's ID badge was prominently displayed even though this wasn't her hospital.

"Surprise!" said Isla quietly. "Sorry we're late. Thankfully Priya knows how to move around a hospital undetected."

Emma grinned at them, wiping her wet cheeks. "I knew you'd come!" she said accepting hugs from her friends.

"Let me see that baby!" said Isla, walking around the bed to where Liam was sleeping, Emma handed him over.

"Isn't he amazing?"

"Yes, he is," Isla said, astounded at how the wrinkly little bundle in her arms was instantly family.

"I'll leave you guys to visit. I need to find some food, and I noticed they had the hockey game on in the lounge," said Andrew. He kissed Emma's cheek and squeezed Isla's elbow. As he walked out, he stopped at the nurse's station and lied to buy them some time.

Priya unpacked her backpack: a bottle of cheap sparkling wine, three tumblers, whipped cream filled eclairs from Emma's favourite bakery, and a small carton of gummy bears. Isla sat in the armchair next to the bed still cradling her nephew. Priya sat at the end of the bed, the food spread out in front of her. Emma bit into a donut, crumbs falling on to her hospital gown, groaning in delight. "You guys remembered."

"Of course we did! We've been planning this for months," said Isla. "I am so sorry we couldn't be here sooner. Janine had a family emergency and I had to stay late."

"Although, you've been late every night this week," Priya stated, with a mouth full of gummies.

"Let's not talk about that," Isla said, changing the subject. "Emma, you had a baby! Tell us all about it."

Both Isla and Priya leaned forward expectantly. Emma looked at her friends and then to her baby. She shrugged, lost for words.

"Did it hurt?" asked Isla, trying not to imagine what happened during childbirth.

25

"Of course it did," piped up Priya. "But you got an epidural, right?"
Emma shook her head. "No, I did it naturally."
"You should've taken the drugs," said Priya.
Emma shrugged again. Everything had gone according to plan. The nurse had said her body was made for birthing babies. It was the most spiritual thing she had ever experienced, but she faltered when trying to tell her friends. They wouldn't understand.

"Why are you staying late at work?" Emma asked, taking the attention off herself.

"New software," said Isla with a scowl, "and every week that goes by things get worse. Knox is such a jerk, he spends his days stomping around intimidating everyone, and yelling about every little mix up. It is impossible! Greg locks himself in his server room, because he's sick of interpreting for us, and Janine is on the edge of a complete break down."

"I'm not following," said Emma. "Who are these people? You've only talked about a Kelly before?"

"Janine is brilliant. She's the accountant I work with, but she's as lost as I am, and Greg is sick of spending so much time teaching us the same thing over and over, and we still don't get it. We are smart women!"

"So, Greg is a jerk?" asked Emma.

"No, Knox is a jerk," replied Priya, still eating gummy bears.

"I'm sorry, I'm completely lost. What are you talking about?" Emma asked looking back and forth between her friends.

"Isla's new boss," said Priya. "He sounds horrible."

"He's the newest partner, son of Ken Harrison, come to be the savior of the lowly Winnipeg office."

"As in Harrison Richards Advertising — that Harrison?" Emma was catching up.

"Yes. And Daddy's little boy thinks he's the grand ruler supreme. He has changed everything, and I despise him," announced Isla.

"Wait a minute, the *son* of a partner? How old is he?" asked Priya.

"I don't know, our age. Maybe a bit older. It's ridiculous, he's younger than most of the staff. Sue doesn't seem to put off by him, but maybe he's just horrible to us basement dwellers," said Isla.

"You despise him, but you haven't told me if he is hot?" asked Priya, her eyes widening.

"Oh my gosh, Priya! You would ask that wouldn't you?" laughed Emma "Who cares if he's good looking if he's not a nice guy?"

"Good looks can cover a multitude of sins," said Priya with an exaggerated wink. She turned to Isla. "So, is he?"

Isla shrugged. "I don't know, not really. —What are you doing? No, Priya! Put away your phone!"

"— Is this him? He *is* hot." Priya held up her phone. In the picture Knox Harrison had a lopsided boyish grin, as if the person taking the picture was someone he genuinely liked.

Isla nodded, annoyed. "Yes, that's him, but he never smiles like that at the office."

"Not bad!" agreed Emma after Priya passed the phone over.

Isla shook her head in dismay.

"Just because *you* like guys who look homeless, with long stringy hair and beards," said Priya. "He's single, according to his profile. Although he barely posts anything and when he does it's only about advertising and hockey. I'm going to follow him anyway."

"No! Please don't! I'm in your profile picture. He'll think I'm stalking him!" Isla grabbed at her phone.

"Fine, I'll just stop by your office one day" said Priya, holding her phone out of reach.

"Again, no! You don't seem to understand how horrible he is. Our receptionist quit on Wednesday, and she's been there, like, forever. He ripped into her about dropping a call, and apparently, she swore at him and walked out. HRA used to be a decent place to work, but now everyone is tense and snappy. No one smiles anymore, and they've even switched the coffee to some horrible cheap brand."

Liam burst into tears, obviously sympathetic to Isla's frustration. Emma rushed to comfort him, giving Isla a sympathetic smile as she put the bundle to her breast "I'm sure it will get better. That's just the way men are, marking their territory."

"Whoa, look at you, nursing like a pro!" said Isla, watching in awe as Liam latched onto Emma's breast and started sucking hungrily.

"Emma's got a point, though. That's how it is at the hospital. Patriarchy, toxic masculinity and all that shit. You've got to learn to deal with it," said Priya.

"I refuse to accept that all men are horrible, or that we, as women, have to put up with it."

"Spoken like the daughter of a feminist," said Emma.

"*Naïvely* spoken like the daughter of a feminist," added Priya.

"I'm not naïve," protested Isla. "Leadership can be accomplished without bravado or cruelty — look at my dad and Andrew, both successful and kind. Michael, too."

"I don't think he counts as being successful."

"Priya" warned Emma.

Priya continued, "I'm just saying that in the real world, hashtag not all men are married to or raised by the Professor. Most men do what they want and say what they want. They don't waste time caring about the feelings of others, their only focus is getting the job done."

"And that's why you're attracted to them?" questioned Isla.

Priya smiled. "Precisely. No feelings to worry about, and they get the job done."

Just then a young nurse slipped quietly into the room, expecting to find a sleeping patient, instead finding three friends devouring a bucket of gummies. Clearing her throat, she startled them. "Visiting hours were over awhile ago," she said, a smile tugging at the side of her mouth.

"We're just leaving," said Priya, quickly gathering up their leftover food containers. Isla kissed Liam on the head, leaving a lipstick mark.

"I am so glad you guys came," said Emma, tears welling up.

Priya uncharacteristically, swooped down and kissed Emma on the cheek. "See you later, Mama Bear."

The two friends crept quietly down the corridor, hoping to escape without confronting another nurse. In the elevator, Priya continued searching through her phone.

"Stop scrolling Priya. What are you hopping to find?"

"Evidence that the infamous Knox Harrison isn't a complete bore."

5.

March 12. Calm, -14C°.

Monday morning, Isla snuck into the office and down the stairs. Once in her office she noticed Janine's bag was there, but her seat was empty. *That's odd*, thought Isla glancing around. She was curious to hear how Janine's son was. She turned back to the door and nearly ran into a wall dressed in a navy suit and a black tie decorated with—were those tiny gold pineapples?

"My office — now."

She trudged behind Knox up the stairs and down the corridor, into the corner office. His office was full of heavy wood furniture with cold marble surfaces, dark grey and brown. The temperature felt five degrees cooler than the hall. Isla shivered and sat on a large, hard wooden chair, her feet not reaching the floor. She felt like a child in the principal's office.

Janine was already seated, anxiously fiddling with her blazer button. Isla tried to catch her eye, but she stared ahead, not focusing on anything.

"Which one of you fucked up pay roll on Friday?" Knox questioned as he sat down in his stiff leather wingback chair, staring at them from across his lacquered wood desk, his arms folded across his chest.

"You are the accounting department, right?" They both remained silent and still. "Nearly half of the cheques are wrong. Overpaid." He placed a piece of paper in front of them and Janine leaned over to pick it up. The paper shook in her hand.

"I did." Her voice was barely above whisper.

"Pardon me?"

"I did," she said, only slightly louder.

"This is unacceptable. A mistake like this will cost me a fortune," said Knox. His voice was harsh, but under control.

Janine nodded and stared at the floor.

Isla could barely breathe. This had to be her fault. How could it not be?

"Janine," she muttered, "tell him what actually happened."

Janine shook her head.

"What actually happened?" Knox questioned Isla.

Janine shook her head again, but Isla spoke anyway. "She had to leave early, so I finished. I made the mistake. I make dumb mistakes all the time. Janine usually catches them." Her words rushed out.

"You left early?" asked Knox, turning back to Janine.

"The mistake was made before I left. It was my fault," she said, picking up the page to show Isla, who wasn't listening.

"Did you have permission to leave early?" asked Knox.

"Permission to leave early? Like a child?" interrupted Isla. All the anger and frustration of the last couple of weeks came up like a tidal wave. "It was a mistake! Everything has changed! You've doubled our workload, we've had no training. A mistake! How dare you sit there on your — throne," she said waving at his massive chair. She realized she had crossed a line, but still she took a breath and persisted "—like a tyrant, yelling at a single mom who had to leave early because her son was being rushed to the hospital! Give her a break, and while you're at it why don't you get us some proper training?!"

"A redhead losing her temper, how original," Knox said. His eye twitched as he struggled to remain calm. He stood up slowly, eyes fixed on Isla. "Pack up your desk and leave. You admitted that Janine fixes your mistakes, and since you care so much about your co-worker, I'm sure you won't mind if we find someone else to do your job."

Janine watched, horrified, frozen in place, unable to triage the escalating destruction.

"I hated this job to begin with, and the day you started, it became intolerable," sneered Isla. She held his gaze for a moment before turning and walking out the door.

"Oh no, oh no, oh no," Janine muttered, as she followed Isla out the door and down the staircase.

When Isla reached their office, she rummaged around until she found a crushed cardboard box. She haphazardly packed her few personal belongings, the picture of her friends, her crooked pottery mug, her paisley pencil case, and favourite eraser.

"We have to go back in there. You can apologise, I can explain what happened — this isn't your fault! I made the mistake," insisted Janine.

"I'm not apologising; he's the worst human being I have ever met."

"You're upset. Take a couple of deep breaths, calm down, and we'll go back and work it out."

"Or we'll go back and both lose our jobs. You need this job, and he is a raging lunatic." *Except I am the raging lunatic*, thought Isla. "I suck at this job. I'm practically incompetent. You know it, I know it, and now he knows it."

Isla paused her hurried packing and took a deep breath. She asked calmly, "How is Kody?"

"He has a broken collarbone and a few bruises. He's in a lot of pain, and out for the season," said Janine, tears pooling in her eyes. "You can't leave, Isla."

"I must," she sighed dramatically. "You'll do brilliantly without me holding you back. You'll get a new co-worker who will be focused and on time, who will get a thrill when the numbers reconcile. You'll be best friends and be the best accounting department in the land."

After her benediction, Isla picked up her box and held her head up high. She straightened her back, thrust her shoulders back and walked out with dignity, clutching her box so her trembling hands wouldn't give her away.

Agitated, Knox paced around his office. He stopped to pick up the payroll printout, crumpled it into a ball and tossed it into his waste basket. The door opened, and Sue came in and stood in front of his desk, her arms on her hips, her hazel eyes livid.

"Knox Reeve Harrison, what is wrong with you?"

News travels fast, he thought, slumping down in his chair. "Don't call me that."

"It's your name. I've known you since you were in diapers; I can call you whatever I want." She sat down across from him, in the same wooden chair Isla had vacated. The scene of the crime.

"Fine then, Auntie Sue, is this going to be a lecture?" Knox knew he was being rude, but continued anyway. "You might as well get on with it."

"This is a business — a family business — not a dictatorship. You can't terminate my employees without first consulting me! Winnipeg is too small to make enemies in. If you don't have good relationships, you don't have anything here. I don't want you to burn the bridges I've spent my career building."

Knox picked up a pen and spun it between his thumb and forefinger, buying himself some time. He wanted this conversation to be over, but he felt the need to justify his actions. "My Dad would've done the same."

"And I would've questioned him too. Your memories of him may not be completely accurate. He built this company through a lot of hard work and by choosing the right people. Yes, he yelled a lot, but he rewarded hard work and he never, ever made rash decisions."

"These are my employees now. Isla doesn't want to work here — she pretty much quit. I doubt an inept bookkeeper has enough connections to hurt *our* business. She was the one yelling at me!"

"You could've avoided the whole situation by offering them some proper training and giving them some time to catch their breath."

"I don't have time for incompetence. I have two years to make this work. I'll do this my way — with or without your support."

"Really? With or without my support? Good luck with that." Sue paused long enough to remember who she was speaking to, and she felt compassion for the man she had known since he was a boy. "I will always support you Knox, you know that, but if you act like a child, I will treat you accordingly."

He winced as he opened his computer. "Are we done yet? I have work to do."

Sue sat for awhile as he typed with his head down, jaw clenched, back and neck rigid.

"Come for supper tonight; Phil's making ribs." It wasn't a question.

Knox nodded and grunted without looking up.

"Six o'clock, not a minute later, and don't bring any work," Sue said as she headed out the door.

6.

March 18. Partly cloudy, -7C°.

The enticing fragrance of coconut and curry hung in the air as Priya rang the doorbell. She had a key, but she preferred to remind her parents of her independence, or maybe to remind herself. Exhausted after a long busy shift at the hospital, all she'd wanted was to go to bed, but instead she'd had one more cup of coffee, peeled off her scrubs, and thrown on the only acceptably clean T-shirt and jeans from off her floor. It was her nephew Taran's first birthday, and nothing short of physical illness or broken bones could get her out of dinner. She waited on the front step, fortifying herself for what was sure to be an evening full of spicy home cooking and passive aggressive guilt trips.

Jasminder Dhaliwal opened the door and stood there with her hands on her wide hips, annoyance written across her face. "Priya, why must you ring the doorbell? This is your home!" Her mother pulled her into her ample chest and hugged her firmly. Priya resisted for a moment but then she surrendered herself to her mother's soft and familiar embrace.

"Why don't you stop by more often? Dee said you were over for lunch a couple weeks back," she demanded with her accented English.

"I was, and then I came here after," said Priya, breaking free from her mother's grip.

"Yes, but you should see us more than your friend's parents," said Jasminder, her hands back on her hips.

"That's why I'm here now Mama-ji!" Priya could hear an edge creeping into her voice. Plastering on a smile, she ventured past her mother into the warm house.

Jasminder was nineteen when Hardeep returned to Jalandhar, after graduating from university. They married right away — an arranged marriage, but that did not mean it lacked love. Six months later they had a boy, stillborn at twenty-two weeks. Aching with grief and the need to escape, Hardeep made plans to immigrate to Canada. Jasminder, reluctant and broken, agreed to leave behind her small village to follow this handsome, smart man to a foreign land, flat and cold as it was. She was determined to build a better life for the next child she carried.

Shortly after arriving in Canada, Jasminder gave birth to another boy. Gurmeet was full of peace and joy, the kind of baby that makes one want to have another. Shortly after his first birthday, Priya came along. She was born screaming and never stopped. Those screams turned to questions, stubbornness, and rebelliousness. Deepa, the youngest, was born five years later, sweet and obedient like her brother.

Canada would never be Jasminder's home. Home was where her mother and sisters lived, where she had held her first baby. Home was the place she scrimped and saved every penny to go back to. Jasminder would always be grateful for the opportunities Canada provided but always felt betrayed watching her children embrace things that were foreign to her.

Hardeep and Gurmeet were nearly identical copies of one another, dark, deep-set eyes framed by unruly brows, and wide smiles hidden in their long beards — Hardeep's nearly grey. Both wore turbans as the outer symbol of their inner faith. They sat on the sofa with poses mimicking each other, watching Hockey Night in Canada, Punjabi edition.

"Kitchen! I need help with the *naan*," Jasminder demanded before Priya had a chance to sit down and join them.

"Come on, Mom! I just got off a long shift, can't I sit and watch some hockey?" whined Priya, indicating the others in the room.

Deepa glanced up from the brown corduroy recliner on the other side of the room. She had large noise-cancelling headphones on and looked surprised to see her sister. She gave a quick wave and went back to her fashion magazine.

"You are not the only woman who works in this house. I'm on my feet the whole day – and besides, if I remember correctly, you need help with your *naan* making. Practice makes perfect."

"I don't plan on ever making *naan* from scratch," replied Priya.

"Of course you will, once you get married."

I am never getting married, Priya thought, swallowing the fight rising in her. "Why can't Deepa help?"

"She can make a round *naan* already. You are right. Deepa — Deepa! Kitchen!" she bellowed, getting her youngest daughter's attention. Deepa glared at Priya who smirked back. They both sulked into the kitchen.

Chadda, Gurmeet's wife was working already, chopping veggies for the dal, her glossy black hair tied back in a long braid down her back. They rolled the traditional flatbread *naan*, frying it in a hot cast iron pan and slathering it with ghee.

Priya's ended up misshapen, while Deepa and Jasminder managed perfect rounds.

"How was work this week, Mama?" Priya asked, through gritted teeth, her lopsided bread rejected once again.

"Beneet and Sahajreet spilled a whole bag of flour!" Jasminder started laughing and switched to Punjabi. Priya followed most of it: the flour had ended up in their hair, making them look like old ladies, or something along those lines. Priya understood Punjabi but lacked practise in speaking it.

Jasminder worked at a large bakery where most of the workers were Punjabi women. Some had been in Canada for years, others had just arrived. Jasminder loved her job because of the connections to her culture and traditions.

"Fancy's son Antar is home from Edmonton," Jasminder said with a knowing look at Priya. Fancy Sandu was Jasminder's closest friend, and her son Antar was a year younger than Priya. He was tall and lanky with an unfortunate nose.

"Is he?" Priya said, uninterested. She rolled her dough.

Antar worshiped Priya, and as teenagers he would announce their engagement at various parties and get-togethers. Priya had threatened to punch him the last time — and he believed her. Determined to win her heart, he'd changed techniques, and had chosen medical school as well. Because of Antar, Priya stayed away from Indian men. Her mother was unaware of this. As far as Jasminder was concerned, Priya could marry anyone she wanted.

As long as he was Indian and Sikh.

"He wants to take you to dinner."

"He can call me," said Priya, knowing rejection would be easier without either of their mothers' interventions.

"Friday night, 6:30pm at the—" Jasminder wiped the flour off her hand onto a tea towel and checked her phone "—at the restaurant on Pembina, the one with the apples."

"Great" said Priya, sarcasm missed by her mother. "Give me his number, Mama."

"Fancy wants to know if you are going."

"I'll call him myself."

"She's not going, Mama," said Deepa, spreading ghee on the hot *naan* as they came out of the pan.

Jasminder threw up her hands in exasperation. "Priya, you must go! You have known Antar since you were children; you should be lucky to have a nice boy like that interested in you. He is going to be a doctor!"

"*I* am going to be a doctor, Mama!" shouted Priya in frustration.

Chadda stifled a giggle, giving Priya a sympathetic look but wisely keeping her mouth shut.

"Then two doctors in the family!" replied Jasminder "I'm sure I don't need to remind you, your younger sister is engaged. Perminder Garwal, got engaged two weeks ago, Mahinoor Chadhar is expected to be engaged by spring, and my Priya, no one. Turning down the only prospect she has ever had, or will ever have, with your hair cut like a—"

"Like a what, Mama?" asked Priya slowly, daring her mother to say what she really meant.

"Short."

Isla burst into her parent's home office. She was looking for a paperclip and was not expecting to find Andrew asleep in the chair with Liam sleeping on his chest.

Andrew slowly opened his left eye.

"Sorry," mouthed Isla.

He grinned and said quietly, "It's okay. He finally fell asleep! Did Emma go for a nap?"

"No, she was wondering where you are."

"She said she was desperate for a nap. I thought if I took Liam, she'd sleep," said Andrew shaking his head. "You're awfully quiet today."

"Aren't I allowed to have a quiet day?" asked Isla defensively.

"Allowed, yes. But I'm not sure you've ever exercised that right before."

Isla gave him a dirty look. "I'm fine, everything is fine. I'm just tired," she said, hoping to deflect any more questions.

"You don't know tired until you've had a baby," he said with a forced laugh. "This little guy was up for three hours last night.

Emma was a complete mess by the time I got up. I wish she'd gotten me up sooner. She insists on doing everything herself and then complains that I don't help — or if I do help, she complains I'm doing it wrong. Sometimes I wish —" he made a show of covering Liam's ears "— I wish things would go back to normal."

Liam slowly lifted his head and turned away from Andrew's face. His eyes peeked open before he closed them again, burrowing into the security of his father's shoulder.

"I shouldn't have said that," he sighed, patting his hand gently against Liam's round bum. "Don't tell Em I said anything. I'm just so tired and frustrated and tired…"

"Andrew, you're a good dad. Look how much he loves you!" Isla said. "Maybe you should tell Emma how you feel. I'm no expert, but isn't that how marriage works?"

"I can't. She's angry with me all the time. She won't go anywhere without him. I don't think she trusts me, or anyone else with him." Liam sighed deeply; his tiny pink lips curled up into a sleepy smile. Isla slid to the floor across from him. The siblings sat in the weight of Andrew's confession. Isla did the only thing she could think of: she also confessed.

"I got fired."

Speaking it out loud made it real.

"Three weeks ago."

First the relief.

"I haven't told anyone."

Then the humiliation.

"What happened?" he asked.

"Vancouver sent us their newest partner, the crown prince. He was horrible, a perfectionist, and he had zero tolerance for any of us making mistakes, even small ones. He was ripping into one of my co-workers and I lost my temper."

"Shocker," said Andrew.

"I told him he was intolerable to work for, which is true, but I could've kept my mouth shut. Also, I called him a tyrant. I thought he was going to fire Janine."

"I guess we know whose daughter you are," said Andrew, not bothering to cover up his amusement.

"It's not funny."

"I'm sorry," said Andrew, regaining himself.

"It was horrible. *I* was horrible." The mid-afternoon winter light shone into the room. Isla felt the warmth on her face, a promise that spring would come.

"What are you going to do now?"

"Besides lying on the couch in my pyjamas watching movies all day long? Luke at Yellow Box Coffee said he had a few shifts for me if I wanted."

"Do you need money?" asked Andrew.

"Probably. Priya isn't going to be able to cover rent without me, not that I've told her," Isla said, tugging at her shirt sleeve, embarrassed.

"You haven't told Priya yet?"

"I told you, I haven't told anyone."

"I can help you out," said Andrew.

Liam's backside rumbled and he startled awake. Andrew and Isla laughed as a yellowish tinge began to creep up his back.

"Oh, gross!" said Isla.

Andrew grabbed the diaper bag and turned to the desk, peeling Liam's sleeper off and changing his diaper like a pro.

"Look at you!" said Isla in awe. "You really know what you're doing."

Andrew grinned proudly, as he zipped the new sleeper up. "This guy is ready for some milk. Should we find your Mama bear?"

"Andy, please don't tell anyone yet. I'm not ready for the lecture Mom is inevitably going to give me," said Isla as she followed Andrew out the door.

"I won't. And I'll write you a cheque after I hand this guy over."

7.

April 7. North Wind, 4C°.

"I'm listening," Isla shouted in the direction of her phone laying on her bed.

"*I said, your father's Aunt Elsa is in the hospital. They think it's a stroke.*" Dee's clear voice rang out of the speaker.

"Okay," Isla responded, distracted by swiping mascara onto her fair lashes.

"*It's so sad.*"

"Have you seen my shoes?" yelled Priya from the other room.

"No!" Isla yelled back.

"*What?*" asked Dee, alarmed.

"Sorry, I was talking to Priya. It *is* sad, but I don't know her, and I'm trying to get ready."

"*What are you getting ready for?*"

"A wedding social."

"*How fun. Do I know the couple?*" asked Dee.

"I don't even know them. It's someone Priya knows from the hospital. I won't know anyone except her, and she is going to be busy flirting with… what's his name? Bryson, Barrett, Ryan?" Isla ducked as Priya threw a pillow at her.

"Brian... Hi Dee!" Priya said, sitting by the phone. "He's bringing some friends — maybe Isla will meet someone."

Isla glared at Priya. "Zip me up. I don't need to meet anyone."

Dee chuckled. "You girls have fun. Don't do anything I wouldn't — never mind. Before you go, I have a question for you about work—"

"You're breaking up — I've got to go, Mom. Bye!" Isla dove on to the bed and hung up before her mom had a chance to respond.

Priya stared at her, wide-eyed. "You haven't told her about being fired?"

Isla grimaced and shook her head.

"Why not?"

"Because when I say it out loud, that makes it real. I'd prefer to live in denial while I process it. She's going to eviscerate me—"

"Yeah, you might as well get it over with."

"I told Andy."

"So Emma knows."

"I don't think so. She would've said something, don't you think?" Isla asked as they left the room. "By the way, I saw your shoes in the bathroom."

They both checked their reflections once more. Isla had on a green sheath dress with a gold belt and nude heels. Priya wore a tight, black dress and had finally found her black heels.

"Cab is here," called Priya, checking the window. "Remember the plan?"

"We're coming straight home for a sensible sleep," Isla said, rolling her eyes. "The most doomed plan ever."

"But you're going to hold me to it, right?"

Priya and Isla rode the rickety elevator to the top floor of an old warehouse in Winnipeg's Exchange District. The door opened to a large room, beautifully decorated with swaths of cream fabric swooping back and forth across the ceiling, and lanterns that bathed the space in golden light. The walls were lined with raffle prizes. On the one side of the room was a huge bar made of ice and in the centre, the dance floor was circled by tables already full of party-goers.

"Wow," exclaimed Isla. The dance floor was packed. The girls circled the room looking for Priya's friends.

"This isn't half bad," said Priya.

Suddenly, Isla skidded to a stop. There, in a maroon blazer with a patterned pocket square, sky blue t-shirt, dark jeans and sneakers, was Knox Freaking Harrison. She let out an audible moan and grabbed Priya's elbow.

"What?"

"It's him," said Isla miserably.

"Who?" asked Priya, looking in the same direction as Isla.

"Knox Harrison! At that table over there." She nodded to a table with five rowdy guys.

Priya grinned and grabbed Isla's hand, pulling her in that direction. "Well, it's your lucky night, because that's where we're heading!"

"No! No! *No*, Priya Kaur Dhaliwal, I cannot go over there!" said Isla as she ducked behind a large, bearded man in a Metallica T-shirt.

Priya laughed at her friend's misfortune and waved Brian over. "Come on, Isla, we've been spotted."

Brian sauntered over, weaving through the crowd. Isla remained crouched behind a table. He pointed at Isla. "Is your friend, ok?"

"She's completely lost it," Priya said, still laughing. "Come on, Isla. Get up! You're embarrassing yourself."

Priya grabbed Isla by the elbow and pulled her up. "What's that thing the professor always says? You can do hard things."

"I think she was talking about standing up to injustice and exclusion, not partying with the guy who fired you," argued Isla.

Brian's curiosity was peaked. "Who fired you?"

Isla stood up and smoothed her dress, attempting to find some dignity. They all stared at the table. The men were all well dressed, all a few drinks in. They were already attracting plenty of female attention.

"Which of your friends is the biggest jerk?" asked Isla.

Brian laughed. "Well, that's a tough competition, but since most of us are lowly minions at the beginning of our careers, the only one in a position to actually fire someone would be Knox."

"Bingo," sighed Isla

"Come on," said Priya, pulling Isla to the table. She beamed at Brian. "This will be fun."

"I hate you," Isla hissed into Priya's ear.

"Gentlemen," Brian said, addressing his friends. "You all know Priya, and this is Isla. This is Chris, Joey, Nate, and Knox, whom you've met already — in his office when the heartless bastard fired you."

This brought an uproar of laughter from the whole table. Knox grinned as the men teased him and slapped him on the back. Isla's face burned with embarrassment. She seriously considered walking out the door and never returning.

"So, Isla what do you do, now that you aren't working for this guy?" Joey asked, smacking Knox in the chest.

"She is an artist," Priya answered to Isla's relief.

"An artist, eh? Do you paint nudes?" asked Chris.

"And would you like me to model for you?" asked Joey leaning in towards her.

"Let's be honest. If anyone is going to model it's going to be me," said Nate, flexing to show off his muscular arms.

"She likes to paint miniature things; I think you all would be perfect," stated Priya.

"Perhaps a group portrait?" said Isla, smiling for the first time.

"These idiots all work with us at the hospital," Priya said, waving her hand around the table.

Lisa Joelle

"Nate is a nurse—" continued Brian.

"I caught Priya when she passed out on her first day," interrupted Nate.

Priya gave him the finger as Brian continued the introductions. "Joey's a paramedic, and Chris sold his soul to the devil — I mean he's a pharmaceutical rep."

"I do it for the money," he said with an unapologetic shrug.

"Guess you're buying then." Priya linked arms with him and asked, "Who needs a drink?"

"Have a seat" Nate said to Isla, pulling out the seat between him and Joey. He had dark curly hair, beautiful brown eyes, and was built like a bodybuilder. Isla sat down and prayed she wouldn't say anything stupid.

"How do you paint miniature things?" asked Nate. "Do you have really tiny brushes?"

"It was a joke, you idiot," said Knox from across the table, his arms folded across his chest.

Isla ignored Knox and flashed Nate a bright grin. "I paint a little of everything. Sometimes flowers and landscapes, but with bright colours and graphic lines. Lately I've been painting more portraits, but I'm still learning." She talked until she noticed Nate's eyes glaze over. He was still smiling at her, but she could tell he had lost interest.

Their conversation was saved by the arrival of a group of women who also worked at the hospital. Soon everyone was engaged in conversation and laughing at inside jokes. Everyone but Isla.

She accepted a glass of something clear and strong from Priya, and as conversation flowed around her, she allowed her thoughts to drift down the path of least resistance: her current painting, her nephew, her terror about telling her parents about her job, and eventually, where it always landed lately, her broken heart.

I hate socials, she thought as she stared at her empty plastic cup, wondering where her drink went.

46

"**D**o you intend to ignore me all night?" said a deep voice in Isla's ear as she waited in line at the bar. She was pretending to be engrossed in her phone, when really, she was taking a quiz: What does your pizza topping choice say about your future children?

"I do."

He didn't leave. Silently they waited as the line got shorter.

Finally, they reached the front. "A double shot of whiskey and water, and she'll have the same?" Knox dared her.

Isla raised her eyebrows and rose to the occasion.

"Your friend really likes Brian, eh?" Knox asked.

"Brian's your friend? I didn't think you were capable of having friends."

"We've known each other for a long time — went to high school together. Roommates at uni—"

"I don't really care," Isla interrupted, as Knox paid the bartender. "And I can buy my own drink."

"You can get the next round," he replied, handing her the glass of dark amber liquid.

There isn't going to be another round, thought Isla as she raised her drink. "*Cheers. I hope the whiskey improves your personality.*"

"And yours," Knox winked, clinking her glass, then downing most of his.

Isla took a sip, turned on her heel and walked away to the door prizes. She bought some raffle tickets, then realized she was being followed.

"Can you explain to me what a social is?" asked Knox, also buying a sheet of tickets.

"It is a Manitoba thing: part party, part fundraiser. Engaged couples throw one to raise money for their weddings."

"They throw a huge party to raise money, in order to throw an even bigger party. Sounds like a nightmare."

"Don't you like parties?" asked Isla.

"I like attending parties. Planning them is the nightmare."

"Socials are usually in an ugly community hall, with drunk uncles serving cheap drinks and teenagers playing DJ. Not like this."

"Sounds like a good opportunity for underage drinking," Knox said with a smirk.

"Pretty much, if you can avoid relatives." Isla smiled, remembering the first social she, Priya and Emma had snuck into. They'd had to spend the evening avoiding Isla's older cousins.

"Seems a bit redneck," said Knox.

Isla laughed. "You should go to one outside the perimeter."

"What do I do with these?" he asked, holding up the sheet of tickets.

Isla ripped the sheet of tickets along the perforated lines. "Put them in the box next to the prize you want to win." She gestured to the long table along the wall.

The table was lined with large baskets, each filled with different prizes donated by local businesses. One held expensive hair products, the next was filled with various car parts and a gift certificate for an oil change.

Knox took his stack of tickets and placed one in each box.

Isla shook her head. "That's bad strategy. You'll end up with something you don't want."

"Okay, wise one, tell me what to do."

"Check out all the prizes and pick your favourite. Put a third of your tickets in now, a third in an hour, and the last third right before the draw." Isla eyed up the generous spa package. She imagined herself and Priya in soft white robes, with glasses of herb infused water, spending the day lounging.

"That's a good prize." Knox interrupted her daydream, pointing at the basket next to the spa: four hockey tickets, centre line, five rows up.

"Hockey? Really? I thought you'd be into the hair products," said Isla. "Besides, everyone is going to want the hockey tickets."

Before he could answer, Priya pinched Isla from behind.

"Hey!" said Isla, rubbing her elbow.

"There you are!" said Priya quietly, before turning to Knox. "Hi. It's Knox, right? I'm going to steal Isla for just a second."

He shrugged and continued putting all his tickets into the hockey ticket box. Priya dragged Isla to the small woman's bathroom. They joined the line for one of the two stalls.

"I don't understand you. I've introduced you to three acceptable guys, and I find you hanging out with the asshole who fired you?"

"We weren't hanging out. He followed me! I was being polite," Isla said defensively.

"Right, whatever. Go for him. He's hot, I won't judge. Or ditch him, and ask one of the others to dance."

"I'm not interested in any of them."

"They're all good looking, successful, nice guys. Get yourself a date!" said Priya loudly as she headed for a stall.

Isla bit her lip so she wouldn't say anything. She needn't have bothered. Priya knew exactly what she was thinking.

"Stop thinking about your ex!" she yelled from the stall.

Isla received a couple of pity-filled looks from the other girls in the bathroom. "You don't need him," one said.

Isla stayed quiet until Priya came out of the stall. "But he lives just down the street! We used to walk by here all the time, have coffee across the street—"

"Don't be pathetic," said Priya, glaring at Isla's reflection in the mirror as she washed her hands and reapplied her plum lipstick. "You don't have to commit to marry anyone; just give someone else half a chance."

Around midnight, the raffle prizes were announced. Knox won his hockey tickets. Once the rest of the prizes were announced,

Isla was ready to leave. The music was loud and her head was spinning. She found Priya entwined with Brian in the shadows next to their table.

"Priya, I'm leaving. I'm reminding you of your plan." She tapped her friend on the shoulder, not caring if she was interrupting.

"Screw the plan," said Priya, barely coming up for air.

Isla shook her head. "I knew you'd fail."

Nothing else would have gotten through to her in that moment, but Priya Dhaliwal does not fail. "Give me ten minutes, I'll meet you at the door," she blinked.

Isla left without saying goodbye to anyone else. She picked up her jacket at the coat check and headed for the doors.

"Whoa, whoa, whoa, where are you going?" Knox asked, meeting up with her on her way out. In one hand he held another double whiskey and water, with the other he waved his Jets tickets in front of her face.

"Home. I have to work tomorrow," said Isla, side-stepping him without pausing. He spun around and matched her step, continuing down the hall with her.

"Tomorrow? What kind of office is open on a Sunday?"

"A coffee making office," said Isla. "Not all of us have a Daddy to hand us a partnership before we turn thirty."

"I earned it," he slurred. He put his arm out in front of her, stopping her and steadying himself on the wall. "So, by 'artist' you meant a coffee artist? You make those stupid coffee swans?"

"I should go," said Isla, making a move around him. Before she could, he placed his forearm on the wall on the other side of her, drink still in hand. He leaned in, towering over her, trapping her.

"Did you have a fun night?" he asked with a sloppy grin, his forehead almost resting on the wall. She could smell the expensive cologne on his clothes and the whiskey on his breath. It smelled like entitlement.

"You've had a lot to drink," Isla said. She pushed back into the wall, trying to create space between them. She looked up to meet his unfocused eyes. This was the terrifying unknown moment when things go very bad, or could be fine. Should she panic, or play it cool?

He shrugged. "I'm fine."

"You're swaying," she said, as he moved closer to her. She could barely see over his shoulder. She tried ducking, but his reflexes were just fast enough to block her.

"Am I? I thought that was you," he joked, his face inches from hers. Then he moved even closer. *Is he going to kiss me?* she thought. Her hand reacted and sailed up into the space between his face and hers. Her intention was just to create a barrier, but, her hand hit his face with some force. He staggered backwards and brought his hands to his face, dropping his drink. As the glass hit the ground, Isla felt whiskey spray on her bare legs.

"Why the hell did you hit me?" he roared.

"I—I didn't mean to—" Isla stammered. "I was — Oh!" A drop of blood was seeping out of his nostril. Isla frantically dug through her clutch trying to find the small tissue package her grandma had given her. There was only one left. As she handed it to him, she started to giggle, not because it was funny but because she was completely overwhelmed.

Okay, it was a little bit funny.

"It's not funny," barked Knox, grabbing the tissue from her hand.

"What did you expect was going to happen?" flashed Isla.

"I thought we were having fun."

"Having fun? Get over yourself! I was being a decent human being, something you seem to have no practise in. You *fired* me, or had you forgotten that after your seventh whiskey? Then you cornered me and thought I'd like a *kiss!*"

"Is everything alright here?" interjected a concerned-looking older man. Standing next to him was an older woman, each sporting hot pink 'parents of the bride' T-shirts.

"Everything is fine," said Isla through gritted teeth.

"You practically asked to be fired," said Knox, holding the tissue to his nose, which was beginning to swell.

"You practically asked to be punched in the face," she shot back.

"You need to calm down, miss," said the father of the bride, stepping between the two of them. "Or else I'm going to ask you to–"

"I have a first aid kit," interrupted the mother of the bride, handing Knox a thick pad of gauze. "David, take him to find some ice. Maybe see if you can find someone sober enough to take a look at his nose."

Then she turned to Isla "Are *you* okay?"

"I—-" Isla took a deep breath to collect herself. "Yeah, I am now, thank you. Umm— I should go, my friend's probably waiting."

Isla started out the door, she glanced back and saw Knox watching her leave, she lifted her middle finger, and hoped she'd never see him again.

8.

"Why don't you keep all your keys together like a normal person?" complained Priya.

Yellow-tinged light from the street flooded the front step of a three-story Victorian house with peach coloured siding and navy trim. Isla and Priya lived on the top floor, the smallest apartment, built out of the attic and full of odd angles and low ceilings. And right now, Isla could not find her keys.

"Shut up. You could've brought yours!" Isla snapped back.

Her evening had continued from bad to worse. They were locked out. Even though it was unseasonably warm, the temperatures in the middle of night were still below freezing. Isla hadn't told Priya about what had happened with Knox. She wasn't sure she wanted to.

"I have to be at work in 6 hours. I could be with Brian right now, warm!"

"It was your plan to come home, I just held you to it. Don't blame me."

"You forgot your keys!"

"So did you!" shrieked Isla. Neither of them was thinking straight, and neither was in any condition to drive. "Let's take the bus to my mom and dad's."

"I'm not taking the bus in the middle of the night," said Priya.

"I'm not paying for another cab! Come on" Isla started walking to the bus stop at the end of the street, thankful there was regular buses between this stop and the stop closest to her parents. They didn't have to wait long.

Bill and Dee lived in a modest split-level from the eighties, largely untouched by time. Renovating would require cleaning up all the books and second-hand treasures that cluttered their home. Their used blue hatchback sat in the driveway covered in frost from the damp cold.

Isla and Priya crept to the backyard. Then Priya accidentally bumped a garbage can as she passed by — the old metal kind, and when it fell, the noise was deafening. A lid rolled away like a wheel, finding its rest under the car.

They paused, their hearts beating loudly in their ears. Then quickly and silently Isla and Priya righted the can.

"Be careful," hissed Isla as she opened the back gate. Once they reached the back door, they found it was locked.

"It's okay, we can get in through that window," said Isla, pointing at a window six feet above the ground. "Mom's been cooking."

The kitchen window had been left open a crack. Deanna Gangon-Peters, PhD, professor of gender studies and international development, fighter of inequality and injustice, was completely devoid of all common sense. She had attempted and achieved scrambled eggs, then forgot to turn off the element and left the plastic spatula to burn in the pan.

"We need a ladder," said Isla through chattering teeth. She headed to the garage, her heels breaking through the hard surface of the snow. She had to shove the side door open with her shoulder, then reach into the pitch black and dig through the mounds of junk her father collected until she found something that was ladder shaped. She hauled it out and back to the kitchen window. They struggled to set the ladder up on the uneven and icy ground.

Isla took off her impractical shoes and took a deep breath. She rubbed her hands together, hoping to warm them up. Slowly she started to climb up the ladder. It wobbled with every step.

"Priya! Hold the ladder."

"Smile," said Priya, filming her with her phone.

"Priya! Shut that thing off," cried Isla.

"This moment needs to be documented! Short skirt, long ladder," she said, still filming.

"Put your damn phone away and hold the ladder, before I break my neck," snapped Isla. She held on to the house to steady herself.

Finally, Isla reached the window. She was able to hoist herself through and slide awkwardly onto the counter, and then lower herself to the kitchen floor. Isla instantly felt the warmth of her parent's house. Silently she tiptoed through the kitchen to unlock the door for Priya.

Once they were both in the kitchen, Isla turned on a light — revealing Bill sitting calmly at the kitchen table smiling at them.

"What the hell, Dad!?" Isla shouted and immediately clamped her hand over her mouth.

Bill chuckled as he stood up and gave Isla a bear hug and a kiss on the cheek. "Welcome home, kid. Next time, use the key under the porcupine boot brush, next to the step."

"How long have you been sitting there?" Isla asked once her heart stopped racing. Bill filled the kettle and put it on the stove. They settled themselves on miss-matched metal chairs around the small well-worn kitchen table.

"I heard a crash—the garbage cans?" he asked, grinning as they nodded. "I snuck down to investigate. You walked right passed me."

Bill poured boiling water over the tea bags in two mugs and handed one to each girl. "I trust you'll make yourself at home. Church starts at nine-thirty," he said to Isla pointedly.

This was the cost of spending the night: sitting next to her parents in the third pew on the left, hungover or not.

Bill wished them a good night and headed back up to bed.

Isla sighed and took a sip of tea, letting the liquid warm her from the inside. She was glad it was her father who had found them. Her mother would not have let them off so easy. Feeling cold and sleepy, they trudged down to Isla's old bedroom. All of Isla's childhood treasures remained except for her bed, which had been replaced by a pull-out sofa. Isla let Priya gush about Brian, choosing to keep her mouth shut about her night. The two friends giggled and whispered as they fell asleep, like they had so many times in the past, amongst their shared memories tacked to the wall.

Isla set five China plates around the formal dining room table. Bare during the week, the glossy ornate oak table had been faithfully covered by a waterproof, faded floral tablecloth each Sunday for the last thirty years. She yawned silently into her arm. Her head ached, and she had fought waves of nausea through singing familiar hymns in four-part harmony.

The family gathered around the table, Isla alone on one side, Priya long gone to her shift at the hospital. Her mother held court at one end of the table. Across from Isla sat Andrew and Emma, Liam asleep in the car seat next to her. Bill sat at the end of the table closest to the kitchen, quietly observing those he loved more than life.

After they finished table grace, Dee feigned ignorance. "What a surprise to have you girls here this morning! Why the sleepover?"

"You know how much I love that sofa bed. I dream about it nearly every night, all the springs pushing up into my back, the sag in the middle. Heaven!" spouted Isla.

"*Sarcasm: the last refuge of the modest and chaste souled people when the privacy of their soul is coarsely and intrusively invaded.* Fyodor Dostoevsky," replied Dee as she poured the rich gravy from the braised short ribs onto her mound of mashed potatoes.

"Fun fact, sarcasm is funny," shot back Isla.

Dee held her hands up in surrender.

"I bet you locked yourself out again?" asked Andrew, serving him self an extra bit of meat.

"We, not I. Priya didn't have keys either."

"Twelve years we've been friends, she should know better," said Emma. "I still carry a spare key to your apartment."

"Great! Next time we'll break into your house," said Isla.

"Our house isn't as easy to break into; the kitchen doesn't need to be aired out as often," said Andrew, indicating to Dee.

"The finer points of kitchen work escape me." Dee gave a dismissive wave of her hand.

"No matter," said Bill with a chuckle. "It was nice to have you here."

"Helena Penner thought your skirt was too short for church," Dee declared.

"I think you mean Mrs. Henry G. Penner," replied Isla.

Dee grinned. "Yes, Mrs. Henry G. Penner—can you believe that woman? She always has something to complain about. Either she complains about not having enough young people in church or she complains about the young people that come to church. She can't have it both ways. I told her I didn't care how short your skirt was — you showed up. Honestly, she wouldn't be happy unless all of us gals were in long skirts like the old days."

"Isla, before your mother launches into her opinions on others giving opinions on how women should dress, can I offer you some more short rib? You've hardly eaten anything," interjected Bill.

Isla's stomach was still churning. She had eaten a few mashed potatoes, but each bite felt like sawdust in her mouth.

"I'm good, thanks, Dad. Mom, my skirt *was* too short! I didn't wear it to church to make a statement; it was this or the old U of W T-shirt I slept in," said Isla. "Had I planned to go to church this morning, I would've worn something different."

"Speaking of planning, you cut our call last night before answering about work," said Dee, calmly scooping mashed potatoes onto her plate.

Isla felt all the blood rush out of her face and pool in her stomach. She was going to be sick. She stood up quickly and grabbed the closest thing to her, which turned out to be the water jug. "Does anyone want more water?"

Her hands shook as she placed the jug under the tap. She turned the stream on low, buying herself time. She splashed some water on her face. How was she going to get out of this? The jug was overflowing before she shut the water off. Slowly she returned to the table. To her dismay, her mother was not distracted.

"I stopped by your office last week," said Dee. "The receptionist is lovely, is she new? She said you were fired three weeks ago."

The professor said it so calmly the significance was almost lost. Isla could feel everyone's disappointment. Even tiny Liam, who was asleep in his car seat, surely now realised what a loser his aunt was.

"It wasn't my fault," she said.

"You yelled at Sue Tremblay!" accused her mother.

"I didn't! It wasn't Sue, it was the new accounts manager, he—"

"Sue Tremblay went out on a limb, hiring you as a favour to your father, and this is how you repay her?" Dee's voice was loud and clear, and continued to ring in Isla's ear.

Isla glanced at Andrew, pleading with him for help, but he stared at his mashed potatoes unhelpfully.

"He is not a nice guy," said Isla. Everything from the night before rushed back to her, the frustration, the unwanted attention, the sound of her palm hitting his nose.

"You can't throw away a perfectly good job because of personality differences. Haven't we taught you anything about resistance? Do you even understand how much privilege you have? Yelling at your boss because he is difficult? Women all over the world must work in deplorable conditions to put pathetic amounts of food on the table for their children. And you can't even deal with a difficult boss. Do you think you're the first person to ever have a difficult boss? Do you know how lucky you are to even have that job? We raised you far better than this Isla Margaret."

There it was, the full name. Invoked to remind her of her great grandmother's struggle to feed twelve children after the death of her great grandfather.

"Isla, are you ok? You look like you're going to be sick!" said Bill.

"She's hungover," said Andrew, as if they hadn't all figured it out.

The professor opened her mouth and closed it again, speechless. Emma smacked her husband's arm. Isla shot Andrew a dirty look.

"Sorry," he muttered back.

"What are you going to do next?" asked Bill, trying to build a bridge between mother and daughter.

"I am going to take two painkillers and go to my shift this afternoon at Yellow Box," Isla answered. She started at her plate, too ashamed to make eye contact.

"The coffeeshop? Really? You're going to work at the coffeeshop?" criticized Dee.

"Yes Mom. The coffeeshop."

"You held that job in high school. You can do better than that. Why don't you go back to school? Finish your degree, at least."

"Dee," warned Bill.

"I don't want to go back to school. You said it was a useless degree, anyway. Maybe a coffeeshop is the best I can do!" said Isla hotly, tears threatening. "Maybe you should all deal with it."

59

Shame had now fully spread through her body. The fight was gone. She was never going to win with her mother, anyway. The only option was to withdraw. Without another word, she got up from the table, leaving a nearly full plate. She grabbed her jacket, put on her heels from the night before and headed out the door to the bus stop.

"I should go after her," said Dee.

"I don't think that would be a good idea. Let her go," said Bill. "She'll figure it out."

9.
April 26, Sunny, 19C°.

Spring had arrived abruptly: two weeks had taken them from parkas to shorts and sandals. The tiny snowsuit Liam had worn home from the hospital sat in the laundry hamper waiting for its final wash, then to be packed up, perhaps for a sibling or friend. Liam had grown chubby, with rolls upon rolls, curls like his mother and colouring from his father. His parents had settled into predictable traditional roles, Andrew going to work and leaving Emma home, a dutiful mother and wife. Supper on the table at six. For Emma, all her dreams had come true. She had the husband, the house, and a beautiful son.

She wondered when it would get easier.

Priya ran on caffeine and adrenaline. She picked up as many extra shifts as she could, learning all she could absorb. Eagerness meant better scores and better references, but sleeping with your supervisor also had its advantages. He had become an addiction. Some of her peers turned to other things, uppers to work, downers to sleep. The prescription drugs were easy to come by. Brian had warned her, he had seen too many students taken down by the temptation. So instead, she clung to his body pressed up against her, in the dark corners and quiet moments. No talk about love or futures — they barely talked at all. He was her release valve, and she was his.

Bill and Dee worried about their children, as all parents do in their spare time. Even empty nesters who are busy living their own lives, giving lectures, and helping non-profits. Those still, quiet moments brought questions. Bill worried about Andrew. Would he get stuck in a rut, day in and day out, doing the same dutiful things he had always done? Would he have enough fun in his life? Would he remember to tell his wife how much he loves her? Dee worried more for Isla. Would she continue to be ruled by impulse and whimsy? Would she ever settle down? Calm down? Commit to anything?

And Isla, well, she was miserable. Nothing was going according to any plan she had ever imagined for her life. Most days she slept in late and then escaped to different worlds of movies, novels, and mindless scrolling. Everyone seemed happy but her. On her easel sat a blank canvas, untouched. Paints had been poured, paint brush put to canvas, only to be discarded in a pile next to the window. Being a tortured artist wasn't working for her. Creating came out of joy, not frustration.

The smell of coffee was the best thing in her life these days. For the first time since returning to Yellow Box Coffee, she was on the morning shift. She couldn't remember the last time she'd gotten up this early. She'd forgotten what a sunrise could do for the soul.

Opening a large bag of Ethiopian coffee beans, she took a moment to savour the aroma, before dumping the beans into the grinder. She hit the switch and leaned against the wall, closing her eyes and listening to the familiar whirl. *Getting up this early is going to finish me off,* she thought as the grinder stopped, *or maybe bring me back to life.* A slight smile tugged at her lips as she thought about coming back to life. She measured the grinds into the filter and pressed start. Time to turn the sign from Closed to Open.

As the day went on, a steady stream of very important people had her moving faster than she thought possible. Six drinks lined up on the espresso machine, six customers waiting anxiously for their order so they could rush off to their very important thing.

The rush eased as the morning continued. Isla took the opportunity to down a shot of espresso, with a dollop of whipped cream. Because her back was turned to the entrance, she heard the door but didn't see who came in. She swallowed her last mouthful of cream and turned around with a big smile, to come face to face with Sue Tremblay.

"Good morning—umm. Hi!" Isla stumbled.

"Hello, Isla, how nice to see you. You have a little something—" she said warmly as she pointed discreetly to the tip of her nose.

Isla wiped her nose with the back of her hand, mortified to see the glob of whipped cream.

"What can I get you?" asked Isla. *Stick to the script,* she told herself, *before you embarrass yourself even more.*

"Have you worked here long? I'm surprised I haven't seen you. I come here much too often," said Sue, without giving an order.

"I usually work the evening shift," she stated, poised at the till.

Eventually Sue ordered an extra hot, extra sweet mochaccino and a black coffee. Then she asked, "How have you been?"

"Fine, I'm good. Life is good," Isla replied with a tight smile. She started up the loud espresso machine and hoped the conversation would stall. Sue wandered around the coffee shop waiting for her drinks.

When Sue wandered back to retrieve her drinks, she asked, "That painting of the iris catches my eye every morning. Do you have any information about the artist?"

It was a trap. The painting in question, a small canvas, with an indigo and blue iris, was Isla's own painting, painted a lifetime ago after a trip to her grandmother's garden. A heart full of love and courage had propelled her to her local coffee shop with an offer that her paintings could go on their walls — free art for them, and the chance to be seen and maybe purchased. Over the years most had sold. The ones that remained taunted her with their optimism and cheerfulness.

Isla busied herself ringing in the drinks. There was an artist biography right next to the painting. Sue knew it was hers. When she finally looked up and met Sue's eye, Sue smiled. "I didn't know you were an artist."

"I'm not really. It's just a hobby, something I do for fun."

"What else do you think an artist is?" Sue asked.

Isla pushed her hair back from her face. "Someone who makes money from their art?"

"Making money is a bad reason to make art," Sue replied after paying. As she headed out the door with her coffee order, Isla realized who the black coffee was for. Knox was in the passenger seat of Sue's car, on his phone. In her mind, she went through all the spiteful things she wanted to say to him, but would never have the opportunity. Thank god he hadn't come in.

10.

May 2. Warming breeze, 16C°.

"Can you start this patient for me? I have to make a call, then I'll be right in," Brian asked Priya, giving her his most disarming smile and handing her the chart.

Priya took it, of course. She would have even without that smile — a chance to see a patient on her own! She was almost done her ER rotation, just four more hours to go. Even though she had enjoyed the company, she knew the ER wasn't for her. She wanted beauty and finesse, not slash and patch.

"Hello, Mr. Foster. What seems to be the problem?" She greeted the couple before her, the man laying on his back on the bed with his hand clutched to his chest, his wife sitting nervously next to him, her hand on his arm. The nurse, having finished her preliminary checks, stood to the side, at the ready.

"I'm having a heart attack, and no one in this sorry excuse for a hospital gives a damn! What do they do? Send me another damn nurse!" he yelled.

Priya preferred her patients under general anesthetic.

"Mr. Foster, I'm Dr Dhaliwal. Can I start by listening to your heart?" said Priya, approaching with her stethoscope.

65

"Don't you come near me with that thing. I want a Canadian doctor."

"I am a Canadian, born and raised," she replied sweetly. With every stubborn bone of her body, she was not going to let him get to her, not today. "Now, I'll just give your heart a listen, sir."

"Don't touch me," he growled.

"What other symptoms do you have? It says here, chest pain and shortness of breath. What were you doing when these symptoms started?"

"I can't understand a word you're saying!" he bellowed. "I want a doctor who speaks English."

"We are speaking English," Priya responded with a fake smile, looking to his wife for help. She glared back.

The door opened and Brian entered. Instantly, his presence eased the tension in the room.

"What do we have here?" he said with his signature smile. "What seems to be the problem?"

"Seventy-five-year-old male, chest pain, shortness of breath..." started Priya.

"Finally! A real doctor. You can call me Al," the man said, reaching for his hand. Brian shook it heartily and then stood back, indicating Priya should continue.

"What were you doing when the symptoms started?" Priya asked, resuming her examination.

The man paused for a moment, looking back and forth between the doctors. "Now that a real doctor's here, does she have to stay?"

"Well Al, Dr. Dhaliwal is a student — a very bright one, I might add." He turned and winked at Priya. "You were lucky enough to have her assigned to you. I'm just here to observe."

The husband and wife exchanged information with their eyes in a way that only those who had spent many years together could.

"My husband would feel more comfortable if she left," replied Mrs. Foster curtly, avoiding eye contact with Priya.

Brian shrugged and relieved Priya of the chart, giving her a half smile. She waited for a moment, wondering if he would defend her. As he turned back to the patient to start the exam, Priya marched out of the room.

She paced the floor outside the exam room. Back and forth, back and forth, wearing a path on the putty-coloured vinyl floor. Her blood boiled. How dare he dismiss her? What a coward!

The door opened and Brian paused, chuckling along with the patient as he backed out of the room. When the door closed, he handed her the chart and said, "likely a panic attack, but we should run some tests just in case. Can you call up to cardiology for a consult?"

"Yes," Priya nodded automatically, used to taking orders of this type. "But can we talk about—"

Brian held up his hand. "I'm totally swamped. We'll talk later, 'kay babe?"

Babe? Something was sinking inside of her — her heart, her stomach, her dignity. She said plainly, "the patient asked me to leave."

"Oh that. Don't worry about that, it was nothing. He was probably uncomfortable with a student doctor. Don't take it personally." He moved to get around her.

"I was asked to leave because of the colour of my skin," stated Priya plainly.

Brian stopped and spun around. "Come on. That is not what happened."

"You weren't there the whole time. You didn't hear everything he said to me."

"Priya, drop it." His supervisor tone came out. "Don't even go there. It was a misunderstanding. Patients are in a vulnerable state, and it's within their rights to ask for a doctor that makes them comfortable."

"He told me he wanted a Canadian, which I am! Who spoke English, which I do! I don't even have an accent!" Priya spoke louder to try and push down the hurt that rose in her chest.

"Sometimes you do," he joked before continuing, "Even if that is the truth, there is nothing you can do about it. He'll be out of here soon."

"You could've done something about it," insisted Priya.

"Stuff like that happens all the time. You need to deal with it and move on. Don't let it affect your performance."

Priya crossed her arms and glared at Brian, "Has it ever happened to you? Have you ever been dismissed by a patient?"

Brian ran is hand through his hair nervously, then he took her shoulders in his hands and kissed the top of her forehead and whispered, "Let it go."

Fuck you, she thought silently, as she watched her lover walk away.

11.

May 5. Drizzle, 14C°.

Emma held Liam as they looked out their front window. She held his hand, making it wave to Andrew as he drove out of the driveway.

"Bye bye, Daddy!" she whispered in his ear. Liam cooed back to her, smiling a toothless grin.

"All right, little guy. Are you excited for your nap? I've got big plans for nap time, mopping floors, taking a shower, starting some laundry..." Emma recited her to-do list in a bouncy sing-song voice, hoping her desperation didn't seep through. She suspected her son purposefully sabotaged her on her busiest mornings. "If you're a good boy and let Mommy finish her jobs, we're going to go shopping with auntie Isla!"

Emma nursed Liam to sleep in the glider next to his crib. She carefully laid him down and tip-toed out of his room, holding her breath all the way down the staircase, flinching when the step third from the bottom squeaked.

Once in the kitchen, Emma sat with her tea and stared at her extensive day planner. Today was Saturday and her weekly list had just one thing crossed off: ~~clean the bathroom~~. She had managed to clean it on Wednesday because Dee had stopped by. Emma had asked if she could shower while Dee watched the baby, but instead she furiously cleaned, unsure of when the last time had been.

She wished she could figure out where all her time was going. Emma took a sip and considered her first task: a shower was non-negotiable. Andrew had made fun of the crusty baby puke she'd found in her hair that morning.

She hadn't found it funny.

Springing into action, she flung toys and junk into the general areas where they belonged. Then as fast as she could, she damp-mopped the dusty, dark hardwood floor, a feature when they moved in, now a daily curse. Next, she loaded the dishwasher. Laundry got started, all while placing toys into random nooks and crannies to get them out of sight.

After forty-five minutes, the house was still far from the picturesque home she had envisioned — but it was better.

Creeping past the nursery into her own room, Emma turned on the shower and, stripped off her dirty pyjama pants and Andrew's old baseball shirt. Then she climbed into the hot spray. For a second, she relaxed and allowed the water to run over her. For a moment, she stood still.

She could feel it, the moment Liam woke up. A tightening of the thread between them.

Emma scrubbed her hair as quickly as she could, then turned the water off and threw a towel around her as she sprinted into the nursery. Liam's face was flushed and his whole body was rigid with emotion.

She picked him up and cuddled him to her wet skin as her hair dripped on the floor. She sank to the pale green carpet and put him to her naked breast. She leaned and waited as his sobs pacified into furious sucking. Tears fell from her face and mixed with the milk leaking from her other breast, onto her bare leg.

"Isla, you have to see how bad this dress is," Priya called into the adjoining fitting room. She stood in front of the mirror, posing to see it from all angles. Isla came out wearing a simple form-fitting navy dress with a herringbone detail. It showed off her curves in all the right ways.

"Pretty," said Priya, whose dress was a much less flattering mint green, dropped-waist potato sack.

Isla joined her on a platform, where she also began to pose. "Is it too tight? I feel like it might be."

"No such thing as too tight," Priya responded. "Not tight *enough*, however, is a real problem." She cinched the fabric around her waist. "How can a dress look so interesting on a hanger and be such a disaster on me?"

Emma stumbled as she entered the changing area. She pushed an empty stroller while balancing her diaper bag on her shoulder and holding Liam on her hip. She greeted them with a simple hello.

"You brought Liam!" squealed Isla, grabbing her nephew out of Emma's arms and nuzzling his neck, which smelled like sour milk and baby soap.

"I thought Andy was going to watch him?" Priya was not nearly as thrilled.

"I had to bring him; he's been so fussy. I think he's teething," said Emma apologetically as she parked her stroller and untangled herself from her bag. Her arms ached and she desperately needed another coffee. "Andy wanted to go to the gym, he hasn't been for awhile—"

"Since when does Andy go to the gym? We've had these plans for weeks!" fumed Priya.

Emma gave Priya a tight smile and tried not to let her get under her skin. Priya didn't understand marriage and she would never understand motherhood. She didn't even try.

"I think it is wonderful that he came." Isla silently begged Priya to give Emma a break.

71

"Isla, that dress looks amazing on you!" said Emma, moving the attention away from herself.

"Do you think it is professional enough?" asked Isla, gazing longingly at the dress.

"Professional for what?" questioned Priya. "I thought you wore a uniform?"

She did. It wasn't that bad as far as uniforms go, a black t-shirt printed with a yellow box, and black jeans. "I don't know. Maybe one day I'll work in an office again."

Before she could say anything else, she was interrupted by Emma's friend, Alicia. She breezed into the changing area pushing a sleek double stroller, both baby and toddler asleep, latte in hand, not a hair out of place.

"Hello, hello!" she sang. "Johnny insisted on taking Charlotte on an adorable daddy-daughter date this morning. Since I only had two, Emma invited me. Girls' Day!"

"What-The-Fuck?" Priya mouthed to Isla, feeling like her head might explode. Not more babies!

Then Liam started crying, not sweetly fussing or whimpering, but full-on screaming. Emma dug in her diaper bag to find something, anything, to calm him.

Without another word, Priya walked out of the change room. But wherever she went, she could still hear his screams. *Babies are so aggravating*, she thought, as she came back with three more dresses — this time her preferred colour: black.

Alicia, whose children slept through the noise, had taken Liam from a stricken Emma. Once in Alicia's arms, he calmed right down.

"Here, try this on." Isla thrust the weird mint dress into Emma's arms as her face crumbled. She pushed her into Priya's changing room before entering hers to continue her dream fashion show.

Leaving Priya alone with Alicia and three small children.

"You're Priya, right? The doctor?" Alicia asked pleasantly.

Priya nodded.

"What is your opinion on baby carriers versus baby wraps? I've been using a wrap with all my children, and I believe they are the safest for the development of the hip joints."

Priya blinked. What the hell was she talking about?

"People have been using baby wraps for centuries in places like Africa and China, and don't even get me started on parents who carry children in car seats! I mean, don't you want to bond with your child? Did your mom use a wrap in India?"

"I was born in Canada," stated Priya.

"Right, right. Of course. But she used a wrap, right?"

"I don't remember," said Priya, searching for a way to end the conversation.

"Does your family practice yoga?"

"We're Sikh."

"You mean *Seek*?" Alicia corrected.

"It is pronounced Sikh."

"Like to be sick?"

Priya tightened her jaw as she turned away from Alicia and pretended to be interested in the framed prints of models frolicking through wildflower fields.

"Well then, happy Ramadan!"

Oh my god, let this conversation be over, Priya thought. "Muslims celebrate Ramadan. Sikhs are not Muslims."

"Interesting. I thought because you both have the, you know—" she made a motion around her head, miming a turban "—it was the same."

"Maybe you should read a book?" Priya said under her breath. She was done with ignorance masked beneath sweetness.

"I'm trying to learn about your culture. You don't have to be rude," Alicia snapped.

73

"Isla! Are you almost done in there?" Priya marched up to the change room door just as Isla opened it. This time she was wearing a grey suit with neon green piping on the seams.

"What the hell are you wearing?" asked Priya.

"A suit," said Isla, buttoning the blazer and smoothing the pants down the front. She liked what she saw in the mirror. Her hair was up in a tight top knot; she could almost believe she was someone important whose life had direction and purpose.

"A little formal for the latte bunch," said Priya, dashing the tiny bit of self-confidence Isla was enjoying.

"I'm dreaming. I'm not going to buy it."

"What brought this on?" asked Priya.

"Sue Trembly is one of my regular customers and she bought one of my paintings—" Isla tried to downplay her excitement.

"Isla! Really? That's amazing! Which one?" interrupted Emma, bursting out of her change room.

"Yeah, she bought the little blue iris. Luke has had it at Yellow Box for awhile. She comes in almost every day. I finally built up enough nerve to ask her to be a reference for me, for a graphic arts course I'm thinking about applying for and," Isla paused, "she asked if I wanted to come interview for the new design position at HRA."

Emma and Priya stared at her, stunned.

Isla continued, "I mean, how ridiculous is that? Like I could ever set foot in that office again."

"You have to do it!" called Priya, retreating to a change room with black clothes in tow.

Isla shook her head. "I think she was being polite."

"She wasn't. If she was being polite, she would've agreed to be your reference. She's handing you an opportunity. You have to do it!" insisted Priya.

"I don't know anything about graphic design! I have no experience — do I have to remind you how horrible it was to work there, for *him*?" Isla slumped down on the pink velvet bench that lined the change room hall.

"But you loved working for Sue! Besides, you're way too talented to pour lattes all day. Graphic design could be something you'd be really good at," Emma said, sitting beside her. Alicia was still rocking Liam. He seemed comfortable in her arms. "Besides, what's the worst that could happen?"

"What's the worst that could happen? I could get the job! That would be the worst!"

"Get over it, Isla. We all work with difficult people. Look at Emma: her boss is cranky, demanding, and poops his pants regularly," said Priya from inside the fitting room. Their conversation echoed across the high ceilings. It was beginning to draw the attention of women around them.

"I can't believe you would say that! Children aren't cranky bosses! They're beautiful souls who need to be gently coaxed into discovering their gifts and talents. It's not work to be a mother, it is a privilege," interjected Alicia.

Priya ignored her, taking off one dress and picking one to try on next. She continued, "You have literally nothing to lose. Go to the interview. If you don't get the job, then go to school. And if you do get it, awesome! You saved yourself the time and money. I'm sick of you moping around and cluttering the apartment with depressing artwork."

"I can't do it," said Isla quietly.

"Why not?" asked Emma. Liam had fallen asleep in Alicia's arms and Emma took him back. She gently cradled him upright on her chest, patting his little bum a few times while adopting the slight swaying bounce that all mothers seem to learn instinctively.

"Knox tried to kiss me," Isla said.

"WHAT?" Priya yelled, charging out of the fitting room in her black lace bra and underwear.

Emma tightened her arms around her baby, deepening her knee bends, patting his back, but he woke up anyway and started screaming.

"When did this happen?" demanded Priya.

Between Priya and Liam, the noise was unbearable. Other customers glared at Emma.

"At the social—when I was leaving, he was drunk, and—" stuttered Isla.

"At the Hunter's social?"

Isla nodded.

"Let me get this straight. Knox Harrison tried to kiss you at the Hunter's social, and you didn't tell me?" demanded Priya, glaring at Isla.

Isla shrugged helplessly, looking down at the stylish suit she was still wearing. It was starting to suffocate her: too tight, too hot, too itchy.

Priya continued, "In the last two months there has never been a moment for you to tell your best friend that a hot guy tried to kiss you at a social?"

"I wanted to forget about it. It didn't exactly end well," Isla admitted.

Emma managed to calm Liam down a little. Alicia's children continued to sleep through the whole outburst.

Does she drug them? Emma thought maliciously.

Everyone was staring at Isla, waiting for her to finish the story.

"You were having fun together" prompted Priya.

"We weren't." replied Isla. "I wasn't— when I was leaving, he trapped me against the wall—"

"Was he violent?" asked Alicia who was listening in with eyes wide. A couple of shop attendants were eavesdropping while precisely refolding rejected clothing.

"No, he was—sloppy. Look, I wanted to go home. I tried to stop him, and I accidentally hit him in the nose. I didn't mean to hurt him, but I didn't want him to kiss me—then his nose was bleeding, and these old people came and tried to help, I was completely overwhelmed. So, I waited for Priya outside."

"It was *you* that punched him in the nose?" Priya laughed, collapsing onto the bench next to Isla. "What a fucking liar, he told us he ran into a door. Brian had to take him to the ER! I don't think his pretty nose will ever be the same."

"Wasn't that the same night you had to break into your parents' house?" Emma started giggling. "Isla, only you—"

Alicia's toddler, Georgianna woke peacefully. Her eyes fluttered open, and she smiled sweetly at her attentive mother, who squatted down quietly and pulled out a snack container with an array of veggies and hummus — homemade, obviously. Alicia reminded her to stay quiet so little Augusta could keep sleeping.

Why is it so easy for her? thought Emma, still jiggling Liam up and down. She had given up on him falling back to sleep.

Isla smiled grimly. "You see why I don't have a chance of getting the job. Not if he has anything to do with it."

"I don't see what the big deal is. So you punched the guy in the face. You need to go to this interview," said Priya. "Besides, he is a nice guy."

"A nice guy? Are you defending him?" asked Isla.

"No, he deserved a punch in the face that night. But he tags along with Brian and me sometimes. I kind of feel sorry for him. He seems lonely."

"Because he's horrible. He should learn some manners and make some new friends," replied Isla.

"I think you should apply. The job is in the art department, right? Maybe you won't have anything to do with him," said Emma.

"I wonder what the professor would say about your dilemma?" asked Priya as she re-entered the fitting room.

"You wouldn't dare" groaned Isla.

"Who's the professor?" Alicia quietly asked Emma.

"Her mother," she whispered back with a sly grin. Louder she said, "if Priya doesn't tell her, maybe I will."

Defeated, Isla trudged back into her change room, again catching a glance of herself in the suit.

Maybe she should try.

12.
May 14. Breezy, 17C°.

Every day was the same. Knox got up, ran five kilometres, worked twelve hours, ate take-out, and went back to sleep. Sundays were the worst — with no work to fill his time, he was stuck at his condo, vibrating with energy. No commitments. No roots.

He'd run for hours. The warmer it got, the farther he went, exploring the city on foot, too quickly to absorb it. An empty horizon made him squirm; he tended to stay among the tall buildings. They helped to keep everything in check.

Finally, *finally*, Monday would arrive. He could work again.

In nearly six months, he hadn't signed any new clients. Things were not going according to plan. He would allow himself a brief moment of doubt — maybe he wasn't cut out for this; maybe the thing he had wanted his whole life was wrong. But then he'd pick up the phone and try again. Self pity never made anyone any money.

Sue wasn't concerned. She had faith in him. She knew the cloth from which he was cut; it rarely tired, it never gave up. She may have chuckled over wine with her husband about Knox's youth and impatience, but she was honoured to walk alongside him and put out the fires the young man failed to notice. *He'll learn*, she thought. *We all do.*

On the day of the interviews for the new graphic designer, she peeked into his office. Her patience had turned to impatience. Interviews were meant to start five minutes ago, and he was still on his phone. He silently waved her in.

Knox held up his hand and mouthed *important.*

She tapped her wristwatch.

Start without me, he silently replied.

A few minutes later, he quietly slid into the conference room and flashed the interviewee an apologetic smile as he settled into the seat. Sue was in the middle and beside her was Ryan, their current and apparently over-worked graphic designer. Sue slid him a stack of portfolios. The top one, belonging to the lady sitting across from him, was—bland to say the least.

Knox wasn't convinced they needed a new graphic designer. What they needed was more accounts. He had spent his whole life immersed in the culture of advertising, and while creative talent impressed him, he knew the cash was in volume. HRA needed more accounts and bigger accounts.

He fidgeted to keep from yawning. The woman they were interviewing used all his least favourite words. Synergy. Go-getter. Utilize. Three strikes and she's out.

The second interview was even worse. The young man was too nervous to make eye contact; he stared at his shoes and mumbled through out the conversation. Knox managed to remain neutral until the door shut behind Mumble Man. He jumped up and immediately began pacing. "Are these the best this city has to offer? Give the job to Kelly and move on."

"Hold on," said Sue. "We're not done. I have one more up my sleeve." Sue handed a portfolio to Ryan. It was in a simple manila folder. Ryan opened it on the table. It was full of scrap paper, and most looked like they had been rescued from the trash. Ryan slowly spread them out on the table and studied each page.

"These are our clients," said Ryan quietly, still looking from one to the next in disbelief. Knox looked over his shoulder and couldn't believe what he saw. zEach piece was a pencil sketch of different logos of current clients.

"Look at this one," said Ryan, holding a sheet up in awe. "This logo is better than what we ended up with. Who *is* this?"

"It's someone — familiar with the company." Sue gave both men a sneaky, confident smile that neither of them dared question. "She's inexperienced, but fearless. I have a good feeling about her."

All that matters in business is first impressions. Knox liked what he saw, enough for an interview at least. Yet something nagged at the back of his neck, slowly creeping up behind his eyes. What is Sue playing at? "Why isn't there a resume? What about a name?"

Before Sue could answer, Knox's phone rang. "I need to take this. I'll be right back."

Knox opened the door with one hand and pressed talk with the other. A split second later, he hung up and slammed the door shut.

Isla was left alone in the hall. All the courage drained out of her body. Her palms starting sweating. She had never felt such palpable hatred in a look. Knox's glare pierced like lasers searching for a target. *Leave*, she whispered to herself.

But something kept her in her seat: maybe curiosity, maybe fear of her mother. Whatever it was, she remained.

"No way," Knox said, rubbing his nose which ached with muscle memory.

"Pardon?" Sue asked, feigning innocence. She tidied the piles of paper in front of her.

"You heard me, not her." stated Knox, moving from the door to face his aunt. "Where did you get those drawings?"

"Janine passed them on to me a couple months back" said Sue, stifling a smile. "We all agreed they are great."

"I fired her," said Knox sharply.

"Yes, you fired her," Sue replied. "And I would like to rehire her."

Ryan looked up from the sketches. "The person who drew these. She used to work here?"

"Yes. Isla Peters—" said Sue.

"She was the bookkeeper responsible for that massive payroll screw up in February," Knox spat out.

"It was a *slight glitch* in payroll, and it wasn't entirely her fault, Knox. Besides, her skills were wasted in accounting," argued Sue.

"Does she have any experience or education in graphic design?" Ryan asked, treading carefully between the warring partners. He realized he might be the deciding vote. Oh joy.

"She doesn't," said Sue, not wanting to lose her ally, "but she is talented and eager to learn."

"She's a loose cannon," interjected Knox.

"So are you, and we put up with you anyway," Sue replied dryly.

Ryan smirked at the younger man, who was pacing back and forth across the room, his fists balled up in frustration. Seizing the opportunity to score a point against the younger man who had been making his life difficult for months, Ryan said "I think we should give her a shot."

"No," said Knox.

"My department, my call," said Sue. "Isla is the most talented applicant. And she's great to work with if you take a moment to get to know her." She matched Knox in stubbornness. "She's awfully brave to show up after the way you treated her."

"The way I treated her? What about the way she treated me?" Knox barked.

Sue ignored his complaint. "Ryan, what's your vote?"

Ryan nodded. "She is talented. She'll be a good contrast to my style. Unless she totally bombs the interview, she has my vote."

"Great," said Knox sarcastically. "I guess my presence here this morning has been a complete waste of my time."

"Stop being dramatic. Your under-articulated argument of '*no*' has failed to change either of our minds. Unless you have something more concrete to contribute, we are going ahead with this interview," Sue replied, elegantly sitting back down in her chair.

"I hope you don't regret your decision," Knox said, his tone conveying the opposite. He collected his stuff and stormed out the door.

13.

May 16. Slight mist, 12C°.

The clock on the stove confirmed what Andrew's body already knew. Bedtime. He made sure every light was out and climbed the stairs to their bedroom. The office light was on. He swung the door open and was surprised to see that Emma was still awake. She had pushed his desk to the side and had set up a folding plastic table. On it, she had placed an ornate mahogany box with the words *William Bennet Peters* engraved across the top. Next to it were smaller boxes, one maple, one cherry, and various notebooks, stickers, markers, stencils, and other craft supplies.

"What are you doing?" asked Andrew, his arms slipping around her shoulders.

Emma jumped. "You scared me! Look, my baby box came today."

"What's a baby box?" asked Andrew.

"Alicia told me about them. She has one for each of her children. It's a system to help document your child's milestones and memories. See, there's a book to document all the milestones, and little cases for the first tooth, and another for first haircut. It's like a baby book, but more encompassing. Alicia has been working on Augustus' since before he was born. She says you must document

84

as it happens, otherwise you'll never remember. Mine only came in the mail today. I'm three months behind already! If I don't start tonight, I'll never catch up."

"It's late. Why don't you leave it for now and come spend some time with me?" said Andrew, nuzzling his face into her neck.

Emma squirmed. "I only have an hour, then Liam will be up again. I haven't even started the pregnancy journal!"

"The pregnancy journal?" questioned Andrew.

"I have to document pregnancy, birth story, and all his firsts, like his first smile and first time he rolled over."

"He rolled over?" asked Andrew. "That is amazing! When?"

"Yesterday. He was playing on his tummy, and he rolled over. I think he surprised himself! He started crying right away, but as soon as I put him back on his tummy he rolled on to his back again."

"I'm sorry I missed it."

"I tried to take a video, but he started crying and the moment passed."

Andrew looked through the pregnancy journal at all the prompts on each page. "Are you going to fill all this out?"

"I hope to," said Emma, taking the journal out of his hand. "Here's one for you. How did Daddy feel when he found out you were on the way?"

Andrew thought back to year ago. "I was happy."

"Just happy?"

"Yes."

"Anything else?"

"No, I don't think so."

"I can't leave the rest of the page blank. Come on, this is for Liam! Isn't there anything else you want me to write?"

For the first time in his life, Andrew wondered if his mother had kept track of anything. He doubted it. If she had, it would be scribbled in the margin of a forgotten book.

"Leave it and let's go to bed."

"I'm not tired." But her body betrayed her with a yawn. "My mom called."

"And how are Sara and Gerald?" Andrew waited, knowing his in-laws wouldn't use overseas long distance for a chat.

Emma looked out the dark window and streetlights. "They're coming for a visit. They want to see Liam."

With every fiber of his being Andrew suppressed a groan. "When?"

"In June. They'll stay with us, mostly, and travel around, visiting supporting churches..." she trailed off, still not meeting Andrew's eye.

"How long?"

"She didn't say," said Emma as she straightened the craft supplies.

"Of course she didn't," said Andrew, rubbing his temples. "Can we nail down when they're leaving this time? We can't afford to have them living off us for months again."

"They're missionaries!"

"With a quarter million-dollar budget! You'd think they could pay for the occasional grocery bill." Andrew rarely got angry, but when he did, his in-laws were usually involved.

"Maybe it will be different this time." Emma turned back to her table and opened the journal.

"I'm going to bed," Andrew announced, hoping she'd come with him.

Emma kept writing.

14.

May 21. Sunny, 24C°.

The heater on the bus hadn't gotten the memo that summer had started, and it was blowing warm air in Isla's face. What little she had eaten for breakfast – two bites of jam toast and a single strawberry—sat heavy, threatening to make a reappearance. Isla took off her blazer—not the expensive one from her favourite shop, but a check-patterned green one she had found at MCC—and folded it gently on her lap. *Stay calm,* she told herself. Instead, she found herself numb with hyperventilation.

Breathe.

Slower.

Three more blocks until she was back at HRA. *Life is weird,* she thought. How had she managed to get rehired after her disgraceful departure? Was this a chance for redemption, or was she a glutton for punishment?

Kelly was waiting for her at the entrance, wearing the very suit Isla had drooled over, grey with the neon green piping. Isla desperately envious, wondered how an intern afforded such and expensive suit?

Kelly led her down the corridor past the conference room, then past Knox's office. Was that a chill she felt?

"Before we go in, here is everything you need to know," Kelly said conspiratorially, stopping just out of ear shot of the large room at the end of the hallway. "Ryan was in charge before Sue became creative director, and he still generally runs the show. He always frames critique as a compliment because he wants everyone to like him, and he hates it if you use all lowercase. Don't ever send him a proof with it, he'll turn it down every single time. And don't ask him about it unless you want a long lecture."

"Noted," said Isla. "No lowercase."

"Angela writes copy. She's a total bitch, and will correct every grammar mistake you ever make. I put cream in her coffee when she specifically asks for skim. Eric handles web design and thinks he is cool, but he's not, he's old. Oh, and he hates coffee, thinks drinking it is a sign of mental weakness. Because you're new, expect everyone to dump everything on you. No one is interested in your ideas or opinions, and they probably never will be. But don't worry, while everyone is running around with their high and mighty heads in the clouds, we are going to have so much fun together!"

The creative space was full of natural light from the large east facing floor-to-ceiling windows. The room contained five different workspaces, and a large butcher block table in the centre with scattered pages and colour chips strewn about. The wall to her left had a large geometric mural. Isla was immediately drawn to the colours. She walked over to touch it, to absorb the artist's meaning through her skin.

"Isla!" A male voice brought her back to her surroundings. It was Ryan, who Isla had met already. He greeted her with a handshake and introduced her to the rest of the team. Everyone smiled before returning to their work.

"Why don't you get settled at your desk? We have a pitch meeting in fifteen minutes, and after that Kelly can get you familiar with the software and we can go from there."

Isla's desk was next to Kelly's in the corner next to the mural, furthest away from the windows and everyone else's. She didn't mind. She felt at home next to the bold shapes and bright colours. She unpacked her few possessions on the empty desk, her sketchbook and pencil case, and her crooked coffee mug. She adjusted her chair a few times, finding the right height for her short legs. She glanced at Kelly for instructions, but she was texting at her desk.

Isla opened her new sketchbook, and sharpened a new pencil. She was ready for whatever HRA had to throw at her. What was the worst that could happen? She could be fired — *been there, done that*, she thought, nearly laughing out loud to herself.

"Kelly," she whispered, "what should I do?'

Kelly shrugged. "Whatever. The meeting is in ten minutes."

Everyone else in the room was concentrating on something. Angela was gnawing on her pen, staring at her screen. Eric's hands flew over his keyboard, his ears covered with large sound-canceling headphones. Ryan had left the room. In the absence of anything else to do, Isla started doodling.

Finally, Kelly stood, her thick black hair hanging halfway down her back like a glossy curtain. She smoothed her pants and checked her appearance with her camera phone. "Coming?"

"Coming where?" asked Isla, looking around in confusion.

"To the meeting in the dictator's office."

"The dictator?" Isla sighed; she knew exactly who Kelly was referring to.

"It sucks. We throw out ideas, and he turns each one down, then tells us to do it his way. A simple email would do, but I guess he likes to pretend we're a team."

The sick feeling that had haunted her on the bus returned with a vengeance.

They were last to enter Knox's office. The only seating left was the wood chair and the middle cushion of the dark brown leather sofa. Kelly quickly claimed the sofa. There she was again on the hard, wooden chair, her legs not quite reaching the ground. She sat uncomfortably, feeling exposed. Sue looked up and offered her a large, welcoming smile.

She nervously played with the hemline of her skirt. There was a thread sticking out that she tried to tug discreetly. She wished she had brought her sketchbook or something to hide behind.

When the meeting began, a new client was introduced — a whiskey distillery, started by brothers, Joel and Ezra hoping to grow their own ingredients on their grandfather's farm.

"We need to come up with everything: logo, branding, print, social media, even a name. What's the story we want to tell? Images, words, whatever comes to mind." Knox had rolled out a whiteboard and was holding a marker waiting for ideas.

Ryan was the first to speak. "Retro farm imagery scores high with our demographic. They love the idea of small farms, ploughing fields, a couple chickens, a cow, a pig,"

"A horse and a red barn, definitely," Angela piped up.

"A farmer — middle aged man, or the grandfatherly type, overalls, carrying a basket of veggies," Ryan continued. "Please say they're organic?"

Before Isla could stop herself, she blurted out, "Isn't that a bit overdone? I mean, have you ever been to a farm? That's not what it's actually like."

The room went silent. Isla squirmed in her seat.

"You mean, like, industrial farms?" Angela asked, narrowing her eyes.

Isla swallowed hard and continued, slightly less confidently. "I mean like my cousin's farm. They're young, they use big machinery, they use modern technology, and they don't wear overalls."

"People don't want their farmers cool and edgy, they want their farmers approachable and relatable," stated Eric.

"But how is an old man carrying a basket of veggies relatable to a whiskey drinker? The nostalgic farmer myth is perpetuated by media types — like us. We could keep telling that story, or we could tell their actual story," exclaimed Isla.

The group was quiet. Ryan fidgeted with his papers. Angela looked out the window, unsure how to respond. Sue's mouth twitched upwards, but she remained quiet.

Knox turned back to the board and started writing. "Grandpa, red barns, horses, tractors, earthy colours, vegetables, chickens. I'll double check about organic. Let's run with this and see what we come up with."

He didn't even acknowledge her comment.

Isla left the office feeling defeated. *Why can't I keep my mouth shut?*

15.

June 9. Sunny, strong wind. 16C°
5:47am

Pain seared in Priya's eyes, even before she opened them. This was going to be rough. Nausea hit the moment she stood up. But stand she must. She had to leave without waking Brian. Somehow, it was inevitable that she would end up at Brian's, but she always left before morning. She liked to sleep in her own bed. Silently she collected her discarded clothing and snuck out of the room, pulling on the mini skirt and tight top. The slinky fabric felt foreign in the early morning light. She saved her shoes until she was in the lobby, their height made her dizzy.

Walk of shame? The only thing she was ashamed of was that she hadn't left earlier.

A cab pulled up on the empty street and Priya slid into the back. The disapproving eyes of the cab driver caught hers for a moment.

"Good morning, uncle," she stated confidently. She didn't know him, but his face was familiar. The Sikh community was not that big. She prayed to no one in particular that cabbies had client confidentiality agreements.

It was hard to say who was more surprised when Priya opened the door and found Isla sitting on their couch, sketching.

"What the hell are you doing up?" asked Priya.

"You weren't home?" asked Isla simultaneously. "I've been quietly sneaking around trying not to wake you and you're not even here?"

Priya shrugged. "Have you made coffee? Do you want some cereal? I need some food in my stomach."

"No and yes please," said Isla turning back to her sketchbook.

Priya came from the kitchen with two bowls, each filled with their own signature blend of bran flakes and fruity coloured loops, milk sloshing as she walked. "Did you know six in the morning existed?" joked Priya.

"I woke up at four with an idea and couldn't fall back to sleep, I had to get it down. I'll go back to bed as soon as it's on paper." Isla held up her sketchbook. "How was last night? It must've been good if you're coming home now."

"I didn't mean to. I must've drifted off."

"Passed out," Isla coughed.

"Whatever."

"Things are getting serious between you two. Are you in love?"

"Oh god, no."

"You are exclusive though, right?"

Priya shook her head, mouth full of cereal.

"But you haven't been with anyone else for like, three months."

"That doesn't mean we're exclusive, I'm a med student — we're together for the sheer convenience of it. You should've come out with us last night. What did you do instead?"

"I worked in front of the TV until I couldn't keep my eyes open. I was asleep before eleven."

"How's work going?" asked Priya, scraping the last fruit O out of her bowl.

Isla wrinkled her nose. "The dictator spoke to me for the first time."

"Hmmm," said Priya. Some of the fuzziness from the night before started to clear. Knox had been there, Michael too. A spilled drink — or was it thrown? Isla kept talking before she could say anything.

"I was complaining — well it was more like ranting — about how I needed a better scale to discern his criticism. Is homespun country shit better or worse than dull and childish? I was telling Kelly that I needed feedback that didn't make me want to jump off the bridge." She paused. "I didn't realise he was behind me."

"Of course, you didn't," laughed Priya.

"He said," she mimicked a smug masculine voice "'Could you wait until next week to jump off a bridge? I need that autobody logo on Monday.'"

Priya laughed harder, making Isla smile too, until they were both giggling.

"Being an adult is hard," said Priya as she headed to her bed.

"We can do hard things," said Isla, dropping her sketchbook on the table and heading back to her own cozy twin bed.

1:13pm

Liam's eye's closed as he snuggled innocently into his car seat. He had just filled his pants. Emma debated whether she should wake and change him, at the risk of him not going back to sleep, or to just leave him until she got to the gym. She sat there and stared, unable to decide, or even string together a clear thought.

She wanted to believe things would get better. Optimism was her natural worldview! Every night she believed, prayed, begged. Tonight, he will sleep, tonight will be better. And every night it was not. She'd stumble into his room and nurse him back to sleep, only to be awoken two hours later to repeat the process. Many nights she fell asleep in the chair, her neck awkwardly kinked, waking up not knowing where in the cycle he was. Feed him or put him down? She'd give up around four and brought him into her bed.

Don't tell anyone.

The unsolicited advice she received most often: don't let him get used to sleeping with you, you will never get him out of your bed. Every time she heard this, she bristled on the inside, outwardly offering a sweet smile and nod of agreement.

She had spent the morning preparing and collecting everything they needed for their afternoon out. The diaper bag was packed, extra clothes for Liam and herself, even the stroller was in the van.

But Emma did not want to go.

Alicia had convinced her to sign up for a mummy/baby yoga class. It had seemed like a good idea. She pictured gorgeous, fit moms and adorable smiling babies all performing simple yoga moves. They would all have cute workout clothes, and fresh colours and cuts. They would all have babies who loved lying on the mat watching Mommy do yoga. And everything was exactly how she had imagined. except for her. Each time Emma had gone, Liam fussed, interrupting each pose. All the perfect, serene mommies wished she could get her act together and stop interrupting their peaceful flow.

In a moment of rebellion, she decided — then she said it out loud for her whole world (one sleeping baby with a dirty diaper), to hear: "I'm not going."

10:37pm

Knox turned off the TV and stretched his neck from side to side. A familiar ache of loneliness sat in his gut, unmoved and unchanged. His phone beeped, announcing an email. He grabbed it quickly from the sofa cushion next to him. In response, he texted Graham *"you're too old to be emailing this late on a Saturday night."*

The response came quickly. *"You're too young to be checking your email on a Saturday night!"* Then shortly after: *"Violet and Max bought you a suit for Violet's grad, I hope you like purple."*

"Purple?" Knox relaxed into his seat and replied, *"After last night it's probably a good idea for me to be at home."*

"They called it navy, but it is definitely purple." Then Graham asked, *"Out with friends?"*

"I'll wear whatever my sister wants me to wear. I only get to go to her graduation once."

He purposefully avoided the friend question. A reply didn't come right away, so Knox got up and refilled his glass, free pouring scotch until a ding interrupted the flow.

"How are you?"

Knox paused. He was not going to answer that question, not truthfully.

"How's work?"

A more comfortable question.

"There are too many women. They drive me nuts. They demand equality and then threaten to jump off bridges when you give them honest feedback."

Graham replied, *"Your honest feedback would make anyone want to jump off a bridge. Why don't you ease up on the honesty and strive for useful feedback? Sue sounds happy with the way things are going."*

"Great," he replied, confident the sarcasm wouldn't translate in text.

"Max sends her love and is demanding I turn off my phone so she can watch tv. Good night."

Knox ached for home. But when he was at home, he ached anyway. He thought the emptiness would be different somewhere else, but it was worse. He drained his whiskey before he headed for bed. He waited for the numbing warmth to start in his stomach. He was fast asleep before it spread any further.

16.

June 14. Windy, 17C°.

A fancy French bistro was not what Isla was expecting when Kelly had invited her to join her and her friend Nadia for lunch. The only thing Isla could afford was onion soup. *It had better be damn good soup*, Isla thought. Kelly ordered a bottle of wine that cost nearly a quarter of Isla's rent. Isla politely refused a glass.

Kelly and Nadia discussed their manicure appointments and most recent clothing purchases. Isla considered sharing her latest thrift store find, but kept quiet. *Where did they get their money?* Even though she was making more than she had at the coffee shop, she was slowly paying her brother back. She couldn't justify manicures or large clothing purchases, not when her car was perpetually on the edge of dying or she could drop a couple hundred on art supplies without thinking. *I guess everyone has their priorities,* she thought.

The first bite of Isla's small bowl of steaming hot French onion soup burnt the top of her mouth, and ruined the rest of them. She slowly ate and tried to savor every bite of soup, every morsel of cooked on cheese, knowing this was all she was getting. The bread wasn't even complimentary.

Kelly and Nadia ate their lavish lunches and leisurely enjoyed their second glasses of wine, like they didn't have a care in the world. Isla kept checking her watch. "We should get the cheque soon."

"Isla, sweetie, is that all your having? Are you watching your weight?" asked Kelly. "Have you tried low carb?"

Isla shook her head. "I'm not very hungry."

Kelly caught her checking her watch, "Don't worry about the time. I have a late lunch deal with Eric — he covers for me when I'm late, and I do the same for him. Everyone wins."

Well not everyone, thought Isla, strangely protective of the company that had employed her in accounting for more than a year.

"I need to get going anyway. I have lots to do," said Isla, catching the eye of their server, a thin man with a wispy moustache and fake French accent.

"You mean for the whiskey account?" Kelly laughed. "Oh my god, don't tell me you've actually come up with something?"

Isla pulled out her file and opened to the page she was working on, showing them her sketch of a field of rye with an uninspired logo in front. "I'm not happy with it, so I'm hoping to rework it a bit."

"What's that one?" asked Kelly pointing to another piece of paper peeking out from behind.

"Oh, it's nothing. Just something I came up with for fun."

"Grid Road Whiskey. That's cool!" said Nadia, as Kelly pulled it out and placed it on the table in front of them.

Isla felt her cheeks redden. "I was fooling around. It is the complete opposite of what the dictator wants. I'm not planning on presenting it, I just needed to get it on paper to get it out of my head."

"It *is* a good idea," said Kelly, picking up the papers and looking at them closely.

"My pitch?"

"No, the grid road one, but I agree it is probably best if you don't pitch it. I'd hate for you to be chewed out again. I've seen how he treats you. You should try to stay out of the line of fire," replied Kelly. The server came up to the table. "Separate cheques?"

"We'll just split it three ways," replied Kelly offhanded.

"No, I'll pay for mine separately." Isla panicked and gave them an embarrassed shrug, hoping they understood.

She left the two of them, leisurely finishing their bottle of wine. Isla had to rush to get back before her lunch hour was up. By the time she made it back to her desk, she was sweaty, her hair was frizzy, and her stomach was hungry. She dug around in her bag and found half a granola bar and a piece of gum.

Isla worked and reworked her mediocre idea. Different colour, maybe a larger font? Nothing she could do could make it better, but her time had run out. Not that it mattered — even if she had the best idea, Knox would never approve it.

When Kelly came in, she dropped her designer bag at her desk and rolled her chair over to Isla. She took her large sunglasses off and giggled, "Isn't day drinking the best?"

"Are you just back now?" demanded Isla, checking her watch. Three-thirty.

"A bunch of insurance guys came in after you left, bought us a couple more rounds. Nadia bailed at two. Anyway, I left our lunch bill with them," she cackled. "I need some coffee. Do you want any?"

"No, I'm good." Swallowing her annoyance, Isla intercepted Kelly before she made it out the door. "I don't think you're going to make it down the stairs. I'll get you coffee — you stay here."

Eric came in before Isla could leave. "I thought you said you'd be just a little late, not three fucking hours! You owe me."

Kelly flashed him her biggest grin. "Aww, Eric, you know I love you."

Except it sounded more like 'wove.' Isla flashed him a look of apology and sat Kelly back down in her own chair and hissed "Stay here."

The next morning, Isla nervously shuffled her papers. She knew her idea wasn't good, and it wouldn't be picked, but she had done her best. Someone else better have a good idea. She was part of a team; all she needed to do was stay under the radar.

Her team sat at one end of the table, Knox was at the other, squared off like a boxing match. In one corner, the dictator: tough, honest, entitled. And in the other corner, the design team: battered, bruised, but trying hard.

Kelly breezed in, showing no ill effects from the previous day. She confidently sat next to Knox with a single file folder and offered a fancy box of muffins to the group.

Angela bravely presented her idea first, then Eric, then Isla, then Ryan. Each idea was safe and eerily similar.

Knox looked bored. He asked, "Is that it?"

They glanced at Ryan to be their spokesperson. "As you can see, we have some cohesive ideas—umm lots to work with. I think we all agree this is the direction we should go."

Then from Knox's side of the room came a soft, humble voice. "I have an idea. It's pretty rough, I don't know, maybe it sucks, and I know it isn't what we talked about, but I couldn't get it out of my head."

Kelly opened her file folder and handed Knox a single piece of paper that looked like it had been ripped out of a sketchbook. Knox stared at it for a moment.

Anyone watching him closely would've noticed his eyes widen ever so slightly as he glanced in Isla's direction. Instead, everyone was staring at Kelly in disbelief.

Angela whispered to Isla, "she has never pitched an idea."

"This is good," said Knox, passing the paper to Ryan. As the paper was passed around the table, Isla felt increasingly anxious. She recognised the paper; it had been ripped from her sketchbook.

When it got to her, she held the paper lightly in her hand, staring at the familiar sketch for Grid Road Whiskey. Kelly was presenting her idea.

"This is really good work, Kelly," Ryan declared.

Kelly beamed. "It came to me in my sleep. I didn't know if I should say anything, but I had a feeling that this was it."

Isla stared straight down, unable to trust her words or her facial expression.

"Okay," said Knox. "Let's run with it. Ryan and Eric, why don't you team up with Kelly on the client presentation."

When Isla got back to her desk, she had a text from Kelly. *"OMG Your idea got accepted! Too bad Knox didn't assign you to the team. I'm sure you have way more ideas for development. Don't worry, I'll tell everyone later, once all the contracts are signed. Maybe then you can work on it with us. Man, it was hard making up all that shit, trying to pull it off as mine. I think you owe me a drink. XOXO"*

17.

June 17. Still windy, 21C°.

It was Father's Day and Andrew was going away, again. To complicate things, her parents had arrived a week early. Angrily, Emma had accused Andrew of planning to work up north while they visited. Andrew denied it — he had no control of the schedule — but his relief was obvious. Both were tense after only forty-eight hours of Gerald and Sara's visit.

The first time Emma had supper at Andrew's family's home, she was overwhelmed with the chaotic and messy environment and banter. Soon she realized they were as free with their love and praise as they were with their teasing and challenging. Emma's home growing up had been precise and sterile, and above all else her family valued hard work and obedience. Once her father had proudly announced to Andrew that the only book he'd ever read was the Bible.

"Please don't leave me," Emma whispered when Andrew kissed her cheek goodbye.

"I'm sorry," he had said helplessly. "I'll be home as soon as I can."

And so, when Sunday morning came, Emma found herself in the back seat of her van with her son. Her father was driving them

downtown to the church she had grown up in. Not the simple, traditional Mennonite church she and Andrew attended with his parents,
with rust-coloured hymnals, wood paneling and its ragtag group of
attendants, with white-haired traditionalists and hipster progressives,
where no one agreed, and yet they loved each other fiercely. This church
was a large warehouse with a dark auditorium, the stage flooded in
creative lighting. The music was loud, a full electric band, dueling
drum-sets. Emma was immediately brought back to memories of
playing under rows of stacked chairs, hide and seek in the back rooms
while the adults lingered after the service.

She was surrounded by people from her past. Some names
returned right away; others had faded, even though it had only
been three years since she walked up the aisle to Andrew waiting
for her.

The music played quietly as Gerald was introduced to bring a
word. And bring it he did. His message was fear, his medium, a long
passionate sermon peppered with Bible verses taken out of context,
out of his mind. Long winded short tempered, full of holy anger
against those who seek to destroy what the Lord had built. Health,
wealth, ask, receive, repent, blessing.

Sara sat in the front row next to the pastor's wife Beth, the seats
of honour. Both were elegant, demure and modest, content as their
husbands orchestrated the service from the stage. Everyone agreed
here, perfect unity, no dissidence. No one was nodding off like Mr.
Penner regularly did. The ease of certainty.

Four years ago, Emma would've said the two churches were
similar. They used the same Bible, they sang familiar songs. "How
Great Thou Art," with or without electric guitar, is still the same
song. Today, everything felt foreign. She'd heard her father preach
before — why did she feel twitchy and uncomfortable today?

When the service was finished, an army of workers cleared the
precise rows of interlocking chairs and set up rows and rows of long

tables to host a community lunch. Everyone was welcome: come for the salvation, stay for lunch.

Sara found Emma in the back and took Liam out of her arms, as if she were doing Emma a favour. She indicated the empty tables needing to be bussed. Coffee mugs with lipstick stains, discarded napkins, post meal flotsam and jetsam.

A group of men were still lounging at their table with coffee and half eaten pieces of pudding and cream cheese concoctions. Gerald was right in the middle. The topic was politics, and the usual suspects spouted the usual talking points. No wonder the neighbours didn't stick around, this salvation required too much.

Gerald called her over, and she wiped her hands on her apron. She plastered on a Sunday morning smile.

"Emma, where is that grandson of mine?" he asked.

"Over there," said Emma, pointing to the back of the room where a group of young women, still children themselves, had corralled all the toddlers and babies and were entertaining them, allowing the young mothers to clean up after the meal.

"Just one child so far?" asked one of the men.

Emma nodded.

He continued, "Once I heard a sermon about that passage in Genesis, you know it: 'Be fruitful and multiply and fill the earth and subdue it; and have dominion over the fish of the sea and over the birds of the air and over every living thing that moves upon the earth.' The pastor had a good point, he said young people these days aren't having enough kids. The church is shrinking, and young people need to do their part."

Emma froze.

"Where is that husband of yours?" The question came out like an accusation. Emma raised her guard before she could formulate a response to the first comment.

"He is working up north," she stammered.

"Well, the Sabbath was created for man, not man for the Sabbath," piped up yet another man, finishing the last of his coffee and handing the cup to her.

"If he works through the weekend he gets home sooner," she explained, as she quickly collected the rest of the cups to escape the conversation. With her full cart, she retreated to the kitchen. Women of all ages flitted around the kitchen. Everyone seemed to know their place. The older women put food away in old margarine containers, the younger women had their arms in the sink up to their elbows in suds.

Apparently, Sabbath was only for some.

"Does it bother you that we have to prepare the meal and clean up, while the men sit around visiting?" Emma asked a friend from childhood, named Jennifer.

"I love it in here, all of us working together. Such a great way to build community. I was having trouble getting little Kelsey to sleep and Mrs. Hamilton gave me great advice."

"Yes, but couldn't community be built just as easily if the men were doing dishes and we were visiting over coffee?" questioned Emma.

The group of women burst into laughter. "Can you imagine the men doing dishes!"

"We'd have to rewash half of them."

"They'd leave the kitchen a mess."

Emma felt her mother at her side. "Emma, the Ladies' Bible Study has just started a new book for the summer, it would be perfect for you. Maybe you should consider joining them? Beth, what was it called again?"

"'The Gift of Submission: A Study of Paul's Instructions to Women,' by Stanley McDowell," replied Beth, who was the pastor's wife.

"Oh Emma, you should join us!" said Jennifer enthusiastically. "I've been looking forward to this study for a while. I have friends who've read it who say it changed their marriages, especially those whose husbands read 'The Gift of Respect: A Study of Paul's Instructions for the Spiritual Leader,' by the same author."

"Ahhh—" stalled Emma. She would love some changes in their marriage, but she was sure this wasn't the book to do it. "I'm very busy."

She wasn't busy at all; her schedule was wide open after quitting yoga.

"Darling, we can go together! It's running all summer and they have childcare. You need a mom's morning out," said her mother.

Emma was caught off guard. How long were they planning on staying?

"That would be amazing. I'll get you a copy," said Beth.

Emma shoved the book into her diaper bag. It was a large, heavy hardcover book, with a classically handsome older white man with a large toothy grin. She would take it home and hide it, maybe in her sock drawer. Isla would laugh, Dee would lecture on the dangerous of internal misogyny, and Andrew would be disappointed, but she didn't know how to say no to her mother.

18.

June 22. Hot and muggy, 30C°.

I sla felt sweat drip at the nape of her neck, under the mess of hair that used to be perfectly straight. She should've known better than to try to straighten her hair in this heat. Her little brown hatchback didn't have air conditioning, so she was showing up to a meeting hot, sweaty, and blotchy.

She reached into her bag for a hair tie and pulled her hair into a messy bun at the top of her head. Her phone beeped. "**Knox is joining us.**" She sat, staring in disbelief. The message was from John Zimmerman, the account manager Isla had specifically approached to introduce Lami and Lolo to. Not Knox! She had very specifically not gone to Knox, and yet he had wiggled his way in.

Isla climbed out of her car. The air was thick with humidity, even in the shade. Isla fanned herself with her phone, to no effect. She took a moment to adjust her sundress, pulling where it stuck to her back. She waved at Lami and Lolo, twin fashion designers and owners of the L2 clothing company. They were friends of hers from high school, which she didn't think was necessary to mention to anyone. They needed some marketing, but their budget was tiny; even so, Isla planned to introduce them to John.

Just John. They weren't exactly the prestigious clients the dictator was looking for.

Isla met up with her friends at the path to the restaurant, an old pumphouse over the river. The air conditioning assaulted Isla the moment she walked in, making her shiver. Knox and John were already seated. She led her friends to the table in the corner. John sat rigid, nervously playing with his straw wrapper and Knox... Well, Isla had never seen Knox in client mode. He had an inviting grin, and his eyes were welcoming and friendly.

False advertising.

Both men rose from their seats to greet them. Knox waved the waiter over and drinks were ordered. They exchanged pleasantries as they sat, the five of them around a large circular table, Isla between Lolo and John, Lami, then Knox.

This was Isla's first client meeting; she wasn't sure how it worked. She waited for the official meeting to start. The conversation seemed to dance over all the important points, almost like some secret language was being spoken. Details were hinted, but nothing was outright said. Lami and Lolo were equally sophisticated and business savvy, charming both John and Knox.

Isla kept quiet. That seemed like the best plan. *Do not open your mouth. Do not open your mouth.* But when she did, she filled it with a sip of white wine, emptying her glass far quicker than everyone else.

"I'm assuming Isla has lots of ideas we can pull off within your budget?" said John.

Budget? Did they talk budget? Confused, Isla nodded her head and smiled confidently. She reached for her sketchbook, ready to present her idea, but before she could, Lolo spoke up with a glance at her watch.

"Sorry to cut this short, but if we don't head out, we'll miss our show. Thanks so much for meeting us on such short notice. We trust Isla completely, whatever she decides is good enough for us."

"Great!" said John, shaking their hands. "Isla has been an asset to our design department since she started."

"It's been a pleasure to meet you, Lami, Lolo. I look forward to working with your fascinating company," said Knox.

Isla fought hard not to roll her eyes. Gathering her stuff, she walked her friends out of the restaurant and up the riverbank path toward the theater.

"I thought you said Knox was a beast, but he was quite pleasant," said Lami.

"It's all show. I guess he can turn on the charm when necessary. I don't even know why he came. He's such a control freak; he thinks everything is going to fall apart without him. Don't worry, though, John is great, and completely capable."

"I hope so. This is going to stretch us. I hope the pay off's worth it," said Lolo, who had always been the more cautious of the sisters.

"I'll do my best," promised Isla, stopping in front of her car as her friends continued down the road. She dug through her bag for awhile before realising the inevitable: she had forgotten her keys.

She walked back into the restaurant, eyeing a plate of pasta as it passed in front of her. John and Knox were still at the table, deep in conversation.

"Sorry to interrupt, I just forgot my keys," she said, flashing John an apologetic look.

While John was mid-sentence, Knox pushed the chair next to him with his foot. The screech on the tile floor indicated she should sit down. She did.

"—- they have a small budget, but they aren't the smallest clients we have. Most of the work we've done in the last ten years has been for small businesses hoping to go national or at least western Canada." John continued what he was saying before Isla arrived.

"And what happens when those clients get bigger?" Knox asked.

John fidgeted with his tie. "You guys poach them. I mean, the main office takes them over."

Knox leaned back in his chair and scratched his head, deep in thought. John glance at Isla, who shrugged, both hoping to be dismissed soon.

"Are you guys hungry?" Knox asked coming back to the moment.

"I need to go; my son's soccer game started fifteen minutes ago," said John, taking the opportunity to get the hell out of there, leaving Isla still sitting in her chair, paralyzed.

Knox handed her a menu. "Everything's good except the squid ink pasta, it's kind of weird."

Isla watched as John crossed the restaurant and left. Slowly she glanced at the menu. Her stomach growled.

"I should go—" she ventured, putting the menu down.

"You should stay and let HRA buy you dinner," he said, not looking up from the menu. He didn't give her an opportunity to reply before waving over the server and ordering a whiskey and coke, a bottle of wine, and a basket of bread.

They sat in uncomfortable silence until their drinks came.

"Are you sharing the bottle with me?" she asked, wary, as he poured her a glass.

"We have all night. You don't have anywhere else you need to be, do you?" he asked, taking a sip of his drink. "I assume you've got some ideas for this campaign?"

I wish I had somewhere to be, she thought, pulling out her sketchbook and flipping to the pages she had been working on, blurry black and white images in the background with models in gorgeous colourful dresses. "I was thinking something along the lines of a woman whose whole life is a disaster. Messy house, bad weather, traffic jam, but she is beautifully dressed in every situation—"

"So, an autobiography?" asked Knox with a smirk.

"Oh good, obnoxious Knox is back. The whole Prince Charming thing was freaking me out," Isla snapped back, slamming her sketchbook shut.

He answered a text on his phone, then said, "Sounds ambitious. What have you promised them?"

"What? Nothing!"

"They seemed excited about the fact that we also represent the largest Canadian owned department store in the country."

"They've done their research," replied Isla cautiously.

"Were you going to disclose that they're your friends? From what I can gather, pretty good friends — friends who you had a disastrous camping trip with last summer."

"How did you —" she started.

He held up his phone with a grin.

"Do you creep all your employees' social media pages?"

"Of course I do. Everything that's on the internet is fair game. Don't pretend like you haven't done the same."

Isla's heart sank. He had opened a door to a world that she didn't want him to be a part of. Her friends, her family, things she'd rather keep to herself. She felt vulnerable. She *had* done the same, but his online presence hadn't exposed anything she didn't already know.

The server came back to take their dinner orders. Isla ordered the squid ink pasta.

"You're going to regret it," Knox teased.

"I'm going to regret this whole evening," she announced.

He threw his head back and genuinely laughed.

Isla's body relaxed ever-so-slightly, settling into her chair. He was on his phone again, texting. Isla thought the polite thing to do would be to ask him about himself. *Tell me about your family, your life in Vancouver?* She practised in her head. But she faltered.

"I hear you're going back home for a couple of weeks?" she finally ventured.

He nodded. "I fly out tomorrow, then we're driving up to the cabin for a couple weeks—" he said, distractedly typing.

I must end this, she thought.

But then her pasta arrived, and it was divine. She said so.

"I know" he replied without looking up, from his steak.

"Then why did you tell me not to order it?" she demanded.

"I was testing a theory; I figure the best way to get you to do something is to tell you not to do it." He looked up with a sly grin.

Isla's head started to spin. He's so damn cocky. And correct.

"I should put this away." He slipped his phone into his pocket and turned his full attention on her. "Do you like your job?"

"That's a brave question."

"Are you going to answer it?"

Isla shook her head. She didn't know the answer herself. Working at HRA was better than working at a coffee shop — at least she was doing something productive, according to her mother. She still dreamed about locking herself in a room and painting all day, but when she did have time to paint, she kept finding ways to sabotage herself. If you want to be a painter, paint, Priya would say to her, although it felt like taunting. Priya never found it difficult to take what she wanted. She never second-guessed herself.

"Why did you let Kelly steal your idea?" asked Knox, trying another angle.

Isla had just taken a bite of bread. She chewed slowly, trying to appear thoughtful and calm. Knox waited patiently for her answer.

Swallowing hard she asked, "how did you know?"

"Three things," he said, holding up three fingers. "One, as we've already established, you enjoy doing the opposite of what I recommend. Two, it was hand-drawn, and you do everything by hand, pencil and sketchbook are always close by." He indicated to her sketchbook which was sitting on the side of the table. "Three, Kelly doesn't have any talent or work ethic."

Isla composed herself, "She was going to tell everyone after—"

"But she hasn't yet, has she?" he interrupted.

Kelly said she would tell, so she will when the time is right, wouldn't she? "She forgot," Isla said, choosing to defend her friend, even though she was starting to have some doubts. "It's fine, all that matters is that the client is happy. And they are."

"Bullshit," he said. His eyes pierced into her skull.

"She didn't do it to hurt me! She liked my idea, and knew I had decided not to present it."

"Why didn't *you* present it?"

Isla's laugh sounded maniacal to her own ears. "Why didn't *I* present it? You — you would've ripped it to shreds, like you have done with every single thing I have presented. What was it you said about my last pitch, 'juvenile and visually repelling.'" Her voice rose in pitch and volume. "She did me a favour, because she's my friend?"

"She is not your friend." His voice was steady, contrasting Isla's growing hysteria.

"What do you know about friendship? You're so full of shit," said Isla, picking up her sketchbook and knocking her keys to the floor.

Knox reach down and grabbed her keys off the sticky floor before she could. He fiddled with them and said, "Kelly wanted your job and would've gotten it if it hadn't been for Sue's power move."

"Give me my keys."

"Sit down."

"Give. Me. My. Keys." Isla growled.

Knox pushed her chair out with this long leg, like he had earlier. "Sit down. Please."

Isla slumped into the chair, crossed her arms, and glared at him. He went back to eating his steak as if nothing had happened.

Isla picked at her black noodles. "Kelly is the only one in the office who's friendly to me. No one else talks to me."

"So what? No one likes me either. I don't give a shit. Do good work, that is all that matters. Don't confuse office colleagues with friendship," he said, wiping his mouth with a napkin. "The only reason she still has a job is that she's the granddaughter of a big client. Good old-fashioned nepotism."

"Nepotism!" Isla sputtered. "Like your whole career isn't built on nepotism!"

"Maybe, but I don't waste my opportunities. Every day I wake up and do whatever it takes to make this company better, more profitable, more efficient. This company is my life. And I have no patience for apathy or entitlement. You should confront her, tell her to create her own content. Give her this attitude you have no problem giving me."

Isla took a long sip of her wine and emptied her glass. Her face was starting to feel numb and her brain fuzzy. "You're awfully intense; do you know that?"

"Yes, I do. I'm also incredibly handsome," he said with a wink.

Isla groaned and put her head in her hands, "I cannot believe you just said that!"

Knox grinned, "it's an objective truth, my face is very symmetrical."

"Ahh that explains it, people with objectively symmetrical faces can afford to be boring."

"I am not boring." He leaned forward, and raised his drink. "I bet you that by the end of the night we'll have fun."

"You're on," Isla clinked her empty glass with his.

Isla realised she was having fun by the time she finished her third glass of wine (maybe fourth, she had lost track). They stayed away from controversial subjects, like work or personal lives. Instead, they spent the rest of the night making up secret lives of the diners around them.

115

"See him?" said Isla, nodding to the man sitting kitty-corner to Knox, "He has a pinky ring, that means he's an engineer–"

"Nah, I don't think he's an engineer" interrupted Knox. "He's an undercover agent, tasked with seducing his tablemate and stealing the contents of her computer."

"Oh, and what has she done to deserve that?"

"Criminal mastermind, obviously. She leads a network of online scammers. She is behind the Nigerian prince emails."

"Scamming and cultural appropriation!" Isla shook her head disapprovingly.

The couple in question were in their mid-fifties. She hadn't liked the menu, too many unfamiliar ingredients. He worried parking cost too much. They should've gone to the chain restaurant down the street from their house. But their daughter had gotten them a gift card. And now the young couple at the table next to them glanced in their direction and laughed.

Later they exited the restaurant as the sun was setting, Isla's eyes were so busy soaking up the heavenly scene that she tripped on the second step ascending the riverbank.

"Whoa, there," said Knox, grabbing her wrist and placing it in the crook of his arm.

"Thanks," she said dreamily.

"So, did I win? Do you regret the whole evening?" he asked, leading her up each step.

"Almost all of it," she said. "Except the food. The food was exceptionally good. I'm totally drunk, aren't I?"

"Yes, you seem to be, and refreshingly chill."

"It's all your fault" she retorted.

"Probably," he said.

"You kept refilling my glass."

"And you kept drinking it. How do you plan to get home?"

"Priya's coming. I'll wait in my car until she gets here," Isla said, leaning into the street where her car was parked.

"How about I wait with you?" Knox said, pulling her out of oncoming traffic. He held her arm more firmly, guiding her across the street when traffic cleared.

They approached her car. "You don't have to say anything," she said. "I know it is a piece of shit."

"I didn't say anything!" He held his hands up defensively.

"Ah but you were thinking it" They both moved to the hood of her car and sat. Isla gestured around, "It's so beautiful tonight— one day past solstice and look, the sun is setting behind those buildings. The city feels alive. Look, people are walking dogs and sleeping babies in strollers. On nights like this, Winnipeggers don't want to go to sleep — just revel in the beauty — it's perfect."

"Are you trying to convince me to like it here?"

"Winnipeg: a horrible place to visit, the best place to live—-" Isla trailed off as she closed her eyes and put her head in her hands.

She felt him move closer, she sensed his frame, the smell of his cologne.

"Welcome back. Where did you go?" he said quietly into her ear.

His words shivered down her spine, it felt like fireworks. Or maybe alarm bells?

"I live around the corner." He continued, "why don't you come over and drive yourself home in the morning?"

Taken aback, Isla blurted, "No!"

He retreated, and stepped away from the car, his face stayed passive.

"Umm—" Isla stammered "I didn't mean to yell. You surprised me. I was surprised. I didn't mean to yell."

"It's fine." Knox crossed his arms.

Isla jumped up, "what I mean is—thank you for the kind invitation, but no thank you."

"Like I said, it's fine. I just thought it would be fun to hook up" He scratched the top of his head, "I'm going to go now. Will your ride be here soon?"

"Umm, yeah." She looked at her phone, it had only been ten minutes since she'd heard from Priya.

He bade her good night with a nod of his head and sauntered down the street, hands in his pockets, nothing amiss. Isla watched, waiting for him to look back, but he didn't. Not even when he rounded the corner.

As the sun finished setting, the streetlight came on over Isla's head. She stared at the corner in disbelief, shivering as if all the heat in the world had vanished with the final sliver of golden light. Fumbling with her keys, she slid into the passenger seat and hoped Priya would arrive soon. *What had just happened?*

19.

June 23. Breezy, 24C°.

His plane hit the runway with a thud; the force lurched Knox forward and back into his seat. Home. When he had left this city, it had been the middle of the west coast winter, raining with dense fog, but today was summer. Not the hot, sticky summer he had left behind in Winnipeg, but warm with a salty ocean breeze. Far more breathable.

The SkyTrain took him into Vancouver's downtown. Views of the mountains peeked between the tall buildings. A cab took him the rest of the way. There were hills — how novel. Up, and then down, and then up again. His thoughts started out sarcastic, but quickly shifted to sentimental as the sights became familiar. He was heading to the closest thing to home he had left. He had always loved his godparents, Graham and Maxine's house. As a child, it had been a magical place, with its flat roof and asymmetrical windows, its minimalist décor and modern artwork. He would play for hours by himself in the small backyard next to the carriage house, or in the upstairs loft where he'd lounge, reading Graham's old comic books for hours while the adults laughed in the dining room below over glasses of wine.

As an adult, the house still held magic. Flutters of excitement surprised him as the cab turned right into their street. There it was: third house on the left.

Home, sort of.

His sister, Violet ran out of the house, two blond tight braids running halfway down her back. She wore a loose, flowy dress in a tiny floral print. She reached him before he could close the cab door and threw her arms around him.

"I'm so glad you're here!" she said, allowing him to pay and wave the cab off.

"Hey! There he is!" Graham yelled from the front door. His booming voice rang across the yard; then came the same corny greeting he had used for years. "When did you get so tall?"

Max was waiting for him in the kitchen in all her grandeur. Not a hair out of place, not a crumb of supper on her pristine apron, fashionable yet understated, petite without playing small.

"Welcome home, Knox," Maxine said, kissing him on both cheeks. Her French accent was still strong, even after years of living in a decidedly not-French city. Playfully, she slapped his hand away from the slice of roast beef he had reached for. Chastened, he took a glass of water, instead, and perched on a stool next to his sister. They were nearly ten years apart in age, but they had identical smiles. In the three years since the accident that killed their parents and nearly killed her, she had gone from being his helpless baby sister to a free spirit who happened to be graduating high school tomorrow.

Knox understood the point of vacation in theory, but couldn't see how relaxation applied to him. Rest? How was that going to achieve his goals? But Violet had insisted (so did Graham and Max, but he could've said no to them). The plan was to attend Violet's graduation ceremony, and then drive to the cabin for two weeks of waterskiing, hiking, and amazing food. He had packed three business memoirs and a textbook from his third year of university to reread. He had also instructed Sue to CC him on every email so that he could keep an eye on everything.

After dinner, Graham found Knox sitting on the back deck in front of his laptop, ignoring the brilliant sunset.

"I love it here," Graham interrupted. He had two glasses and a bottle of their favourite scotch. Graham poured a generous two fingers for each of them and pushed Knox's laptop closed with a click.

"To sunsets," Graham said, holding up his glass. Knox clinked his glass, took a sip, and felt his body relax a little. He watched the sky change colours as the clouds passed in the breeze.

"How was the date?" asked Graham, breaking the spell.

"What date?"

"The redhead? Last night, you texted *I finally got the redhead to agree to dinner*," Graham replied with a sly smile.

"Shit," Knox scowled, "That wasn't meant for you."

"I figured as much," said Graham, laughing. "So, who is she?"

"That text was for Brian. I meant to blow off my plans with him," Knox said. "She's nobody."

"Nobody?" Graham leaned forward eagerly. "You don't actually expect me to believe that?"

"It wasn't a date. I was trying to get Brian off my back." Knox shifted uncomfortably in his seat. This conversation could not end fast enough. "She's one of our designers. We had a meeting with a client, and that led to dinner. That's it."

"This redhead — does she have a name?"

"Isla Peters."

"Ah! Sue's prodigy."

"Sue's pain in the ass."

"Ooo, you like her!" Graham made kissing noises.

"It was not a date. It was a business dinner." Knox enunciated every word to make his point.

121

Graham was quiet as they watched the sun drop beneath the horizon, illuminating the clouds with a glow of pinks and oranges.

"So are you going to ask her out, again?"

Knox sighed. Apparently, this conversation wasn't going to end until he told the truth. "She made it pretty clear she wasn't interested."

Graham grinned; he had finally broken through. He leaned forward in anticipation. "Continue."

Begrudgingly, Knox offered up the bare minimum. "We had fun at dinner and when I suggested-- more, she literally yelled 'No' at me."

Graham burst into easy laughter. "Wait a minute – did you ask her back to your apartment? The shit you think you can get away with– she technically works for you! Slow down or you're going to get yourself in trouble. Dates, gifts, *time*— Max didn't sleep with me for almost a year!"

"I didn't need to hear that," said Knox, covering his ears. Hearing about Graham and Max's sex life was almost as bad as hearing about your own parents.

"That's how you know it's love," said Graham with satisfaction, "when you don't mind waiting."

"Yeah, well, this is definitely not love. I was bored."

"I think you mean lonely."

"I'm not lonely."

"Are you going to try again?"

"Not a chance."

"So, you're checking out?"

"She talks a lot and has annoying opinions. She's not really my type."

"Right, I forgot. Your type is beautiful and dull," said Graham sarcastically.

Before Knox could defend himself, Violet and Maxine came out on the deck.

"Just in time! We're discussing Knox's love life," announced Graham.

"Have you met someone?" asked Max hopefully.

Knox glared at him. "Don't listen to the old man. He's gone delusional."

"Can I have a taste?" Violet lifted Graham's glass to her nose. Graham nodded.

"Oh, hell no, sissy!" Knox jumped up and grabbed the glass out of her hand.

Graham laughed. He took it back and returned it to Violet. "Go on, bottoms up."

"I leave her here with you for six months, and she's drinking scotch?" Knox objected.

"I turn nineteen in a few weeks, Knox," reminded Violet.

"Don't be so hypocritical! Remember when you were eighteen," added Max.

Graham laughed. "I seem to remember finding you hungover in the basement numerous times. You'd sneak in and spend the night here so your dad wouldn't kick your butt."

"What about that time you puked all over our front step in the middle of a snowstorm? It took weeks to clean it up!" reminded Max.

Knox shuddered. "That was a long time ago."

Violet giggled and then took a sip and choked.

"Keep going. Apparently, you need the practice," teased Knox.

"Yum," Violet sputtered, handing the glass back to Graham.

Knox yawned and looked at his watch.

"Who's the old man now?" said Graham. "It's only ten."

"It's midnight at ho—in Winnipeg. Besides, it's a big day tomorrow!" he said, giving Violet a high five. "Anyone care to join me for a run at six?"

"In the morning? Oh god, no," replied Max.

"All that exercise can't be good for you," said Graham.

"There are worse things I could be doing. Only eight kilometres tomorrow," said Knox. "Goodnight, all."

"It *will* be good, because I won't be sleeping alone," Graham announced, lifting his glass to Knox as he left.

20.

June 24. Humid and still, 34C°.

Emma closed Bill and Dee's back door behind her. The first thing she noticed was the dark clouds coming in from the west; the air was thick with humidity again. After four days of unbearable heat, relief would come with a storm. This afternoon would be a doozy. The second thing she noticed was that Isla had pulled a deck chair on to the lawn, in the shade of the evergreen tree which was conveniently out of sight of any of the house's back windows. Emma knew she was preoccupied over a boy who wasn't worth it. Not that Isla cared about her opinion; Isla did whatever Isla felt like.

"I found your hiding place," said Emma, carrying another chair off the deck.

"Come hide with me," said Isla with a smile. "How bad is it?"

"Well, your mom made the mistake of bringing up the woman pastor at her church—"

"That was no mistake."

"Ha! Then my dad quoted First Timothy—"

"Predictably."

"Your mom argued that women have the right to representation and to have the scripture interpreted from their perspective. Then my dad replied that if a woman doesn't understand scripture, she should ask her husband."

"And the professor's head exploded?"

"Yeah, something like that. And then your dad calmly said, 'what if the wife is smarter than the husband?' My dad prescribed more prayer and Bible study—"

"—presumably to dumb down the wife and smarten up the husband," finished Isla, making a puking motion.

"I had to leave at that point. Why did your parents invite them for lunch anyway? They can't stand each other. Dad thinks your parents are liberal snowflakes destroying the world with compromise, and your parents think he is a right-wing extremist destroying the world with legalism — and in some ways, they're both right, but they are both wrong too," said Emma exasperated.

"Gerald is batshit crazy."

"Yeah, well— it puts me in an awkward position. Andrew is stressed out; he keeps hinting that they should book flights home, but you know my dad. He doesn't listen, or chooses not to hear anyone."

They sat in the relief of the shade for a while, Isla checking her phone every five seconds.

"Stop doing that!" said Emma, "what are you expecting anyway?"

"I don't know" said Isla "it was such a confusing evening. I keep thinking there should be some sort of follow up. Shouldn't there?"

Emma shrugged. Just then a breeze picked up and they both sighed in relief.

"Do you think my mom is happy?" asked Emma.

"Yes, of course she is," Isla said. "Because she isn't allowed to have a thought or action that doesn't originate with Gerald, she doesn't have to think about how unhappy she is."

Gosh, Isla. Don't hold anything back, thought Emma "But she seems content and actually happy! She was ironing my tablecloths the other day, and when I told her she didn't have to she said she counted it all joy to help me keep my home."

"Do you believe her?"

Emma shrugged. "I guess. I don't have a single memory of her ever complaining or even being tired. I've seen my dad get angry, but never her, not even about bad traffic or mix ups. She's always positive and upbeat. I don't know how she does it."

"I couldn't be married to him," said Isla, checking her phone yet again.

"I know my dad isn't an easy person, but I wish I knew her secret. I'm married to Andrew, and I complain all the time." Emma sighed, disheartened, but Isla was only half listening. "Stop checking your phone."

Then it buzzed, startling Isla. *Pick up some TP on your way home.* It was Priya.

There was a rumble in the distance. The birds stopped chirping and the slight breeze from before stopped blowing. The calm was unsettling.

"Look who's up!" called Dee from the back door. She carried Liam across the yard to the friends' hiding spot. As they approached Liam yawned and rubbed his eyes.

"Did you wake him up?" accused Emma.

"I was just checking on him, and he opened his eyes," Emma's mother-in-law defended herself.

"He was only asleep for forty-five minutes! You should've put him back to sleep," Emma said. This had happened before — in fact, it seemed to happen regularly at this house. She took Liam out of her mother-in-law's arms and immediately put him to her breast. Maybe he'd fall back to sleep.

"I'll go get a blanket," said Dee. "I'd hate for him to get chilled."

He was already wrapped in a white muslin one with rocket ships printed on it.

"It's sweltering out here." Emma spoke quietly so Dee wouldn't hear her on the way back to the house.

Isla laughed. "Come on, let her think she is being helpful. That's what grandmas are for."

"It's annoying, and it's not just her. Everyone seems to think they know how to raise my child better than I do."

"I don't," said Isla. "I think you're doing great!"

"I'm not," admitted Emma, but Isla was distracted, checking her phone again.

Suddenly, a gust of cold wind brought a wall of rain and flash of lighting, forcing them to race for the house. They entered with childish giggles. The storm had come and brought respite, if only for a moment.

21.

July 9. Sunny, 25C°.

Isla dropped her bus pass and cracked her head on the money box when she bent to pick it up. Cracked it hard enough that the people around her were alarmed. A large goose egg started forming on the right side of her head. She tried covering it with her hair, but it was too prominent. At least Knox wasn't back yet — or was he? She replayed their conversation over again. He had said three weeks, right?

Not that it mattered. He hadn't texted. How could he not text? Maybe because she had yelled 'NO' at him.

If she would've remembered her keys, the whole situation could've been avoided.

She paused at the lobby elevator; maybe she'd hit her head harder than she thought. Pain pulsed through her head, and her palms went clammy. *Maybe I'll pass out right here. Who would notice, who would call the ambulance?*

"Isla! Hey girl!" came a call from behind her.

Isla spun around. "Kelly, hi."

It wouldn't be her.

Kelly casually threaded her arm through Isla's. 'Work besties' she had called them last week, even though she had yet to confess to stealing Isla's idea. Even when Ryan had complained that they were struggling to develop the idea because she hadn't been able to produce any follow up.

"How was your weekend?" she asked. Before Isla could answer, she continued, "Mine was amazing! Saturday night we ended up on this pub crawl and you will never guess who I ran into?"

Do I care? thought Isla. She was already weary of this conversation. She left the elevator first, pausing to hold the door for Kelly. Megan the receptionist waved them through.

"Knox! Can you believe it?" Kelly exclaimed. "My friends and his friends hung out for the whole night, drinking and dancing. Oh my god it was so fun! We got so drunk and stayed out all night; I was so hungover the next morning."

Isla pasted a smile on her face. *He's back.* Why did she feel slightly nauseated? Oh, right. She probably had a concussion.

"Hey, Knox!" Kelly cried, grabbing Isla's arm again. He emerged from Sue's office carrying a large file box. Isla reluctantly allowed Kelly to drag her down the hallway. Probably best not to prolong this.

"Hey," Knox said, giving Isla a quick smile.

"Hey." She looked up just long enough to catch his eye.

"Oh my god, Knox, I was just telling Isla all about the pub crawl on Saturday—"

"Excuse me," said Isla quietly, leaving Kelly prattling on to Knox who shifted under the weight of his box.

Once at her desk, she quickly loaded her project and put on her headphones. *Do good work; that's all that matters.*

As the morning wore on, she settled in. Copy, paste, crop, pick a colour, pick a font. Every decision mattered, right down to the finest detail.

Finally, Kelly walked in and perched on the edge of Isla's desk, narrowly missing a stack of sketches and a stick of charcoal. She picked up Isla's framed photo of Liam and then put it down, and then studied the photo of Priya, Emma, and Isla from tenth grade. Isla tried to look busy. If she didn't make eye contact, maybe Kelly would go away.

"Would you hook up with him?" Kelly asked at last.

"Pardon me?" said Isla, taking her earphones off.

"Knox. If given the opportunity, would you hook up with Knox?" Kelly asked.

No. Even though his eyes crinkled when he laughed. *No.* Even with her arm tucked tightly in the crook of his elbow. *No!* The way their bodies repelled apart like the same end of two magnets. No, she hadn't. And there probably would not be another opportunity.

"Don't think about it too hard. It isn't likely to happen. I mean, he's a solid nine and you're like a six and a half…" She gave Isla a once over, "maybe seven. But would you?"

Isla slammed her laptop shut and shouted, "You are such a cow!"

(She didn't actually do that, but she wanted to.)

"I totally would, I mean I know he can be a prick, but he is so hot—"

"I wouldn't," Isla interrupted.

Kelly stared at her, dumbfounded. "Really? Why not?"

Why not? Because being hot isn't a good enough reason.

"I have work to do," Isla pleaded. "Don't you need to get your grid road proofs to Eric today?"

"Yeah. You're going to help me, right?"

"No, I have my own stuff to work on. I've got the L2 photoshoot this afternoon." Isla's patience was wearing thin. "You presented the idea; you do the work."

"Pretty please?" Kelly gave her puppy dog eyes.

Isla shook her head.

"God, you're pissy today." Kelly hopped off her desk. "I thought we were friends."

Isla didn't reply. She put her headphones back on, turned her music up loud enough that it could be heard by those around her, and focused on her screen.

Again, she was back in the groove, copy, paste, move the image to the left .01mm, move it back, when she felt a tap on her shoulder.

She ignored it.

Tap tap tap.

"What?" shouted Isla, louder than necessary due to her headphones. She whipped around in her chair and immediately regretted everything.

"Whoa!" said Knox, holding up his hands in mock defence. "Hi!"

"Hi," said Isla, taking off her headphones, slowly placing them next to her laptop on the desk, trying to compose herself. She was the most awkward person in the world. Why couldn't she handle this with composure? *Cool, calm, collected.* No, she was instantly sweaty and lightheaded, not to mention the now purple goose egg on her forehead.

"Are you ready for this afternoon?" he asked, cool as a cucumber.

"Yes," said Isla timidly.

"John will be there, and hopefully I can stop by if I have time."

"Ok." Stick to one-word answers.

Knox stood for awhile, maybe waiting for her to say something else. She couldn't, nothing intelligent came to mind.

Knox scratched his head. "About what happened, before I left..." he trailed off. "It's cool, K?"

Isla nodded expectantly, but he didn't say anything else. Then he left.

It's cool? she thought. *What the hell does that mean?*

Cool.

22.

Priya had been awake for awhile, lying still, staring at the ceiling fan go 'round and 'round. Brian was snoring loudly next to her, his dark hair sticking out in every direction. During the day she thought he was adorable; currently she was considering suffocating him.

This is the way it had become between the two of them now that she wasn't working in the ER anymore. She'd started staying over. They didn't talk about it, it had just happened one night. He'd wanted to make her breakfast the next morning.

"I'm famous for my eggs," he had said.

They were bland. She pretended to like them.

Now she slept over regularly.

The birds had started to sing around five. *It must be seven by now*, she thought, checking her phone. Six-fifteen.

Shut up, shut up, she silently cursed the birds, who continued their morning conversations. Priya rolled over and covered her head with her pillow. Mercifully, she fell back to sleep. She slept for another hour or so, ate the bland eggs, and kissed Brian good-bye.

Autumn had started announcing itself part way through August. The mornings were cooler, and the air had lost its humidity. The plants were drying down, preparing to survive what was inevitably coming. Priya shivered as she stepped out of Brian's building. The cool breeze of change.

"Hey! Excuse Me! Can you hold the door for me!" yelled a perky blond woman walking quickly towards her, carrying a huge bouquet of multi-coloured helium balloons.

Priya shrugged and held the door for her. It wasn't her building.

"Thank you so much! I was hoping I could get in undetected. I'm surprising Brian McAlister — Dr. Brian McAlister," she said, emphasizing the *doctor*. "Do you know him?"

Priya smiled sweetly. "Fourth floor, second on the left, 406. How do you know him?"

"I'm his fiancé!" she held her left hand up, a large princess cut diamond on the ring finger. "I just flew in this morning. When we talked last night, it was so hard not to spill the beans!"

That's how curiosity killed the cat: with a shot to the heart.

The woman standing in front of Priya did not look like she'd just gotten off a plane, her hair in flawless long waves, make-up perfectly applied.

"I'm Athena," she said, holding out her free hand. "Are you neighbours?"

Priya didn't take her hand, leaving it hanging awkwardly. "We work together."

"Oh, are you a nurse?"

"Doctor," she said, purposely not giving her name.

"Nice to meet you," Athena replied cheerfully as Priya marched away.

Priya had driven Isla's stupid car and she had to get the key in the stupid lock in order to enter.

"Hold it together, hold it together," she whispered to herself. Her eyes clouded with tears, making the keyhole harder to see.

She dropped the keys a second time and shouted, "Fuck you!"

Still fumbling with the keys and the lock, the tears she had been desperate to hold in suddenly spilled over.

"What are you looking at?" she snapped at an innocent bystander. Finally getting into the car, she slammed the door and pealed out of the parking lot as fast as the little hatchback could take her.

Isla slept in gloriously late, then lounged in bed, checking her social media feeds. It was nice not having Priya around in the mornings. She was too perky and energetic, banging around the apartment. Isla checked her clock. 11:17am. It was the need for caffeine that got her out of bed. She planned to brew a pot and bring the mug right back to her cozy bed.

The last thing she expected to see was Priya lying on the couch, staring at the blank TV in old gym shorts and a ratty t-shirt. Mascara streaked down her face, giving her a grotesque horror movie look. Beside her on the floor was a tumbler containing a small amount of amber-coloured liquid.

"Good morning, Pri," Isla said gently as she knelt on the floor beside her.

"The DVD player isn't working," mumbled Priya, her nose stuffed and voice hoarse.

Isla picked up the glass and tasted it, mostly whiskey and a couple melted ice cubes. "Oh sweetie, it's hard to work technology when you're drunk. What is the matter? How long have you been here?"

"I'm not drunk," Priya said, rolling over and away from Isla.

"Priya, what's wrong?" When she didn't answer, Isla sat on the floor. This was not the Priya she knew. The Priya she knew was always on the move and never cried on the couch. *I'm the one that cries on the couch*, thought Isla. Then, more productively, *what does Priya do for me when I'm feeling gross?*

"You should get up," she started kindly, "and have a shower, and then the two of us can go for a walk. We can walk…to the river and get donuts and go to a movie," continued Isla, doing her best Priya imitation: bossy, and upbeat (this was asking a lot, considering Isla still hadn't had coffee). "Why don't you tell me what happened?"

"Go away," growled Priya.

How rude, thought Isla. Although to be fair, that was how she would react. Isla grabbed the tumbler and dumped it down the kitchen sink. She started a pot of coffee.

"If you don't get off the couch, I'm going to call—-umm" she thought hard, and then called from their small kitchen, "your mother."

No response from the couch. That threat didn't carry as much weight when it was Isla saying it.

Priya sat on the couch, waiting to attack. She glared at Isla as she came in from the kitchen with two mugs in hand.

"Guess who has a fiancé?" she hissed.

Isla held her breath. Nope, she was not going to answer that question.

"That shithead! Five months!" Priya unleashed. "We've been together for five months and the whole time he's so happy about not being *tied down*," Priya gestured with exaggerated air quotes, "and all this time he's been *engaged* — and not engaged to any normal girl, but a perfect one with perfect hair and perfect teeth and no wrinkles in her dress. She's named after a goddess!"

Regrettably, Isla couldn't help but ask, "Weren't you happy with not being tied down as well?"

If Priya was angry before, she was near eruption now. "How *dare* you take his side? He lied to me! He betrayed me!"

A fresh set of tears rolled down Priya's cheeks. Isla was shocked. She couldn't remember the last time she'd seen Priya cry — grade eleven maybe, when she got a C on an English paper?

Then Isla asked quietly, respectfully, empathetically, "Are you in love with him?"

"Of course not!" Priya sat back, silently wiping her face with the backs of her hands. "How the hell should I know? I don't fall in love. I'm not naive like you."

"Ouch. Ok, I'm going to let that slide, because you're my best friend and right now it is not about me," said Isla.

"It's irrelevant whether I'm in love with him or not; you should've seen this girl! Trophy wife material in every way. Elegant, cheerful, and sweet – oh-so-sticky-sweet. Did I mention she's white? Have a fling with the exotic dark-skinned girls — but marriage must preserve purity. I hate her."

Isla rubbed her back while she screamed into the pillow. "Don't be mad at her. She didn't know. Channel all that hatred towards him. He is the villain. Well, actually, patriarchy is the real evil here—"

Priya wasn't listening. She was formulating revenge.

137

23.

August 16. A dry heat, 27C°.

Emma's mini van sat in the parking lot of Brian's apartment building. They were close enough to the door to see anyone who entered or exited, but were far enough to be discreet.

"I don't think we should be doing this," said Emma. She slouched in the driver's seat, clad in all black, including a black ball cap and big sunglasses.

"You didn't have to come; we just needed your van," said Priya from the passenger seat.

"What if someone sees us?" asked Emma.

"You're the only one who looks suspicious, dressed in black from hat to toe on a hot day in August," said Isla. She wore jean shorts and a blue tank and sat in the back seat, feeding Liam tasteless baby crackers. Isla had worked hard all week in order to take the afternoon off. She would be forever grateful that Sue hadn't asked any questions about her sudden 'illness.' She was such a bad liar she would've told the truth immediately and thrown herself on Sue's mercy. Thankfully, Sue was not interested in the personal lives of her employees.

They began the afternoon at Isla's cousin's farm picking up some necessary supplies. Once they finished at Brian's, they were going to Emma's for takeout pizza, all on a Thursday, making them feel like they were teenagers again.

"Are you sure they're going to leave?" asked Emma again.

"Of course!" said Priya, losing patience. "What kind of a fiancé doesn't take you out on your last night in town?"

She said *fiancé* with the type of venom usually reserved for loathsome creatures: snakes and spiders and mice.

"How do you know it's her last night?" asked Emma.

"She's been spying," said Isla.

"Have you been stalking them?"

"It is called research. It would be stupid of us to do this without proper research. I have some contacts in the ER willing to ask some questions for me."

"So, you haven't actually talked to him yet?" asked Emma.

"Why would I talk to him? I know everything I need to know," replied Priya.

"Get down! There they are." Isla pointed toward the door and all three girls ducked down quickly.

"Emma, check to see if they're gone?" asked Priya after a while.

"I don't want to look," squeaked Emma.

"You're the only one he hasn't met. Casually look up. Pretend you were looking for something and now you've found it."

Emma held her breath and rummaged around the floor a bit before sitting up and exhaling. "Coast is clear."

"Good. Take off that ridiculous hat. Let's go," said Priya.

"I am really uncomfortable about breaking into his house," said Emma.

"For the last time, we are not breaking in! I have a key. I am returning my key, and his stuff, and leaving him a parting gift. You're welcome to stay in the car."

"Come on Em, it'll be fun," grinned Isla. She pulled a big cardboard box out of the trunk, containing Brian's hoodie, several textbooks, a stuffed mouse, and a couple of old mouse traps.

Priya grabbed the box out of Isla's hands and marched towards the door like she owned the place, leaving Isla behind to deal with a shoe box with holes poked in the top. Emma tip-toed behind Isla, Liam in her arms, her eyes darting back and forth conspicuously.

Once in the apartment, Priya placed the big box obviously on the coffee table and arranged the stuffed mouse on top.

Priya had no final words, or ceremony. The three friends left as quickly as they came. Five field mice explored their new home, freed from the shoe box as a last parting gift.

24.

August 26. Cooling after a hot day, 24C°.

Time stopped. The cereal bowl slipped out of Andrew's hand and hit the side of the dishwasher before crashing onto the tile floor. Shards of ceramic scattered across the floor, shattering the peace they'd been working so hard to keep.

Emma grabbed the broom out of the closet and shut the door with purpose, her sweeping exaggerated, cleaning the whole kitchen instead of just the corner where the bowl had been dropped. Andrew stared at her, wide eyed. Each sweep was calculated and precise.

"You should've told me they were planning to stay," he said again.

"How many times do I have to tell you? I didn't know!" Sweep, sweep.

"I find it hard to believe that your parents spent the whole summer in our house without mentioning that they planned to move back to Winnipeg."

"Are you implying that I am lying?"

Andrew tilted his head ever so slightly, implying that very thing.

Emma stopped sweeping. Hurt welled up in her, and her voice shook as she said, "I have never lied to you, Andrew."

"You lied about the book study!" he challenged.

141

"That wasn't a lie, I –I just didn't tell you because I knew you wouldn't understand."

"You're right! I don't understand why you would go to a book study on marriage that promotes the oppression of women."

"I didn't go for the book—-" Emma started.

"—Would you rather I boss you around and demand you serve me? Cook me steak! Fold my laundry! Kiss my shoes!" Andrew was yelling now. "Is that what you want, Emma? Because I want a partner, not a servant."

Emma shook. In all the years they had been together, she'd never seen Andrew so angry. These last few months, everything had been stretched to the point of breaking. Andrew was busy with work, staying extra late to avoid spending time with his in-laws who had long overstayed their welcome. Emma felt trapped. Her mother's constant companionship kept her locked behind a façade of pleasantries.

In order to avoid conflict with her parents, she went along with them, smiling and nodding, letting them believe they were right. And as every week came and went, they remained. A steady spiral of polite death.

Then this morning, Gerald and Sara announced to their congregation that he had accepted the pastor of mission's position — they were staying in Winnipeg. Emma and Andrew found out when Gerald sent a text message: *Big News!* Alongside was an attachment with the announcement on video.

"I went because I needed a break!" Emma yelled.

"A break from what?"

"From this!" she said, indicating the room around them. "We might have a partnership in theory, but you still get to go to work everyday while I'm stuck here keeping a baby alive, doing all the laundry, all the cooking, all the cleaning. Plus, I do it all with a baby strapped to me because he will not let me put him down. I go to the stupid book study because they have childcare, and Liam actually enjoys it. I get to put him down and for sixty glorious, magnificent minutes, I don't have a child clinging to me, draining me of all joy."

"But isn't this what you wanted? You wanted to be a mom. You said that's all you ever wanted!"

"It was — it is. It's just — I don't have any friends—"

"What about Isla and Priya?"

"They work during the day," she said.

"What about Alicia? And all those women at your baby shower?"

Emma deflated. "I stopped going to yoga and I haven't heard from any of them since."

"Have you contacted them?"

"You don't understand."

"You can't say you don't have friends, when you're not putting in the effort." He kept interrupting her.

"That's not the point! Before mom and dad came, I would go all day without talking to another adult. Of course I don't enjoy the book study. The only thing I have in common with those women is the fact that we're mothers. But someone takes him out of my arms for one hour, and it's the best part of my week."

"What I don't get is that you'll leave him with them, but you won't leave him with me?" Andrew snapped, "I'm his father, and you don't trust me."

Emma felt like she had been slapped in the face. His words stung. *That's not true,* she wanted to yell back. But she couldn't. It *was* true. Anytime she had left Liam with Andrew she'd been racked with fear, sending text after text after text, quick check ups, making sure they were okay.

The truth was, she didn't trust anyone with Liam — barely even herself. He was so perfect and fragile. What if they screwed him up for life? What if he got sick or hurt? What if he grew up and went to therapy and blamed everything on her?

Tears streamed down her face as she stared at her husband, her Andy. When was the last time she had really looked at him, really seen his face, those hazel eyes, flecked with gold?

"I can't do this. I am failing every single day," she choked out.

The front door opened.

Emma quickly wiped the tears from her eyes and Andrew busied himself finishing the dishwasher. He touched her hand, a brief reassurance.

"Well, well, we sure pulled that surprise off, didn't we?" boomed Gerald. Andrew winced as he pounded him on the back. "How exciting, huh? Getting to spend more time with the grandson."

To Emma, Sara looked happier than she had all summer, like a weight had lifted. She gave Emma a side-hug and said, "Isn't it wonderful, sweetie? We'll start looking for our own place, but we're so grateful that you've put up with us this long."

"What are we going to do, kick you out?" Andrew said. Then, just loud enough for Emma to hear, he added sarcastically, "we wouldn't dream of that."

25.

August 31. Strong south wind, 28C°.

The thing about Fridays before long weekends is that everyone has already checked out.

Sure, they're in their chairs, computers on, but all anyone is thinking about is the cold drink on the deck or the canoe on the lake. The last thing anyone wants is a curve ball. So when Sue walked into the creative office with her sensible summer blouse and pursed lips, holding a battered file with loose papers jumbled together and remarkably thin, no one noticed. Just like no one noticed the two empty desks.

"We have a problem," Sue announced.

Isla startled out of her daydream with a blink and a shake of her head. She looked at her supervisor. Slowly, a sense of dread filled the room.

Sue stood by the table in the middle of the room while everyone gathered. "Last night, Knox had to fire Kelly and Eric for engaging in inappropriate behaviour at the office."

Angela masterfully turned a chortle into a cough. Ryan looked horrified, but ventured, "Can I ask what kind of inappropriate behaviour?"

Sue clasped her hands in front of her, conflicted. Finally, she said, "Against my best judgment I will tell you that they decided to toss the whole Grid Road pitch, and then engaged in mood-altering substances to 'enhance their creativity."

"They were high?" Isla blurted out.

Sue nodded. "All they accomplished was destroying the file containing all of the work from the last six weeks."

"No. that can't — this can't be right! No—" Ryan shook his head. "There has to be a backup on the server."

Sue turned her focus to Ryan. "I had understood the three of you were finishing the pitch last night."

Angela caught Isla's eye and smirked. Isla felt comradery with the woman for the first time and gave her a small smile back.

"They just had two things to finish when I left at eight," Ryan defended himself. "I wouldn't have left if I thought they were going to blow everything to pieces!"

Ryan grabbed the file and flipped it open, muttering to himself. "This can't be it." He flipped through each page, again and again. Page one: the digital logo. Page two: a couple of paragraphs of text. Page three: Isla's original sketch.

Finally sinking into the nearest chair, he said, "this is a disaster."

"I agree," Sue stated. "What are we going to do about it? Joel and Ezra were supposed to come in at two this afternoon. We've managed to push it to four."

Isla took a deep breath, but before she could speak, Ryan sprung into action. "Isla, you need to redraw this digitally."

He handed her the digital printout and continued, "Angela –"

Isla interrupted him. "This one is wrong. I'd like to go back to the original."

"Excuse me?"

Isla put both logos side by side. Pointing to Kelly's, she explained, "this one is all wrong—"

"All wrong? We don't have time to do anything new," snapped Ryan.

Isla took a deep breath and confessed, "I drew the original sketch."

The room was silent. Everyone gaped at her.

"You drew the original?" questioned Ryan.

Isla nodded. "Kelly stole it out of my sketchbook and presented it as her own."

"Ah—" sighed Sue. "Why didn't you say anything?"

"I'd barely been here a month and I didn't want to make a scene — another scene."

Sue looked around at her staff and took charge. "Isla will do the logo, her way, as fast as she can. Angela, you try and make heads or tails out of this jumbled copy. Ryan and I will work on the website. No breaks, no lunch until this is done. Do you understand?"

They nodded. Suddenly there was a new energy in the room. Mission impossible, clock ticking. The pre-long weekend daze was behind them.

Isla was alone, sitting at her desk, munching on a bag of chips, finishing the final details of the logo when Knox approached. "I hear you finally told everyone Grid Road was your idea."

They had barely spoken since his declaration that everything was in fact, cool.

"I did, yeah. I think we've pulled it off: a new logo, decent copy, a functioning website." said Isla "Do you think I should ask Sue if I can come to the client meeting?"

"Nope," he responded.

"Why not?"

"Because I said so."

"Are you kidding me? This whole idea was mine!"

"I am the managing partner, and I say no." he smirked.

Isla whispered *arrogant shit* as she turned back to her computer.

He heard her, as she'd intended.

"Okay. I'll tell you why."

She braced herself.

"Your dress."

"My dress? There is nothing wrong with my dress!"

"It isn't professional. You look like Anne of Green Gables—"

Isla looked down at her sundress. It was loose fitting and had a tiny floral pattern on a light blue background, with ruffles on the bodice and tiny puffed sleeves.

"—when she was twelve."

Anger boiled through Isla's veins. She clenched her fists and tried to come up with a calm, reasonable response. Nothing came.

"Now if you were wearing yesterday's dress," he continued with a grin as he relived the memory, "that would be a whole other story."

Yesterday's dress? The dress she had decided against wearing to work ever again because of the multiple catcalls she'd received on her way home. The dress that was tighter, shorter, and lower cut than the dress she currently was wearing? Isla stood up to look Knox straight in the eye. "Do you honestly think I dress for your benefit? I will wear whatever the hell I want, for myself, not for you or for anyone else!"

"*Ahem*"

Knox whirled around. Sue stood in the door. Neither of them knew how long she had been there. "Isla, can I talk to you in my office, please?"

Isla stormed out of the room, down the hall and into Sue's office.

As Sue followed her, she took a couple of deep breaths and tried to imagine her chair on their cottage deck overlooking Lake of the Woods. Phil and the boys had already left; she was supposed to take the afternoon off to join them. Maybe she was too old for this.

Isla was pacing when she entered.

"I cannot continue dealing with the drama between the two of you," she told Isla.

"Knox was completely out of line!" blurted Isla. She was too angry to sit, even as Sue primly took a seat at her desk.

"Can you sit down, please?"

Isla sat in a huff.

"I agree that what he said was inappropriate, but why did you ask him about the meeting instead of me?"

"I was going to ask you, but he knew about my sketch, that Kelly took it."

Sue raised her eyebrow. "How long has he known?"

"He said he knew the moment Kelly presented it," replied Isla. "He tried to convince me to speak up, but I didn't."

"I have a hard time imagining you unable to speak up for yourself."

"Kelly was—is my friend. I mean, I wanted her to be my friend. I don't care what Knox thinks about me. Actually, I know what he thinks of me and I'm quite sure there isn't anything I can do to lower his opinion."

Sue sighed and asked, "Do you want some tea?"

Isla nodded.

Sue busied herself with her electric kettle and placed tea bags in a delicate antique tea pot with pale pink roses on it. "What he should've told you, was that we've decided the two of us — as partners — will handle the meeting together, to show them that we're taking them seriously and we want their business."

Then she sat across from Isla, leaned across her desk, and asked, "Is there more to this story? Anything else you want to tell me?"

Isla quickly decided not to share any more details. She shook her head.

"Okay. I'd like you to fill out a harassment complaint."

"A harassment complaint? Against Knox?" questioned Isla. "Do you really think that is necessary?"

Sue looked Isla directly in the eye. "I want to stop this behaviour before it gets worse. Ken would have similar conversations with female employees, and it got him in trouble. Knox's father's shadow looms large over him, and grief makes memory selective."

Isla's body involuntarily jerked. "Is Ken *dead*?"

"You didn't know?" asked Sue, surprised.

Isla shook her head. "I assumed he was retired."

"Ken and Iris, Knox's mother, both passed away in a car accident three years ago last winter. His sister Violet was also seriously injured, but she has recovered." Sue spoke in her usual, efficient tone, but Isla sensed a deep sadness in her. "I guess you also wouldn't know Ken was my stepbrother. Our parents married each other late in life. We were both only children; we quickly realised the value of extended family. Knox is like a nephew to me."

Isla took a sip of hot tea and listened.

"He puts far too much pressure on himself to be just like his dad, who was a bull in a China shop. He made many mistakes, and Knox was shielded from the fallout. I don't want to minimize what happened— I care about him enough to expect better from him. If Knox thinks he can handle being a partner, then I will hold him to the standard of behaviour of a partner."

"If I make a complaint, he'll be even more annoyed with me."

"We've all had to work with people who annoy us from time to time. Trust me, he'll get over it. What I don't want, is for you to feel disrespected and leave because of it. I'd like you to write, in your own words, what happened. I'll present it to the other partners and recommend he take some sensitivity training — and that he formally apologises to you."

26.

September 5. North wind, 19C°.

"She made a harassment complaint against me!" Knox announced before sitting down on the brown microfiber couch.

Harold sat calmly in the matching chair across from him. "Shall I assume 'she' is the same 'she' you've been ranting about all summer?"

Knox nodded miserably. Therapy was required for his employment. He had stubbornly said the bare minimum for the first five months. Every session would begin with Harold asking if he wanted to talk about his parents; every time he declined.

"I'm a nice guy! I'm not a creep," Knox defended himself. "Sue put her up to it — she even admitted it. She is determined to make sure I fail."

"What was the complaint for?" asked Harold.

"I was teasing her; I made a comment about her dress."

Harold waited. When Knox didn't say anything else, he said, "I think you got off easy."

"Pardon me?"

"You have described in our sessions at least two other incidents that could have ended with complaints."

Knox started to defend himself and then stopped. "But I'm a good guy."

"I'm not saying you aren't, but I wonder if maybe you should stop trying to conquer this young lady and start treating her like a human."

Knox sat in silence for a long time, his body fidgeting, toe tapping, hands crossing and uncrossing. He scratched his head a couple times. Harold waited, and then asked, "What's making you uncomfortable?"

Knox shrugged. "I don't want to talk about it."

"Okay. But can I make an observation? Normally when you don't want to talk, you sit very still and stare at the painting behind me."

Knox adjusted his body, trying to find a comfortable position. "I remembered something about my dad."

Harold waited.

"I must've been nine or ten. My parents were fighting. I had never seen my mom that angry. They fought about things I didn't understand. I didn't know what 'sexual harassment' was at the time. Mom took us to her mother's for the night, maybe longer? That's it — that's all I remember."

Harold paused. "How does that memory make you feel?"

"My whole life I've been told –you're just like your dad, apple doesn't fall far from the tree, his mini-me. I want to believe it; he was a great man."

"He was human."

"You don't understand. He came from nothing and built a multi-million-dollar business. People adored him. Newspapers wrote articles about his business sense. He didn't even have a university education." Knox looked everywhere and anywhere to avoid Harold's piercing gaze.

"The thing about being human is that we're all both great and deeply flawed, sometimes at the same time," said Harold.

"Do you know what happened after your mom took you to your grandmother's?"

"I don't know. Something must've happened. Violet was born when I was ten." The cadence of his voice slowed as he finished his sentence, recognising the significance of it.

"She went back to him because she was pregnant."

"Or maybe they worked it out and a baby was the result. I think you should ask some questions, investigate a bit. Part of grieving a loved one is coming to terms with the not-so-great things we remember. Remembering your father as someone perfect does a disservice to him, and to you, especially if you think you have to live up to a life that didn't exist."

That night Knox paced in his apartment. Even after a long run, he felt jumpy. He poured himself a couple of fingers of whisky, and stared at his phone. He had done the easy research. The internet had helped him find a damaging article, "Respected Businessman Accused of Inappropriate Sexual Conduct," but not much else.

He took one sip, then dumped the rest down the drain as he called up the courage to dial Graham's number.

"What do I owe the pleasure of a phone call?" Graham answered, chipper as usual.

"I want to know about my dad and his assistant."

Graham had been expecting this conversation ever since Sue had called him earlier in the week. He had been dreading it, even though he knew it was necessary. "What do you remember?"

"Lots of fighting. Mom and I went to grandma's for awhile."

Graham sighed. "You lived there for almost two months. She had one foot out the door, permanently, when she found out she was pregnant with Violet. That changed everything."

"She stayed with him because of Violet?"

"No, he changed. They'd started trying for a second child right after you were born. Nine years and three miscarriages later, they were both miserable, drowning in their own grief, separately. Your father started putting all his energy and free time into the business and made a couple of good decisions that skyrocketed him to the next level. Iris put all her time and energy into you, micromanaging every aspect of your over-scheduled life. Hockey, soccer, art classes, extra math tutoring. It was ridiculous for a nine-year-old to be doing grade eight math. You excelled, and she kept you both busy. Meanwhile, your father hired an attractive, young assistant who was abysmal as an employee. Your father was lonely as hell, and felt invincible at the office. And, well, it was a different world back then.

"Ken swore he didn't have an affair. Iris never believed him." Graham paused. "I'm not sure if I ever did either. It was messy and complicated. Your father said she wanted something, and he wouldn't give it to her; she said he pursued her against her wishes and threatened to fire her if she didn't comply. Ken was ready to fight to clear his name until Iris told him about the baby. She told him she was prepared to do it on her own, and she would've succeeded. The thought of losing her and the baby and you—" Graham took a few seconds to compose himself.

"Something changed in him. I could barely believe it myself. The young, brash, stubborn man who had been my best friend for better or worse decided to change his life. He threw all his energy into reconciliation and marriage counseling. He settled with the young lady, gave her everything she wanted. He owned up to his mistake in front of his company. He hired Adam to be his next assistant — he was not nearly as attractive, and far more competent. Your mother was hesitant, and she didn't know if the pregnancy would hold. They had had so much heartbreak. It would have broken our hearts if your mom had left and taken you away with her. But by the time

Violet was born, they had reconciled enough for her to move back in. Full healing took years. But Ken was a changed man. For so long he believed he had to be a certain kind of man to be successful, and he *was* that man, he was brash and demanding, but he softened enough, he lost his sense of entitlement. He realised how easily he could lose it all."

Knox was silent. Grahams final words, *lose it all*, echoed around his head until grief choked him.

"He did lose it all," Knox finally said.

"When he died, he had everything he ever wanted."

"No, he didn't. He had a fuck-up for a son."

"Knox," Graham implored. "Don't say that. You know that's not true."

"I should've been there that night. I should've been with them. Violet had a recital, and mom wanted me to come home for supper. She tried bribing me with a lemon pie. Dad and I had gotten into a big fight on the weekend, over my commitment to school."

Ken had insisted on a master's in business before Knox could join the company. Knox had one semester left and had resented every moment of it. Six years of university so he could join his father's business, when his father didn't have any post-secondary schooling. In a moment of anger, Knox had threatened to take his master's degree somewhere else. Ken had matched his anger and bravado and double dared him to try.

"I didn't go to supper. Do you remember, it was one of those rare sunny days in the middle of winter? The sun feels so good after weeks of rain. Some buddies and I went to the beach to drink beer. When I didn't show up for supper, dad called, and we fought again."

Knox's voice wavered; he didn't know if he could say the next thing that needed to come out of his mouth. He had pushed it down and denied it for three and a half years. "I told him to butt out of my life and leave me alone — then I hung up on him."

155

Knox dropped his phone to the tabletop so Graham couldn't hear him cry. Graham let out an audible moan. The pain of this young man whom he loved as a son radiated down the phone connection, straight through his heart.

27.
October 17.

The middle seat in the back row of the plane felt far more comfortable than the alternative — even though the alternative was an aisle seat in business class. The roar of the engine, the proximity to the bathroom, the chattering flight attendants...Isla put on her headphones and decided yes, this was better.

Isla had been dreading this day since Sue assigned her the role of creative representative to the HRA annual meetings. She'd been excited at first: a trip to Vancouver just as Winnipeg was sinking into cold, ugly autumn weather. Three nights at a luxury hotel sounded good to her. But the only other Winnipeg staff attending? Knox Harrison. No way. Full stop.

But somebody had to go. Sue couldn't because of her sick mother-in-law. Ryan's baby was going to make an appearance any day. Angela had the days booked off for a friend's wedding. That left Isla: bottom-rung Isla.

Fine. She'd go.

But a three-hour flight next to Knox?

In the end, she couldn't do it. As she walked up to the gate, she had noticed an elderly woman being wheeled to the gate by airport staff.

Would she like to trade seats?

"This is a business class seat, ma'am. Are you sure?"

Yes, she was so sure.

She had all she needed: music in her headphones, a good book to read, and Priya had snuck some snacks into her bag.

The look on Knox's face when she'd boarded was enough to make her second-guess her decision. But he had been nothing but horrible to her since the day they met; she wasn't going to let him get to her. He hadn't spoken one word to her since Sue made her fill out the harassment form six weeks ago.

Not one word.

He'd even stopped attending meetings she was at. Sue had promised things would get better, but the more time passed, the more anxiety welled up in her. And now they were on a plane together, on their way to meetings and workshops. She wouldn't be able to avoid him the whole time, nor he her.

Knox scowled when she entered the plane. Next to him sat an elderly woman who hadn't stopped chattering at him since she sat down.

Couldn't she take a hint?

"There must be a mistake," he had said to the flight attendant. "This is my co-worker's seat."

"No mistake, sir," she replied, showing the boarding pass with the right seat number on it.

Her name was Louisa and he had already seen pictures of her great grandchildren and her single granddaughter.

"Are you single?" Louisa had asked.

And then Isla boarded the plane with a smug look on her face. She never could hide her true feelings, and she looked delighted to see how miserable he was. He'd promised Sue that he would finally talk to her and apologise; he'd been planning to do it on the plane, and now she'd messed everything up.

He hated when a plan didn't go his way.

Once the plane landed in the mist of the lower mainland, Isla deplaned and found her way to an escalator. Knox was waiting for her, arms crossed and furious.

"Nice stunt," Knox snapped.

"Did you and granny enjoy the flight?" Isla countered.

"She didn't stop talking the whole flight, so we're basically best friends now. She's even going to knit me a scarf."

"A scarf, how nice. Maybe she'll put a big fat 'K' on it, so everyone knows whose it is."

"We're late," stated Knox, as he turned towards the doors leading outside.

"Wait! I need to get my luggage," said Isla, looking around for the baggage claim.

"You put luggage underneath? Are you an idiot? I have to be downtown in forty-five minutes."

Isla recoiled. "Don't you have luggage? Is that all you brought?"

All he had was a laptop bag and a small duffle bag. Suddenly she became aware that her ideal flying outfit was vastly different than his. He had on a navy suit; she had leggings, a band t-shirt and a long cardigan.

"I should change."

"You think?" Knox retorted as he took off towards the luggage carousel. "Don't you need your luggage for that?" he called back as they weaved through the crowds.

"I have extra clothes in my bag," she called, holding her tote bag up slightly. He had stopped in front of a large carousel. It was turning but held no baggage.

"I can go change while you look for my suitcase," she said. "It's pink with polka dots."

"Of course it is." Knox rolled his eyes. "Fast. Please."

Isla rushed to refresh her makeup and change into a simple grey jersey dress borrowed from Emma. Perfect for travel, she had said. Three-inch emerald, green heels added some personality. *Not bad for ten minutes*, she thought, checking herself out in the mirrored wall.

When she found Knox, he had hauled her bright suitcase off the luggage carousel. Wanting nothing to do with it, he pushed the handle towards her and walked away.

Pulling the heavy suitcase, Isla struggled to keep up with his long stride. Weaving in and out of crowds, she broke into a trot a couple of times.

"Can you slow down?" she called to him from behind.

He ignored her. Isla was forced to take off her shoes and sprint after him. She caught up to him as he reached the revolving door and headed outside. She followed, though her feet were still bare.

The air was damp, even as the sun peeked through the clouds. A crisp north wind blew through the covered roadway. Isla shivered.

She finally caught up to him at the SkyTrain kiosk. He bought tickets just as the train rounded the corner into the stop. He handed her one. "Put your shoes on, you're embarrassing yourself."

Isla, red faced, lips pursed and ready to explode, followed him onto the train. *He is so horrible and rude and thoughtless and mean.* She struggled to pull her suitcase on, then sat across the aisle from him. She leaned over and hissed, "Go to hell."

Only then did she put her shoes back on.

It was a long, quiet train ride over the Fraser River and into downtown.

Graham was waiting as they emerged from the elevator into the GHRA foyer. On the seventeenth floor, large windows offered a spectacular view of downtown, with Stanley Park in the distance.

"Hello to my favourite prairie dwellers!" Graham reached up and pulled Knox into a bear hug. He turned to Isla and thought about a hug, but pulled back to offer a hand instead.

"Ms. Peters, how nice to finally meet you! I've heard so much about you," he said with a mischievous wink.

Isla warmed to him instantly. "And you, Mr. Richards. I am so glad to be here."

"Please, call me Graham. I'm not old enough to be a Mr. yet." He pointed to a man in his early forties, dressed in a navy suit with a neon green shirt, with a tie that had a wild print that somehow pulled the outfit together. "That's Adam Parker; he'll show you around and get you set up with a desk before the workshops start after lunch. I'm glad you're here, Isla; Knox has told me so many good things about you."

Knox cleared his throat and Isla gave a reluctant smile. Adam came over and introduced himself before leading her away.

"How was the flight?" Graham asked, following Knox into Ken's old office. They hadn't updated it when the rest of the office had been renovated two years prior. It still had the original nineties décor; a forest green pillow sporting a handsome mallard sat on the chocolate brown leather sofa. Ken had wanted his office to look like the hunting cabin of his dreams — the one he was going to live in once he retired. Neither Graham nor Knox had had the heart to change it.

"Fine," Knox responded flatly, unpacking his laptop and slipping into the worn leather desk chair.

"I can see why you like her — those bright eyes! Have you two made up, or is she still sore at you?" asked Graham.

"She's still mad as hell. And as I told you before: I don't like her." Knox turned his seat away from where Graham was perched. Silently, he urged his computer to be ready. *Damn updates*, he thought, as he watched the download bar move slowly.

"She switched seats with an old lady to avoid sitting with me on the plane," Knox finally elaborated.

Graham laughed. "Really? She is a clever one, too."

Knox ignored him and started working.

"Have you tried apologising?"

Knox could feel his neck tightening. He asked, "Don't you have work to do?"

"I cleared my whole afternoon so I could harass you," the older man said, giving Knox a nudge.

Knox sighed. "I have more important things to worry about right now."

"Tomorrow's meeting will be fine. You'll do fine! We all have rough patches—"

"Things are worse than we thought," Knox interrupted.

"You've only been there nine months—"

"Don't go easy on me. It pisses everyone else off. My dad wouldn't let a partner get away with a revenue drop this significant — especially me." Knox leaned back in his chair. "Right now, we're barely breaking even. There aren't new clients to be found, not the size we need. Winnipeg is full of small businesses with tiny budgets, but very few national companies."

"Stick with the small companies. That's how Sue made it work."

"Yeah, well, she wasn't exactly moving forward. It's probably best she isn't here."

28.

October 18. Sunny, 18C°.

The next morning was so glorious, Isla couldn't resist walking to the Harrison Richards office. At every turn she found something beautiful to gape at, views of the ocean through the sea of skyscrapers, pots of flowers not yet killed by the first fall frost (unlike the flowers in Winnipeg, which were long gone). She stopped to treat herself to a coffee before she found her way to the creative office. She liked it here. The space was big enough that it wasn't dictated by one personality or bad mood. The energy was different. Still professional, still mostly grey suits and blue ties, but the occasional pink shirt and white tie made Isla feel like she had found her people. The large creative staff absorbed her effortlessly, not forcing her to prove anything, and not threatened by her. Adam led the group with exuberance and optimism. The morning meeting was fun and inspiring; she found herself wishing her Winnipeg colleagues were there with her.

The afternoon was the complete opposite: long and dry, an overview of every single account. Isla flipped back and forth between utter boredom and sheer terror, anticipating their turn to speak. She noticed on the agenda that she and Knox had been given a block of time, and they had no plan — not one she was aware of, anyway. She hoped she wouldn't have to say anything.

When it was their turn, Knox called her up and introduced her. He handed her his laptop and launched into the list of accounts they had, while she scrambled to find the proper visual to go with each client. After awhile she caught on to the flow. What seemed like an erratic order started making sense; Knox was hiding the underperforming accounts among the more successful accounts. She started guessing which account would come next, and was successful over half the time. Eventually there were only two accounts left, Grid Road and L2. Isla was anxious, as she felt personally responsible for both accounts. She picked Grid Road thinking he'd end with L2, since it had had the fewest hiccups.

"Isla has more to say about both of these clients than I do, so I'll hand it over to her."

There goes my plan to keep my mouth shut, thought Isla.

She found the Grid Road slide and started talking, following Knox's lead in deciding what to share and what to leave out. She made it through and looked to Knox for - what, she didn't know. Some encouragement, acknowledgement, maybe just eye contact?

She got nothing.

He opened the L2 slides, and she continued. When she was done, Knox opened the floor for questions and comments. The onslaught was quick.

"Only two new clients! Have you been on vacation for the last nine months?" called a man who looked more like a linebacker than an account executive.

Isla noticed Knox's calm facade falter. "Orson, you know as well as I do, progress takes time. We have a few big things coming up in the new year."

Do we? questioned Isla, fidgeting with her hands, unsure of what to do next.

"Fashion and whiskey? Not exactly our target clients — but some of your favourite things, no doubt," replied Orson with a smirk. A titter of laughter scattered around the room. "What about real clients, who have real businesses? Not just pipe dreams."

"In your summary," started another man, "in the last year you have lost four clients and only gained two. What is your plan to stop the hemorrhaging?"

"Three of those clients were poached by the Vancouver office," said Knox. "It's not entirely fair to call them losses. Secondly, Winnipeg is doing what it has always done: taking small ideas and branding them successfully, preparing them for larger audiences. These small companies either get bought by bigger companies, or grow beyond our capacities."

"But you said you were going to stop that from happening, make Winnipeg a stand-alone agency. I don't see that happening, not with these numbers."

Isla found herself moving toward the side of the room. These questions were not for her to answer. She was on the outside looking in, like watching a car wreck. She found herself next to Graham. He had a pained look on his face, but he kept his mouth shut. Knox continued to answer the questions that were lobbed at him like grenades, keeping his cool, answering as vaguely and confidently as he could, until everyone had had their say.

Finally, the assault ended, and the meeting moved on to the next item. Isla wanted to sink into the floor in a puddle. She found it hard not to take the criticism personally — this was her office, her colleagues, her clients. If she were in Knox's position, she would have fled the room in tears. She envied his fortitude.

Graham finished the meeting with an invitation for everyone to meet at the pub down the street. Dinner and drinks for all spouses, dates, even blind dates were invited.

Isla took a few moments in the ladies' room to catch her breath. She had not anticipated the meeting to be as stressful as she had found it. Any rose-coloured glasses she had on regarding HRA or business in general had disappeared. She sulked back to the creative area, feeling jumpy and defensive. She wasn't sure about going to the pub. Maybe just a long walk back to the hotel and room service, like she had done the night before.

Adam was waiting for her. "I need a date. My husband Jeffery is stuck with a patient — a lovely lab who swallowed, well he is not sure, but you know labs — will you be my date?"

"Sure," said Isla, who knew nothing about dogs. "As long as Jeffery won't mind?"

"Well, he shouldn't, but we won't tell him how pretty you are, ok?" said Adam with a wink.

They walked down Cambie Street towards Gastown, meeting up with some other colleagues who were happy to finally be out in the sun after a grueling week. When they arrived at the dark pub, they all headed straight for the bar.

"Shall we start with shots?" Adam asked.

Isla laughed. "No! I'll be under the table before we eat."

Disappointed, Adam ordered them a couple of beers, and they joined a table. Shortly after, Graham arrived, followed by his wife Max, whose arm was linked with a beaming young woman. Isla recognised her smile: Knox's sister.

Behind them were Knox and his date. Unlike some women who are beautiful but seemingly unaware of it, this woman was completely aware of how beautiful she was. She walked into the room with an expectation of attention. Jet black hair, dark brown eyes, and cream coloured skin, she had high cheekbones and a practised pout, high heels, high waisted white pants, and a tight black cropped shirt. Isla couldn't keep her eyes off them, as the two of them glided across the room, greeting other tables. It was like watching a magazine cover in motion.

"Striking couple, huh?" Adam said, interrupting her thoughts.

"Are they—-a couple?" stumbled Isla, embarrassed to be caught staring.

"I doubt it. He isn't the coupling type. He likes to keep his options open, which, let's be honest, if I were his age and looked like him, I would be the same way. Well, until it gets you shipped off to the middle of nowhere, am I right?"

"Right," responded Isla, even though she had no idea what he was talking about.

Adam caught on to her lack of comprehension. He was ecstatic with the prospect of sharing new gossip. "You haven't heard why he was exiled to Winnipeg?"

Isla shook her head. "You mean it wasn't his choice?"

Adam grinned wickedly. "No way, my dear. He was voted off the island. I can't believe you don't know about this! I thought everyone knew."

Isla shrugged. "Maybe everyone knows, but no one tells me anything. They barely tolerate me."

"That can't possibly be true; you are downright enchanting."

Isla grinned. "Flattery will get you everywhere."

Adam leaned forward and started his story. "Every year we attend this big networking event, lots of big clients, lots of potential clients, seminars, speakers, you name it. The office goes silent that week. Everyone who's anyone attends the conference. Apparently, Knox got bored and decided to skip out on his afternoon session, instead choosing to go to the hotel bar, where he meets an attractive older woman. They get drunk and go to her hotel room, where they get busted by her husband—"

He paused for dramatic effect — "who was, emphasis on *was*, one of our clients."

Isla was stunned.

"We lost the account immediately, and the partners shipped Knox to Winnipeg as punishment."

"Punishment? You think being in Winnipeg is punishment?"

"I'm sure Winnipeg is lovely, but what else could they do? He was a liability, and becoming more so as time went on. Don't get me wrong, he's a great guy, but he's struggled. The death of his parents — one doesn't bounce back from that. From what I've seen, Winnipeg has been good for him. He seems less—" Adam paused to find the right word — "smug."

There it was. She finally knew something personal about him, it didn't feel nearly as good as she thought it would.

Adam looked back towards Knox and his date. "That's Gabby. He's brought her to other events. I think they're friends."

"Friends?"

"With benefits — booty calls, fuck buddies, I don't know what you kids call it these days."

"She looks like a model."

"She is, and she won't let you forget it. Some sort of influencer, fashion blogger, makes money endorsing diet teas and face cream. Imagine using your MBA to sell crap like that."

"It would be nice to look like that," sighed Isla.

"Nah. You're far too interesting to be beautiful."

"Is that meant to be a compliment?"

"Interesting *and* beautiful." Adam corrected himself with a bow of apology. "Now come on, beautiful, lets get some food and another drink."

Adam hopped up energetically, held his hand out to Isla, and guided her through the tables of loud conversation.

At the poutine bar they filled their plates. Isla chose classic brown gravy and fresh cheese curds. Adam chose a little of everything, creating a mountain on top of his fries. "Let's not tell Jeffery about this.

He keeps trying to get me to lose weight; I tell him I'm in my forties, I am who I am. The perils of being married to a younger man."

They stopped at the bar to refill their beers, Isla balancing her full plate of fries and gravy in one hand and her beer and phone in the other. As she turned around, she bumped into Knox.

"Whoa! You don't want to lose any of these," he said, steadying her plate and helping himself to a fry.

An intimate gesture, all things considered.

"Hey!" she said, jerking her plate away as he reached for a second.

"Adam, darling, how are you?" Gabby's voice broke through, drawing Isla's attention back to Adam, who was receiving air kisses on each cheek.

"How is Jeffery? Is he here?" she looked around hopefully.

"He got caught up at work and couldn't make it. But I have a worthy replacement," he said, gesturing to Isla.

Knox murmured introductions.

"Nice to meet you." Gabby gave her a perfunctory glance. "Too bad Jeffery couldn't make it; I would love to see him again! Does he have anything big coming up? Maybe the film festival?"

"I guess you haven't heard, he finished school and is a veterinarian now. No more events," replied Adam.

"I'm sure he still has connections," continued Gabby. She accepted her drink from Knox, double vodka soda with lemon. "Thanks, babe."

He also had a drink, a whiskey and coke, if Isla had to guess. He looked uneasy, checking his watch and fiddling with his straw. "We should get some food."

Gabby pulled a face. "I doubt there is anything I can eat. I'm a keto-vegan now, far better for your health than regular keto—"

"Of course you are," Adam interrupted. He didn't want his night ruined by a speech on the benefits of vegetables. "Knox, I see Violet is here. Didn't she just turn nineteen?"

Knox readily changed topics; he wasn't interested in Gabby's current diet either. "Yeah, in August. She graduated in June and started School of Music at UBC. I'm glad she chose UBC and not somewhere on the other side of the country."

"That's fantastic! I think we should celebrate. Isla, now its shot time." Before Isla could reply, he turned to the rest of the crowd and announced, "hear ye, hear ye! Our very own Ms. Violet Harrison has a belated nineteenth birthday to celebrate!"

The crowd whooped and cheered as Adam walked over to where Violet was sitting and offered her his hand, which she bravely took. Then he walked her to the bar at the centre of everyone's attention. "This calls for tequila shots all around, and a toast!"

The bartenders rushed to fill shot glasses and cut limes, handing them out to the crowd along with saltshakers. Graham and Max looked on in amusement. She accepted a shot; he did not.

Isla didn't take a shot either. She could barely smell tequila without feeling nauseated — that one night when she was twenty-two had cured her forever.

"I'm nervous, I've never done this," whispered Violet to Isla. "What if I miss my mouth?"

Isla grinned. "Don't worry, just take it slow."

"I'm Violet."

"Hi, I'm Isla."

"I know, I've been hoping to meet you —"

Adam called the crowd to attention, interrupting Violet.

"A toast" Adam held his shot up, and those around him did the same. "Smart, sophisticated, friendly, and beautiful... Now that's enough about me. My dearest Violet, may you make better choices than those who have gone before you! Happy birthday!"

Everyone cheered and licked their salt, shot their tequila, and sucked the lime. Isla took a sip of her beer. Out of the corner of her eye she saw Gabby take both her shot and Knox's, with her camera in hand, filming. Knox watched with a stiff back and pinched smile. No doubt who Violet was supposed to make better choices than.

Violet took her shot like a pro, her cheeks pinking with the heat of the tequila. Then she turned back to Isla. "I'm glad to meet one of Knox's friends from Winnipeg. I mean, I know it is weird to worry about your big brother, but I do."

"Oh, we're not friends," corrected Isla.

"You're not?"

Isla felt an immediate affinity towards Violet and didn't want to disappoint her, but also wanted her to know the truth. "We sometimes work together, but that's it. Did he say we were friends?"

Violet shook her head. "Graham said something about it; don't worry, it's no big deal."

The party atmosphere continued to grow as the evening went on, the hum growing louder as the hours went on. Isla stuck close to Adam, who enjoying being the centre of attention, telling story after story, each one more ridiculous and over the top.

"Tell us about that time in Greece," someone would call, and he'd launch into another. Isla yawned; it was late, Winnipeg time. Feeling virtuous, she ordered a water instead of another beer, and sat down in an empty chair on the edge of the storytelling circle.

After awhile, Gabby came up next to her, leaned in and slurred, "He isn't looking for a girlfriend."

The vodka sodas, tequila shots and an empty stomach had caught up to her. Isla gave her a polite smile and turned away.

"Hey, Lyla, I'm talking to you!" Gabby grabbed Isla's face and turned it back towards her until they were face to face, a few inches apart. "I know what you're thinking, a handsome, successful guy like that. But don't get your hopes up. He is not the marriageable type."

"It's Isla, and I am not interested in Knox. Maybe you should have some food, or a glass of water."

"Fuck, why are you so obsessed with food?" Gabby sneered. "Listen, I'm warning you; I'd hate to see a sweet clueless girl like you get your heart broken."

"Like I said, I am not currently interested in Knox, nor will I ever be," Isla stated, realising too late that Knox was standing right behind Gabby.

"Excuse me," Isla said, downing her last sip of water and turning away.

She wanted to say goodbye to Adam, but he was in the middle of the crowd and the last thing she wanted to do was draw more attention to herself. She found her coat and bag and called a cab. The wait time was twenty-five to thirty minutes. With one last glance at Adam, she waved and went to the foyer to wait. Isla looked up from her phone mid-yawn, as Knox and Gabby entered the foyer. She looked down immediately and hoped they'd leave her alone.

"Thank god we're finally leaving. What a boring group of morons."

"You look tired," said Knox to Isla as he held the door for Gabby, who stumbled out on to the sidewalk.

"So do you," replied Isla.

Knox shrugged. "It's past midnight at home. Do you need a ride?"

"No thank you, there's a cab on the way." There was nothing Isla wanted less than to get into a car with Knox and Gabby.

"It's Friday night, it will take awhile," he stated, leaning against the open door, letting the ocean breeze waft in.

"I'll be fine. Go enjoy the rest of your night," said Isla, waving him out the door.

Once he left, she opened the book on her phone and continued reading. A few minutes later, the door opened again.

"You're back," she said.

"Yeah," said Knox, joining her on the bench.

"Did you forget something?"

"No," he replied. "Sort of."

He sat beside her in silence, shifting awkwardly. Finally, he spoke. "I'm sorry about Gabby. I wish I could say tonight was out of character for her, but it isn't. I'm usually tanked alongside her." He paused. "I don't know why shit like this keeps happening between us."

"Maybe because you're a shitty person," Isla said, more aggressively then necessary.

Snapping at him had become more habit than anything. Knox's body tensed, then he huffed out a sigh. He was trying, and she wasn't going to make it easy for him, Isla added, "I didn't mean that."

He snorted. "Of course you did."

"Maybe a bit, but it was harsh."

They could hear the party inside. Adam must have come to a particularly funny punchline, as the whole crowd roared.

"I've never made a formal apology before, so I'm not exactly sure what to say or how to say it." He paused and scratched the back of his head. "You did good today, at the meeting."

"Thank you," she responded cautiously.

"Actually, you do good work most days."

"*Actually?*" she started, but then stopped to let him continue.

"I'm sorry I teased you about your dress instead of telling you the truth."

Isla inhaled slowly.

"And for generally being an ass."

Isla stared ahead, slowly exhaling. "Is that all your going to apologise for?"

"Well—I" Knox faltered, as his phone rang; he declined the call.

"You trapped me against a wall and tried to kiss me!"

"I–"

"—-Also, you got me drunk and then expected me to go home with you."

Knox hung his head and quietly said "I misread those situations."

173

"You misread the situation?" Isla's voice raised sharply. "You trapped me against a wall! You're like a foot taller than me. Even if I was tall like— like your sister—it still would've been scary!"

His sister thought Knox. He stared at his shoes, as his right foot tapped anxiously. "I hadn't thought about it like that."

"Maybe you should've." Isla said quietly, suddenly she felt really tired.

They sat in silence, until his phone rang again. He declined it.

"You're right." He sat up and looked at her. "I owe you an apology for all of it. For trapping you. For trying to kiss you. For being unprofessional at dinner. For thinking you'd enjoy being teased instead of respecting you with a straight answer. I am sorry, for all of it, you didn't deserve any of it."

Against her better judgment, she hoped his apology was sincere. But she wouldn't give him resolution, not yet.

His phone rang a third time. She glanced over; it was a call from Gabby. He declined it again.

"You should go. Gabby is waiting for you."

"She can wait," he said, fiddling with his phone. "Do you think we can be friends or something?"

Not what Isla expected. "Someone once told me not to confuse office colleagues for friendship."

"That guy is wrong sometimes." Knox gave her a half smile. "How about: I'll stop treating you horribly, and you'll stop expecting me to treat you horribly."

"Okay," replied Isla. "Truce."

"Truce," He stood up. "Shall we shake on it?"

He held his hand out, and she shook it.

29.

November 10. Light snow -12C°.

After the dim ballroom, Priya's eyes took awhile to adjust to the brightness of the cloakroom. She found her coat and bag amongst the rows of winter coats — winter coats that had been pulled out of attics and basements far too early, considering the official start to winter wasn't for another six weeks. She made her way to the back of the room where she found a carpeted ledge hidden behind jackets. Perfect, she thought. She undid the cap of her water bottle and took a quick sip of the vodka and Red Bull she had poured in earlier. Drinking in secret wasn't a habit she usually participated in, but her younger sister's wedding called for drastic measures. She wanted to be pleasantly tipsy, enough so the passive aggressive criticism rolled off her back. The Red Bull was to keep her from yawning; she had covered a last-minute shift between the *mehndi* last night and the wedding. Against her mothers wishes.

"The least you could do is get some sleep the night before your sister's big day," demanded Jasminder earlier in the week.

Priya leaned her head back, took another gulp, and closed her eyes for a moment. She was jarred back to reality when someone stepped on her foot.

"Hey," she cried.

The coats opened before her like a curtain, revealing a handsome, unfamiliar face.

They assessed each other quickly. She was in a traditional black and coral sari, contrasting with her short hair and freshly shaved undercut. He wore a modern, charcoal checked suit, classic crisp white shirt, navy tie, and his face was clean shaven, no turban.

"Do I know you?" she asked.

"I think I would remember if we had met," he answered, grinning. "Sorry for interrupting. I needed something from my jacket."

He found his wool coat, pulled out a scrap of paper and stuffed it in his pocket. "I'm Samarpreet Singh, but most people call me Sam."

He had an accent, one Priya couldn't pin down. Definitely Punjab, but also British? Maybe South African?

"Nice to meet you, Sam," she said, not offering her own introduction.

"What's in your bottle?"

"Water."

"Interesting," said Sam, sitting on the ledge next to her. "If I were hiding in the back of the closet at a Sikh wedding, my bottle would contain something far more exciting than plain water."

Priya took another sip and handed it to him.

He took a sip and said, "That's more like it."

"How do you know Deepa and Kavan?"

Sam shook his head. "I don't know them. I recently moved to Winnipeg and my mother took it upon herself to contact a friend, who called an auntie, who called another auntie, and scored me an invitation. She doesn't trust me to make friends on my own."

Priya smiled. "Where are you from?"

"All over the world."

"Do you think being vague makes you more interesting?"

"You're the one who hasn't even told me your name. May I?" He reached for another sip. "I lived in India until I was twelve, then we immigrated to Edinburgh, Scotland. I went to King's college in London. I spent a few years in Cape Town South Africa, finding myself. My family moved to Toronto, so I followed them to Canada."

"What made you move to *this* frozen wasteland?"

"Pure economics. I bought a brand-new condo with a fifteen-minute commute. For the same price in Toronto, I would have a twenty-five-year-old condo with an hour commute. With the savings, I can afford a car and multiple flights to see my family—"

"You're boring me with all this talk about economics," interrupted Priya. "Are you going to tell me what you do?"

"No. If you're going to be tight lipped, I can be too," he said with a grin. "How do you know Deepa and Kavan?"

"She's my younger sister."

"Ah, the vodka in the closet makes far more sense now. Downing your sorrows because she beat you?"

"Beat me to the only option for a woman's happiness? No. I'm just trying to survive the aunties."

Sam laughed. "Oh god, those aunties. They're the same all over the world."

"You would know; apparently you've been all over."

"Are you going to tell me your name before or after our first date?"

This time Priya rolled her eyes and shook her head. "Smooth. I hate to break it to you, but I don't date."

"That's unfortunate."

Priya shrugged. "Med school doesn't allow much down time."

"Med school? Smart *and* beautiful."

"You don't actually think these lines are going to get you anywhere, do you?"

"Would begging work better? I'm not below getting on my hands and knees."

"Give me your phone," Priya said, rolling her eyes.

Sam signed in with his fingerprint and handed it over. Priya entered her number under the heading 'doc'.

"There. For emergencies only."

"Doctor?" He asked, "what constitutes an emergency? Falling from heaven? Because you are an—"

"Shut the hell up with that or I'll delete my number. You were telling me what you do for a living."

"Computer programming, website building, tech support. Shocking for an Indian, but what can I say? It's good job security."

Priya took the last sip from the bottle. The vodka was catching up with her at last.

"Shall we get back to the party?" he said, standing up and offering her his hand.

She took it and allowed him to help her stand. He was only a couple of inches taller than her. They stood face to face; he still held her hand and his thumb caressed her palm. When their lips met, it was hesitant at first, then Priya pressed in more fiercely.

"Priya! Priiiyya!" Jasminder Dhaliwal's voice pierced through the layers of coats. "Where is she?"

Priya and Sam were still, except their pounding hearts.

"Priya is it?" he whispered in her ear, sending shivers all the way down to her toes. She nodded, putting a finger up to his lips.

Then they looked at each other with strangers' eyes again. The spell had been broken. She used her thumb to wipe off the plum lipstick that was left on his mouth.

"Duty calls," she said quietly, adjusting her sari. "Make sure you get all that lipstick off before returning."

She exited the cloakroom and immediately tripped on a floor mat. Act sober, she admonished herself, catching the doorway to steady herself.

"Priya! Your mother is looking for you," called her mother's closest friend, Fancy Sandu.

"Thank you, auntie-ji. Where is she?"

"Over there. I'll come with you," said Fancy, linking arms with Priya.

"Look who I found," announced Fancy to a group of Jasminder's friends.

"Priya where were you?" questioned Jasminder.

"I was – finding — looking for something in the jacket – closet." Her words slurred and came out in the wrong order.

"Are you ill, Priya?" asked another auntie.

"I'm great! Just a little tired," said Priya with a giggle.

Jasminder's face fell as the truth dawned on her. She grabbed Priya by the elbow and pulled her away from the group, "Have you been drinking?" she hissed. "You smell like a bar."

"How would you know?" shot back Priya.

"Don't talk back to me. You are drunk."

"Of course not, Mama-ji, don't be silly." Priya allowed herself to be dragged away, the effects of the vodka rapidly advancing.

The loud colourful room swirled around her; she suddenly felt extremely hot. She stopped walking and leaned against the wall. Jasminder whirled around and grabbed Priya's face between her hands.

Priya had always admired her mother's hands. They were soft, and the nails were neatly trimmed and filed. She closed her eyes and was transported back to childhood, watching her mama rub heavy cream into her hands after the final dishes were washed – a ritual to mark the end of the day.

"Look at me," Jasminder said sharply. "You disrespect your father and I by drinking alcohol at your sister's wedding. You are selfish and bad-mannered. Nothing was required of you except to be a decent daughter and sister. Does it make you happy to humiliate me, in front of my friends?"

"Mama-ji—" Priya tried to pull away, but couldn't. She wanted to shrink down through the floorboards.

"Get out." Jasminder said it so calmly, it broke Priya's heart.

"No, mama, please. Let me stay."

"Go home, Priya." Only then did she remove her hands. "You are a disgrace. I don't want anyone to see you like this. What will they think about your father and me?"

Priya burned with shame. She had had plenty of disagreements with her mother. She usually felt justified and superior to her mother, but not this time. She felt like a child, small and empty.

"I'm sorry."

"No, you're not. You never are," replied Jasminder. "Don't apologise until you are prepared to be a better daughter."

Jasminder returned to the party without another word, leaving Priya breathless. She touched the side of her face. It felt like it had been slapped.

She looked up and saw Sam. He had seen everything. Priya took a deep breath, smiled and shrugged.

"I'm so sorry," he said.

"You have nothing to be sorry for. That was twenty-five years in the making."

"But still..." He trailed off.

"Do you want to get out of here?"

"Yeah sure. Do you want to go talk somewhere?"

"Go, yes. Talk no. Why don't you take me to that brand new condo of yours? I'm sure we can find something to do besides talk."

"Priya, are you sure you're alright?"

"I'm fine," she said brightly. "Don't worry about me, that was nothing."

But that was a lie.

30.

November 21. North wind, -22C°.

A cry woke Emma. A sharp pain radiated from her throat; every muscle in her chest ached. She was tangled in a blanket and couldn't figure out how to free herself. Everything was blurry. Where was she? It took her a moment to realise she was on her living room sofa. Liam kept crying. She was freezing.

What time was it?

Emma grabbed her phone off the console by the front door as she stumbled up the stairs to Liam's room.

Two-thirty in the afternoon.

She had barely been asleep for ten minutes. Seeing a missed call from Isla, she pressed redial.

"Hey," Isla answered.

"Hey. Say hi to Liam." Emma hit speaker phone and set the phone on the shelf above the change table.

"Hi, baby boy!" came Isla's voice, loud and clear, causing Liam to stop whimpering and look around. Emma lifted him out of his bed. He was drenched with sweat and burning up. When was the last time she had given him meds? Ten-thirty? Eleven? When did she eat last? Was that her breakfast?

"What's up?" asked Isla.

"You called me," said Emma.

"You called first, this morning—"

"Oh right," said Emma, without a clue why she had called. "How's your day going?"

Emma laid Liam on the change table. He cooed softly. Emma peeled the clammy sleeper off him and reached for a clean diaper. The basket was empty.

"Not bad, I guess," replied Isla. "I have a client meeting this afternoon, I—-"

"No, no, no!" Emma said, sounding desperate.

"Emma, are you okay?"

She kept one hand on Liam, and with the other she dug through the other basket under the change table. "There has to be one!"

"Hello? Emma?" asked Isla's voice through the speaker.

"Diapers, I'm out—-"

Then Emma noticed Liam's arm jerk, an unnatural movement. With her full attention back on her son, she saw that his eyes were rolled back into his head, and his whole body twitched.

"Liam!" Emma screamed.

"Emma," Isla called, "what's happening?"

"He's twitching, his body—like a seizure! What do I do?" Emma yelled. Suddenly he stopped and his whole body went limp.

"Emma!" called Isla, responding to the desperation in her voice, "call 911! Emma, do you hear me? Hang up and call 911!"

The trip from the HRA office to the Health Sciences Centre was only ten minutes, but each red light felt like torture.

Emma had texted, *The ambulance is taking us to the Children's Hospital, can you come?*

Without a second thought, Isla had closed her computer, told Angela she had a family emergency, and walked out the door. Now she waited for the longest light at Notre Dame and Balmoral. She could hear her phone ringing from her bag on the floor. She prayed it wasn't Emma.

"Can you tell me anything about my nephew?" Isla asked at the emergency room desk. "Liam Peters, he's a baby, his mom is here with him. She is Emma Peters."

The nurse took her time typing in the names before responding, "the baby is being seen by a doctor." She indicated to the Children's Hospital hall. "Emma Peters is also being seen by a doctor." She indicated in the opposite direction, to the adult ER.

"Wait — Emma is being seen by a doctor? What happened?"

The nurse read the intake chart thoroughly. "Presented with a high fever. That's all I've got. You can wait. I'll send someone to talk to you as soon as possible."

The waiting room was full of coughing and sneezing, even some blood. The whole area made Isla's skin crawl. She was too jacked up to sit, anyway. She paced. She should call Andrew, but he was hours away. What good would that do? She was the worst person for dealing with this kind of stuff. She was the artistic one, not the person who you call in an emergency.

Priya's the one who would know what to do. She's the one to call in an emergency. Maybe she was already at the hospital? Isla pulled her phone out of her bag and was annoyed to see three missed calls, all from the dictator. She hadn't changed his name in her phone yet.

She sent a quick text to Andrew, trying to sound positive and upbeat, then she sent a desperate text to Priya, expressing the terror she was feeling.

Why was Emma seeing a doctor too?

The phone rang again. She watched it ring. She could let it go to voice mail again, but Knox didn't seem to be giving up. Isla shored herself up and answered by launching into a defence. "I'm sorry I

183

left! I had to go to the hospital, my nephew Liam, he's a baby, he had a seizure and now I think Emma is sick too, she is my sister-in-law. I don't know what's going on and I'm the only person here, and no one has told me anything and I'm waiting in the waiting room, and no one is texting me back and I don't know anything…"

She rambled incoherently before coming to an abrupt stop.

"Hi," said Knox.

She took a big breath. "Hi."

"Angela mentioned there was a family emergency. I wanted to see if you needed anything."

His unexpected thoughtfulness brought tears to her eyes, and she slid down the wall, landing on the floor in the hall.

"I don't know what to do. I'm totally freaking out," she admitted, wiping her eyes. "How did the meeting go?"

"It doesn't matter. I'll fill you in later—"

Then heaven's curtain parted, and Isla saw Priya walking down the hallway towards her.

"I have to go," she said to Knox. "Priya's here to save me."

"Priya? Brian's Priya, right?"

"She was never Brian's anything," stated Isla.

"I forgot you guys were friends."

"She's my *best* friend. Ride or die."

"Right. So I guess he should thank you for the fifteen mice he trapped in his apartment."

"I don't know what you're talking about."

Knox laughed. "You're a horrible liar."

"Fifteen! I swear we only left five," she insisted.

"You better hope he isn't the doctor treating your sister-in-law, you'll have guilt written all over your face," Knox teased.

Priya sat down next to her and asked, "Who are you talking to?"

Isla shushed her and turned away.

"He totally deserved it," replied Isla.

"Yes, he did, but still. Fifteen mice, that's disgusting," said Knox.

"You're such a city boy."

"I'm sorry, but you don't exactly scream country girl."

"Yeah, but a couple of harmless mice don't bother me."

"Right." Then his tone turned serious. "Listen, let me know if you need anything. Call or text, anytime."

"I will — thanks," said Isla as she hung up.

"Who was that?" Priya demanded.

"Knox."

"Knox? All that flirting was for *Knox*?"

"It wasn't flirting!" said Isla defensively.

Priya raised her eyebrow in disbelief.

Isla shrugged. "It's a shaky ceasefire at best."

"Right." Priya stood and offered Isla a hand up off the floor. "Do you know anything else?"

Isla shook her head. "No, just what I texted."

"Come on," said Priya. "I can find out. Have you heard from Andrew?"

"Not yet. Do you think I should try to call her parents?"

"No way. Let's find some info before we call anyone else. Have you talked to the professor?"

Isla shook her head; she was so panicked she hadn't even thought to call her own parents. "What if Brian is Emma's doctor? Knox said he killed fifteen mice."

"Fifteen! How fortuitous." Priya smiled. "He's a great doctor even though he's a horrible human being."

Following Priya down the hall, Isla said, "Hey! You should go out with Knox."

Priya stopped and turned to Isla. "I don't think so."

"Why not? You guys would be perfect together! You have so much in common: you're both workaholics—"

"I don't think I'm his type," interrupted Priya.

"Of course you are! You're beautiful and ambitious—"

"Based on the conversation I just witnessed, I think he prefers redheads." Without missing a beat, Priya turned her attention to the intake nurse. "I need information on Liam Peters, infant, brought in by ambulance. And his mother, Emma Peters."

Emma sat in a wheelchair, in a hospital gown. She had an IV in her left arm, and she couldn't catch her breath. Where was Liam? The nurse pushed her down the hall towards the children's wing. Emma thought over what her doctor had said. She had bronchitis and was severely dehydrated. Had she even noticed she was sick? Caring for Liam had taken her whole week. She couldn't remember the last time she'd had more than two hours of sleep in a row.

Once they entered the room, Emma saw Isla holding Liam, who was sucking on a bottle. Priya was talking to the nurse and reading a chart. She greeted Emma with a smile. "Everything is okay. He suffered a febrile seizure, which can happen to infants when they have a high fever. He has bronchitis. They've given him antibiotics and fluids, just like you, I see."

"I told you all would be well," smiled the nurse as she headed out the door.

When the door closed, Emma burst into tears.

"Sweetie, how did you miss that you were so sick?" asked Priya kindly, rubbing Emma's back as she coughed.

"I don't know! I mean, I knew I had a cold. I took some cough medicine. What is wrong with me? I should've known — where is Andrew?" Emma looked around franticly. "I thought he'd be here."

Isla caught Priya's eye and grimaced. "He's not coming. By the time I got a hold of him, we knew both of you were fine. He thought it would be best if he finished the day at work. He'll be home late tonight. I'll stay with you until then."

Based on the look on Emma's face, they could clearly see that he'd made the wrong decision.

"My mom and dad are on their way — I didn't have a way to contact your parents," continued Isla.

Emma did not want to see Dee and Bill. She was even less interested in seeing her own parents. Still disoriented, she asked, "Why is he drinking from a bottle?"

"The nurse said he was hungry, so we tried."

"But he doesn't like bottles," stated Emma.

"He seems to like this one," replied Isla brightly.

"He doesn't like bottles."

Isla looked at Priya helplessly. Priya shrugged.

"Give him to me." Emma held out her arms.

Isla gave a tug on the bottle in Liam's mouth. He sucked harder. Isla tugged harder. Liam let out a wail. He kept wailing while Emma tried to place him on her breast. He didn't want it; he didn't want her.

Finally, Priya took Liam and handed him back to Isla, who was ready with the half empty bottle.

"You should call Andrew," said Priya, dialing and handing Emma the phone. Emma hung up and dropped her head into her hands and sobbed.

31.

December 2. Clear and bright, -22C°.

On the menu this week was roast chicken, goat cheese mashed potatoes, and Grandma Peters' broccoli salad with lots of mayo and raisins. Everyone was in their seats, Priya included. She took a second scoop of the creamy, tangy salad, hoping it would dull the guilt she felt at not being at her own family's house.

"You and Liam seem to be feeling much better," Dee said to Emma, as she passed the mashed potatoes.

Emma forced a smile. "Only a few more days of meds left for both of us. Liam has been sleeping much better."

"I didn't even hear him once," interrupted Andrew, his mouth full of chicken.

"Of course you didn't," Emma said under her breath.

"What's that?" asked Dee.

"Nothing," replied Emma.

"I thought you said Liam was up four times," interjected Isla.

"It was *only* four times," Emma said with a tight smile. "That's a lot better than it has been."

"Why aren't you getting up" Dee demanded of Andrew. He winced and stumbled over his answer.

Emma answered for him. "I'm nursing, so there's no point in both of us getting up."

"I'm sure Liam would be fine with a bottle or a cuddle with his father. He is almost nine months," replied Dee.

"I like nursing. He's only a baby once," said Emma, stifling a yawn.

Andrew squeezed her shoulder, then glanced at Isla. "Mom, I think it's time."

"Time for what?" asked Isla.

"Do you think now is the right time for that juicy tidbit?" Dee said, a wicked smile forming on her face.

"Juicy tidbit? What is going on?" demanded Isla.

"Your brother and I had lunch together last week," answered Dee. "As we do once a month or so."

"Why don't you invite me?" Isla asked her mother.

"Andrew initiated it."

"Because I was working downtown."

"*I* work downtown!" said Isla.

"You could have lunch with us if you would stop being so self-absorbed and invite us for lunch," needled Andrew.

Isla scowled at him.

"We can have lunch anytime you want," interceded Bill.

Dee gave Andrew a conspiratorial look and started her story. "We always meet at this darling Vietnamese place on Ellis; it's in the front room of a two-story house. It's quaint and popular."

"I've been there! I love that place," said Isla.

"Stop pouting and let mom tell her story," replied Andrew.

"Anyway, it was packed. We had a table for four next to the entrance, and we had just been served our pho. Oh, it was delicious, so aromatic and full of veggies, perfect on a cold day, and the—"

"Mom, your story," interrupted Isla.

"Right, well these two handsome young men came in. Because it was so busy, they were told to wait. I could tell they were in a hurry.

The taller fair fellow came over and asked if they could share the table with us. Obviously, I said yes; I couldn't resist lunch with three handsome young men."

Andrew rolled his eyes, but he was grinning like a kid on Christmas morning. He couldn't wait for the punchline.

"We each continued our own conversations, but it was very hard not to — overhear."

"Eavesdrop?" laughed Bill.

Dee took a bite of her chicken and chewed it methodically, building suspense.

"What happened, mom?" asked Isla impatiently.

"They started talking about Grid Road Whiskey! I had to interrupt. I told them my daughter designed the Grid Road logo."

"Naturally," said Priya.

Isla's heart rate rose as the puzzle pieces fell into place.

"The taller one replied that he was the account manager, and introduced himself, Knox Harrison, and his companion Sam Singh."

"Oh my god. No." Isla put her face in her hands. "This cannot be happening."

Priya's body also tensed, but no one noticed.

"So, I explained that I was your mother and introduced your brother and we all had a lovely lunch together."

"You didn't! Mom!" protested Isla. "I'm afraid to ask, but what were you wearing?"

"Why does that matter?" demanded Dee.

"Her orange shirt with the daffodils and teal pants," interjected Andrew, not bothering to hide his amusement.

"Mother! Must you dress like you're colourblind?"

"This is hilarious," said Priya, thankful no one had noticed her shock. Why were Sam and Knox having lunch? How did they even know each other? She was desperate to ask, but not desperate enough to risk having to explain how she knew Sam.

"I think your mother dresses nice," said Bill, forever the peacemaker.

"She dresses like a four-year-old. I cannot believe you had lunch with Knox and Sam. Did you say anything embarrassing?"

"Mom told Knox that he's not nearly as handsome as she was expecting."

"You did not!"

Priya, seizing her opportunity, asked, "Who's Sam?"

"He's the new Eric, except way better. He has his own company: website design and tech support — all that stuff. We contract out our website stuff to him; he's in a couple of days a week. And he's great! Fun to work with, and for whatever reason he likes Knox. They have some sort of bromance going on," answered Isla. She brought the conversation back to the issue at hand. "I need you to tell me everything you said to them, word for word."

"I don't know why you're so exasperated with me. Your brother is the one joining their ball hockey team," deflected Dee.

"Ball hockey? Like, the sport? You hate sports!" Isla turned on Andrew.

"I don't hate sports!"

"He's just bad at them," said Priya.

"I thought maybe I should do something active. I've been feeling—sluggish." He patted his non-existent belly.

"How often does this team meet?" asked Emma quietly. She rarely spoke up once Dee and Isla got into it.

"Once a week, with the occasional tournament."

"You can't do this, Andrew!" said Isla. "Emma, tell him he can't do this! You can not be friends with my co-workers."

"Why not? Are you scared they'll like me better than you?"

"I don't need my personal life mixing with my professional life."

"Your lives won't be mixed; you're not the one playing."

"They were lovely young men," Dee mused. "We should invite them over for Sunday lunch one of these weeks. Priya, you should meet Sam! He's terribly handsome."

"Just because he's Indian, you think I should meet him. Dee, isn't that a bit racist?"

"I hate this city," moaned Isla. "This would never happen in a bigger city."

32.

December 17. Thick cloud, -10C°.

Sue waved her hand in front of his face. "Hello? Anyone home?" Knox shook out of his daze and leaned back in his chair. "Good morning."

"Why are you here?" Sue asked.

"I'd go squirrelly at my apartment, you know that."

"You could've gone back to Vancouver."

"The Atchison meeting's this afternoon. I know how important they could be as a client."

"I could've handled it."

"I know." Knox nodded. "It's been four years. I'm in therapy and I've been doing good these last few months. I thought this year would be easier. I thought it wouldn't hurt as much —" He turned away so he wouldn't have to look Sue in the eye. "It hurts as much today as it did the day it happened."

"I know it hurts. Do you think it is supposed to get easier? Do you actually want it to feel easier to not have parents?"

"You're right." He sighed, "if it were easy it would feel like betrayal."

Sue sat and crossed her legs. "Can I make an observation?"

He nodded.

"Where were you last year on this day?"

"At my apartment"

"And what were you doing?"

He tapped his hands on the desk and grimaced. "I was working my way through a bottle of very expensive whiskey."

Sue nodded. "You're feeling it this year because you're actually feeling it. You're not trying to numb the pain, and I'm proud of you for that."

Lunch, Isla decided. She needed lunch. She shut down her laptop completely, hoping it would reset and everything would work properly when she started it back up. If it didn't, she'd throw it out the window.

She grabbed her bag and headed down the stairs to the empty lunchroom. Many of her colleagues had been using their lunch hours to finish holiday shopping. Isla had been done her gift acquiring for a while. In an effort to rally against capitalism, her mother had implemented a thrift or make gift-giving policy a couple of years earlier. Isla had gotten Liam to scribble on two canvases with black marker and had turned each piece into an abstract landscape, one for Bill and Dee, and one for Emma and Andy.

She settled into the coveted table by the window but found the silence unsettling, so she turned on some music and spread out her belongings in front of her: her ham sandwich and container of apples cored and sliced, one cookie, and her sketchbook. She was working on her last gift, shading the portrait of Priya's grandfather. Even with the music coming out of her phone she heard someone come into the room.

Knox held a large paper bag with grease stains seeping through the bottom. Isla quickly turned off her phone, before he could mock her choice in music.

"Hey, can I sit with you?" he asked, sliding into the chair across from her. Indicating to her sketchbook, he added, "nice work."

"I guess it would be weird if you sat at a different table," she replied, tidying her clutter to make room for him. "Thanks. I erased a hole through the last page, so I'm trying again. It's for Priya, but I don't know if I'll be able to do it justice."

He took wrapped packages out of his bag. He opened a package of ketchup and squeezed it on his box of fries, then another packet of ketchup, then another, and then a fourth.

"Do you think you have enough ketchup?" said Isla, making a face. Knox purposefully held eye contact while opening his fifth and final packet, and slowly squeezed ketchup on any empty spots that remained.

"That's gross," stated Isla.

"I'm glad you think so. I didn't want to share."

"Don't you usually eat out?"

"Dad would always take Violet and me out for greasy fast food. It seemed appropriate for today."

"Why, what's today?"

"Uhh," Knox faltered. He hadn't meant to bring it up so casually. In his experience, nothing could ruin a good lunch like being thrust into someone else's sad story. "Nothing. I just miss them today."

"Why today?" asked Isla perceptively.

"It's the anniversary—" he trailed off.

"Of the accident? Oh, Knox, I'm so sorry. I had no idea."

"It's fine," he said, brushing it off.

"It's not fine. It's something."

"Ok, it's something." He sighed. "I'm kind of regretting not flying home early for the holidays. I should be with Violet today. A phone call just isn't the same."

"Why didn't you? You've probably worked enough overtime to take the whole month of December off."

Knox shrugged. "I almost booked a flight yesterday. I would've made it home by eleven tonight. Not really worth it."

"Uh, so, speaking of Violet, she started following me on social media. Are you ok if I follow her back?"

"Yeah, sure. I don't care," he said, distracted by putting more ketchup on his burger.

"Interesting — all her posts are shirtless guys and keggers she attends," said Isla as she pretended to scroll.

Knox's head shot up. "What?"

Isla laughed. "Just kidding. Mostly selfies, with her and a cello?"

"Anita."

"Anita?" asked Isla.

"Her cello's named Anita. Cello is everything to her. She's in the School of Music, hoping to play professionally someday," he said with a heart full of pride.

"Does she live with Graham and Max?" asked Isla.

"She's in dorm now, but yeah, she has since the accident."

"Did you live with them?"

He shoved a gloppy fry in his mouth. After chewing thoughtfully, he said, "I spend a lot of time there. Being away from Violet is the hardest thing about moving to Winnipeg. I mean, besides working with you."

Isla rolled her eyes. "Ha."

"Just joking," he said, flashing her a rare grin. "She and I are really close. I don't know what I'd do without her." He paused. Isla was about to ask another question when he added, "she almost died in the accident as well." He set his burger down. "She was only fifteen. Her recovery was long; she missed a whole year of school. At first, she couldn't physically play cello. Her old cello was destroyed in the accident. Graham went all the way to Germany to buy her Anita. Even once she was physically able, she didn't play for a long time.

Then one day, she started playing again. She played for hours. I was so relieved, it's like she was ready to start living again."

"That's beautiful." Isla imagined young Violet in the middle of a large, empty concert hall, playing by herself and absorbed in the music and the rhythm of the bow. "Maybe one day I'll get to hear her."

"It's pretty incredible to hear her now, considering how painful it was when she started," answered Knox. "I can send you a link to watch her if you want."

"That would be great! What about you?" asked Isla, nibbling on her single cookie. "How did you know you were ready to live again?"

He stopped midway lifting his burger to his mouth. "You assume I have?"

"Sorry," she said, quickly. "That was too personal; we can talk about something else."

"I know the moment I realised nothing was going to be normal again: in the weeks after the accident, I'd wake up around two every morning, and toss and turn. I wouldn't be able to fall back to sleep. So I'd go to the cemetery. They didn't have the large granite headstones that they do now, just plastic markers in the dirt: Iris Elizabeth Stanley-Harrison and Kenneth David Harrison. I'd sit in the wet grass drinking beer until I'd fall asleep. I missed a lot of morning classes. One morning I woke up and an old guy was standing over me. He nudged me.

"Are you okay son?" he asked.

"Uh. Yes, sir," Knox said, pushing the empty beer bottles out of sight.

"Based on the quality of that jacket, I'm going to guess you have somewhere more comfortable to

sleep. I like coming to visit my Mabel early in the morning too. Usually the place is empty, the way I like it," he said pointedly.

"Sorry," said Knox, still half asleep and unsure why this man was speaking to him.

"My Mabel has been gone for seven years. Still hurts like hell. I try to come a couple times a week when the weather allows. Are those your parents?" the man guessed.

For the first time since the accident, Knox felt tears welling up in his eyes. The back of his throat burned as he tried to push the emotion down. He nodded, looking away from the man, away from the graves.

"Nothing shameful about crying. If you're going to do it, this is the best place." said the man, turning to walk away. "I'll leave you in peace."

"Does it get any easier?" called Knox, wiping his face with the back of his hand.

"If it does, I haven't reached that point yet. I'm a grumpy old man though — you might have better luck."

The whole time Knox was telling his story, he stared down into his fries. He expected to see pity, maybe even judgement in Isla's eyes. Instead, there were tears.

"I am so sorry," she said, wiping an escaped tear.

"Most people don't get it" he continued. "Most people think I'm lucky or spoiled, the golden boy who became a partner straight out of university. They don't understand what I lost. I would give it all up, in a heartbeat, to have my parents back."

Isla considered for a moment before asking, "Are you in therapy?"

Knox eyes widened. "Are you always so blunt?"

"Sorry, yes I am. It's just — that's a lot to deal with. The loss of your parents, almost losing your sister. I can't imagine—"

Knox's phone beeped and he leaned back, suddenly remembering where they were.

"I've been in therapy since I was a child," she offered.

"Really?" His attention refocused on her.

"Not for anything traumatic. My mother was, and is, obsessed with being the perfect progressive parent. Pre-emptive therapy. It's good, I guess. We all need someone to talk to."

"I am in therapy," he answered reluctantly. "Sue and Graham strongly suggested I start when I moved to Winnipeg."

"Because of what happened at the conference—" Isla trailed off, watching Knox's face flash from anger to annoyance to simple resignation.

"I should've known someone would tell you. Let me guess, Adam?"

"Yeah."

"Well, great." He put his head in his hands. "You asked when I knew I wanted to live again?"

Isla nodded.

"The last three years, but especially this past year have been a series of me drinking too much, fucking up, and then completely regretting everything the next morning. It got to the point where I had to choose if I wanted to fall down an even darker hole, or start living again. I quit drinking and decided to take therapy seriously. It's been—" he trailed off.

"Good?" asked Isla,

"—impossibly hard."

"Oh, right. Of course," responded Isla. "Will you tell me something about each of them?"

"My parents?"

Isla nodded.

"Umm… Mom loved flowers and plants. Our house was like a greenhouse, she was always propagating something. She had elaborate gardens, she was constantly changing things around, moving plants back and forth. She always complained about having dirt under her fingernails. And dad was so competitive. He'd turn everything into a competition: who could run to the mailbox the fastest, or slurp their spaghetti noodle the fastest — he'd always win of course, but if Mom or I or baby Violet ever won, he'd be even happier."

He looked sad and lost. Isla wanted to reach out to him and squeeze his hand. Understanding how completely inappropriate that would be, she packed up her empty lunch containers instead. "Thanks for telling me all this."

"Thanks for being a good listener."

She laughed. "I've never been called a good listener before."

Just then, Sue entered the room. She glanced at the two of them, laughing together at the only occupied table. *This is an interesting development*, she thought.

"Sue," called Knox. "Come join us."

"I see your father passed his disgusting eating habits on to you," she said, eyeing the empty ketchup packets. "I thought we should review the agenda before we meet with Atchison, but it can wait."

Isla stood up quickly. "Go ahead. I should get back anyway. Hopefully all my technology problems magically solved themselves during lunch."

33.

December 31. Light mist, 5C°.

Gabby's familiar condo was packed full of acquaintances, any new faces were the same as the familiar ones, each one desperate to impress. New jobs, new cars, new wives. One friend had been married, divorced, and re-married in less than five years. All of it seemed foreign to the slower, less glamorous life Knox now led in Winnipeg.

He didn't belong with these people anymore.

"Knox! Hey, man!" Brian offered him his hand and then pulled him in for a quick, masculine hug.

"Hey," replied Knox.

Brian's partner Athena threw her arms around him and squealed. "We were hoping we'd see you! We have a wedding invite for you; can you believe I finally got Brian to settle on a date?"

Knox narrowed his eyes at Brian briefly. Brian shrugged with the confidence of a man who knew he'd gotten away with something he didn't regret.

"When's the big day?" Knox asked politely. Whenever it was, he would make sure he was busy.

Before Athena could answer, Brian steered him away towards the drink table. "Funny how we live in the same city, and only see each other while we're home for the holidays. Sue must be keeping you busy."

"Yeah, busy. You know how it is." He declined a tumbler of whiskey, still working on his first beer. He had made a deal with himself; he couldn't remember his last seven New Years, and he wanted to remember tonight. After explaining the situation to Violet, her seasoned advice had been to take the first drink and nurse it the rest of the evening. She was right. The moment he sat the bottle down, someone tried to shove another drink into his hand, so he picked it back up and had spent the last hour or so carrying around a warm beer.

Brian knocked back a good portion of his whiskey before asking, "I need another groomsman. Athena is insisting on six attendants. Do you want to do it?"

Knox stared at his old friend in disbelief. "I don't think that would be a good idea."

Brian led him further away from anyone who could overhear. "Come on, buddy. Are you still mad at me for lying about Athena?"

"Lying, cheating, more lying… I want nothing to do with any of it."

"You're going to ditch me in my time of need?" Brian lowered his voice. "How else was I going to survive three years away from home? As if you and Gabby are any different."

"Gabby and I are totally different! I've never made any declarations of commitment to her, much less given her a diamond ring," clarified Knox.

"Athena and I were on a break when things started with Priya—"

"—And then you asked Athena to marry you, while you continued things with Priya."

"Dude, why do you care so much about Priya? I told you before, you're welcome to her — unless you're still hung up on her friend, the redhead?"

"I care because Priya and Athena are human beings, and you're a piece of shit that doesn't deserve either of them. I don't want to be a groomsman, and I won't be at your wedding."

"You're going to throw away a fifteen-year friendship over a couple of chicks?"

"Yeah, I am." Knox walked away.

Brian called after him, "I'll tell Athena you're busy that weekend."

Knox wandered to the window overlooking a courtyard decorated with Christmas lights. He opened his phone and looked at his Winnipeg friends' names, wondering what they were doing for New Years. He started a text, but then noticed how late it was.

He had started a text every day since his arrival in Vancouver. And he hadn't sent one.

"Knoxy," said a voice from behind, as a pair of sparkly arms slipped around his waist. He quickly put his phone back in his pocket and wiggled out of Gabby's grip. She was dressed like a disco ball, silver reflective sequins covered her jumpsuit, and she was tipsy already.

"Come on." She grabbed his hand and pulled him towards her bedroom, shutting the door behind them. His heart rate rose as she threw her arms around his neck. Before he could stop her, her lips were on his; she pushed her body against his so hard he was forced to take a step back.

After the way they had left things in October, this was unexpected. It took him a moment to gain his bearings.

"Gabby," he breathed, as she continued kissing him.

"Gabby!" he pushed her away and looked her in the eyes. They were glassy and heavily made up, covering shrunken dark circles.

She stood up straight and put her hands on her hips. "Guess what everyone wants?"

Knox stared at her blankly, distracted by her appearance. His phone vibrated in his pocket, and his hand immediately went for it. It was Graham; he'd sent a blurry photo of a group of his friends. A finger covered half of Max's face. Knox could hear the party through the door. Someone had started a countdown. He looked at his watch — it was only eleven.

He was ready to leave.

"Aren't you going to guess?" sang Gabby as she shimmied back towards him.

"Why don't you tell me," Knox said impatiently.

"Us." She stepped towards him.

"Together," Another step.

"Officially," Her arms were around his waist again.

"Gabby—" he started, but he couldn't come up with anything better than a flat "— no."

He tried wiggling out of her arms, but she held on tight.

"I know you're scared," she whispered, "but it's okay. We belong together. We're soulmates."

"Stop." Knox unwrapped her arms from around his waist and took a couple of steps back. He paced back and forth in the small space. They had been friends in university, *real* friends who had considered dating but decided it was better to just be friends. His parents' death had changed everything. The first time they'd slept together had been after a long night of drinking, and at that point, they morphed into friends who slept together regularly. They'd never been exclusive. She dated other guys, and he was happy to tell girls his sad story and then take them home at the end of the night. He was always amazed at how well pity worked.

"Come on, babe, we've been through so much! All our friends are waiting for us to make it official. It's inevitable. I love you. You must know how much I love you." She looked at him expectantly. "I know you better than anyone else; you know me—"

The only thing he felt as he looked at her was trapped. "I can't. We can't."

"Tell me you don't love me," she demanded. "I know you. You're scared, scared if you love someone they're going to leave. I'm not going to leave. Tell me you don't love me." Her voice grew shrill as she begged. "Everyone knows we belong together."

"I don't love you," he replied quietly. "If we were meant to be together, we would be already."

The weight of his confession hit him hard. He knew he wasn't in love with Gabby, he'd known for years, but he hadn't stopped to consider her feelings. Not once. She slid onto her bed, her head in her hands. Tears poured down her face.

"I'm sorry."

"Get out!" She looked up, her angry face smeared with make-up. He didn't need to be told twice.

34.

January 1. Cloudy. -14C°.

Emma rocked back and forth, patting Liam's back, silently begging him to fall asleep. She was in a room she had never been in before, in her husband's grandparent's house. The midwinter light shone through the thick seventies floral curtains. The din of the family filtered up the stairs. She could hear bits of conversation and greeting, but she was as far away from the action as she could be, while still being in the same building.

She and Andrew had planned the drive to the family gathering around Liam's nap. He was supposed to sleep during the drive and then he'd be awake for all the doting aunties, uncles, and cousins. But he hadn't slept at all, instead fussing and screaming for the long drive.

Then she'd forgotten Andrew's cousin's wife's name, the one with the curly brown hair and the sweet smile, the one who'd been so excited to see them. Emma had completely blanked. She was so tired from the disastrous New Years girls night out, the night before.

Just like every day, she was pleading with Liam to fall asleep. She had tried everything, read every parenting book. She had tried letting him cry it out, but she hadn't realised how hard and how long one child could cry, or how long or hard she could cry. She considered weaning him, but then something in her universe would remind her that breast was best.

The universe meant well.

Holidays weren't for mothers. Emma guessed correctly that eighty-three-year-old Grandma Peters had spent days cooking and cleaning, and was currently buzzing around the kitchen making sure everyone was happy. And Grandpa Peters? He'd be playing cards, likely with Andrew.

Kaylee! That's Andrew's cousin's wife's name, Emma thought as she drifted off to sleep.

Isla filled her plate: turkey, stuffing, mashed potatoes, sweet and sour meatballs, broccoli salad, and carrots in cheese sauce. Everything mashed together in the best possible way. It tasted like it had every holiday gathering that she could remember. Each year the hardest part was choosing what kind of pie to have for dessert. Today's choices were pumpkin, apple, chocolate, or coconut cream, all homemade. She was planning on pumpkin until she saw the coconut; now she couldn't decide. Where was Emma? Maybe they could share a couple of pieces.

Before she sat down, Isla felt her phone vibrate in her pocket.

Happy New Year! It was from Knox.

Isla put her phone screen-side down on the table. She didn't need to respond to an obligatory group text.

There was Emma, descending the stairs with a wide-awake Liam. Andrew, who was deep in conversation with their cousin Tyler, didn't notice until Liam was dropped in his lap.

Isla's phone buzzed again. She hesitated before checking it quickly.

I saw your posts from last night. Funny.

Isla sent a grimace emoji and was surprised when he responded right away.

I feel like you're the type to lock your keys in your car regularly.

Everyone's attention was on Liam and Emma. Aunties popped up from their plates to find highchairs and fill plates, or refill platters of food. When no one was looking she typed: *Ha. It was so cold! The whole night was a total disaster, Priya had planned an epic night, but nothing worked out. Emma complained the whole time. Finally, we decided to grab hot chocolate and catch the fireworks, but I locked my keys in the car. Did I mention it was freezing?*

As Isla waited for a reply, she caught her mother's glare from across the room at the adult table. She put her phone down quickly and returned to the feast on her plate. Her phone buzzed again.

She had to check it. What if it was an important work question? Isla decided to escape her mother's gaze. She slid her phone into her pocket and climbed the stairs towards the bathroom, stopping in the hall just out of view, and sat down. Free to concentrate on her conversation.

That sounds more fun than the night I had. He had replied.

Did you work all night? she typed back.

I do have a life outside of work.

Do you? she asked.

I went to a party, it was boring, so I left early. Got made fun of by some cops at the sky train station for being sober and alone at midnight.

Ah, so no New Year's kiss. Oh no! Why did she send that? She tried deleting it, but he was too quick.

No kisses this year. Graham and Max didn't get home until 3am. The two of them have been nursing red wine hangovers all day.

Amateurs. When do you fly home? I mean here.

Before he could answer, the professor grabbed Isla's phone out of her hand.

"Come, on mom! Give it back. It was important!" cried Isla.

"If it's that important you should make a phone call. Nothing important should be discussed with texts." For all her progressive views on many things, the professor was decidedly negative about cell phones — mainly she believed they should remain in one's bag only to be taken out in case of emergency. To have one at the dinner table was strictly prohibited.

"Please?" Isla begged, as her phone buzzed in her mother's hand.

"Back to the table," demanded her mother, tucking her daughter's phone into the cargo pocket of her full-length khaki skirt.

Isla's phone was not returned until all the dishes had been done, the pie had been served, card games played, and all the aunts, uncles and grandparents had been kissed goodbye. Only when Isla climbed into the back seat of her parents' car, was she able to read the final text, sent four hours earlier.

Tomorrow. Isn't there an app or something that stops you from forgetting your keys???

Sam's arm felt heavy around Priya's curled up body. She could hear him breathing deeply. Carefully, she lifted his arm and slowly sat up. The moon shone through a crack in the curtain, causing a stream of light to fall across the floor where her feet hit the ground. She yawned, rubbed her eyes, and found a clock. Half past two.

Sam rolled over, touching her back gently with the tips of his fingers. "Where do you think you're going, Doc?"

"Home," she replied, moving forward so that his fingers dropped to the bed.

"Stay," he said sleepily.

"I can't."

"You can. It's the middle of the night, and freezing, and New Years. I don't think buses are even running."

"I'll call a cab."

209

"I'll drive you home in the morning," said Sam, wrapping his sturdy arms around her. "I'll even make you breakfast. Stay."

Priya's resolve crumbled. It was a cold night and she had spent too much time in the cold the night before. Maybe Isla wouldn't notice. Priya turned and glared at Sam. "This doesn't mean anything."

"All it means is you don't want to go out in the cold, that's it."

"What are you going to make me for breakfast?" she asked, crawling back in beside him.

"Rice pudding."

"Mmmm." She gave a sigh of approval. She hadn't had rice pudding for a long time; the dish had sustained her through her childhood.

"You are never allowed to meet my parents," she mumbled.

"You won't let me meet anyone. Are you afraid they won't like me?"

"The total opposite. They'll have us married before the end of the year. I've spent my life purposely choosing completely unsuitable mates. Besides, you know everyone already."

"What do you mean, I know everyone already?"

"Well, you work with Isla, and you're buddies with Andrew. You've even had lunch with the professor. Since my parents and I aren't really talking, there isn't anyone else."

"Don't worry. I am completely, utterly unsuitable. I mean, if I were suitable, wouldn't I be married by now? I'm thirty. If you stick around long enough, you'll discover all the unsavoury bits."

"Such as?"

"Romantic comedies make me cry. I eat too much meat and I am an utter wimp when it comes to blood. Shall I go on?"

"No, that's enough. Thanks for the heads up," Priya said with a grin. "Just so you know, I'm practically perfect in every way."

"I know," he said, giving her a quick kiss on her forehead before they both settled back to sleep.

35.

January 10. Snowing big fluffy flakes. -7C°.

"Hold the elevator." called a voice as the door slid closed. Isla reached out and pressed the open button repeatedly until the door opened again, revealing a grinning Knox. "You're going out for lunch? I thought you usually stayed in."

"My mom's taking me out."

"Special day?" he asked.

"Ah yeah—" Isla replied hesitantly. It was always weird to announce to people, but she wanted him to know. "It's my birthday."

"Happy birthday!" he said. "Take an extra thirty minutes if you want—"

"Aw thanks, you're such a benevolent dictator," Isla sassed as she got off at the lobby. He waved and continued on to the below-ground parking. Isla pulled her hood up over her head and headed toward the café on foot.

"Your grandma said to tell you happy birthday and she's proud of you for going back to school to finish your degree," announced Dee as their server placed their drinks in front of them: an earl grey tea for her, and a latte for Isla.

"I'm not going back to school."

"I thought you said you were," replied Dee, stirring in her milk.

"That was months ago! Sue wants me to take an online graphics course to get my skills up-to-date. I looked into whether they count as credits towards my degree, and they do not."

"Oh," said Dee, clearly disappointed.

"Do you think if you just say it out loud enough, you can manifest me finishing my degree?" asked Isla, clearly annoyed.

"Well, would it be such a big deal for you to go back? Who knows what kind of doors it could open?"

"But I like my job. I'm getting good experience and making good contacts. Not having a degree hasn't stopped me yet — maybe one day it will be a barrier, and then I'll go back."

"Do you think you'll stay at Harrison-Richards long-term?" asked Dee.

"I don't know. For now, I guess. I want to take it one day at a time."

"Are you happy?"

Isla took a sip of her latte. She wasn't prepared for an interrogation over her birthday lunch. She should've been. Every other conversation with her mother turned into one. She took another sip of her latte, delaying her answer. *Am I happy?!* As if she could take stock of her life and place a single emotion it.

"I guess so," Isla answered finally.

They moved on to more neutral topics. How is Grandma? What book are you reading? What latest piece of junk has dad rescued from the dump? Isla assumed that her grilling was over, but as soon as their soup and sandwiches came, round two started.

"Any new lovers?"

If Isla expected this question, she wouldn't have taken a large mouthful of sweet potato peanut soup, which was too hot and burned her throat as she fought to swallow instead of spewing it across the table.

"No, mom! I do not have a lover." She sputtered. "I don't have 'lovers.' Priya does."

"Does Priya have one currently?"

"I think so. She hasn't been home very much, but she doesn't seem too keen to talk about it."

"What about Chippy Neufeld?"

"No one has called him 'Chippy' since he was ten," Isla said. "For Priya? I don't think they're a good match."

"No, for you! I saw you guys were flirting at church last week."

"We were not flirting!" Isla insisted. Well, maybe just a little.

"I always thought you two would make a nice couple."

Isla took a sip of water to soothe her burnt mouth. "When did you think that? When we were children? When I was dating Michael? Because neither time seems appropriate."

"Doesn't matter. He's a very nice guy."

"He *is* a very nice guy, but I'm not interested."

"Not good enough." Dee waved her hand, indicating that Isla should continue.

"Do you want an itemized list?" Isla asked.

"Yes. Please explain to me why a handsome, smart, successful man who was clearly excited to see you, and dare I say, was flirting with you—"

"He wasn't flirting."

"I'm just saying what I saw. Why not spend some time with him?"

Isla paused to collect her thoughts. She could see her mother's point. There wasn't anything wrong with Carson. He was cute and he was flirting, but she wanted butterflies and rainbows. She wanted big, amazing romance — not just a nice guy.

"He's moving to Alberta after he graduates," Isla pointed out.

"With his masters."

"Yes, Masters of Divinity. I'm definitely not pastor's wife material. I'm too loud and much too opinionated, thanks to you. I don't even go to church most weeks. Besides, I can't leave Winnipeg, it's my home! I love it here. Why would I get involved with someone where that was even an option?"

"I hate to break it to you, but when you fall in love you'll move across the world if necessary."

"What I want to know is, why is the loudest, most opinionated feminist I know so eager to pair me up with someone?"

Dee paused, which is not something she often did. "Because — I believe in partnership and companionship, and I want you to be happy."

There was that word again. "Do you think I can only be happy if I'm with someone?"

"I'm your mother. I'd like to think I know you better than you know yourself. You need someone to ground you, otherwise you'll float away."

"I'm not going to float away. I have Priya."

"And when Priya moves away for her residency?"

"Mom, I don't think I'm as flighty as you think I am. Besides, Emma can keep me grounded too."

They were both quiet for a moment. Both thinking of Emma. How was she? Neither of them wanted to admit that they didn't know. Finally, Dee spoke. "Have you talked to Emma recently? It feels like it's been a while since we've had a heart to heart."

"She's fine —I think?" replied Isla.

"Is she still upset about New Years?"

"Ugh, I don't want to think about that night. Sometimes she can be so— "

"So?"

"I don't understand why they always have to be at each others' throats. Emma criticizes, and then Priya is rude and mean. I hate being in between the two of them."

"You always have been."

"Yeah, but it seems to be getting worse."

"Friendships don't always last as you get older. But don't give up on them too quickly, and don't let them give up on each other." Dee took a sip of her tea and continued, "Don't think I don't see what you are doing here, changing the subject – tell me about the other men in your life."

"There are no other men in my life, mom," sighed Isla.

"What about Knox and Sam? Both handsome, kind, single men," said Dee with a big grin.

"No."

"Knox is tall. You like tall guys, don't you?"

"Please stop talking." Isla held her hands up, as if she could physically muzzle her mother.

"Okay — back to Chippy then. You could be Mrs. Reverend Carson W. Neufeld!" Dee burst out laughing. "It might not be that bad."

"You're a nut."

Priya entered their apartment in a flurry of activity. She dropped her bags while peeling off layers of clothing, hopping on one foot in the direction of her room, her work pants trailing behind her. She paused long enough to notice Isla sitting on the couch, empty popcorn bowl and candy wrappers beside her, wearing a gloomy expression.

"Oh, shit! Fuck, goddamn," she said, coming to a full stop. "I forgot it's your birthday."

With a dramatic sigh, Isla shook out her ponytail and retied it up on top of her head. "You and everyone else. I was entertaining fantasies that everyone was busy and ignoring me to keep from ruining a surprise. It's almost nine o'clock and here I am feeling sorry for myself, binge watching a show I've already seen, halfway through a bottle of wine I bought for myself."

"I am so sorry," said Priya, sitting next to her on the couch wearing only her t-shirt. "I won't go."

"Where were you going in such a hurry?" asked Isla.

"It doesn't matter. I'll cancel, and we'll finish that bottle and have some fun."

"You have a date, don't you?" accused Isla. "Who is he?"

"Excuse me?" said Priya, looking up from her phone.

"Your date! I wish you would tell me who he is."

"What makes you think I have a date?"

"You haven't slept at home all week!"

"I've been on nights."

"No, you haven't. You just took off your work clothes. Who are you meeting?" demanded Isla.

Priya stood up and walked to the kitchen.

"Who is he?" Isla asked again.

"I'm going to get a drink," Priya said.

"Have some of my wine," said Isla, lifting her half-full bottle.

"Nah, I don't feel like wine." Priya returned with a coke, presumably with rum added. "You don't know him."

Isla waited for her to elaborate. When she didn't, Isla shouted, "that's it?! That's all your going to tell me?"

"Shhh," laughed Priya. "It's late."

"Why won't you tell me more?" said Isla woefully. "Who is he? How did you meet? What does he look like? Is he a doctor?"

Isla peppered her with questions, trying to gage her reaction, but Priya remained straight-faced. She had considered telling Isla about Sam. Many times, she had tried. She'd even practised some opening lines —'You know Sam, that guy you work with?' Each time, she faltered. It killed her to admit to anyone else how she felt. No, she wouldn't be able to do that until she admitted it to herself.

"Let's call him Mr. X. It sounds so mysterious," said Priya, refilling Isla's glass.

Isla pouted. "He isn't married, is he?"

"Fuck, no! I'm not an idiot." Priya shuddered. "I wouldn't touch that with a ten-foot pole."

"Well, there must be some reason you're not telling me. There's something embarrassing about him—is he unemployed?"

"Yup, that's it," replied Priya quickly.

"You're lying."

"You'll never know," said Priya. "You could've saved me some gummies."

"They were a gift," said Isla, with a dreamy look on her face.

"From?" Priya asked.

"Knox."

"When are you going to admit you like him?" demanded Priya.

Isla sat up straight. "How many times do I have to tell you? I don't have feelings for him. There's nothing to admit to. We're friends — just friends."

Priya lifted her eyebrow. "I call bullshit."

Isla was insulted. She did not have feelings for Knox.

Just because she'd reread every text he had ever sent.

Just because she'd hung his *Happy Birthday* post-it on her mirror, next to other important paper scraps she had collected in her life.

Oh.

"Oh no! I *do* have a crush on Knox Harrison!" She hid her face in the pillow. "This is a disaster! What am I going to do?"

"Umm, ask him out?"

"No!" cried Isla. "Besides, this will pass quickly. It has to. We're doing a big project together, I can't — this is a catastrophe!"

Priya rolled her eyes. "Chill the hysterics for one moment — what if it doesn't pass quickly?"

"I'll get over it. Knox and I won't ever be a thing, he's too—"

"Too what?"

"Well — he's a solid nine. I'm a six, maybe seven."

"Who the hell told you that? That is complete shit. You don't honestly think he's too good for you? If I remember correctly, he's made a move on you at least twice."

Isla leaned back in the couch and sighed. "Both times he was drunk and regretted it all the next morning."

"Did he tell you that?"

"Sort of."

"He is *not* too good for you — you're too good for him! You are kind, empathetic, creative, and a fucking cool bad ass! His life would be significantly improved with you in it."

"Thank you," said Isla. "But I don't think I can do the whole casual dating thing—"

"Yeah, that might be a problem. You're definitely a relationship person."

"And he definitely is not."

Priya shrugged.

"So, you agree. I need to wait it out until I'm over this crush."

"Let's be honest: the only way you're getting over your crush is with a broken heart. To minimize the damage, you need to ask him out – like, right away. You need to be clear about your expectations, not letting him string you along like some other loser I won't mention. And then when he can't meet your expectations—*poof!* Crush gone."

"That is not helpful, Priya."

"But it's the truth. That's what I do: tell the truth!"

"Why don't you tell *me* the truth about Mister X?"

"Who?"

Priya ducked as Isla threw a pillow at her.

36.

January 11, still snowing. -11C°

Is it always so bright in this elevator? thought Isla as every bone in her body vibrated, from her feet to her skull. At least the world had stopped spinning.

Or had it? She reached for the wall and paused to catch her breath before entering the office.

Knox happened to be walking by. He looked at his watch. "You look like you had fun last night."

Isla groaned.

"A big party in your honour?"

Isla gave him a weak smile. "No party. Priya and I stayed up too late, and I consumed too much red wine for a Thursday night."

"Sounds like a winning combination. How is your head?" he asked.

"Not good," she replied.

Knox turned back into his office and grabbed a bottle of pain killers.

"My hero." As Isla grabbed the bottle, their hands grazed, causing her to drop the bottle.

"Sorry," she said as it rolled down the hall.

"I got it." He grinned. He picked it up and tossed it to her. "I'll save you a seat."

Knox headed to the conference room and Isla dropped her jacket and bag at her desk, threw back two pills, and chugged as much water as her stomach would allow, hoping it wouldn't come back up during the meeting.

She was the last to arrive in the conference room, sliding into the chair next to Knox. *He smells so good*, thought Isla. She positioned her chair far enough from him that she wouldn't be distracted. A full two feet, that should be good. She should be able to concentrate at this distance.

Maybe a bit further, just for good measure.

While they waited for Sue to work through some tech issues, he leaned over and whispered, "Guess who I had lunch with yesterday?"

Isla's stomach heaved. She took a deep breath and waited for him to go on.

"Kelly Morgan," he said, "and her grandfather, Jim Walker."

"Kelly?" said Isla sharply.

"Yeah." He grimaced like he had a bad taste in his mouth.

She silently screamed, *Why? Why would you have lunch with her?!*

"She's starting a company, something to do with image consulting. It sounded like a pretty weak idea, but Jim is backing her. And she wants you to do the logo."

"Me?" Isla hissed.

"You." Knox moved his chair closer to hers until they were shoulder to shoulder. Isla froze.

Knox continued unfazed. "I told her you were too busy, but she begged and said you were the best. I agreed, but when Jim wasn't at the table, I told her I didn't want her stealing your ideas and playing it off as her own."

Isla's eyes widened. "You think I'm the best?"

"Ryan's on parental leave, so you're our only designer. By process of elimination—" he shrugged.

She shot him a dirty look.

He grinned and continued, "She called you naïve because you let her get away with it."

"But she didn't get away with it," replied Isla. "She lost her job."

"I wanted to give you the option of doing it if you want to; otherwise, I'll ship it to Adam. He can get his intern on it."

"I'll think about—"

"Don't think too hard. I don't want you wasting your time. I don't know what she's playing at, but I don't want you in the line of fire."

Sue's presentation flickered on the screen, and the room got quiet. Then the screen flashed off again, and everyone returned to their conversations.

"Do you have any plans for tonight?"

Why was he asking? Was this it? Was he going to ask her out, during a meeting? That's not very romantic.

"I think we're good, let's get started," announced Sue as her presentation flashed on to the screen. About three slides into her presentation, the screen went black again. Isla watched Sue's composure falter just for a moment.

"Tonight—?" Knox was in her space again. "You should come to our game. Andrew said Emma wants to come, if she can find someone to help with Liam."

"Your ball hockey game?" she clarified.

"Yeah, we can always use more in our cheering section."

She closed her eyes and the room started spinning again. Opening them, she said, "uh, maybe. Are you any good?"

"God no. We've only won one game."

"That's what you get, playing sports with my brother."

"It's fun! A bunch of us usually go for drinks after—"

A bunch of you, huh? "I'll talk to Emma."

Sue gestured for Knox to come to the front and take over. Watching him walk across the room in his perfectly fitting suit, Isla was finally able to take a deep breath. This was unbearable.

37.

January 17. Bright sun, -18C°.

For someone who gave lip service to missing her grandson, Sara kept herself busy doing other things besides interacting with him. In the six months since returning to Winnipeg, Sara hadn't offered to babysit and she seemed to have an endless supply of excuses whenever Emma asked. She had plenty of time and energy for Bible study and church related activities, however. On the rare occasion she did spend time with him, she'd stare with confusion and say, "I just don't know what to do with boys."

Emma used to marvel at the energy her mother had. She never stopped; from sun-up to sundown, she barely sat down. Now, Emma found it exhausting. Sara was straightening the books in Emma's living room bookshelf, making sure each one was lined up to precisely two inches from the edge of the bookshelf. All the while, she made pleasant conversation, providing updates from church families, church missionaries, church controversies (most recently: which shade of grey to paint the foyer). Sara left the living room mid-sentence and returned with a dust cloth. She continued to adjust the bookshelf, this time taking the books down and wiping each one.

"Mom!" said Emma sharply. "Could you please stop and sit down?"

"I'm almost done," said Sara brightly. "It's pretty dusty up here. We all get behind once in awhile. I haven't gone through my bookshelves in a couple months! They're disgusting, too."

In all the time they had lived in their house, Emma hadn't even thought to dust her bookshelf.

"I could make you a copy of the list," said Sara as she stared the next shelf down.

The list. Emma immediately flashed back to the master cleaning list her mother had laminated and posted by the back door. It had three categories: weekly, monthly, and bi-annually. From what she could remember, she was lucky if the weekly list got done in a month. The monthly list got done maybe once a year. The yearly list, like defrosting and organizing her freezer? Ha!

"I've always lived by the list, and it has never let me down," continued Sara happily. "The best way to show our families love is by giving them a clean house."

Emma had grown up in a very clean house.

Emma watched as her mother kept cleaning. Every swipe of the cloth and adjustment of a book made her heart race and her breath sharper. Emma looked around and almost grabbed a cloth herself. She couldn't sit still while her mother cleaned; she'd have to join her, but dishes sat in the sink and a basket of clean laundry sat by the stairs, waiting to be folded. There was so much other work to do — why the bookshelves?

Emma tried to release the tension building in her arms by making fists and then straightening out her fingers.

Why won't she stop cleaning?

Sara moved to the second bookshelf.

Emma stood up and marched to the laundry room only to find that she hadn't started the dryer and her dry clothes were still wet. How long? She sniffed.

Days.

She loaded them back into the washer and turned it on again. *I can't even finish a simple task like laundry.* Tears stung her eyes as she slowly climbed the stairs. *I'm so stupid.*

"Emma, are you okay?" asked Sara as Emma returned to the living room and slumped on the couch.

Emma started to cry. "I can't do this."

"Do what, sweetie?"

"This. Anything! I'm so tired and I can't eat, and I cry all the time. I can't — I feel like I'm drowning."

"Emma, honey, it's normal to have a couple of low days here and there." Sara folded the rag on the table and straightened it so it was parallel to the table's edge.

"It's been more that a couple of low days—"

"In the Bible it says, 'cast your cares on Him because He cares for you.'"

Emma stared blankly at her mom.

"When you were young, it was so important for me to have my daily quiet time. I would read the Bible and do a gratitude list. Do you have a gratitude list? Maybe that's what you need, to count your blessings." Sara stood back up and continued her work on the bookshelf.

Clenching her fists and opening them again, Emma asked with a shaky voice, "Do you mind if I take a shower?"

"Go right ahead, sweetie," Sara replied without even looking up. "I'll keep an eye on Liam."

Emma locked her bedroom door and headed for the bathroom. She started the shower, her whole body rigid and shaking. She struggled to take off her clothes; her hands felt numb. Climbing into the shower, she slid down and sat with her head between her legs, the searing heat of the water rolling off her back. Tears rolled down her face as she fought to regulate her breathing. Her world continued to spin out of control.

38.

January 24. Strong east wind, -7C°.

Isla hadn't been at Ag Days since she was a child. Her father would keep her and Andrew home from school and drive them to the big agriculture trade show, two hours away in Brandon. They'd meet up with her uncle and cousins and spend the day running around big machinery and eating corn dogs as big as their arms.

When deciding who would help him with his presentation, Knox had said, "Isla is our resident farm expert."

"Am I?"

And that's how she became a presenter at Ag Days Manitoba.

More like the presenter's assistant — Knox was handling most of the presentation. She had a small portion at the end about visual storytelling. They had practised many times, and their presentation that morning had gone over well. They had just begun their final presentation; Isla was far more nervous for this one since Uncle John and her cousins Tyler and Shawn were attending. They had already spent a good part of the morning texting her about the embarrassing questions they planned to ask.

Knox launched into his opening anecdote. He gestured to his audience, who were mostly farmers. "Like you, I was born into an industry, branded the moment I was born. A man named Knox Reeve was my father's hero; he was the first advertiser to use storytelling instead of just describing the product. He told stories about how the product would make the customer feel, selling a dream of who the consumer could become. People don't want facts, they want a human connection, they want to *feel* something. Lazy marketing taps into the easy emotions like fear. It is lazy, but unfortunately, effective."

Isla glanced around gauging the audience. They seemed to find him compelling, laughing at all the right points, nodding when they agreed, pursing their lips when they disagreed. This second seminar was packed, and Isla grew more nervous. As Knox spoke, she looked over her notes, and took a few deep breaths. How badly could her family embarrass her?

He made his final point and introduced her, calling her to the mic.

Then he winked at her.

Isla stood and immediately tripped over a cord, flinging the laptop off the side of the table. She lunged for it and caught it, but in the process, knocked a paper cup of cold coffee all over her cream floral skirt.

The room chuckled with amusement. Their host jumped up quickly, armed with napkins, and helped Isla blot her skirt.

"I'm so sorry, folks. This is so odd and completely out of character for Ms. Peters." Knox could barely get the words out before he laughed out loud.

"Not true!" yelled Isla's Uncle John from the back.

Jerks, all of them.

But there's nothing like an embarrassing moment to break the ice and create trust between a presenter and audience. The rest of the presentation went smoothly, with a robust question and answer period.

Thankfully, Isla's relatives refrained from embarrassing her any further, and took them for dinner after.

The first snowflakes started to fall just as the lights of Brandon faded behind them. Isla was busy fielding texts from her mother.
Drive safe!
Knox was planning to drive like a maniac, but since you texted, he has changed his mind.

The snow quickly got significantly worse. Isla must have looked worried, because Knox stated, "I've driven in snow before."

"I thought when it snows in Vancouver, the whole city shuts down," she replied.

"Yes, it does, but that doesn't mean I've never driven in snow. We have a cabin in the interior," he said, as if that explained anything.

"Prairie snow with wind is a different beast." She was trying to express the magnitude of the situation without annoying him.

"Don't worry, what's the worst that can happen?"

The worst that can happen came within the hour. Snow drifted across the highway, cascading over the windshield with every gust of wind. With each whiteout, Knox tensed. Both wondered how they were going to make it back to the city.

By the time the landscape opened to bald prairie, there was zero visibility. They crawled along until Portage La Prairie. There, the highway was closed and RCMP were diverting traffic into town.

Knox pulled into a dated hotel with a suspiciously full parking lot.

"Here?" Isla asked, her heart sinking.

"Would you rather spend the night in the car?" Knox replied. "I'll go see if I can get us two rooms."

When he returned, he handed her a key. "Last room in the whole city."

"Last room or rooms, plural?"

"Room."

Her face must've shown her apprehension.

"I'll sleep on the floor," he stated.

The room was small — really small — a bed and an oversized desk and chair crammed into the corner. It smelled like wet dog.

Knox sat on the edge of the bed and flipped through channels on the TV. He didn't notice when Isla took a selfie with him in the background. She quickly posted it, before texting her parents and Priya to let them know what had happened. Then she stood by the closet, supremely uncomfortable — and not just because she had spent the day in heels. Surveying the room, she grabbed the spare pillows from the closet and stripped the bed of its blankets.

"What are you doing?" Knox asked absently. She was interrupting his hockey game.

"Making a wall," said Isla as she placed the pillows down the centre of the bed.

"I told you, I'll sleep on the floor," said Knox.

"This works. Besides, the carpet smells like dog." She remade the bed on top of the wall of pillows. She stood on the other side of the bed, still unable to sit on it. He sensed her hesitation but was at a loss as to what to do about it.

"Are you hungry?" he asked, grabbing his wallet out of his bag. "I can go find us some snacks."

She shook her head.

Once he left, she quickly took off her itchy tights, which had seemed like at good idea thirteen hours earlier. Pants would have been much wiser. She climbed onto the bed. The polyester quilted blanket felt weird on her bare legs, so she climbed under the blankets. She had her novel and was rereading a page when Knox returned, carrying a bag of cheezies and an apple.

"How do you know Mike Stevens?" he said, staring at his phone.

"Who?" said Isla, surprised to hear the familiar name. "Michael?"

"He just sent me a DM referring to us being here," he said, indicating the cramped room. "You didn't post something, did you?"

Isla grabbed her phone off the side table, and groaned. She had fourteen new comments. Looking up from her phone, shamefaced, she asked, "How do you know Michael?"

"I don't know him; he bartends at a restaurant I used to go to. It's horribly pretentious, but they have a great burger. I didn't realise he followed me. How do you know him?"

"We dated," she said, trying to sound casual and upbeat, maybe even confident. Definitely not heartbroken.

"He still follows you?" he asked with a sideways glance and raised eyebrow.

"He stopped, but then he started again a little while ago."

Knox flopped down on the opposite side of the bed and opened his bag of cheezies. "He doesn't really seem like your type."

"My type? What would you know about my type?" demanded Isla.

"I figured you appreciated those who were gainfully employed."

"He *is* employed."

"He's a bartender."

"A mixologist."

"A pretentious bartender, then — how long ago did you break up?" asked Knox, slapping her hand away as she reached for his bag. "I thought you weren't hungry?"

She glared at him. "A little bit more than a year ago."

"Did you break it off?"

"It was mutual."

"So, he dumped you. People always say it's mutual when they don't want to admit they were dumped."

Isla snapped, "I guess you're an expert in that — dumping people?"

"I haven't really dated anyone for awhile," he replied lazily as he threw a cheezie up in the air and caught it in his mouth.

"So just lots of hook-ups, then?"

He glanced away, paying attention to his hockey game once again. Isla waited a beat before returning to her novel. Apparently, the conversation was over.

"Why did he break up with you?" he asked at the next commercial break.

Isla closed her book slowly, unsure of how to answer. She had asked herself this same question many times over the last year. Michael had never given her a satisfactory answer. "I suspect he didn't like that I worked for an advertising company. He said the best products would sell themselves. Marketing was a capitalistic ploy to make us buy stuff we don't need to fix problems we don't have."

Knox laughed. "He isn't wrong."

"Yeah, well, he had some big ideas and ideals. He wanted to be an entrepreneur. He tried lots of things, but nothing worked out. I think after awhile, it was hard on him that I was making more money than him."

"How very masculine of him." Knox offered her the apple. "Does he have his BA?"

"Ha, no — he believed education is for those with no imagination."

"You're kidding! I'm sure your parents loved that."

"They didn't know that part," said Isla sheepishly.

"He sounds like an idiot."

"He's not an idiot. He reads a lot," she replied. "And he was really fun, and spontaneous and romantic. He bought me flowers all the time, always planned elaborate celebrations. We were together for a long time."

Isla's emotions were running high. This whole situation was so ridiculous. She never in a million years imagined she'd be trapped in a hotel room with Knox. Why was he asking so many questions about Michael?

"How long?"

"Three years, sort of, off and on," she said, mortified to hear the sadness in her voice. "We've known each other for longer though."

Feeling the need to escape, she took her apple to the bathroom to wash it. She scrubbed it until she broke through the skin. She looked at her reflection in the mirror: blotchy and red. Why must her skin always betray her? She splashed some water on her face; only when her mascara started running did she remember that she still had make up on.

"You are a hot mess," she said to her reflection. She scrubbed the rest of the make-up off her face. What did she expect, anyway? That he'd make a move on her? *Calm down, lady.*

Fortifying herself with a few deep breaths, she twisted her hair into a messy bun at the top of her head. and returned to the room. This time, she avoided the bed and took the chair next to the window.

After awhile he asked, "Would you get back together with him?"

Isla tried to shrug nonchalantly. "He asked me to go skating on the river next Saturday."

"He did? Skating? How *romantic*."

Isla ignored him and read her book.

"Are you hoping he's going to see the wrong of his ways and beg for forgiveness?" he asked. "Oh baby, I'm so sorry."

Isla slammed her book shut. "Stop being such a jerk."

He smirked and picked up his phone. "Do you want me to reply?"

"No," said Isla.

"What did you post, anyway?" he asked. "Now Violet is texting me."

"It was just a selfie that happened to have you in the background. No big deal," she said defensively.

"Can I see it?" he asked.

"No." She wasn't about to show him all the suggestive comments from her friends. She was already embarrassed enough that Violet had seen them.

Knox finished his cheezies and the game ended. He turned off the TV and he crawled under the blankets on his side of the pillow wall. Before he turned his light out, he asked, "Are you planning on sleeping in the chair?"

"I guess not," Isla replied. She got up hesitantly and crept back to the bed. By the time she settled herself under the blanket and looked over, he had fallen asleep.

It took Isla much longer. Somewhere around four o'clock she fell asleep with her book in hand and light still on.

39.

February 2. Completely still -8C°.

The stairs by the Johnston Terminal used to be their spot. The place they would meet, winter or summer. The Forks had always been their favourite place to eat a gooey cinnamon bun, walk together, and forget the rest of the world existed. Isla paused as the steps came into view. There he was. She hadn't seen Michael in person in more than a year. He looked different, or maybe less familiar. His hair was longer, his peach fuzz beard had filled in, but his clothes were still two sizes too big. His whole face lit up when he saw her.

"Isla!" He rushed to her and threw his arms around her, drawing her into an unexpected bear hug. Her arms were pinned by his, preventing her from hugging him back, even if she had wanted to.

Isla shrugged him off. "Hi—Michael."

"You look amazing! I've always loved when you wear green!"

"Green is my favourite colour," she stated, as they walked towards the river to find a spot to put their skates on.

"Yeah, I remember that! Remember that time I surprised you and put green food colouring in everything for your birthday?"

She did. It had been revolting. "Yeah, it was hilarious."

They arrived at the river and found a bench. The sun was out, and the wind was lazy, so the trails were full of families skating and enjoying the winter afternoon.

"Did you survive your ordeal with Harrison?" Michael asked coolly as he tied his hockey skates.

"What ordeal? We got storm-stayed. It wasn't anything."

"Yeah—but—"

"Yeah, but what?"

"Look — I'm just saying. You should stay far away from him."

"Why?"

"He's the kind of guy who thinks he can get any girl, anytime. He and his buddy — the doctor — used to hang out at my restaurant. You know how guys like that are." He finished with his skates and indicated to hers. "Do you want me to tie yours?"

"I can tie my own laces," she said, annoyed that he'd even asked. "What do you mean, 'guys like that?'"

"You know, lots of booze, lots of girls, thinking they're entitled to everything because their fathers have money."

"You know nothing about his father."

Michael shrugged. "One night they were at my restaurant and they were drinking a lot — totally out of control. I had to ask them to leave, and Harrison punched me in the face. I could've pressed charges, but I'm not like that. I let it go."

"He punched you?" questioned Isla. "That doesn't sound like Knox. He's usually fairly —contained."

"Yeah, well, you weren't there. How well can you really know your boss, eh?" Michael grinned. "I'll race you to the first shack."

Isla took off. She loved the feeling of skating fast, to her it felt like flying. As a child she'd despised playing hockey, even though her mother continually pushed it on her. *You're a Canadian! At least try to like it.* Dee would sit in the change room pleading with Isla to get on the ice until they were both in tears. But she always loved skating on the river trail, skating until her legs burned. Isla threw her hands in the air and squealed. She slowed to find Michael was having trouble keeping up with her.

"I forgot how amazing you are at skating," Michael said, trying to sound charming while he struggled to catch his breath.

Isla grinned. "This is my first time this winter. In fact, I'm not sure I went last winter either."

Her grin faded as she remembered the last time she skated. Two years ago, Michael had brought her skating to talk about something important. She was expecting a proposal; what she got was another fantastical speech about his latest dream. Isla pushed away the unpleasant memory and forced a smile.

"Do you want to keep going, or head back?" she asked.

"Let's head back," he said, not wanting to admit his lungs were burning. "We can go for a drink or something — better atmosphere for talking."

Isla started back, not as fast as before, but making sure she left plenty of space for the hard memories between the two of them.

Sam sat in the snow psyching himself up to stand on skates for the first time. It was a mystery why he let Knox talk him into this. He was sure he could live in Canada very happily without learning how to skate, but his friends seem to think it was a prerequisite to stay in the country longer than two years. He didn't understand the physics of it. Two blades as sharp as knifes strapped to shoes? Not to mention the idea of standing on a frozen river! All he could picture was breaking through the ice, and how cold it would be to freeze to death.

Andrew was happy to leave the house. He had even brought Liam along to give Emma a chance to do something fun. She snapped at him for even suggesting it. *Don't you know how much house cleaning*

I have to do? Andrew placed Liam on the chair they had brought for Sam to use for balance. When — if — Sam ever decided to get up.

Knox wanted to skate in the central area of the trail. It was the best chance they had of running into Isla and Michael. He was proud of himself for thinking of a reason besides obvious sabotage to be at The Forks. He skated over to give Sam a hand up.

"Please promise me I won't die," said Sam.

"You won't die, I promise." Knox glanced up in time to see Liam crawling on the ice towards a redhead in a bright green wool jacket, skating fast towards them closely followed by a skinny man with a scruffy beard and longish hair swept up into a bun on top of his head. Bingo.

"Whoa, Liam!" Andrew grabbed his son before he could get in the way of the skaters. Then he noticed his sister and scowled when he saw who she was with.

Isla's face lit up as she saw her nephew. "Liam! Hey buddy!" She grabbed him out of Andrew's arms and gave him a huge hug and kisses all over his face. He giggled.

"What are you guys doing here?" she exclaimed, looking around for Emma. Instead, she saw Sam clutching an old chair, moving his feet back and forth like a saw. Knox was beside him, giving him directions.

"Michael." Andrew gave a curt greeting.

"Andrew," said Michael with the same feeling.

"What's going on, Andrew?" Isla hissed.

"You tell me," he hissed back, his eyes darting to Michael.

"Good day for a skate," Knox yelled, guiding Sam towards the group.

"Knox thought today would be a good time for Sam to learn to skate," Andrew replied.

Michael scowled. "We should leave—"

Knox took one look at Isla's expression, and knew he was busted. Politely he asked, "What brings you two here?"

"Oh, you know. Just two old friends catching up..." Michael started.

"Can I have a word?" Isla interrupted. She grabbed Knox's sleeve and skated him out of earshot.

"What are you doing here?"

"We thought it would be fun to go skating. Sam needs to learn if he's going to live here," he said, suppressing a grin.

"Skating. Today? You thought *today* would be the best time for you and my brother to teach Sam how to skate?! You are so infuriating!" said Isla. She drew herself up, all five feet and two and a half inches, and looked him directly in the eye. "Why are you really here?"

"I told you, to teach Sam how to skate."

"So this has nothing to do with my date with Michael."

"Of course not," he shrugged. "He's an asshole."

"You're an asshole!" she shot back.

"That's true, I am." He smiled confidently "And you don't need two of us in your life."

"I don't need *any* of you in my life!" Isla yelled. She desperately wanted him to give her a reason why she shouldn't be on a date with someone else. "Tell me why you care?"

His cool blue eyes didn't give anything away. "We're friends, aren't we?"

"If we're friends, then you should've told me the real history that you have with Michael. You should've told me that you punched him." She glowered at him, and then turned to skate back towards everyone else.

"Hey—" he said, grabbing her arm before she could skate away. "Don't believe everything your *ex* tells you."

"—leave me alone!" she said, wrestling out of his grip. "I can take care of myself."

She grabbed Michael's hand and skated towards the entrance and their boots. Michael shot Knox a triumphant look and a quick salute as he skated away.

"Ah, shit," Knox said under his breath.

"What was that about?" asked Sam, now sitting on his learn-to-skate chair.

"Did you know she was going to be here — with him?" Andrew asked angrily, ignoring Sam's question.

"She might've mentioned it last week," Knox admitted.

"You do realise that if you tell Isla not to do something, she will do the very thing you tell her not to do?" Andrew snapped.

Knox nodded.

"Here, take Liam." Andrew handed Liam to Knox, who suddenly realised he had never held a baby in his adult life. "I've got to make some calls."

Andrew cut through the snow, finding firmer ground to make his phone calls.

Sam, still sitting on his chair in the middle of the skating area, held his hands out for Liam. Knox quickly turned him over.

"Do you want to tell me what that was all about?" asked Sam, adjusting Liam on his lap comfortably.

"That was Isla's ex—" He pushed the learn-to-skate chair, with Sam and Liam still on it, over to a bench on the frozen riverbank.

Sam climbed out of his chair and onto the bench, happy to be on firm ground again. "Did something happen between you and Isla when you got stuck in Portage?"

"What do you mean?" asked Knox.

"You know something — romantic?"

"Ah. No."

Sam scrutinized his reaction and body language; he didn't believe Knox.

"Nothing happened! Nothing *can* happen. I'm her boss—"

239

"And you like her." Sam had Liam standing on his lap; they were doing shimmies to the left then to the right to unheard music.

"I—" started Knox. He took his time finding the right word. "I think she is remarkable—"

"But?"

Knox cleared his throat and indicated to Andrew who was returning.

End of conversation.

"I got a hold of mom and Emma, but Priya didn't pick up."

"I think Priya works until five today," said Sam absently, still dancing with Liam.

"What?" said Andrew and Knox simultaneously.

Sam stopped dancing and stared at his friends, wide-eyed.

"How do you know Priya's schedule?" asked Andrew.

"Who?" asked Sam blankly.

"Priya! You said she works until five," said Andrew. "Why do you know Priya's schedule? How do you even know Priya?"

Sam looked miserably at Andrew and then back to Knox, who smirked because he had just guessed the reason. "Oh, bloody hell. She's going to kill me."

"The tube of lipstick I found on your coffee table makes far more sense now," laughed Knox.

It took Andrew a couple more seconds for the pieces to fall into place. "*You're* the secret boyfriend?"

"She called me her boyfriend?"

"Emma mentioned that Priya had been spending many nights away from home but wouldn't say a peep about where she was staying."

"—it's more like friends with benefits, but without the friend part."

"Do you know what you have gotten yourself into?" questioned Andrew.

Knox laughed. "The last guy she was with ended up with fifteen mice in his apartment, all thanks to Priya and company."

"She cannot know that I told you. You cannot tell Emma! And you," Sam said, turning to Knox, "cannot tell Isla."

Knox agreed. Andrew was still dumbfounded. "I don't think anyone would believe me. This is weird! She's like a sister to me, a more obnoxious sister, but still."

"Time to get back on the ice," Knox said, clapping Sam on the back. "Might as well learn to skate before Priya murders you."

40.

February 2, later.

Isla settled into the booth at Michael's restaurant. The décor was so clichéd: pictures of chickens walking through long grass, a chalk board menu... If she had to guess, her drink would be served in a mason jar. After pining away for Michael for so long, she was surprised how unattractive she found him now, how annoying he was. Had he always had such bad taste in music? And did he always talk with an upswing at the end of every sentence?

She knew who she really wanted, yet she was with the other guy.

"Two Frida Koolio's," said Michael, setting down two jam jars filled with a pale golden liquid and large springs of rosemary.

"What is a Frida Koolio?" asked Isla.

"Like the artist, Frida Kahlo. Its small batch tequila made with organic agave, house-made orange liquor, fresh lime, fresh pineapple juice, one organic free-range-egg white, and a rosemary skewer."

"I hate tequila," Isla stated.

"No, you don't," he replied.

"Yes, I do."

"You'll love it, give it a chance," he said lightly.

Isla took a small sip as he watched, eagerly awaiting her reaction.

It was horrible. She swallowed quickly and shook her head. "I'm sorry."

His face fell. She felt like a horrible human being. "I really thought you'd like it. I thought of you when I created it. Have another sip, maybe it will grow on you."

She took another and fought a shudder. There was no way she was having a third.

"Tell me, what is Isla up to these days? Have you been painting much?" Michael asked.

"When I have time. I've been slowly working on a series of portraits. I'm working on Priya's grandpa still."

"Wow! Amazing! I'd love to see them!" The next instant he switched from enthusiasm to disapproval. "And how is Priya? Still Priya?"

"What do you mean by that?" demanded Isla.

"You know what I mean. She's so different from you. I mean, you're a really nice person, and she's a total b—" He faltered.

"A total what?" questioned Isla.

"Bitch."

"—and by 'bitch' I think you mean smart, ambitious, determined — shall I go on?" countered Isla.

"I'm just saying, she fits right in with Harrison and his crew. The way she goes through men, she's probably dated all of them by now."

Isla gaped at him. "What the hell Michael? I didn't come here so you could bad mouth my friends."

"I assumed you weren't as close anymore."

"Why would you assume that?"

"Never mind," he said with a dismissive wave of his hand. "Have you heard of Johnny Watson yet?"

Isla shook her head and thought about why he would think she and Priya wouldn't be friends anymore. Was she missing something?

"He's a ground-breaking entrepreneur. We've been working together for a few months, and he wants to partner with me. It is such a fantastic opportunity! We're going to open a holistic lifestyle complex, with a gym, spa, life-coaching, organic free trade clothing and housewares. And I want you to come on board with us."

Isla paused, stirring her drink with her rosemary skewer. She was seeing clearly now. The whole afternoon had been a lead-up to this pitch. Unimpressed she asked, "what do you want from me?"

"We need a designer: logo, branding, all that sort of stuff. I thought we could use your paintings as art and give people the opportunity to purchase them! It would be like having your own gallery!"

"Hmm…" she said, digging in her handbag. "That sounds interesting. What kind of time frame are you looking at?"

Michael's face lit up. "Well, we'd like to start right away. Social media — full on campaign. Website, flyers, the whole nine yards. We want to get our branding on point before starting construction."

Isla finally found what she was looking for. She wrote a number on the back and handed her business card to him. "Great! Email your info to my HRA address and I'll send you an estimate."

She pointed to the number she had written on the back, and added, "that's per hour."

"Isla—" He grabbed her hand. "Come on, babe! We don't have to do this through HRA. It could be a side project! Come on, help me out — as an old friend."

"Don't call me 'babe'." Isla pulled her hand back and held his gaze. "I'll do it on the side for time and a half."

Michael narrowed his eyes and threw his hands in the air. "I should've known you'd do this! After all we've been through — remember, we weren't going to become like this, Isla. We were going to be different, not settle for boring paycheques. We were going to chase our dreams, live the good life! Now you're trapped, serving the corporate gods."

"There is no more *we*. You were the one who made that choice. And it was never about my dreams. Only yours."

244

"You've changed. The old Isla would've helped a friend out."

"I *have* changed — and the new Isla knows her worth." She rose out of her seat. "Michael, you haven't changed a bit. Good luck with your life."

Isla hadn't planned how to get home. She started walking in the direction of her apartment. She crossed the eight lanes of traffic at Main Street and walked down Broadway. Dark clouds had covered the sun and the wind had picked up, whipping against her face. Gone was the pleasant afternoon. The sun had almost set when she arrived at the bus stop down the street from the HRA building. She stopped walking and sat in the bus shelter. Her teeth chattered as she waited, her coat inadequate for the changing weather. Only then did she hear the ping of her phone. She pulled it out and saw she had four missed texts from Andrew, three from Emma, five from the professor, plus two missed calls and fourteen missed texts from Priya. All verging on the edge of hysterical. This is why she'd told no one except Knox, from whom she had zero new texts.

Isla made it home before it started snowing, but she was chilled to the bone and ready for a hot shower and maybe a good cry. She opened the apartment door and entered the living room.

"Why the hell would you go out with him? Are you stupid?" spat Priya as she jumped off the couch and stormed towards her.

Isla took a deep breath and looked around. "What are you doing here?"

Her mother waved from their large, overstuffed pink chair. She had a cup of coffee in her hand.

"How long have you been waiting for me?" demanded Isla.

"Are you forgetting the months — I mean, *years* — of heartache that loser put you through?" interjected Priya. "Why the hell would you spend the afternoon with him?"

"Why didn't you tell anyone except Knox?" asked Dee.

"Wait. Knox knew?!" yelled Priya.

Isla pointed at Priya, who was still fuming, and said to Dee, "exhibit A."

Priya gaped at Isla. "Please tell me you have a reasonable explanation for why you spent the day with Michael."

"I went because I was curious," she said. Curiosity was the only thing she was willing to admit to out loud. Deep down, her reasons were much murkier. Maybe she had hoped he wanted her back, not because she wanted him, but so she could believe *someone* wanted her. "Knox knew about it because it came up last week — by accident. I wouldn't have told him if I knew he was going to show up and tell all of you."

"Tell us what Michael wanted," said Dee, returning from the tiny kitchen with another cup of coffee.

"What makes you think he wanted something?" said Isla, accepting the coffee and curling herself up on the sofa. "Maybe he just wanted to catch up."

Dee gave her a questioning look.

"Fine. He wanted me to come up with a logo and branding for his new stupid business," Isla grimaced. "For free."

"You told him to shove it up his ass, right?" interjected Priya.

Isla laughed. "Yeah, something like that. It was pretty horrible. He started by serving me a tequila cocktail."

"Even *I* know you hate tequila," said her mother.

"He wouldn't shut up about how much he hates Knox, and then he started in on you, Pri. I kind of got the feeling I was missing something." Priya was avoiding eye contact, studying the water stain on the ceiling.

"I considered telling you, I really did, but in the end I couldn't. It was so nasty. I didn't want to hurt you more than you were already—"

"What happened, Priya?" interrupted Isla.

"Last spring, when I was with Brian, we went out with a bunch of his buddies including Knox. Michael had finished his shift and being Michael, he joined us. All of us had a lot to drink and he was bullshitting about all his plans. At first Knox seemed genuinely interested and the two of them seemed to be having a good conversation but then everything switched, quick. Knox probably asked too many questions. Michael started ragging on him about being a trust fund baby and having everything handed to him. I kind of lost it on him and told him to get the hell away from us. But he wouldn't leave. He told Brian to shut his woman up. I shoved him, and he threw a drink at me and told me to calm down."

Isla stared at Priya in open-mouthed disbelief. Priya continued, "Knox grabbed him by his shirt and dragged him to the bar. I think he settled up and then we left quickly, before any other staff got involved."

"When?" Isla asked struggling to take it all in. "When did this happen?"

"Just after you started working for HRA again," said Priya quietly.

"I can't believe you didn't tell me."

"I know you, Isla. You would've concocted some story in your head about how Michael still loved you deep down and — well, he didn't ask about you. Not at all."

Isla absorbed that in silence. How could he hang out with Priya and not even ask about her? "I am *so* over him. And I'm a little insulted that you're all flipping out over today."

Priya sighed. "You were a wreck, for a long time. None of us want you reliving that."

"So, Knox didn't punch him?"

"No! I was about to, though."

"Where was Brian in all this?"

"Enjoying the show, the bastard. I can't believe I ever gave him the time of day. Knox was great, he paid. Knowing him, he probably tipped, and he got us out before things got even more ugly. He's the one you should be spending the afternoon with."

Isla sighed deeply. "Well, he didn't ask me, did he?"

"It has to mean something that he tried to sabotage your afternoon," stated Priya.

"I think you should ask that young man out on a date," added Dee.

Isla looked at her mother like she'd forgotten she was still in the room.

"I think that's a great idea," agreed Priya.

"But he's my boss—"

"I thought Sue was," replied Priya.

"But — he's not interested."

"I think he is," said Dee. "He sabotaged your afternoon."

"Because he hates Michael."

"Because he likes you," said Priya.

"No, because we're friends—"

"Enough of your excuses. I'll do it for you," offered Priya.

"Don't you dare."

41.

February 4, Plus wind chill. -28C°.

By the time Isla entered the large glass doors, her face had gone numb with cold. Her frozen eyelashes melted the moment she entered the warm building, mascara now streaming down her face. She whipped her hat off and untangled her scarf. She had only crossed the street and walked in the wind half a block. Her parka kept her alive. The fact that she'd worn a skirt and tights was a mistake. Even if they were cute blue and purple plaid tights.

She stopped in front of the mirrored wall and wiped the running mascara from her eyes. She'd have to fix the rest upstairs.

"Hey," said Knox. He was waiting at the end of the mirrored wall, in his navy suit, camel coloured wool jacket unbuttoned. Nothing cold about him.

"Good morning," replied Isla, looking around. "Are you waiting for someone?"

"You."

"Me?" she replied. Ugh. What had she done now?

He held out a small, black-and-white striped cardboard box tied up with a hot pink bow. "An apology cupcake."

"An apology cupcake?" Isla took the box and opened it. Nestled inside was a chocolate cupcake with a generous swirl of mocha-coloured buttercream and a chocolate covered coffee bean on the top. "It looks like someone tasted the icing."

"I bought two. I had to figure out which tasted the best."

"So you could eat the best one."

"So I could give *you* the best one!"

"What was the other flavor?" she wondered.

"Cherry cola."

Isla took a swipe of the mocha flavored icing. "You made the right choice."

Knox made a move to head toward the elevator.

"Dude! I want to hear the actual apology."

"Just a cupcake's not going to cut it, huh?"

Isla shook her head and indicated with her hand that he should get on with it.

"I'm sorry I crashed your date with Mike."

She waited.

"More?"

She nodded. "Do you think I'm going to let you off the hook that easy?"

He sighed and ran his hand through his hair. "Showing up with your brother was immature and unnecessary."

"Yes, it was," Isla agreed. "Priya totally flipped out on me and then told me about what happened between you guys and Michael last spring."

"Ah. I hoped she would—tell you the story, not flip out. See? I had a good reason."

Isla evaluated him. He looked appropriately chastised.

"Okay, apology accepted." Isla turned and marched toward the elevators. He grinned and followed. There were four elevators and since it was first thing in the morning, a crowd was waiting.

"So, how *did* the date go?" he asked as they joined the queue.

Isla scowled. "Not great. He asked me to do a bunch of design work for him and when I made it clear I wouldn't do it for free, he got pissy. He accused me of selling out to the corporate gods."

Knox started to say something, but Isla held her hand up. "You were right, I did want him to want me back. I imagined how satisfying it would be to turn him down and break *his* heart for once. Instead, he confirmed that he doesn't even respect me enough to pay me for my work."

"Whether your work is good or not, you deserve to be paid — and your work is excellent,"

Knox said as the elevator to their left opened. They entered and six more people followed, relegating them to the back corner.

"And I'm sure you've had lots of opportunities to break hearts." He said this softly, so only she could hear.

"I don't think I've ever broken anyone's heart. I have a pathetic habit of falling hard for anyone who shows me even the slightest bit of attention. I've had my heart broken by guys who barely know I exist." *Alert! Alert! Overshare alert!*

"Breaking hearts isn't as satisfying as you'd imagine," Knox replied.

I bet, thought Isla.

After a couple of stops the elevator emptied, leaving the two of them to travel the final few floors. They barely noticed, remaining close in the back corner, talking quietly. Knox told her about teaching Sam to ice skate. As he talked, he leaned against the handrail. Isla tried to pay attention; she really did. But all she could think about was how close her hand was to his. What would happen if she inched her hand to his and their fingers touched? Best case scenario: he'd hit the big red stop button, press her up against the wall, and kiss her passionately. Worst case scenario: his hand would recoil in disgust.

The searing pain of rejection was not something Isla was emotionally prepared for on this bitterly cold Monday morning.

"I want you—" he started.

Isla snapped back to reality.

"—to look at the proofs Adam sent regarding Kelly's account. She's sent a new list of frustrating requests; it's like she is purposefully trying to be difficult."

"Yeah, for sure." Isla caught her breath as the elevator door opened to the HRA lobby.

"Keep track of every minute you spend on it; I'll make sure you get paid." Knox held the door for her, and as their eyes met, he gave her a grin that made her regret not moving her hand those last two inches in the elevator.

42.

February 16. Breezy, -21C°.

The awful sound of retching interrupted Isla's first sip of coffee. She called out, "Pri— are you ok?"

Priya moaned, flushed the toilet, and splashed cold water on her face before returning to the living room, were she sunk down on their couch.

"Please don't say the stomach flu?" asked Isla, her index fingers crossing in front of her to ward off germs.

"I wish," groaned Priya.

"Hungover?" prodded Isla, leaning against the kitchen door frame. "I thought you had a shift last night?"

Priya's face crumpled into tears as she shook her head.

"Oh my god, Priya!" Isla sank down beside her as Priya pulled her knees up and buried her face in them. She began to sob while Isla rubbed her back. "Maybe you're just late?"

"Not late. I took a test, I'm eleven weeks already." Priya's words were muffled; she kept her face buried in her lap.

Eleven! No. No. No, this can't be happening, thought Isla. *What do I do? What do I say?*

"I'm assuming the father is your mystery man?" asked Isla hesitantly. "Are you going to finally tell me who he is?"

Priya knew it was time to come clean, especially to Isla. She needed someone to know. Keeping the secret for so long had been more difficult than she imagined. Priya looked up at Isla and took a deep breath. "Samarpeet Singh."

"Samarpeet Singh?" replied Isla, surprised. "Like, my friend Sam?"

"Your friend Sam, Andrew's friend Sam, Kavan and Deepa's friend Sam. He's a very friendly guy," Priya snapped.

"I can't believe it! He isn't even really your type. How did you meet? How long have you been together?" Isla blurted out every question swirling in her head. "Did you plan this? Why didn't you use protection?"

"This wasn't fucking planned!" cried Priya.

Isla shut up. She stood up and walked to the kitchen where she took a couple deep breaths before returning to the couch. "What are you going to do?"

The girls sat in silence for a moment.

"I can't keep it," whispered Priya.

Silence echoed around the room. In that moment, the last shadows of childhood disappeared. Confronted with no clear answer, there was no way forward except hopelessness.

"What does Sam think?" Isla finally asked, not trusting herself to share an opinion.

"He doesn't know, and I'm not planning on telling him. He'd probably do something stupid like ask me to marry him."

"You have to tell him," urged Isla.

"My body, my decision. No one else can know! No one."

"What about Emma?"

"Especially not Emma!"

"But she's had a baby," reminded Isla.

"She *wanted* a baby. This is a completely different situation!"

"But — it's her birthday! We're going out tonight."

"I know. And you are going to keep this secret," Priya threatened. Or else.

"But she's your best friend!"

"Just because we took a best friends forever pledge at sixteen, doesn't mean she's going to understand," Priya cried. "Promise me!"

"I promise." Isla was close to tears herself. She asked, "Have you thought about keeping the baby?"

"No."

"But—"

"But what? I don't have a choice. I graduate in the spring and start my residency in the fall. I am on the brink of achieving my lifelong dream of being a doctor, and I am not about to throw it away on motherhood. I don't want to be a mother. I've never wanted to be a mother," explained Priya.

"But Sam would be such a good dad."

"He should find someone else to have a baby with, then. Someone he could marry and settle down with. I'm not wife material and I'd be the worst mother in the world. You don't understand. *You* want the husband-and-three-kids-in-the-suburbs life. I don't."

"I don't think you'd be the worst mother in the world," murmured Isla.

"Stop." Priya held her hand up. "Imagine if I did keep this thing. It would be the end of my relationship with my parents, not that things are good now, but this would be the nail in the coffin."

"I don't think it would," said Isla. "Your parents love you."

"They are perpetually disappointed in me. When I was younger, I overheard them talking about a cousin in India whose daughter had gotten pregnant. My father was ruthless. He said horrible things about her and about her parents. This would kill them — I don't have a choice. It should be called pro-not-having-any-other-choices."

255

Fresh tears fell from Priya's eyes. "Please don't judge me. Not all of us have parents like yours."

"I'm not judging you."

"You are, I can see it in your eyes. You think I'm wrong to even think about ending this pregnancy. I guess your pro-choice stance is only in theory," snapped Priya.

Isla exhaled, "Pri—I promise no matter what you choose, I am always on your side."

Isla and Priya were already seated when Emma arrived. It was unusual for her to be the last to arrive. Isla gave her a perky smile and peppered her with the usual questions regarding Liam: what was he learning? Had he said 'aunty Isla' yet? How was he sleeping?

Emma's answers were clipped and precise. "Walking along furniture. No. He's not."

They sank into silence. The three of them hadn't been together since New Years, and apparently there were still hard feelings. The silence was interrupted by an overly friendly server asking for drink orders. Emma ordered a soda water, Isla ordered a white wine, and Priya ordered a rum and coke. Isla choked on the water she'd been sipping, and then bit her lip to stop herself from speaking.

Emma's phone rang and she left the table to find a quieter spot.

Isla wasted no time. "Rum? You're having a rum and coke?"

Priya glared at her. "Who cares? It doesn't matter."

"It matters."

"I am dealing with the most stressful crisis of my life, and you're telling me not to have a drink?"

"But you're pregnant," hissed Isla.

"I won't be for long."

"What if you change your mind?"

"I'm not going to change my mind, but if I do, one rum and coke isn't going to hurt the fetus."

Emma cleared her throat. "It's Dee," she said, handing Isla her phone. "She wants to know why you wouldn't answer your phone."

Emma had overheard their conversation.

"I'll call you back," Isla said, hanging up before her mother could reply.

She had betrayed Priya's secret. Why did she have such a big mouth?

Emma sat down and turned to Priya. "You're pregnant, and based on the looks you're giving each other, I guess you weren't planning to tell me?"

Priya didn't look at Emma. She was glaring at Isla, who mouthed, "I'm so sorry."

"I guess I'd find out eventually," stated Emma.

No one spoke.

"Please tell me you know who the father is?" asked Emma.

Isla sucked in an audible breath.

"You really do think I am an irresponsible whore, don't you?" snapped Priya.

Emma's eyes widened, before growing dark. "Is it Sam's, or some other guy?"

"You know about Sam?" Isla asked.

"I've known for weeks! Andrew said Sam let it slip."

"I can't believe I'm the last to know," whispered Isla.

"This isn't about you Isla," said Priya.

The server delivered their drinks, and Priya asked for a few more minutes before ordering. As he walked away, Priya took a long sip of her drink.

"Doesn't that have alcohol in it?" questioned Emma.

"Do you think I give a shit? I am not keeping this thing."

"But that's murder," said Emma. As she said it, something in Priya shifted, closed, armoured up. Emma braced herself.

"I knew you wouldn't understand. I knew this is exactly how you'd react. You're so proud of your high moral standards and your perfect life that has unfolded exactly as you planned. You've always judged me. News flash — I'm not you. I never have been. Don't hold *me* to your impossible standards. I will do what is best for me. Your opinion doesn't affect me at all. I do not care what you think." Priya spat the last few words with such vitriol that Isla shivered.

It was too much. Emma looked at her friends and couldn't take their disgust anymore. She fumbled with her wallet and threw some cash on the table. Emma could feel it start in her fingers; the tips grew numb. She grabbed her bag and jacket and headed to her car. The numbness spread as her breath sped up. She managed to drive to a residential street before she pulled over and retched into a snowbank, her body going through the familiar motions even though her stomach was empty. Tears poured down her face. No one followed her. No one would check up on her.

43.

February 21. Strong south wind, -28C°.

To avoid speaking to Sam, Isla had glued herself to her desk chair, headphones on, back turned to the group. She took her break later than everyone else and appeared to be very focused on her current project. But she was procrastinating by searching the Internet for balloon bouquets. She'd got in in her head that it would be funny to celebrate the one-year anniversary of being fired. Are balloons the appropriate thing to buy the man who fired you one year ago and whom you currently have a giant inappropriate crush on?

Maybe she should get some real work done.

Except she needed the swatch book that was currently sitting on Sam's desk, and she couldn't grab it without speaking to him. How did anyone expect her to keep this secret? Sam's phone rang. Isla noticed him check the ID looking confused, then excuse himself to take the call in the hall.

When it was safe, she grabbed the swatch book and returned to her desk and her headphones.

"Isla," said Sam, before she had a chance to put them back on. "Can we talk?"

Isla prayed the panic she felt wasn't visible on her face.

"Privately," he added, indicating to the hall.

He knows.

Sam steered her to a conference room. He shut the door and stared at her, his face full of hurt and confusion.

"I just got off the phone with Emma," he stated.

"Emma?" Isla choked out. "Emma called you?"

"Is it true?" he asked quietly.

"Sam, I—" Isla shook her head. There was nothing she could say.

"Is it true?" He raised his voice.

"She had no right to tell you—" replied Isla.

"It's a good thing she did, since Priya won't answer her phone, and you obviously had no intentions of telling me," snapped Sam.

"You don't understand—-"

"You're damn right I don't understand! I deserve to know that my girlfriend is pregnant."

Sam's raised voice caught the attention of Knox, who happened to be walking by. He let himself into the room quietly.

Isla pressed her hand to her head, a dull ache starting in her temples. Without acknowledging Knox, she said to Sam, "it's not my news to share, and it wasn't Emma's either."

"Emma said she's going to get an abortion," he said, his voice cracking with emotion.

Isla glanced at Knox; his eyes widened slightly as he understood. She turned back to Sam. "Priya made me promise I wouldn't tell anyone — especially not you. I couldn't betray her. You don't know what she's like when she is mad! There's no in-between with her: either you're on her side, or you're the enemy. She needs people in her life to support her."

"*I* am that person," insisted Sam. "I am the person that should be supporting her."

Isla shook her head. "Not if she doesn't want you to be."

"What am I supposed to do? Walk away and pretend like none of this is happening? I can't do that! Do you think I should be cut out of this?"

"No of course not—" Isla's voice cracked.

"She hasn't returned a text or a phone call in over a week. What should I do?"

Isla shrugged her shoulders and sighed. "She's off today. I guess you could try going to our apartment. But she's going to be pissed."

"I won't mention we talked," said Sam.

"Sam — she's scared, even though she'd never admit it. And when she's scared or upset, she aggressively cuts people out of her life. I don't know what to do, but I don't want her to end up alone."

Sam startled when he saw Knox. He hadn't realised he was there. "I'm gone for the day."

Knox nodded and patted Sam's back as he left. Isla started toward the door, but Knox closed it before she could leave.

"Wow," he said quietly, taking a step closer to her. "Are you okay?"

She shook her head, tears welling in her eyes. "This is a mess, and I don't know what the right thing to do is."

Knox moved to touch her shoulder, but someone was coming down the hall, so he dropped his hand to his side. "Is there anything I can do?"

Isla slid down the back of the door until she was sitting on the floor. "Can you count to sixty?"

He slid down next to her and started. "One, two—"

Isla wrapped her arms around her knees, bowed her head, and cried.

"—- fifty-eight, fifty-nine, sixty," finished Knox.

Isla lifted her head, took a deep breath, and wiped her face with the back of her hand.

Knox moved a bit closer and asked, "should I keep counting?"

Isla sighed and leaned her head back against the door. Finally, she turned to him, "We should get back—"

"We can stay a bit longer," he replied.

"Okay." Isla leaned her head on his shoulder. "Count to sixty again."

Andrew came into the house from the garage. He was hungry and tired, and not prepared for the scene that lay before him. He looked around the kitchen, confused. Dishes, toys, and clothes were strewn around. The milk was out, and it had soured after spending the day on the counter. He saw the breakfast dishes on the table, and no signs of lunch dishes.

"Emma?" he called; silence was his answer.

Then he heard a call: "da-da da-da" coming from upstairs. He found Liam in his crib, playing with some toys. He had a full diaper, but was in good spirits.

"Emma?" he called again as he changed Liam's diaper. He could hear voices coming from their bedroom. He knocked before entering. Emma was lying on her side, back to the door. She was still in her pyjamas, an empty bag of ketchup chips and the laptop perched beside her with a movie playing.

"Babe, what's going on?" asked Andrew.

Emma didn't respond.

Liam started screeching.

"He's hungry," murmured Emma, still not moving.

"Let's go get a snack," said Andrew. "What should I give him?"

"I don't effing care!"

Andrew stared at his wife's back in disbelief. In the thirteen years he had known her, he had never heard her swear. Ever. Not even fake swears. And for all of Liam's eleven and a half months on earth, Andrew had never fed him anything without Emma's supervision.

Andrew carried his son downstairs, placed him in the highchair, and opened the fridge. Pickings were sparse, no fruit except an abandoned lime that had grown brown and shrivelled. He dug in the pantry and found some soda crackers, and filled a sippy cup with water because milk wasn't an option. Then he called a local pizza chain and ordered a large pepperoni with extra mushrooms. What was going on? He knew Emma had been struggling the last couple months, but this worried him. How long had Liam been in his crib?

After Liam had had his fill of soda crackers, Andrew carried him back upstairs and put Liam on the bed. He immediately crawled over to Emma, wanting to nurse.

"No!" Emma snapped.

Liam started to cry as she pushed him toward Andrew and turned her back towards them.

"Emma, what is going on?" Andrew barked in frustration.

"Leave me alone."

"I ordered a pizza," he said.

"Good for you," she snapped.

Andrew stood up and lifted Liam on his hip. With all the grace he could muster, he asked, "can I bring you anything?"

Emma didn't reply. Silent tears rolled down her face as she heard the bedroom door close.

Andrew paid for the pizza and cut small pieces for Liam, who shoved them in his mouth as fast as his two teeth would let him. Andrew picked at his piece and considered the situation he found himself in. Should he call someone? Isla? His mom? His mother-in-law? Something told him bringing in outside opinions wasn't going to help the situation. He noticed the house was in need of cleaning; the dried-up rice and peas on the floor were from five days ago, and dirty dishes lined the counters until there wasn't any space left.

When had this become normal? Yesterday they had spaghetti, then he had gone to practise, and beers after with Knox and Sam. The night before? He had worked in his office, catching up on emails. Emma always seemed to have everything under control.

Andrew put Liam to bed and tried to enter his own room, only to find he was locked out.

"Emma?" he knocked.

No answer.

Andrew felt sick to his stomach.

He returned to the main floor, and he did the dishes and rewashed the load of laundry that smelled like it had curled up and died in the washer. He started putting toys away, at first worried whether he was doing it right, but after awhile he didn't care. Emma and her stupid systems! What did she expect, anyway? He couldn't read her mind; how was he supposed to know which toy went where? How was he supposed to know what her problem was if she wouldn't talk to him?

44.

February 22. Big, fluffy snowflakes, -3C°.

Priya could feel the heat seep out of the water. She had turned the faucet warmer three times, but eventually she was going to have to get out of the shower and face the day. Her appointment was in two hours, and she had managed to avoid Sam for three days since Emma had ruined everything. Just thinking about her made Priya want to hit something. Maybe she should take up kick boxing, she thought, closing her eyes and imagining kicking a bag with Emma's face on it.

She sat on the tub's edge with the towel wrapped loosely around her and let herself drip dry. This was the most still she had been in the last three weeks. She sat until she could feel her throat constricting. Time to move again.

With the towel wrapped around her hair and her robe around her body, she stepped out of the bathroom and was surprised to see Sam on the couch.

"Where's Isla?" Priya demanded.

"She had a meeting this morning." Sam answered calmly, determined not to be drawn into an argument. He was there and wasn't going to leave.

Priya marched into her room and slammed the door.

"*Priya let me explain—*" started Isla over the phone.

"What the hell is Sam doing here?" Priya screamed.

"*What else was I supposed to do? He wants to be there for you—*"

"First Emma, now you? Why won't you listen to me? Let me deal with it my way. I'm going to call a cab. I don't need you. I don't need anyone."

"*Bullshit.*"

"Go to hell."

"*I know you're mad at Emma and me, but Sam deserves to be part of this.*"

"Emma did exactly what I knew she would do. I expected her to betray me. I thought I could trust you."

"*Trust me to do what, exactly? Not do what's best for you? You need people around you, despite what you think. You can't do this by yourself. We all care about you too much to let that happen.*"

"Sam's going to want to keep it."

"*You don't know that! Have you talked to him?*"

Priya hung up and threw her phone across the room. It hit the door with a thud and fell to the floor. Priya sighed. She would never really end her friendship with Isla. No one knew her as well as Isla and still liked her.

Sam heard the conversation through the paper-thin walls. Things were going about as well as he expected. He remained on the couch, working on his laptop, until it was time to go.

Priya walked out of her room, dressed and stone-faced. Sam looked up from his laptop and said, "I don't want you to do this by yourself."

"But you don't want me to do this?" she challenged.

He paused. "I didn't think you cared what I want?"

"Do you want me to terminate this pregnancy?" she demanded.

"Honestly, no," he said. "But I'm not here to change your mind. I want to be here, for you and for the baby."

"Fetus."

"Fetus," he said.

She knew she was going to have to go with him, they wouldn't let her come to the appointment without someone responsible to take care of her and bring her home. That didn't mean she liked it, or she was going to talk. He followed her out the door and opened the passenger side of his car for her. She got in silently.

Sam found a parking spot across from the clinic. But Priya didn't get out of the car. Instead, she stared out the passenger window. Snowflakes lazily floated by, resting on the window before melting. She stared at the snowflakes, frozen.

Three songs played on the radio before either of them spoke.

"We should go if we are going to go," he said.

It was supposed to be simple, a quick in-and-out. But she couldn't convince her legs to move. Of course, this was the best option. It was the *only* option, wasn't it?

"Priya?" asked Sam tenderly. "What do you want to do? What do you want right now, in this moment? If you go in, I go with you. If you stay, I stay with you."

She was barely twelve weeks pregnant. She could still come back. She didn't have to decide yet. She still had time. "I'm hungry."

"Yeah, me too," replied Sam, holding his breath. "What would you like to eat?"

"I want a cheeseburger."

Exhaling, Sam smiled and turned the car back on. "Cheeseburgers, coming right up."

They got cheeseburgers and returned to Priya's apartment. Sam walked her to the door. "I am going to be here for you. Anything you want — cheeseburgers at three in the morning? I'll come. I promise."

He took a step towards her. He wanted to kiss her, but he would've settled for a hug. Priya shook her head slightly. Sam stepped back. Message received.

Priya slowly walked up the stairs, fighting back tears. For the first time in her life, she didn't know what to do next. All she knew was nothing would ever be the same again.

45.

March 10. Sunny and breezy, 4C°.

Their house was fuller than usual for a Sunday lunch. Bill had cooked up Liam's favourite meal, macaroni, and cheese, with a buffet of more adult-friendly toppings: bacon, pickled jalapenos, roasted cherry tomatoes. The dining table was extended to accommodate the extra guests. There was also a bucket full of ice with beer and gourmet sodas on the side table. They rarely had alcohol or pop at lunch, but on this occasion, Dee had insisted. It's not everyday your only grandchild turns one.

Isla and Priya were the first to arrive. Thrilled with the bucket of drinks. they helped themselves and sprawled out on the lumpy, mismatched couches. Bill was struck by the passage of time; they could've been ten years younger, doing the same thing.

Emma and Andrew arrived with Liam dressed in his birthday outfit, tiny skinny jeans and a black t-shirt with a stylized one on it. Emma had bought it months ago. She used to dream about his party, balloons, cake smash with a cute backdrop, and a professional photographer. But now that it had arrived, she felt nothing. She hadn't even thought about it until Bill called last week and insisted on hosting so she wouldn't have to worry about the details and cleaning. Emma had hung up the phone and shrunk to the floor and wept. It wouldn't live up to her dreams, but at least he'd get a party. That night in front of Andrew she'd made a big deal about how his parents insisted, and wasn't that just like his mom to want to take over. She didn't know why gratitude was so hard.

When Gerald and Sarah arrived, they sucked all the lightheartedness out of the room. Dee offered them a beer, just to revel in their disapproval.

The final guests, Sam and Knox, were the ones Bill was most curious about. He'd heard so much about them but had yet to meet them. Isla jumped up to get the door. She found two nervous-looking young men, with a gift wrapped in a shopping bag. It was a book about fire trucks, and they had spent thirty minutes debating about it at the bookstore.

Knox handed the gift to Emma with a slight bow and apology. "We've never been to a baby's birthday before."

Bill could tell Emma was touched. Her eyes shone for a moment.

Bill had three tasks to perform that afternoon: stop Dee from picking a fight with Gerald, make sure the food was perfect, and get to know these two young men. Knox, whom his daughter seemed to be quite fond of. And Sam, well Bill didn't know what to think about Sam. Priya was like a daughter to him, and this unexpected pregnancy had shaken everyone. But he knew his only role was to offer support no matter what was needed.

Lunch managed to be diplomatic, with everyone on their best behaviour, although some best behaviour was better than others. Bill watched his wife fight to keep her mouth shut, biting hard on her lip every time Gerald spoke up.

Isla was crawling out of her skin with nerves. Bill could appreciate that having Knox in her parent's house was a complicated thing. Knox and Sam, on the other hand, had warmed up instantly and were now completely comfortable, enjoying comradery with

Andrew — a comradery that seemed to be lacking between Priya, Isla, and Emma.

After lunch was finished, Andrew offered up the cake that Sara had made, dates and black beans masquerading as chocolate. Once the leftover cake had been sufficiently hidden under napkins, Dee offered everyone coffee with Irish cream, creating the desired effect: Gerald and Sara's hasty departure.

"You shouldn't antagonise them so much," Bill had admonished Dee as they waved goodbye.

Isla offered to do dishes, and no one was surprised when Knox volunteered to dry. After the flurry of food being put away and dishes being stacked, Knox and Isla found themselves alone in the kitchen.

They created a comfortable rhythm; she'd clean each plate and put it in the rack, he'd dry and stack it in the cupboard. It was the first time Isla was grateful that her parents didn't have a dishwasher.

Then he snapped her with his damp towel.

"Ouch!" she yelped.

He laughed self-consciously. "Sorry! I didn't mean to do it that hard."

"I'm going to have a welt!"

He took her arm in his hand and bent over to look at it more closely.

"Should I kiss it better?" he asked, off handed. Then realising what he said, he dropped her arm and picked up the next dish.

Isla forgot how to breathe as she picked up a stoneware serving dish from the eighties and shoved it under the soapy water. Now or never, she thought.

"What are you doing tonight?" *Was that calm enough, or did I sound maniacal?*

He answered, "Probably the same thing I do every Sunday night: order in, answer emails, call Graham and Max."

"Uh-huh," Isla said, nodding furiously as if those were fascinating, riveting plans.

Knox lifted the serving dish she had just finished and turned to her. "What are your plans for tonight?"

Isla felt his eyes on her but wouldn't look up to meet them. *Play it cool,* she told herself.

"Priya and I have tickets for the New Lightweights concert tonight, but she's pretty tired so—" she faltered, and closed her eyes for a mini pep talk. *Take courage.* "So I thought – wondered – if maybe we could go together? You and me. Like, on a date?"

She opened her eyes and finally looked at him. He dried a dish, face passive.

Quickly Isla continued, "Or as friends! Or, you know, work colleagues, or not go at all—"

He watched her intently, his lips pursed. She couldn't tell if he was deciding how to let her down easily, or holding back a smile.

"Aren't you going to say something?" she demanded.

Then his face broke into an easy grin. "Not yet. I'm really enjoying each shade of red your face turns."

She shoved him off balance. As he took a step back to balance himself, he grabbed her wrists and leaned forward slightly, "You and me on a date, eh?" he asked as his hands moved to her palms then intertwined his finger into hers. "That sound's like a good idea."

Isla stomach flipped, as his eyes glanced down at her lips.

"I am going to kiss you now, is that all right?" he asked.

When Isla nodded, he let go of her hands, and leaned in closer. His index finger traced the bridge of her nose all the way down to her lips. "Your freckles slay me." His finger then slid past her lips to the tip of her chin, which he lifted and kissed her lips lightly. "I've thought about this moment for a long time."

Isla stood on her tip toes and wrapped her arms around his neck. "You could've done something about it."

"I couldn't." His arms wrapped around her waist. "Did you forget? You have a harassment complaint against me."

"Oh yeah–right. I guess that complicates things."

"I couldn't risk being shut down again. Professionally or quite frankly, my self-confidence."

"So you were just going to wait for me to be brave enough to make a move?"

"Took you long enough—" This time when he leaned in to kiss her, she met him halfway.

Momentarily, they forgot where they were, in the heart of the home Isla had grown up in. The kitchen where she had made cookies and stirred soup. The room where she had thrown a water glass at her brother after he called her moody (it missed him and shattered all over the stove).

"It's about fucking time, you two."

Go away, Priya, thought Isla as they separated sheepishly.

"You're never going to finish the dishes at that rate."

"You're welcome to take over!" Knox leaned easily against the counter.

"The engineer, lawyer, and computer programmer seem to need your help putting together a toddler toy," said Priya, pointing to the family room where everyone else had retired.

"Yes ma'am," he said, with a mock salute. He tweaked Isla's elbow and headed out the doorway.

Priya stopped him. "You break her heart, I'll destroy you."

"Oh, I know," he said gravely.

Once he was safely downstairs, Priya turned to Isla. "I guess I'm out a ticket for the show tonight?"

Isla squealed and pumped her fists in the air as she danced in a circle.

"Way to play it cool," Priya said. "So I'm stuck giving Sam a ride home."

Isla stopped her happy dance. "Like that's a hardship! You seem to be getting along fine — otherwise you would've been home Friday night."

"We slept together, that's allowed!"

Isla gave Priya a questioning look.

"We are having a baby," said Priya. "I think."

"You think?"

Priya shook her head, "I don't know, we have a few more weeks before we have to decide."

"Why won't you admit that you're in love with him."

Priya glared at her. "I'm not in love with him."

"Why not?"

That's a good question, thought Priya as she deftly changed the subject. She picked up Knox's discarded towel and changed the subject again. "I'm worried about Emma."

"You are?" asked Isla.

"She's lost a lot of weight and seems really detached. When was the last time you saw her without make up? Even when we visited her at the hospital when Liam was born, she had mascara and lip gloss on. She's not taking care of herself."

Isla thought back to the recent times she had spent with Emma, her messy hair, and clothes hanging off her. Everything had seemed just a little bit off, but she hadn't been able to identify why. "What should we do?"

"She needs to see a doctor. I talked to Andrew; he seemed pretty overwhelmed."

"Why don't you talk to her?"

"No," said Priya. "I'm still angry."

"Angry or hurt?"

Priya glared at Isla. "I have a lot going on. You and Andy can handle it. She needs to see a doctor — and maybe try and convince her to see a counsellor. Also, keep her away from her parents. All the gaslighting and guilt-tripping can't be good for her."

Isla turned to look at Priya. "It's almost like you care."

"Of course I care! I'm graduating in two months. I have to swear an oath to do no harm! This isn't personal, it's professional. I personally still hate her."

"Hate is pretty harsh. You're here, aren't you?"

"And miss you finally asking Knox out? Not a chance. Besides, Bill is a damn good cook." Priya took the last pot out of the sink and dried it with her damp towel. "Promise me you will try to talk to her."

Isla nodded.

"But first, have fun tonight. Don't do anything I wouldn't do."

"So, getting pregnant is acceptable?"

"Ha. I want you to have fun, and not be nervous."

"I'm not nervous. I *was*, but now I feel good, like something in the universe aligned."

"Like some magical correction in the space time continuum?" said Priya, raising her eyebrows. "god, you're delusional sometimes."

"And yet you insist on being my friend."

"Someone's got to keep you in reality."

Emma stood at Liam's crib patting his tummy. He was asleep, but she wanted to make sure he stayed that way. And she hoped that the longer she took, the more likely Andrew would get into a movie, so she'd have an excuse to go to bed alone.

He had said something unexpected and strange in the car on the way home from his parents.

"Do you have a one-year appointment with your doctor?"

"Liam had one last week," she'd responded.

"What about you? Do they do one for you, too?"

"No, why would they?" Didn't he know anything?

"What if something was wrong?"

"Nothing is wrong" she'd snapped.

He hadn't pursued it, but it had shaken Emma. Because something was definitely wrong.

Of *course* something was wrong, but she didn't need to see a doctor, she needed to buck up, be thankful, get back in the habit of exercising! She needed some will power, a glass of water, and some sleep.

When Liam was asleep, he looked like the beautiful baby they had brought home from the hospital. Not a one-year-old. Tears welled up in her eyes. She hated this time of night so much. He'd fall asleep, and she'd pray fervently that he'd stay that way. Inevitably, in two hours he'd be up, inconsolable. And the cycle would continue until six, when he'd be up for the day. Emma would hear him playing in his crib happily, because he'd spent the night exactly how he wanted, in the arms of his mother.

Emma tip-toed out the door.

"How did he go down?"

Emma was so startled that she clamped her hands over her mouth so she wouldn't scream. Andrew was standing outside Liam's room, waiting for her.

"Can we talk?" he asked.

Emma started down the hallway to their bedroom. "I'm really tired, and Liam's going to be up at midnight."

She hoped he'd give up, but she didn't give her husband enough credit. He wasn't going to be deterred.

"It's important." He followed her and sat on the unmade bed.

"Fine," she said, intensely searching her drawer, looking for the perfect pyjamas.

"Can we please talk about what is going on?" he said quietly. "I know something is the matter and you won't talk to me."

"Nothing is the matter," she said, raising her voice.

"Yes, something is. The house is a mess, we've eaten frozen pizza and canned spaghetti for weeks now, you don't go out of the house, ever. And you don't talk to your friends—"

"My friends hate me," she interrupted.

"They don't hate you, Emma. They're worried about you. I'm worried about you. You're not yourself anymore."

"Not *myself* anymore? What does that even mean? Because the house is a mess? Is that all you like about me, that I clean your house?"

"Our house."

"Your house! Your money pays for it!"

Andrew gaped at her in disbelief. "Emma, what is going on?"

Emma couldn't take it anymore. All the fight dissolved. She looked at her husband, her Andy, with his brown eyes and dirty glasses, and held back the pain that rose in her chest. But it was too big, and had been pushed down for too long. She collapsed on the floor in a heap, her face in her hands. "I can't do this anymore. I hate being trapped here every day! I hate this house, I hate you for being able to leave, I hate being a mom. I'm so bad at it! I thought I'd be a good mom, but I'm not. I'm a complete failure."

Andrew rushed to her and wrapped his arms around her, pulling her into his lap. Quietly he said, "it's ok, Emmy, it's ok."

When they were kids, he would tease her by calling her Emmy. She pretended to hate it only to prolong their conversations, only to make sure the next time they saw each other in the hall, he'd have something to say to her.

"I have these moments that I—" she faltered, unsure she'd be able to admit how bad things had actually gotten, unsure of how he'd react. "I have trouble breathing and then I throw up sometimes."

"You're throwing up?" said Andrew, alarmed.

Emma melted into his arms which were still wrapped tightly around her, keeping her from falling. *Maybe she had said too much? This is gross. She didn't want Andrew to think poorly of her.*

"Every day?" he asked, still not deterred.

She was scared, but something had to change. And something about how Andrew tenderly stroked her back gave her courage. She felt something different, as a huge sob rose in her, was it relief? Tears fell down her face as the dam broke. "Not every day. I'm nauseous nearly all the time. I struggle to eat much. I've been making decisions about what to eat based on how it tastes coming back up. And for a moment I feel better, but then the whole world crashes down on me and I'm back here, stuck, miserable and completely unable to do anything about it."

"Why didn't you tell me? Or anyone?"

"I did." She sucked in a ragged breath. "I talked to my mom. She told me to stop feeling sorry for myself and to turn my feelings into gratitude. She gave me a list of a thousand things to be grateful for and told me to pray every day."

Andrew had some choice words planned for his mother-in-law. "Did it help?"

Emma shook her head. "I don't think God cares about me or my gratitude. If he cared, he'd make Liam sleep, wouldn't he? The more I pray, the more I don't even believe in God anymore."

"The God I believe in doesn't require gratitude as payment for suffering," said Andrew softly.

"I'm so scared" she said. "I don't want this life anymore. I have everything I ever wanted, the exact life I've always dreamed of! And all I want is — out."

"Out?" replied Andrew. Fear grabbed him. "What do you mean, 'out'?"

"I don't want to feel like this anymore, like a complete failure. Like garbage."

"You're not garbage. Look at me" he said. "You are not a failure and I love you."

He stared into her eyes until she couldn't take the intimacy of it anymore and turned away.

"Priya wants you to see a doctor. She wouldn't recommend that if she thought it was a personality flaw."

Emma started crying again.

"She took me aside today. She thinks you might be depressed, and you should see a doctor. This isn't something you need to beat yourself up about. It might be something outside of your control – and we can do something about it."

Those words broke something open in Emma. What if these feelings really were something she couldn't fix through prayer or happy thoughts? What if they were out of her control?

She felt a glimmer of hope for the first time in months.

46.
March 15. Windy, 8C°.

Bored, Isla sat cross-legged on the floor in Andrew and Emma's family room. Liam was content playing by himself if his auntie sat right beside him, watching — not reading, not drawing, not scrolling her phone. She tried to drive one of his vehicles, to join in his play, but quickly got the message that she was doing it wrong. She glanced at her phone. It was nearly seven and she was starving. Knox said he was going to bring food, but he had texted that he was running late.

Ignoring her hunger, Isla lay down and allowed Liam to drive over her with his garbage truck. She remembered their date — their first real date. The concert itself was fantastic, and standing next to him had made everything magic. She loved how her hand felt in his, fingers intertwined, a connection that announced to everyone, *he's with me.*

The last kiss goodnight, on her doorstep in the cool March weather, had sustained her through the busy week. They had decided to keep it (whatever the undefined *it* was), a secret at the office. It was his idea, Isla agreed. Office gossip would be far more damaging for him than her, anyway.

Tonight, they had offered to babysit for Emma and Andrew. Andrew had taken a week of sick days and they managed to get Emma in to see a doctor and to line up some counselling appointments. Andrew hoped doing something fun would be a good way to finish off a difficult week. Emma looked exhausted when Isla arrived, but was game for an evening out.

Andrew had written the list of what to do for Isla; it was short, compared to the lists Isla had seen Emma write. So far, she had fed Liam some mashed spaghetti and squash. Next up: bath time.

Isla's stomach growled. She hoped Knox would show up soon.

She gave herself the same pep talk she had been giving herself all week. *Don't rush in; play it cool.* Once, she had been told that she was too much, too soon, and it had stuck with her for years because she knew it was true. Her natural inclination was to rush in and smother with her feelings and actions. Love was easy for her; restraint was the difficulty.

Finally, the doorbell rang. Isla scooped Liam up in her arms and they answered the door together. Knox handed her a bag of groceries.

"What is this?" Isla asked looking inside and seeing a tomato, an onion, some raw sausage, and a bag of frozen shrimp.

"Supper," Knox said, juggling another bag and a bottle of red wine.

"These are groceries."

Knox gave her a sideways look and said, "—to cook supper with."

Isla's stomach collapsed with hunger.

"Are you hungry?"

She nodded.

"I'm sorry I'm late. I should've ordered in, but I really wanted to cook for you. This will only take an hour or so."

"An hour? I need food now!" she said, showing him to the kitchen. She dug around to find some crackers and cheese. She offered a cracker to Liam, as he sat on the counter next to her. "I didn't know you could cook."

"Shouldn't every person over the age of thirteen know how to cook?" he asked, raising an eyebrow.

"Knowing how to cook is different than wanting to, and being good at it. And for your information, neither of those things applies to me."

Knox laughed. "I've met the female role model in your life so that doesn't surprise me. My mom taught me. She didn't want to send me into the world useless and pampered like my father."

"Well, I'm not useless or pampered, but I could get used to someone cooking for me."

Knox got to work, sautéing onions and sausage. Isla gave Liam a bath and then prepared his bottle and read him three books. Once Liam was tucked tight in his crib, Isla ventured back to the kitchen, where Knox poured her a glass a wine and indicated to the stool at the island.

Isla sat, sighed, and took a big sip. Knox checked his pot, the heavenly smells of paprika, garlic and peppers wafted through the kitchen.

"You look tired," he said.

"—and hungry," she replied. "How does anyone take care of a baby, like all day? It is simultaneously stressful and boring."

Knox opened a couple cupboards before giving Isla a quizzical look. she pointed to the cupboard with plates; Knox retrieved two and scooped out two portions of the fragrant Jambalaya. He headed to the living room. Isla took her glass and followed him.

"Emma wouldn't approve of us eating in the living room," she said, dropping into the leather couch.

Knox stopped. "Oh, we could—" he indicated back to the kitchen.

"We'll be careful and clean up before they get home. We have until nine or so; besides, you promised to watch my favourite movie."

They settled into the sofa, plates on the coffee table.

"Oh my god, this is so good!" Isla exclaimed.

"You had doubts?" Knox responded.

"I'll never doubt you again."

Knox was bored by the movie. He was tired and didn't feel like reading subtitles, but his basic French kept the storyline going while he closed his eyes, dozing off here and there. What he really wanted was to kiss Isla. He leaned over and crept his fingers from her right shoulder across the back of her neck. She giggled and resisted just long enough to make it interesting for him. He turned her face towards his, pressing his lips to hers while she adjusted herself to him. It didn't take long for them to lose themselves in the feel of lips, hands, and bodies.

"Wait!" Isla cried.

Surprised, he pushed himself on to his forearms, taking his weight off her body.

"We can't miss this scene, it's my favourite," Isla said, scrambling up from under him and righting herself back on the couch. He slowly righted himself, and watched her watch her favourite scene.

After a while, he stood up and collected their dishes. He kissed her on the forehead and said, "nothing was going to happen; it's your brother's couch."

Isla sat pinned to the couch. Great it was their second date and already she had done the wrong thing, why was she so bad at this? Was navigating romantic relationships easy for other people? She picked up their glasses and entered the kitchen.

"I'm really sorry," she said. "The whole thing on the couch, and stopping — I don't think I can do casual," she blurted, slamming the glasses on the counter harder than necessary.

Knox stood up from the dishwasher as she fidgeted and paced, obviously grappling with what to say. The whole uncomfortable conversation played out on her face before the words even came out of her mouth.

"I mean, I don't want *us* to be casual," she said. "I thought I should clarify my expectations before anything else — um, before we proceed."

Isla braced herself for the inevitable broken heart. She had hoped they could have fun for a little bit longer before forcing the issue, but here they were. In her brother's kitchen, cleaning dishes, barely a week in.

It had been fun while it lasted.

"Did I say or do something to make you think I want something casual?" he asked, taking the glasses and finding a spot in the dishwasher.

"I don't know, maybe when you wanted to hook up last summer—" she retorted.

"Are you trying to pick a fight with me?" he asked, sincerely confused. "Last summer was a different thing altogether. I know you well enough now that I would never agree to go out with you if I didn't want to actually be with you."

"Oh." Isla relaxed a tiny bit.

"I don't know what the right word is — relationship? Whatever it is, I'm all in." Knox closed the dishwasher and came around the island until they were standing face to face. "Do you think I'm angry about what just happened?"

Isla nodded, embarrassed. "I don't think I'm ready to have—"

"—have you ever?"

"Yeah — with Michael. But it was always complicated, and if I tried to talk to him about it, it would be even weirder. Sometimes we'd even fight."

Knox dropped down to a stool so they could see each other eye to eye. He grabbed her hands and shook his head in disbelief. "I can't believe you put up with him for as long as you did."

"I was so in love with an idealized romantic future, one that I had imagined for so long. I ignored how miserable our present was," Isla said. "I don't want to do that again."

"You've always told me exactly what you think and feel about me. I don't want that to change. I'll listen. Please don't pretend something is fine or good if it isn't." Knox brought her hand to his lips and kissed her fingers one at a time, index, middle, ring, then pinky. "I'm willing to wait as long as you need. Besides, I'm nervous too."

"Why are *you* nervous?"

"I've never been with someone like this before, someone I really care about. I've got my own list of baggage and issues — I don't want to mess this up either. We can take as long as we want to figure things out."

47.
March 17. Raining, 14C°.

Graham settled into his favourite chair in the living room. Sunday mornings were his favourite. He'd make love to his wife before she headed to mass, then pour himself a large mug of coffee with a splash of Irish cream and read his Sunday papers, one at a time, until she returned. As he leafed through the financial section, his favourite notification dinged on his phone.

The group chat with Violet, Knox, and Max. It took Knox moving halfway across the country and Violet moving into dorms for Graham to truly embrace texting. Up until then, he'd exclusively used his phone for voice calls.

Knox had sent a selfie of his and Isla's grinning faces. They were cozied up next to each other, and though cut out of the frame, Knox's arm was clearly around her waist.

Violet replied immediately. *"WHAT IS THIS? WE NEED DETAILS!"*

She's yelling, thought Graham; he had been schooled in text etiquette enough to know that.

Max replied before he could even formulate a response. *"Beautiful, but an explanation please??"*

286

Graham's chubby thumbs couldn't keep up with his thoughts, so he hit the video chat button. This was too important to text.

Decline

Decline

Decline

"At mass!"

"At brunch!"

Then, finally, Knox's bubble appeared, typing.

All three held their breath in anticipation.

"I'll call tonight."

Was that it?

"NOT GOOD ENOUGH" yelled Violet's icon.

"We're waiting with anticipation," wrote Max.

"Yup," Graham managed to type.

Knox's typing bubble came up again.

Graham waited and waited. *Maybe it's like waiting for a pot to boil*, he thought, turning his attention back to the paper.

Ding.

"Isla and I are together."

Violet immediately sent five or six of those short video loops — *what were they called again?* thought Graham, *jiffies?* Each of them had someone cheering: a woman in the street, a toddler pumping his fist in the air, a crowd doing the wave.

Graham managed a happy face before Max said exactly what he wanted to say: *"Lovely, she seems like a wonderful woman. When did it happen? Is this a casual thing or more serious?"*

"Can we tell people?" asked Graham.

Nothing.

"You asked too many questions — scared him off," wrote Violet.

Finally, Knox responded. *"Chill out, it's all good! I'll call tonight. Don't tell anyone."*

Too late.

Graham had already forwarded the picture to Sue with an *FYI*. He quickly followed up with *"Please don't tell him I told you"*. He shut off his phone and leaned back with satisfaction, his heart bursting. Moments like this, he was so grateful he got to be a stand-in parent. Sudden grief crashed on him like an unexpected wave. He was overwhelmed by the need to talk to Ken. He missed his friend.

Today on the lunch menu: al pastor tacos, rich flavorful meat with all the toppings one could find in the middle of a long winter. The avocados weren't perfect, neither the tomatoes, but the slow cooked meat made up for the lack of seasonality.

Liam sat in the second-hand highchair Bill had found at a recent trip to MCC. It didn't exactly scream up-to-safety-standards, but it allowed Liam his own spot at the lunch table. He sat with a tray of unfamiliar food in front of him, picking at the tortilla shell. The avocado was a hit; the tomato was not.

Andrew and Dee were deep into it over healthcare cuts and infrastructure costs.

Politics: the first thing a proper family would avoid talking about.

Isla figured religion was right around the corner.

"The infrastructure is crumbling! What if a bridge collapses? Then what?" Said her brother.

"Well, at least frontline workers will be around to help the injured. The only option is to raise taxes on the rich." Replied her mother.

"That sounds good in theory, but not in action. We need to cut back on bureaucracy. Do you know how many people I have to report to?"

"Cuts always end up hurting frontline workers, nurses, EMTs—"

Bill leaned over and touched Isla's hand; she tipped her head toward him. "They'll go on forever. What should we change the subject to?"

"Pastor Tom's interpretation of the text this morning?" Isla joked. "I don't know, I don't mind listening to them. At least I'm not part of the argument. Let Mom fight with Andrew for once."

Liam threw some tomato on the floor and Emma startled out of her thoughts. She got up to grab a cloth, murmuring, "we don't throw food."

Liam threw some meat on the floor for good measure.

"Liam!" scolded Emma when she returned. "Andrew, could you do something with your son?"

Suddenly the focus turned from budget cuts to the baby, who was munching on tortilla and systematically throwing every bit of meat and tomato he could find on the floor.

"I guess he doesn't like the meat," said Andrew.

"Make him try it," Emma huffed. "He needs protein."

"If I remember correctly, it's perfectly normal for kids to throw food on the floor. He's learning about gravity! We don't mind cleaning up when he is done," said Dee.

Emma sat down with the same straight empty face she had on earlier, not angry or sad, but not happy, either.

"So, Isla, you and Knox left the party *together* last Sunday... Do you have anything to tell us?" asked Dee.

Isla blushed as the whole table turned to stare at her. "I can't believe it took you that long to ask."

"I can't believe you didn't offer anything," replied Andrew.

Isla was trying to seem nonchalant. She caught her dad's eye; he was beaming.

"Is he your boyfriend now?" Dee asked directly.

"Yeah, I guess so—" she finished her sentence with a shrug.

"You guess so?" questioned Dee. "Maybe you should clarify that?"

"Yes, he is," replied Isla with more confidence.

"I feel weird about it. Do you think he hung out with me to get to you?" pondered Andrew earnestly.

"Are you kidding me, Andy?" Isla laughed as she gestured to Emma. "Like when Emma would walk six blocks out of her way to our house so you could give us *cough cough* her a ride to school? Honestly, I wouldn't know what that feels like."

289

"That was different!"

"How was that different? Emma was my friend first, but if it makes you feel any better, I think he genuinely likes spending time with you. I don't know why, but he seems to."

"Stop it, you two," said Dee. "How does Liam feel about Uncle Knox?"

Isla rolled her eyes.

"Liam likes him just fine. He's one year old, he likes everyone. He thinks the garbage man is his best friend," said Emma.

"The garbage man!" Dee laughed as if this was the funniest thing she'd ever heard.

"How will your relationship affect things at the office?" Bill spoke up for the first time.

Isla chewed on her lip. "We're going to try to keep it a secret. I think if people knew, it would be pretty awkward. So far, so good."

"Does your health plan cover birth control? If it doesn't, your father and I can help you out."

Everyone at the table froze. Emma's mouth dropped open; Andrew looked like he'd forgotten how to swallow; Bill's face turned red.

"*Mother!*" screeched Isla.

Silence fell. Bill downed a full glass of water.

They'd thought religion was right around the corner, but they'd thought wrong. It was sex.

48.

March 19. Turning cold again, −6C°

Emma was shown into the most perfect room she had ever inhabited. It was cozy without being sloppy, colourful without being loud, warm without feeling forced. Behind her entered Alice. Alice her new counsellor. Alice the one who was going to fix her.

Emma had gotten dressed in real clothes: a buttoned, collared shirt that used to be her favourite. Now, she felt uncomfortable in her own skin — how was she expected to feel comfortable in anything?

Andrew had made all the arrangements. He had driven her there and would be waiting when she emerged, in one hour.

She'd be fixed then, right?

"What would you like to talk about?" asked Alice, her face warm and passive.

"I don't know. What should I talk about?" responded Emma. She was edgy and suspicious, and she didn't know why. Maybe it was Alice's passive, open face, like her mother's face. Even when she was angry, Sara's face rarely expressed anything.

Alice waited comfortably. She was used to silence and knew most people started talking because they grew uncomfortable with it.

"Do you believe in abortion?"

291

That caught Alice off guard, although it wasn't the most outrageous opening comment she had ever heard. "I don't think abortion is something that requires belief. It's something that happens. Why would you like to talk about abortion?"

"My friends are really irresponsible."

Alice waited. So far, she wasn't following the train of thought, but she understood the process.

"My friend Priya got pregnant by her secret lover." Emma used air quotes with the word *secret*.

Disheartened, Emma took a deep breath and started over again. "My parents used to take me to pro-life rallies when I was a kid. We'd stand around with candles and yell – 'abortion is murder!' Over and over until we were hoarse."

Emma paused and closed her eyes; she was brought right back to those feelings of fear and confusion. Why was everyone so angry? "I called my best friend a murderer, and then betrayed her and told the father about the baby. And I don't know why I did it. I guess I thought I was doing the right thing. As soon as I heard the word 'abortion,' something took over my body. I became judgemental and parroted all the things my parents taught me."

"Do you still think it was the right thing to do?"

"I don't know. Actually I'm fairly sure it was wrong of me to tell Sam — the father — but Priya is keeping the baby now, I think. We haven't exactly talked since. I think I've broken something beyond repair."

"Do you feel regret?"

"I don't know. That's the problem, I don't know anything anymore. I don't trust myself. I don't trust my thoughts or ideas. What if everything I think or believe is from my parents, or husband or friends. Do I think abortion is wrong? I have no idea. I hadn't given it any thought until my dad's voice took over and I hurt my friend. I don't know anything — and honestly, I don't know if I care." Emma stopped talking and looked directly at Alice.

Alice held her eye until Emma couldn't stand it anymore.

"They weren't even going to tell me about the pregnancy. I found out by accident." Emma started crying.

Alice knew they were getting close to something important. She handed Emma the box of tissues on the table and asked, "Did you feel left out?"

"Left out — yeah. Like I'm trapped behind glass, watching life go on without me. Then something inside me snapped, and a monster emerged. I did the meanest thing I could think to do, and I pretended it was because I had a strong moral conscience. But I just wanted to hurt her."

"There it is," said Alice finally.

"There what is?"

"The real thing."

"The real thing?"

"We hurt people because we are hurting. Everything else is a distraction to avoid saying the hardest thing."

"Which is?"

"I am in pain."

49.

March 21, the end of a spring blizzard, -5C°.

Emma carried a bouquet of flowers and a bakery cake up the three flights of stairs to Priya and Isla's familiar apartment door. Just as she jiggled the lock with her spare key, the door flung open.

"What the hell are you doing here?" Priya waited at the door with her arms crossed.

"I didn't—" Emma stammered. "I didn't expect you to be here."

Emma could feel Priya's eyes assess her, Emma knew she still looked too thin and too pale, she gave Priya a half smile anyway.

"Umm — can I come in?" asked Emma. She considered turning around and ending her mission. She knew how quickly her peace offering could be turned into a confrontation.

"Is that shit for Isla?" asked Priya.

"No, it's for you." Emma breathed deeply, waiting to be asked to leave.

Instead, Priya stepped aside and allowed Emma into the apartment.

"It's your favourite, caramel pecan with vanilla cream cheese frosting," said Emma, heading to the kitchen in the familiar apartment. She had spent so much time there that she might as well have lived there. She found a dusty old vase and gave it a rinse before placing the flowers in it. She considered the letter she had written, still in her bag. She could leave the letter and leave the apartment. She probably should.

Then Priya handed her two plates, and said, "I'll take a large piece." Completely unexpected.

Emma found the serrated knife in the drawer and cut two slices out of the cream-coloured cake, one large and one sliver for herself. Her hand trembled as she handed Priya her piece.

"I'm sorry," she said.

Priya said nothing as she took her first bite.

"I shouldn't've told Sam about your pregnancy. Please forgive me?"

Twelve words, three sentences. That was all she'd come to say. Emma stood in the kitchen for a moment longer. She knew she deserved Priya's full wrath; she also knew she didn't have the strength to withstand it.

Time to leave.

"Did Isla put you up to this?" questioned Priya before Emma had a chance to step away.

Emma shook her head. "She doesn't know I'm here."

"Where's Liam?" asked Priya.

"Bill has been taking him a couple of afternoons a week — to give me a break, or so I can go to appointments."

Emma watched as Priya shoved large bites of cake into her mouth, with her mouth full she shrugged, "the baby wants what the baby wants."

Emma waited for a clue whether she should leave or not. Her own piece of cake remained untouched, her appetite still non-existent. So rarely was it just the two of them without Isla there as their buffer. Emma felt tears well up in her eyes.

"—I was drowning, and you were the only one who noticed."

"Everyone else noticed," Priya said. "They were scared and didn't know what to do. I gave them unsolicited advice, that's all."

Emma wiped a tear from her cheek. "I thought you hated me."

Priya looked down, unable to meet Emma's teary eyes. "I did it for your family. They love you and they need you."

"You are part of that family," whispered Emma.

Priya swallowed her final bite.

"I'm so sorry, Priya. I was scared, and I wasn't thinking straight, and I thought I knew what was best for you. I was wrong. Please forgive me. I can't imagine my life without you in it, even though you drive me crazy sometimes."

Priya didn't respond right away, and the silence in the room dragged on for what felt like eternity. When Emma couldn't take it anymore, she stood and moved towards the door, not receiving what she had hoped for.

Forgiveness.

"Who is your OB/GYN? I guess I should start seeing someone."

There it was — or at least, the best Priya could offer. An invitation back in.

50.

Isla glanced back as she pushed open the heavy glass door. None of her colleagues were in sight. She quickened her pace and headed down the street in the opposite direction than usual. She kept her head down as she dodged other pedestrians. With one last glance around her, scanning for familiar faces, she reached the exit of the parkade. Knox's car was second in line to exit. Isla pulled out her phone seemingly to check her messages, all the while glancing around to make sure they wouldn't be seen. Her heart was racing, terrified that they would be caught, and she'd have to come up with a lie on the spot. As Knox's car came to a stop, she lunged for the passenger seat, slammed the door shut, then ducked and shouted, "go! Go! Go!"

Knox shook his head and laughed. "You know, you're a total weirdo."

"And you like it."

"Against my better judgment, I do." He turned left onto the street and out of the parkade.

"All this cloak-and-dagger stuff is fun, even if we didn't have to keep this secret" Her voice was muffled, as she remained hidden from sight.

"You can sit up now," said Knox, turning right onto Portage Avenue. "Do you mind if we stop at my apartment? I need to change. Then we can walk from there. We won't be able to find parking much closer to the arena, anyway."

"Sounds good," she said. "I can't wait to snoop around your stuff."

"I hope you're not disappointed. It's a sublet full of my land-lords' stuff."

She pouted. "No secrets or oddities?"

"Sorry to disappoint. What you see is what you get."

Knox found parking on the street, and they rode the elevator up to the eighth floor.

"Ooh it's beautiful," Isla said, as the heavy oak door opened into a modern, industrial space. Floor-to-ceiling windows overlooked the river.

"Snoop away. I'll be in—" he pointed to the opening to her right, his bedroom.

Isla took off her jacket and examined the random slips of paper stuck to the fridge by small silver magnets. Receipts and a couple of takeout menus. She opened the fridge. Nothing out of the ordinary, except a small carton of cream, still sealed, due to expire in five days.

He doesn't take cream in his coffee.

Closing the fridge door, she continued around the kitchen. Everything was neat and precise. Isla paused to take in the view of the river before a flash of indigo caught her attention.

"What the—" Isla blurted, walking toward the wall dividing the living space and bedroom. "Where did you get that?"

She heard Knox snort in the other room. He entered wearing only a pair of jeans. The sight was almost lost on Isla as she gaped at the most out-of-place object in the skillfully decorated space: a small square painting of an iris, with deep blues, purples, and greens. It sat between the TV and window. It was too small, and didn't go with the neutral colour scheme.

Knox came over and tilted his head at the painting, as if he too was seeing it for the first time.

"That is my painting!" Isla exclaimed.

"Is it?" questioned Knox with a grin.

She gaped at him, waiting for an explanation.

"Sue bought it for me last spring for my birthday. She knew my fondness for irises," explained Knox.

"Did you know it was mine?" asked Isla.

"I did not. Not until I was in your parent's house and saw its twin. I checked the signature, made the connection, and then checked mine when I got home." He pointed at the IMP in the right-hand bottom corner.

"Isla Margert Peters," she said quietly, unable to take her eyes off the painting in front of her. It was as if she was seeing it for the first time, with the more objective eyes of a viewer, not the creator. "I remember Sue buying it; she said she had the perfect spot for it."

"It doesn't really go with the rest of the space, but it reminds me of my mom."

"Do you think—" she started.

Knox glanced at her. "What?"

"Never mind, it's silly."

"Tell me."

"Do you think it's a sign? Or like, fate or something?"

"I don't know," he said, wrapping his arms around her from behind. "Either that, or Sue has a sick sense of humour."

Isla leaned back against his chest. His chin rested comfortably on the top of her head. They continued to stare at the little square painting.

"You are a very talented painter," he whispered.

"Painting breaks my heart," she sighed. "—Not to be dramatic or anything."

"No, you're never dramatic."

299

Isla ignored him and continued, "I start with a picture in my mind of how I want something to turn out, and no matter how it turns out, it's never as good as I imagined."

"You *are* a talented painter — I wouldn't say it if I didn't believe it."

"Please tell me a million times," said Isla, turning around. Still wrapped in his arms, she put her hand on his bare chest and murmured, "You should put some clothes on."

"Maybe you should take some off," he whispered into her ear. His hands cupped her face, and he drew his mouth to hers.

"Maybe later," she breathed, pulling away slightly.

Knox stood straight up. "Really?"

"Ah - yeah," she said, grinning. "I'd like to stay tonight, if you want—"

His mouth was on hers again. She stepped back until she felt the weight of the wall behind her. He pushed himself against her and fumbled with the hem of her shirt; she shivered as she felt his hand on her bare back. When his fingers found the bottom of her bra, Isla sighed. "What about the game?"

"Fuck the game," Knox murmured.

She pulled back briefly. "You've been looking forward to this for weeks!"

"And by *this* you mean...?"

"The game!" she laughed.

"I've been looking forward to *this*," he indicated to the two of them, "for a whole lot longer."

"Those tickets were a lot of money—"

He interrupted her protest by kissing her again, before pulling away reluctantly. "Fine, I'll go get dressed."

He returned wearing the signature green and blue of the opposing team.

"A Vancouver jersey?" she said. "I'm going to pretend I don't know you."

"C'mon," he said, holding the door open for her. "Winnipeg is going down."

"Honestly, I just hope everyone has fun."

They exited his building and hustled through the streets of downtown, joining more and more fans all headed in the same direction. Knox received a couple of rude looks, gestures, and words, but they survived the game without a major altercation.

Isla did spend the night, and was delighted the next morning to find out the small carton of cream in the fridge was stocked just in case she needed it. She wondered if anyone had ever been that thoughtful ever before.

Operation Don't-Fall-In-Love-Too-Fast was an official disaster.

51.

March 30, windy -2C°.

"Nothing fits me anymore," complained Priya, pulling off the fourth shirt she'd tried on. "I thought I would enjoy being a couple of cup sizes bigger, but this is ridiculous." She turned to Isla who was sitting on her bed, already dressed in a bright, triangle-print dress. "Do you have anything I can borrow?"

"You're going to have to buy some new clothes," said Isla, leaving the room. She returned with the box Emma had dropped off.

Maternity clothes.

"Get that shit away from me," growled Priya. If she had any friends at the end of this, it would be a miracle. "I still haven't even decided if I'm going to keep it."

"You're running out of time—"

"You think I don't know that?" Priya flashed.

"I meant, for *tonight*," said Isla. "I'll go look in my closet."

She returned with a flowy green tunic. Not Priya's style, but it would do.

"Remember how big Emma got? By the time Liam was born, even her maternity clothes didn't fit." Isla sat back down as Priya pulled the tunic over her head.

"Ugh, I look pregnant," she complained, smoothing the tunic over her tiny baby bump.

Isla winced. "How do you want me to respond to that?"

Priya shot her a dirty look but didn't reply.

Isla's phone dinged. "Knox is here."

Knox drove them to the restaurant where they met Sam, Emma, and Andrew. It was something the guys had cooked up — as if a triple date would solve everything.

When their first round of drinks arrived, Priya sipped her lime and soda water, disappointed it wasn't stronger. She dug deep and put on a fake smile as the waiter brought their appetizer, a cheese and charcuterie board with various crackers and breads, jams, and mustards to eat with it.

Priya was tired, and the restaurant was warm, and she couldn't bring herself to join the conversation around the table. She'd felt this way pretty much since she'd taken the pregnancy test. Any energy she had, she poured into her work. She hadn't told anyone at the hospital yet, and even worse, she hadn't told her family.

Emma passed the time on her phone texting the babysitter, their thirteen-year-old neighbour. How had she let Andrew talk her into leaving their baby with a thirteen-year-old girl she wondered. *She's still a child herself! And she has her own cell phone — probably tic-toking all night and ignoring our child!* And so, Emma texted to check in every thirty minutes. *At least it will keep her focused!*

Isla was keenly aware that neither Priya nor Emma was present to the conversation around the table. She felt alone as the guys dominated the conversation, talking about financial markets — a topic she neither understood nor cared to learn about.

As dinner progressed, entrées were ordered, and drinks were refilled. When Priya's entrée came, seared duck breast with apricot and basil chutney, she couldn't bring herself to even taste it. What was appealing twenty minutes ago now brought nausea.

Why do they call it morning sickness when it lasts all day?

Priya picked at the goat cheese mashed potatoes, which were the only appealing thing on her plate. She offered her meat to Sam, who insisted she try a couple bites — for the baby.

Priya rewarded him with a forced smile and tentative bite. She chewed and chewed, hoping she would be able to swallow without gagging. By the time the waiter took their dinner plates away, Priya was exhausted. She leaned her head on to Sam's shoulder and closed her eyes, letting the noise of people having a good time lull her to sleep.

"Hey – Doc," Sam whispered in her ear.

Groaning, she snapped out of her catnap.

"You fell asleep. Are you OK?" he asked quietly.

"I'm just so tired," Priya said. Sitting back up, she realized everyone was looking at her worriedly.

"Well, it's time for dessert!" Sam said, a little too loud.

"I'm not really hungry for dessert," Priya said. She was ready to go home.

"I am," said Knox, reaching for the menu. "We should all order one and share."

Priya glared at him, as Sam and Andrew agreed.

Emma checked her phone again. When she wasn't actively typing, she was tapping the phone against the table or flipping it in circles, as if her constant vigilance would protect Liam from any harm. She just wanted to go home, and Andrew also wasn't receiving any hints.

The server placed a large platter in front of each of the couples, saving Priya and Sam's dish for last, the plate held a small chocolate cake decorated with fresh fruit and white chocolate curls, with a small pitcher of salted caramel sauce. In front of the food lay a gold ring with a huge, princess-cut diamond. Written on the plate with chocolate sauce were the words '*Will you marry me?*'

Time stood still. For the first time in Priya's life, the smell of chocolate was offensive.

No.

A silent scream echoed in her head, but she couldn't say anything out loud. Sam took the ring and got down on one knee, drawing the attention of all the other diners. Priya looked at her friends. Andrew and Knox were beaming; they knew this was coming. But Isla's eyes were wide, and her mouth was open. *She better not have known this was coming,* thought Priya. *Surely, she would've stopped it had she known.*

Priya looked at Sam, and swallowed. She was seconds away from humiliating this good man.

"Priya?" Sam noticed the panic in her eyes.

"Please don't make me answer," she breathed, so only he could hear. She wouldn't meet his eyes.

Priya stood up and said a little louder, "I'm sorry."

She walked through the restaurant and out the door, leaving him alone, still on one knee. The wait staff and other diners politely returned to their own business. Sam stood up stiffly, staring at the door. He had expected that to end differently.

Isla rose to go after her.

"No," said Sam. He shoved the ring in his pocket. Without saying anything, he grabbed Priya's bag and followed her.

Isla dropped back down into her seat, fire in her eyes. "I guess neither of you thought it would be a good idea to let me in on this little surprise."

"Don't, Isla," warned Andrew.

Isla looked back and forth between Knox and her brother, who were shamefaced and embarrassed. "For future reference, talk to the best friend before planning clichéd, surprise proposals."

"Friends," echoed Emma. "I would've told you it was a bad idea, if you had bothered to ask."

The cold air stung Priya's hot face. She looked around for something to hit. How *dare* he ruin everything? She turned back towards the door as it opened, and Sam barrelled out.

"Let's go," he commanded. Without waiting for a response, he walked towards the parking lot, trusting she would follow. He held the passenger side door of his car open for her and slammed it shut after she got in.

Priya had never seen Sam angry, and in a weird way she was relieved. Seeing him sad would have done her in.

His door slammed shut and she started, "I'm so sorry—"

"That was humiliating" he spat out.

"I know—"

"I did it for *you*—"

"What makes you think I want to get married?"

"It's the right thing to do! I love you, and we are going to have a baby together."

"Would you have asked me if I wasn't pregnant?" demanded Priya.

Sam paused and rubbed his face. "I don't know. Maybe. Maybe, before that I'd ask you to admit to the world that we are together."

Sam started the car and tore out of the parking lot. After driving in silence for a time, he asked, "What the hell do you want from me?"

Priya looked out the window, gnawing on her lip.

"Do you want me to leave?"

"No," she admitted.

"I thought we were doing this together," he said, gesturing at her stomach, "but you refuse to talk about the future."

He approached an intersection. A right turn would lead them to his apartment, left to hers. He signaled left. She answered, "My whole life I've had a plan. I was going to become a surgeon, a brilliant surgeon, and I wasn't going to get married, and I was *never* going to have children. My whole life is falling apart! All my goals are ruined. I'm nauseous all the time. I'm so tired that I randomly fall asleep. None of my clothes fit me anymore. I fucking hate it, and—" she paused and rubbed her temples — "I am completely terrified."

Silently, Sam navigated his way through the most confusing intersection he'd ever seen. He turned onto her street, and parked. He took his phone out of his jacket and read, "Week sixteen: your nausea and tiredness should end soon."

Priya looked at him. "Excuse me?"

"This app says your nausea and tiredness should end soon—"

"What app?"

"When I found out you were pregnant, we started developing an app for new dads. It sends weekly updates: the size of the baby, how mom should be feeling, and things dads can do, like cooking healthy suppers. I'm testing the prototype; hopefully we can launch it…" he trailed off when he noticed a look of amazement on Priya's face. "—what?"

"You are *such* a nerd."

Sam gave her a grin and a shrug. "So far we are calling it *info-4dads* until we can come up with something clever. There is so much information out there for moms, but very little for fathers. Haven't you been reading or researching?"

"I'm in med school, I think I know enough—"

"Did you know the baby is the size of a softball?" he interrupted.

"A softball?"

"Yeah, or a pear. We're not sure if we should do food or sport metaphors."

"What else do I need to know about week sixteen?"

"The baby's circulatory system is fully working. The heart is pumping about forty-two pints of blood around their body every day," Sam read, "and they can close their hands to make a fist."

"Really?" asked Priya, her hand instinctively moving to touch her stomach.

"You won't be able to feel it for a few more weeks."

Priya settled back into her seat, her hand still resting on her stomach. "While I've been in denial, working obsessively and hoping the whole thing will disappear, you've been thinking this through, haven't you?"

Sam paused. He didn't want to admit how much he had been thinking, researching, and planning — and how excited he was. Being a father was something he had wanted since he was a small boy playing cricket with his own father. "I thought maybe we could buy a house with a yard. I always wanted a yard growing up. You can take a semester off school and start back where you left off. You can't be the first med student to get knocked up. Then I can take parental leave and stay home with her or him."

"You would stay home with the baby?"

"Yeah, I think it would be fun. I like kids."

Priya thought for awhile. She had assumed he was as stressed out about the pregnancy as she was, but he was excited. And he loved her.

His love scared her, but not as much as her love did.

"I think we'll add a 'no surprise proposals' to week sixteen for Things Not To Do" joked Sam.

"How are we going to afford a house with a yard? I have student debt."

"I have a little money saved up for a down payment."

"What about our families?" asked Priya. "My parents will be furious."

"Maybe it won't be that bad."

"You don't know them."

"I have strict traditional Indian parents too—"

"Then you *know* this won't go well—"

"—I know strict Indian parents love their children."

Priya sat back and closed her eyes. How did she get here? She wasn't someone whom life happened to; she was someone who made life happen. And yet here she was, completely out of control of her own life. *Is this love?* she wondered. Here she sat with the one person on earth she could completely crush. The one person who could also completely crush her. He was still waiting for her to answer his real question. *What do you want from me?*

"Get out of the car," she demanded.

Sam raised both eyebrows.

"Please," she added.

Sam got out of the car and met her at the hood.

"Samarpreet Singh, will you be my boyfriend?" she proposed.

He shifted from one foot to the other and gave a slow nod.

"Okay," she said, wrapping her arms around his neck. Before she kissed him, she whispered, "I love you so fucking much."

52.
April 4. Sunny, 8C°.

"*Your dress is pretty.*" Isla glanced at the text from Knox as she slid into the only open chair in the conference room. It was their weekly afternoon staff meeting, and she was late — really late, even by her standards. The quick and easy errands she had planned for her lunch break completely backfired when her car wouldn't start at her second stop. It wasn't entirely her fault, but she was very late and really hoped everyone would be in a forgiving mood.

"*Your eyes are pretty,*" buzzed her phone. She glanced at it and sent Knox a confused look. They were keeping their relationship a secret by ignoring each other most days. Why the flirting?

"*Your smile is pretty.*"

"*Your shoes are pretty.*"

She typed, "*Stop it.*"

"*Your teeth are pretty.*"

What? thought Isla, replying, "*Your tie is pretty.*"

"*I'm pretty sure you are late.*"

She sent a dirty look both as an emoji and in real life.

John was in the middle of his sentence when Sue interrupted. "Knox and Isla, could you please stop texting? We all know you are

310

in a romantic relationship, but we'd prefer it didn't interfere with our meeting. Do you mind passing me your phones? Then we can give our proper attention to the matter at hand."

Isla melted into a puddle of embarrassment and passed her phone down the line of shocked observers. Knox managed to remain stoic. He handed Sue his phone before calmly indicating to John to continue.

Isla spent the rest of the meeting staring down at the ground and avoiding eye contact with everyone. Knox happily ripped her design to pieces, removing any doubt about his ability to remain professional.

He caught up to her after the meeting and steered her into his office.

"Did you know she was going to do that?" she demanded.

"I did not. That was really embarrassing."

"What are we going to do?" Isla could hear her co-workers snicker as they walked by.

Knox went to shut the door.

"Don't you dare!" she yelped. "That will make things worse!"

Sue appeared in the doorway, holding their phones out to them.

"That was fun," she said.

"How did you know?" asked Knox.

"Graham has been keeping me updated. I thought it was about time for everyone else to know. You've been doing too good of a job not letting on. I have to say, I'm a little insulted you didn't tell me." She was addressing Knox.

"I didn't think you'd approve," he responded, his eyes on the floor. Isla watched, fascinated by the power dynamic. She had assumed these two partners were equals, but Knox clearly deferred to his aunt. Her opinion mattered to him.

"What I don't approve of is texting during meetings. You two—" she gestured between the two of them and shrugged — "you'll either make it work, or go up in flames. Either way, you should probably come to dinner on Friday."

It wasn't a question.

Isla nodded and watched her boss leave the room. She turned to follow her, but not before Knox stole a kiss in the doorway, in full view of everyone still lingering after the meeting.

53.

April 9. Very windy, 2C°.

Emma was back in the perfect room, still feeling as broken as she had the first time. Maybe a bit more comfortable with being broken. Was that progress?

She told Alice how she had smoothed things over with Priya, maybe? The apology hadn't solved everything. It had barely solved anything. Emma still felt lost and hopeless most of the time. Her meds had helped to settle her panic, but had replaced the panic with numbness. At least the panic attacks reminded her she was alive. Now each day bled into the next in a blur. She made a checklist, and some days she crossed most of it off.

1. Get out of bed before Liam wakes up

2. Shower

3. Eat something

4. Move your body

5. Take a nap if you want

Andrew was back at work, but had quit anything extra so he could be home as much as possible. Bill and Dee checked on her daily, and 'borrowed' Liam a couple of days a week. Emma hated feeling like a burden, like everyone had put their lives on hold for her. But as much as she tried, she couldn't function enough for it to be any different.

She had spent that morning lying on her bathroom floor. The cool tiles woke up her brain a bit, enough to think things through. She examined her memories from the last year, trying to pinpoint where it had all gone wrong.

"How are you this week?" asked Alice, sitting comfortably in the chair across from Emma.

Emma shrugged. "I laughed on Tuesday," she replied after a beat of silence.

Alice smiled. "What was so funny?"

"Liam smacked Andrew in the head with his dump truck. I shouldn't've laughed, but it caught me off guard. If he would've hit me, I would've gotten angry and disciplined him. But Andrew laughed, too. He fell over, and let Liam climb all over him." Tears welled up in Emma's eyes. "I wish I could be that easy going. Instead, I would've freaked out because he acted — like a baby."

"Tell me more about that."

"If I say any more, you'll think I am a horrible person."

"I've heard many confessions in this room. I don't believe anyone is awful, just hurting."

"When I was a little girl, all I wanted was to be a wife and mother. I remember adults complimenting me – *Emma, you'll make such a good mother!* — after I'd babysit or watch the babies at church. It's the only thing I've ever wanted, and the only thing people ever told me I'd be good at. And I am horrible at it. Most days, I hate being a mother."

Emma shifted uncomfortably in her seat. "I remember when we were in grade ten, we did a project where we had to describe our five life goals. I've accomplished all of them — before the age of twenty-six."

"Would you like to tell me what they were?" asked Alice.

314

"Number one was to see the Rocky Mountains. Isla, Priya, and I did that the summer after we graduated. Number two was to marry Andrew, which I did three years ago."

"You knew who you wanted to marry when you were in grade ten?" Alice blurted, unable to hide her surprise.

"He's Isla's older brother. I loved him from the first time I met him." Emma paused. Did she still feel that way? She shook off the thought. "Number three was to finish my Bachelor of Arts. Which I did. Number four was to live in a brand-new house, which we moved into two years ago. And number five was to have a baby. That's it. All five. I've done it all."

Had she arrived at some sort of finish line? It didn't feel as good as she imagined.

Alice waited.

"Isla's dreams were ridiculous. She wanted to find the perfect shade of lipstick, eat crickets in Thailand, and sell art on Venice Beach. She hasn't done any of them, and she doesn't care. She dreams up new stuff and keeps living life. And Priya, she sets the biggest goals she can imagine, and crushes them. Then she sets another one. Isla is the creative one, Priya is the rebel, and I don't know what I am. Probably the boring one. I thought if I did everything right, I'd have a perfect life — but I feel empty."

"When was the last time you had fun?"

Emma thought back over the last year. There were moments that were supposed to be fun, in theory, like New Years Eve, or Andrew's birthday, or taking Liam to the zoo for the first time. She had wanted those to be fun, but they weren't — they were exhausting, and layered with constant worry. Did Liam have everything he needed? What would she feed him? When would he go to sleep? When she thought of those moments, it was like she was locked in a room, watching through a dirty window. Everyone was having fun, and she was separate from them.

"I don't know. I guess I'm a failure at that as well."

"Motherhood can be overwhelming and isolating. Just because you feel those things, doesn't mean you failed; it means it's a difficult job."

Emma nodded, but didn't trust herself to say anything.

"It's time for you to dream, Emma. Make a few more goals! Allow yourself to imagine who you can be, beyond being a mother and dutiful wife. Dream big and little. What are some silly, accomplishable things you can do? Like finding the perfect shade of lipstick, or eating something new and different. And then, dream big. Even if you have more children, they will grow up. Who do you want to be when there are no more children in your house? Do you want to be involved with your community? Or have a career? Or go back to school? The fun of dreaming is that it doesn't have to be realistic or possible, but it will give you hints and direction. Nothing in life is predictable, but we need things that make us feel alive — maybe because they're fun, but even more so because they're hard and interesting and worthwhile."

"That all sounds lovely and impossible. I'm barely sleeping, barely functioning."

"It's the best time to start. You can't become what you can't imagine. Pay attention to what makes you feel human. Enjoy food, move your body, connect with those you love. Start there. The dreams will come."

54.

April 18. Foggy, 8C°.

Priya's stomach continued to grow, and at nearly twenty weeks she could no longer hide it. She continued to live in denial and panic. Whenever her supervisor wanted to talk about the future, she found a reason to deflect the conversation. She refused to wear maternity clothes, sticking to long t-shirts and threading a hair elastic through the buttonhole of her increasingly tight jeans to keep them together.

She had been to one doctor's appointment, and was scheduled for an ultrasound next week. She dreaded it. Inversely, Sam had printed out a paper calendar and posted it on the fridge. He had circled the appointment date with a big red heart — he couldn't wait. He waited on her hand and foot, cooking meals, giving her foot rubs, taking care of all the details she was happy to ignore.

Sam had bribed her to join him grocery shopping with the promise of a sweet, overpriced coffee. And while arguing about the sugar content of her favourite cereal, Jasminder and Hardeep turned into the aisle.

"Priya? Is that you?" Jasminder asked, seeing her daughter from behind. Even after months of not seeing her middle child, she would never forget the curve of her neck or her stubborn stance.

Priya inhaled sharply, and grabbed the box of cereal out of Sam's hand. She turned around slowly, hoping the box would provide cover. "Mama-ji, Papa-ji-"

Hardeep gave her a stiff nod of greeting. Nothing had been repaired in the months since Deepa's wedding. It had been six weeks since they had even seen their daughter — she'd shown up late for a family supper, and left early, remaining quiet in the time in between. Hardeep didn't notice his daughter's protruding midsection. But her mother did. Jasminder missed nothing.

"—Do you remember Samarpreet Singh, from Deepa's wedding?" She spoke pleasantly, but her hands trembled where they gripped the box.

"When are you due?" asked Jasminder plainly.

Priya glanced at Sam for help. All the colour had drained out of his face; he looked like he was about to pass out.

"How are you? How is everyone?" Priya tried.

"When are you due?" repeated Jasminder.

Priya considered denial. Telling a bold-faced lie. But she found that she couldn't. "September seventh."

"We will plan a wedding for mid July. We'll have it in the yard, small, only family. It might be hard to find a caterer — but it will be small." Jasminder looked at the ceiling while speaking, accessing the part of her brain where the check-list for daughters' weddings was stored. "We can wrap the sari to hide the tummy — maybe we won't have time for a custom sari—"

"Stop!" interrupted Priya. She was still holding the box in front of her, although it offered her no protection. "There won't be a wedding."

Sam found his voice. "Maybe we should go somewhere else to discuss this?"

His diplomacy was ignored.

"Don't talk back to your mother!" said Hardeep, as he glared at Sam. "Do not protect this man if he will not do the responsible thing."

318

"*I* am the one who doesn't want to get married! He has asked me — multiple times."

Hardeep's anger prevented him from hearing his daughter, he continued his interrogation of Sam, "What is stopping you from doing the respectable thing? Do you need money?"

"Will you listen to *me* for once in my life!" Priya shouted at her father. "We are not getting married. You don't get a say — now or ever. If you want a chance at a relationship with your *grandchild*, you're going to shut up and not say another word about marriage, or how ashamed you are to have me as a daughter."

Hardeep took a step back, as if her words had physically struck him.

Priya continued, "You have never let me be myself. You try to dictate who I should be, and you've never accepted me for who I really am."

People had come into the aisle and hastily retreated. They could do without cereal for the week. A store employee stood at a distance, ready to alert security if needed. Sam was keenly aware of all of it.

He touched Priya's shoulder, "I think we should go."

"It is you who has never accepted us," said Jasminder quietly.

Sam took Priya by the arm and escorted her out the door, leaving their cart to be dealt with by the staff. Once they were in his car, Priya screamed: one loud, angry burst of sound.

"I am so sorry," said Sam. "That was the worst possible way for them to find out."

"I'm giving up my dream of being a surgeon to have a baby with an Sikh man and that still isn't enough for them. Nothing will ever be good enough for them! The only thing that will make them happy is if I give up all control and let them dictate the rest of my life."

"You're *not* giving up your dream of being a surgeon," insisted Sam. "I won't let that happen."

Priya looked at him with fire in her eyes. "I have everything against me. Woman, immigrant with dark skin, unmarried mother: three strikes. I'm out."

"Not one of those things is going to stop you."

Priya let her head drop into her hands. "What if I can't do it?"

"I have no doubt you can become a surgeon."

"I know, but what if I can't be a mother? I clearly suck at being a daughter. You deserve to raise this baby with someone who is more maternal. Someone nicer, calmer and less bitchy."

"C'mon Doc. I love you because of who you are, not despite it — and so will our child. We will cheer you on, and support you, always. I promise. There is no one else on this planet I'd rather do this with. Let's call my parents tonight. We can follow up with your parents in a couple of weeks once everyone's had a chance to calm down — maybe not in a store. They'll come around. I know you miss them."

Priya started to protest, but the words stuck in her throat. She did miss them. She missed her siblings and her nephews, too. She missed being in their home, she missed her father's random questions and corny jokes. Mostly, she missed her mother's strong arms around her.

55.

May 4. A few fluffy clouds, 16C°.

To Isla, nothing felt more lovely than this moment. She and Knox, and Sam and Priya, were at Andrew and Emma's house for dinner. Like a real grown-up dinner party. Knox and the guys were heading to the deck to barbeque hunks of meat Knox had been marinating all day.

Emma moved around the kitchen with a new bounce to her step. She was purposeful but not labored; she ripped various greens into a large wooden bowl as Priya cut cucumbers, tomatoes, and black olives to add.

Isla wasn't doing anything helpful for the meal preparation. She had picked out the wine and defrosted the rhubarb pie her grandmother had forced her to take last time she visited. Her job was done.

"Okay, I have news," announced Isla, double checking to make sure the door had fully shut behind the guys.

Emma looked up. Priya paused chopping to wave her knife, indicating the dramatic pause had been long enough.

"Knox told me he loves me!"

"Ahh," said Priya knowingly. Emma grinned.

"—Except I don't know if it counts."

"Why wouldn't it count?" asked Emma.

"Well… most mornings he gets up ridiculously early, and I don't hear him because it's, like, the middle of the night. He usually goes for a run and then wakes me up after his shower, but this morning I was awake. He turned off his alarm, rolled over and kissed me on the cheek and whispered, 'I love you.'"

"What did you do?"

"I pretended to be asleep," Isla said sheepishly.

"What if he knew you were awake?" asked Emma.

"I don't think he did."

"Do you think it was the first time he said it?" questioned Priya.

"Whoa." Isla's eyes grew wide. "What if it wasn't? But isn't it too soon?"

"Three months is long enough," said Emma.

"He's practising," replied Priya.

"So, you think I wasn't supposed to hear him?"

Priya shook her head. "I don't think so."

"So, what do I do now?"

"Nothing. Or you could say it first, assuming you do love him."

Isla paused. She had been avoiding the "L" word for a long time, too scared to blurt it out at the wrong time, knowing how easy her emotions got away from her. Was it possible that she loved someone who loved her back, and there was no need to wait years to say it?

"Of course, I do."

"Words mean nothing unless actions prove them, and based on his actions, I have no doubt that he loves you," said Emma.

"Even if it takes that chicken shit another year to say it properly," added Priya. She jumped up and headed to the entrance. "Are you done? Because I have news, too."

"I'm done," said Isla. As Priya walked away, she gave Emma a confused look.

Emma shrugged.

Priya returned carrying a piece of printer paper with a grainy black and white photo on it.

"You had your ultrasound!" squealed Emma, grabbing the paper out of her hand.

Priya tried to contain her smile. She felt happy, happier than she ever imagined she would. "It's a girl. Sam is beyond—well, he's completely lost it. He bought a bunch of clothes and set the crib up."

"And how are you feeling?" asked Isla cautiously.

"Like it's real," Priya answered, placing her hand on her stomach. "I can feel – her — moving now. I'm starting to be able to picture what life could be. I talked to my supervisor, and she approved pushing my residency back by six months. We're going to look for a house. I might have to take up gardening or renovate a kitchen or something."

"It will be weird not to live with you anymore."

"It's not like you're ever there! You'll barely notice."

"I have some news too," said Emma. "I mean if you're both done."

Priya shot Isla a questioning look; Isla shrugged.

"I got a job."

Priya and Isla gaped.

"Doing what?" asked Priya.

Emma straightened the cutlery she was collecting and answered, "nothing big, just a part-time administrative assistant."

"Finally going to use those obsessive organizational skills, huh?" asked Priya.

Emma nodded. "It's just two mornings a week."

"What does Andrew think?" asked Isla.

"He's really supportive. He also took a new job. It's not a promotion, actually he's getting paid a little less, but he'll be working in the city now. No more trips up north, so he'll be around to help."

"This is amazing!" said Priya, astounded. "I never thought you'd ever do anything."

Emma lifted her eyebrow.

"You know what I mean — you only ever wanted to be Susie Homemaker," she added quickly.

"And I never thought you'd be a mother, and yet here we are," Emma shot back.

Priya grinned.

Emma continued, "It's not that I don't like being a mom, but it turns out being Susie Homemaker is a lot of work and very lonely, and I'm not sure I'm cut out for it. Maybe being a working mom will be even harder, but I feel like I need to try."

"This is so great," said Isla. "I'm sorry this year has been so hard. I wish I'd known, so that I could've helped more."

Emma gave her a half smile. "It's taken me awhile to figure out that people can't just sense what I need or how to help. It's really hard for me to ask for help."

"What do your parents think?"

Emma scowled. "They strongly disapprove. Mom said I should have another baby if I'm bored."

"She thinks you're *bored*. Did she miss the post-partum depression diagnosis?" asked Isla.

"You know you're on the right track if Gerald and Sara disapprove," said Priya.

"It's weird. I've never really done anything that they disapprove of, at least not outwardly or obviously. Telling them about this, knowing they would hate it felt—liberating."

"Congratulations! The professor has always told us we're not adults until we do something to piss off our parents."

"How would you do that? Your parents support everything," said Priya.

"Well, I didn't finish my degree." She thought for a bit. "I guess Andrew isn't an adult yet."

Emma said, "Priya's been an adult since she was seven."

They all laughed, but Priya felt a stab of grief. What do you do when you ask someone to stay out of your life — and then they actually do?

They had called Sam's parents to tell them about the baby and received a cool reception at first, but they were warming to the idea of their first grandchild, even if it wasn't under the circumstances they preferred. Priya could relate. These weren't her preferred circumstances either, but it was happening, and the more she settled into the idea, the more she also warmed to it.

Priya was aware of how selfish she could be, caring only about her own success and happiness. Except that wasn't exactly true — she cared about her friends' success, and she wanted them to be happy. She cared about Sam (oh, did she care about Sam!). She cared if he was happy, she cared if she made him happy. At one time, she couldn't fathom loving a child, and now she could. She could picture a toddler with dark eyes and black pigtails. She could picture coming home from the hospital and being greeted with squeals and slobbery kisses. She could picture a school-aged girl all gangly-legged and buck-toothed, who would know that nothing would stop her from being who she wanted to be — not her gender, not her skin colour.

Priya stared again at the grainy ultrasound photo and hoped this child would have Sam's temperament, though.

Let's be honest.

56.

May 16. 12C°.

"Hey, girl!"

Isla snapped out of a daydream as Kelly dropped her designer bag on the table, pulled out a chair and sat down.

"Hello," said Isla warily.

"Look at you! You look great! Have you highlighted your hair, or did you stop shopping at the thrift store?" laughed Kelly.

Thanks a lot, Isla thought.

Before she could respond, Kelly gushed, "That logo! So fab! I knew you were the best person for the job."

"Yes. I—" Isla started. She regretted her assertion that she could get this meeting started herself.

"But — could we tweak the colour, so it's less aggressive but more 'girl boss'?"

Isla nodded, and wrote *girl boss* on her file. The waiter took their orders, coffee for Isla, white wine for Kelly.

"I want pink, but the right pink. Not a girly pink; bold but not off-putting, you know? I miss collaborating with you! You're so talented."

Isla looked down at Kelly's original instructions in her file. In capital letters it said ABSOLUTELY NO PINK. This logo project was a nightmare, dragging on far too long. "Sounds good. I'll pass that on to Shyla."

"Who's Shyla?" Kelly asked, with a slight edge creeping into her voice. "I thought you were doing my logo."

Isla pasted on what she hoped looked like a sincere smile. "We've been short handed since Ryan took parental leave, so we had to ship it to the Vancouver office—"

Kelly nodded. That sounded important.

"Shyla is their intern."

Kelly's face hardened. "I specifically asked for *you* to do it. This is a very important logo. I'm starting my own company and it must be perfect. Not the shit that interns produce."

Isla let her rant — did she realize what she was saying? Thankfully, she noticed Knox approaching the table.

Finally.

Isla caught his eye long enough for him to wink. Then he kissed her firmly, and long enough to make it awkward.

Kelly stopped talking and gaped. "Do I get one too?"

Knox ignored Kelly and kept his eyes on Isla.

"Hi! What are you doing here?" Isla acted surprised — as planned.

"I was in the area. I'm going to grab myself a coffee. Do you need anything?" he asked, glancing at her half full mug.

Isla shook her head. "I'm good."

As Knox walked away, Isla turned her attention back to Kelly, whose expression had gone from condescending to dumbfounded. "Are you two — a thing?"

Isla nodded.

"But you said you weren't interested in him."

"That was a long time ago."

"This is unbelievable," sneered Kelly.

Knox returned to the table with a steaming mug of black coffee and a menu. He moved his chair next to Isla's, so they were sitting shoulder-to-shoulder, facing Kelly.

"How's it going? Are we making progress on the logo?" He was in client mode: upbeat, relaxed, and charming.

Kelly smiled sweetly and addressed Knox directly. "Wonderful! We were just discussing the finishing touches."

"Fantastic. Did Isla mention we've been swamped? It will be nice to move on."

"You have no idea how maddening this process has been! If you had followed my instructions instead of passing it off to a useless intern, we'd be further along."

"Did you bring the cheque?" asked Knox, leaning forward.

"Pardon me?" she replied.

"As I'm sure you remember, we bill by the month. You've been sent three invoices and Shyla won't do any more work until those get paid. Here are some copies, in case you've misplaced yours." He laid out three pieces of printer paper in front of her.

She glanced at them. "You're a savvy enough businessman to know that one shouldn't pay for incompetence."

"If incompetence were the issue, I would deal with it. My competent, talented designers will address your every whim; however, they will be compensated for it. Next month's invoice will be addressed to your grandfather. If I remember correctly, he is the one investing in your business." Knox spoke calmly.

Kelly drained the rest of her wine and glared at Knox, continuing to ignore Isla altogether.

"That won't be necessary. A cheque will be in the mail, asshole." She gathered her bag and jacket, and spat out, "I guess your strict 'no dating employees' policy was bullshit."

As she stormed out, Knox casually opened his menu. "I guess it's just the two of us for lunch. What should we eat?"

"What—was—that — all about?" asked Isla, wide-eyed.

"What was what?" he asked, still looking at the menu. "Do you mean the disdain and open hostility?"

"Yes, that," replied Isla. "And the ridiculous kiss. That wasn't part of the plan."

"I deviated from the plan," he said. "I had my own point to make."

As the server arrived and took their orders, Knox's phone rang and he stepped away from the table to take the call.

Isla sipped her coffee and wondered what point he wanted to make. A memory from the previous summer started niggling at her brain.

When he returned, she asked point blank, "Did you sleep with Kelly?" She wasn't sure she wanted to know the answer.

Knox took a long sip of coffee, then cleared his throat. He shook his head. "No. I didn't…"

"But?" She could tell by the look on his face that his sentence was incomplete.

"But I almost did."

"Oh." Her heart dropped. "What stopped you?"

Knox grimaced and scratched his head. "She puked all over me in the cab." He had stopped the cab, given the driver $100 cash to take her home and to clean the vehicle, and stumbled home on foot.

"The pub crawl last summer?" Isla asked, already knowing the answer.

Knox nodded. "It was Brian's birthday."

"You said she was entitled, and had no talent or work ethic," Isla argued, accepting her eggs benedict from the server.

Knox was about to take a bite of his chicken and waffles, but he put his fork down. "Oh shit, you're mad."

"I'm not mad," she declared. "I just want to understand. You didn't like her—"

"I didn't."

329

"But you were going to sleep with her?"

Knox nodded slowly. "I was really drunk. It was a stupid mistake—"

"Was it a stupid mistake when you wanted *me* to sleep with you two weeks before that?"

Knox sighed. "It *was* a mistake, and you knew it! Isn't that why you shut me down? Please don't be mad."

"I'm not mad!" Isla snapped.

Knox gave her a look of disbelief.

"Fine, I'm mad." Isla threw her hands in the air. "I thought I was special—"

"You are—"

"—but I wasn't then, was I? I was some chick you got drunk in order to hook up with."

Knox flinched because she was right. He took a few seconds to reply, hoping she'd cool down, before asking, "Did you know you were the first girl that ever turned me down?"

"—not to brag or anything," she mocked.

He held up two fingers. "Twice."

"You thought I was an easy target."

"No, I was fascinated by you, so I tried a second time. It was a bad idea, but I thought I could convince you. I should've realized I didn't stand a chance." He shook his head. "One of the many things I admire about you is that you know exactly what you want. You don't compromise anything about yourself in order to impress anyone, and you don't care whether people like you or not."

"That's not true! I care way too much if people like me."

"Not enough for it to change who you are," said Knox.

Isla picked up her fork and stabbed it into an egg yolk, watching it ooze onto the English muffin below. Finally, she asked, "What happened after that night with Kelly?"

"I woke up on my floor covered in her vomit, hungover, and disgusted with myself. Something had to change. I did not want anything like that to happen again. That's one of the reasons I stopped drinking." Knox sighed. "Kelly was — persistent. So I told her I had a strict policy against dating coworkers. After I fired her, it had to expand to include past employees."

"She persisted even after you fired her?" asked Isla in disbelief.

"Yeah. She tried again when we had lunch in January. I lied and told her I was seeing someone." He gave her a half smile and reached for her hand. "I'm not proud of who I was when we first met. It's not who I am anymore."

"I shouldn't be upset. I had no claim on you then," she said, playing with her empty coffee cup.

"Hey." Knox reached over and took the cup out of her hand. "I love you. You have full claim on me now."

"Finally!" she blurted, snapping her hand to her mouth in embarrassment realizing what she had said.

Knox was surprised, but a smile curved at the edges of his mouth. "Excuse me?"

"I heard you when you thought I was asleep. I heard you say you loved me."

Knox shook his head sheepishly. "I've been practising for awhile."

"Awhile?" asked Isla. "I only heard you once! When was the first time?"

"It doesn't matter." He brushed crumbs off the table on to his palm and then dumped them onto his saucer.

"Yes, it does," Isla insisted. "I want to know!"

"The night of the snowstorm in Portage. I woke up and you had fallen asleep with your book on your face. I thought, *I think I might be in love with you.* Then you moved, and I realised I might've said it aloud. I freaked out! I don't think I've ever been in love before. Honestly, I didn't think I'd ever have the guts to tell you."

Isla took his hand. "I love you; I love you; I love you. And I love that you waited until you were ready."

57.

May 28. Sunny, calm, 26C°.

Anything they could do; she could do better — even pregnant. When it was suggested that Priya should sit down and take a moment to rest, she'd growl back that she didn't *need* to rest. If her male colleague Dr. Wong could stand for a whole shift, so could she. At twenty-six weeks, she had plenty of energy, and her belly wasn't big enough to be cumbersome. She only had two weeks left in her rotation, and she wanted to make the most of it.

"Dr. Dhaliwal?" Dr. Wong asked. "What do you think would be the best course of action?"

Priya looked at the elderly patient in the bed in front of her, his eyes watery and unfocused. She could tell he was in pain, probably more pain than he would admit. Priya wiped sweat off her brow. Was the air conditioning broken? She'd been hot all day.

"EKG, CT scan—" she started rattling off the standard course of treatment, but suddenly her vision started to swim. She casually grabbed the end of the bed to steady herself.

"Dr. Dhaliwal?"

Priya inhaled sharply as a cramp nearly brought her to her knees. Dr. Wong reached for her as she swayed.

"Priya — are you okay?" He gestured to the nurse to hold her while he checked her pulse.

The room disappeared. Priya put her hand on her stomach.

Move. Please move.

Isla was happy with how the meeting had progressed. She could never predict how first meetings would go. Often clients who claimed to want innovation were the least likely to take risks. Those who were less assertive seemed far more open.

So far, her ideas and mock-ups had been presented and discussed. She sat back comfortably while Sam took his turn presenting the digital plan.

Angela interrupted with a knock on the door and apologetic look on her face. "Sorry to interrupt. Isla, your phone has rung seven times in a row — I wondered if it could be an emergency?"

Isla glanced at Knox; he gave her a slight nod. She sent an apologetic smile to the clients and excused herself. As she walked into the hallway, her phone rang for an eighth time.

"Hey, what's up?" Isla answered, happy to see it wasn't one of her parents calling.

Sam followed Knox's lead and kept the mood lighthearted, but he couldn't keep his eye off his friend in the hallway. As her body wilted, he caught Knox's eye. They knew it was bad news. Then she looked directly at him, and his heart broke.

"She's gone. There's no heartbeat."

"Oh — Priya no!"

"I can't bear to tell Sam."

"I will."

"Can you come?"

"Yeah, as soon as we can."

333

58.
June 14.

Two weeks had passed. Two weeks of tears. Two weeks of disbelief. Two weeks of unimaginable pain.

Emma spent every waking moment at Sam's apartment. She sat with Priya as she lay curled up on the couch, back to the world, unmoving and silent. Emma did dishes and helped Sam pack up the tiny baby things into boxes.

Sam couldn't sit still, but he couldn't focus, either. Emma sent him on walks to the corner store. *We need milk*, she'd say. *We need chocolate.* Any little errand to keep him moving.

Bill kept them fed, casserole after casserole, all made with little Liam in tow. Andrew, Isla, and Knox came over in the evenings. And the six of them sat around the small table with supper on their plates, eating very little.

What was there to say? How many times could you say *this is so awful* before you sounded trite?

Yesterday, Sam returned to work. Priya hadn't moved since supper the night before. She flinched when he bent over to kiss her cheek. She said nothing.

Today, Priya was alone for the first time. She texted Emma and told her she'd be fine, not to come, and then she turned off her phone. She had a plan. Nothing was going to distract her.

As the day progressed, Priya started packing boxes. There were only three, but they were heavy, full of clothes and broken dreams. She walked past the nursery. The disassembled crib sat in the corner.

It had been stupid of them to buy it so early.

She wouldn't go into the empty room. Every time she walked past, it reminded her that it would remain empty. But she couldn't close the door, either.

There was no sentimentality when she left. No final walk through, and no note. She carried each box down to Isla's car, one at a time. Her body was sore; her arms ached with emptiness.

Sam was sitting on the hood of the brown hatchback waiting for her when she returned with the last box. He looked deflated and resigned. He had been waiting for this day. Deep down, he'd always feared that one day he'd come home and find her leaving, and now it was happening.

He took the last box out of her hands and set it down on the ground. "Please don't go."

"I have to," Priya responded, staring at her box. She refused to look him in the eye.

His left hand brushed her hair from her cheek. His right hand coaxed her chin up to look at him. "I love you. We belong together."

She took a step back, out of his reach. Her eyes welled up and she looked away; she wouldn't let him see the tears.

The past weeks, all they had done was cry, both together and apart. Priya was done with crying. It was time to move on. Maybe if she moved quickly enough, the pain wouldn't keep up.

"Did you at least leave a note? Or were you just going to leave?"

"Why don't you just call me a bitch and get it over with? Say all the horrible things you've thought about me, tell me you hate

335

me. Get it over with now. It'll be better for both of us if you tell me the truth."

"Don't pick a fight with me," said Sam. "I refuse to fight with you, Priya. I will not let you justify leaving by being an asshole. I love you. You know I do."

Priya walked towards the driver seat. He stepped between her and the car door and repeated, "I love you."

"I can't do this, Sam," she said quietly, reaching for the door handle.

"I love you and you love me," he said again, his body right beside her, close enough to smell her coconut shampoo.

"I don't love you," she replied coldly.

"You do love me."

"I lied."

"No. You're lying right now."

"Let me go! This hurts too much."

"I know it hurts," he said. "Please stay. I'll do whatever it takes. We can go to therapy. We can move, find a different condo. I'll come with you wherever you get placed."

"You don't understand — I can't be with you. Being with you reminds me of her," Priya said tightly. "It's time to move on."

"I don't want to move on!"

"Find a girl who loves you and is desperate to give you babies. Find her and love her, and let me live my life."

Sam flinched at the thought of loving anyone else. From the moment he had met her, he'd known there would never be anyone else.

59.

July 8. Already hot and humid. 29C°.

"I'm leaving in 10 minutes, whether you're ready or not!" Knox called from his kitchen. Isla was still in bed. She rolled over and buried her head in the pillow, groaning. The clock said 6:45am. A certain cheerful morning person was getting on her nerves.

Knox dove onto the bed next to her.

"Go away," she mumbled.

"You wanted me to get you up, remember? Last night you declared you were turning over a new leaf and getting up early." He grinned, quite used to evening-Isla making plans morning-Isla didn't appreciate. Isla snuggled into his side, willing him to stay a bit longer.

"I've got to go. I have lots to do before the staff meeting this morning." He turned and held her gaze. "Don't forget I'm taking you out for lunch."

Knox leaned over and kissed her. Isla perked up as she responded to his kiss, but then he pulled away. "Seriously, I've got to go. Save that for later."

He called from the door, "Don't be late!"

"I'm up," Isla called back. When she heard the door slam, she lay back down. She still had at least a half hour.

While everyone's attention was on Sam and Priya, Knox's stress had been mounting. He worked longer and longer hours with a growing sense of unease in the pit of his stomach. Now, the time had come. He was not looking forward to navigating office dynamics over the next couple of days. Worst of all, he didn't know how Isla was going to react, and it was creating an unbearable buzzing in his brain.

There was a soft knock at his door. a quick glance at the clock told him it was just before nine. Sue walked in, followed by a grim-looking Graham and their fourth partner, Tomas Cunningham.

"We have a problem," said Graham.

This is not good.

"Mac Williams is putting out a press release at nine thirty this morning."

"What?" said Knox, jumping up. "He can't do that! He said he wouldn't say anything until tomorrow."

"Well, he got it in his head that today is the day. It's too late — we have to make the announcement this morning," stated Tomas.

"We can't," said Knox.

"Why not?"

"I haven't talked to Isla yet." Knox slid back into his chair.

Graham looked sympathetic, but before he could respond, Tomas spoke. "I know she's your girlfriend, but she's also an employee. You agreed to tell no one until things were finalized."

"And I haven't, but I wanted her to hear it from me." He put his head in his hands. This was not going to end well. "Let me go tell her quickly before the meeting."

"She's not here yet," replied Sue sympathetically.

"I'll wait for her."

"We don't have time," Tomas said. "The release is going out at nine-thirty, and the news will be all over within the hour. This is business, Knox. The fallout will be a lot worse than a simple lovers' quarrel if you don't break the news to the staff now. Come on. Everyone's waiting."

Knox looked to Sue for help, but she shrugged apologetically. "We have to do it. We don't have a choice."

Graham let Sue and Tomas leave the office ahead of him. When they were gone, he said, "Isla loves you, Knox."

"I guess we'll find out." Knox sounded more optimistic than he felt.

Isla made it just in time, rushing to unpack her bag and grab her notebook for the meeting. As she neared the conference room, she did a double take. What were Graham and Tomas doing here?

As she found a spot, Isla thought back on the last couple of weeks. They had been crazy, but surely, she'd remember if Knox had mentioned that Graham was coming.

Graham caught her eye and winked. She waved back but noticed he looked stressed. Knox avoided eye contact with her. He had his business face on. It was all unsettling.

"Good morning." Knox's greeting called everyone's attention to the front of the room. "Before we start our monthly meeting, we have some news we need to share. You all remember Graham Richards and Tomas Cunningham."

"Why don't I take it from here?" Tomas said, quietly but firmly. Turning to the gathered staff, he began. "First off, I would like to announce that Sue Tremblay has decided to retire. She has been with HRA from the very beginning: hired by Ken and Graham as a copy writer, making her way up through the ranks to partner, and then successfully running shop here for the last twenty years. She will leave us to enjoy spending time with her grandchildren and traveling with her husband."

There was riotous applause as the office showed their appreciation for her. She rose to say a few words, but Isla was having a hard time concentrating. She was still unable to catch Knox's eye. She sent him a quick text: *What's up?* She watched him check his phone, and not reply.

Tomas continued. The clipped tone of his voice forced Isla to pay attention. "As you know, Knox started here a year and a half ago. He came with a specific goal for this office, and we are happy to say that he has accomplished it — like a typical Harrison. Knox has been so successful running this office that we've caught the attention of Williams Marketing in Calgary, who have made us an offer we cannot refuse. Knox..." he invited Knox to speak.

Knox stood up slowly and faced his staff with a pained look on his face. He caught Isla's eye for the first time and quickly looked away.

"We've sold the Winnipeg division to Williams Marketing. They will be keeping the office, just as it is, and I assure you that everyone will be keeping their positions." He paused to let everyone take it in. "Except for me. I will be moving back to Vancouver to rejoin the team there—"

Isla felt the air being sucked out of the room. She slammed her notebook shut and stood up. Knox's sentence trailed off and the room went silent as she walked out.

Everyone was stunned for a moment, but then the questions started flying.

"What's Mac Williams like?"

"Will this affect my vacation time?"

"Are you taking any clients?"

Knox tried to answer as many as he could, but he kept an eye on the hall. He watched Isla head towards the elevator with her bag slung over her shoulder. He turned to Sue. "Take over."

He caught up to Isla as she was waiting for the elevator.

She heard him come up behind her; without looking, she hit the down button repeatedly, willing the elevator to come quicker. "You should have told me."

Knox put his hand on her shoulder, and she flinched and took a step away.

"I couldn't. I was going to tell you at lunch."

"Lunch? You should've told me sooner!" Her voice grew shrill, and tears began to fall.

The elevator door opened.

"Don't go. Let's go to my office and talk."

"How about you 'don't go'?" she spat back, walking into the elevator and slamming the 'close door' button hard.

The door shut, leaving Knox alone.

Later that evening, Knox arrived at his apartment, exhausted. He had been searching for Isla all day. She wasn't at the apartment she shared with Priya, or Emma's, or at her parents'. He checked her favourite coffee shops and restaurants. He even drove across town to check the art store. He had filled up her voicemail and sent multiple texts. He even texted her friends. Emma hadn't responded, and Priya simply texted back, *you're a dumbass.*

He should've known better than to expect Priya's help.

He unlocked his door and was surprised to see Isla's tote bag in the entrance. He walked into his bedroom and saw her sitting in front of her easel. She was chewing on the back of a paint brush and had some Payne's grey smeared on her left cheek. She didn't turn when she heard him enter the room.

"I've been looking everywhere for you," said Knox wearily.

Isla took the brush out of her mouth and pretended to concentrate on a fine detail.

"Not going to talk, huh?" He took off his tie and jacket, and sat on the bed across from her. "Are you willing to listen?"

She didn't respond.

"I'm sorry," he said. "Mac jumped the gun on the announcement; he wasn't going to say anything until tomorrow. I planned to tell you at lunch. I know that was a horrible way for you to find out."

Isla picked up her paint water and brushes and walked out of the room. She did not want to have this conversation. Knox followed her out of the room, into the kitchen where he filled two glasses with water, setting one next to her as she furiously cleaned her brushes. Tears pooled in the corners of her eyes.

"I don't want to go by myself." He leaned against the counter and watched her. Isla turned and glared at him, making eye contact for the first time. He gave her a hopeful smile. "Do you want to come with me?"

"Move to Vancouver? You want me to pack up my life, leave my friends, and my family? Priya is a mess! I can't leave her. Why can't you stay here? Why did you have to sell out to that stupid Calgary firm?"

"I came to Winnipeg to sell the business. That was the plan the whole time."

"You should've told me!"

"I told you many times that I planned to move back."

"You should've told me!" she shouted.

"I couldn't. You're an employee — we couldn't risk it getting out."

"I can keep a secret!"

"The partners made me promise," he said. "I am so sorry."

"I thought you liked it here."

"I do, but it's not my home. I need to be in Vancouver. My *business* is in Vancouver."

"This is *my* home! My whole life is here! Do you love your business more than me?" Isla spat out angrily.

"Don't make me choose, Isla," he said quietly. He turned and walked back to the bedroom. In that moment Isla understood. He would choose HRA. It was more than a job to him, more than a business — it was his only connection he had left to his father, to his family.

He returned holding a small box in his hand, and held it up to show her.

"What is that?"

"An engagement ring."

"Are you asking me to marry you?" Isla stammered.

"No—not yet," he replied with a small grin. "I want you to know how serious I am about us. I wouldn't ask you to leave your friends and family unless I thought we had a future together."

Stunned, Isla stared at the box in his hand, weighing the implications of his words. "Can I see it?"

As she reached toward the box, Knox lifted it out of her reach. "No! You'll have to wait until I actually ask you."

"Just a peek?" She jumped up and tried to bat it out of his outstretched hand. "Please?"

Shaking his head, he wrapped his other arm around her, trapping her against him.

He whispered in her ear, "Will you think about coming with me?"

"I wish you would've told me sooner."

"I know, I'm sorry."

"I'll think about it."

"Okay," he said, easing up on his grip.

She pulled away slightly. "Now can I see the ring?"

"No."

"Pretty please?"

"You're not going to change my mind."

"Boo."

"I love you." He kissed her forehead.

"What would I do in Vancouver?"

"I know a guy," Knox grinned.

"Ha."

"Actually, Adam has been threatening to offer you a job for months. And my condo has a second bedroom, maybe we could make it into a studio."

Isla pressed her face against his chest. She could hear his heartbeat and she knew. She knew what he had already figured out. Home was each other.

60.

July 17. Still hot and humid. 32C°.

Priya walked laps around the living room, back and forth on the old rainbow rug that she and Isla had found on the side of the road on Free Day. She fantasized about rolling it up and tossing it out the window, so its cheerfulness wouldn't mock her anymore. Twenty-two and a half hours until the meeting that would determine her future.

"Anywhere but here," she said out loud.

It was the end of an era. Isla was moving at the end of the month, to her new glamorous life in downtown Vancouver. Maybe she'd get a placement on the west coast?

Not likely.

She was expecting the reject placements no one else wanted, Thunder Bay or Red Deer, or even worse — Moose Jaw. She didn't care, as long as it was somewhere else.

What time was it? She checked again. Two-thirty.

It was always two-thirty when she thought of her mom. This time, she marched to her room and grabbed her sneakers and the keys to the ugly brown hatchback she seemed to inherit.

She drove past Bill and Dee's. Their house would always be a refuge, but it wasn't home. She turned down the next street and slowed. Like clockwork, her mother's car drove into the driveway, two forty-five.

Priya watched Jasminder climb out and lock the doors once with the remote.

Beep beep.

Then a second time, just in case.

Beep beep.

Jasminder entered the house without noticing the brown car parked two doors down.

This time, Priya didn't drive away like she had many times before. She took a deep breath, mustered all the courage she could, and walked to the front door.

Jasminder answered the timid knock, quickly suppressing any shock she felt at seeing her daughter on the top stair.

"Mama-ji," Priya said with a slight bow to her head. "I'm so sorry—"

Jasminder took in her daughter's slim figure and the dark circles under her eyes. Nothing needed explaining. She was brought right back to India. Right back to the day she and Hardeep had boarded the flight to Canada. They had planned for an uncomfortable flight with an infant; what they endured was emptiness.

Jasminder gathered her daughter in her arms and held her. Priya surrendered every last drop of resolve, sunk into her mother's embrace, and sobbed.

"She's gone, my baby is gone—"

"I know — I know." Jasminder rubbed her daughter's back.

"I don't know what to do."

"You survive." Jasminder guided Priya into the house.

"How?"

"You just do."

61.

August 2. 25C°.
1:23pm

Emma lifted the final pan from the breakfast and lunch dishes. She couldn't believe the freedom of leaving the breakfast dishes to wash with the lunch ones, especially on the days she went to work. Sometimes her mothers voice would intrude in her head *We show faithfulness to God by being diligent in our housework.* On those days, she'd pause and take ten long breaths and say *I am good inside,* just like Alice taught her. It stopped that panicked feeling, Emma couldn't believe how well it worked, instantly and almost magically.

Emma left her dishes to drip dry, while she glanced at her very long to-do list. She heard the garage door closing. She turned and was surprised to see Andrew walk in. "What are you doing here?"

"I took the afternoon off," he said, wrapping his arms around her from behind and burrowing his face into her curls. "You smell good."

"I think that's the curry squash soup I had for lunch." She giggled as he nibbled her ear.

"You smell good all the time," he whispered, sliding into the chair beside her. "How was work? How *are* you?"

346

Emma smiled, "really good actually, the more I settle in there the more I really like it. I like the work and the people." She paused as he reached for her hand. "I think I'm going to be okay, Andy. I think you can stop worrying that I'm fragile and going to break."

They had some version of this conversation regularly.

"I'm not going to stop checking in." said Andrew as he kissed the center of her palm. "I'm so proud of you Em. How long until Liam wakes up?"

"I just put him down—"

"—do you want to go upstairs?" said Andrew.

Emma hesitated; it was the middle of the afternoon, and she had so much left to do.

"I'll help later," Andrew murmured. "Come on, Emmy."

Emma felt a flush of excitement and daring. This all felt very improper. "Okay, but we should go down to the guestroom, so we don't wake him."

Andrew stopped in the doorway and kissed her with the same intensity and love that he felt when they first fell in love. He took her by the hand and led her down the stairs. For the first time in a long time, every part of her felt alive.

6:10pm

Isla opened the door, Priya and Emma stood with confused looks on their faces. "Why did we have to come in?" demanded Priya.

"We have to find the ring!" Isla said. "We have 20 minutes until our reservation; the three of us can cover the whole apartment. I've gone through most of the bedroom, just the closet is left. Emma, you start with the bookshelves and Priya, you search the kitchen. It's a blue velvet box."

"What's the end game here, Isla? What happens when we find it?" asked Priya.

"I get to see it."

"And then what?"

"If I like it, we put it back and go on with life."

"And if you hate it?" asked Priya.

"Then you two," she pointed at her friends, "apply pressure to see it, and then tell Knox you don't approve. He'll have to get something better."

"But what if it's his mom's ring?" asked Emma.

"Oh no! What if it *is* his mom's ring — and it's ugly?" Isla slid onto the sofa with her head in her hands. "I didn't even consider that."

"He has the best taste of any guy we know," reassured Emma.

"Yeah, because Max picks everything for him," replied Isla.

"Presumably she also had a hand in this," said Emma.

"I guess. Okay, less talking, more looking!" said Isla as she returned to her search in the bedroom.

"This is stupid," said Priya with her head in the lower corner cupboard.

Fifteen minutes later, the search came to an unsuccessful conclusion.

"I think he's smart enough not to hide it here," said Emma.

"I know, but I already searched his office and his car," said Isla. "Maybe Sam has it?"

"You have lost your fucking mind," said Priya. "Let. It. Go."

6:37pm

"She searched my office," said Knox, laughing. He was sitting at Andrew and Emma's kitchen island with Liam in his lap. Liam pushed his dump truck across the island to Sam, who caught it and pushed it back across to him.

"You don't know what you're getting yourself into. My sister is obsessive about gifts. She used to find all the Christmas gifts and tell me what I was getting even when I didn't want to know," said Andrew, grabbing ketchup and mustard out of the fridge and setting them on the counter. "She will not stop until she finds it."

"It's completely safe," said Sam, "in my sock drawer."

"Yes, but she'll try to weaponize Priya to gain access to it," explained Andrew.

"And I'm a sucker. If Priya ever showed up, I'd lead her right to it—"

"Well, Priya and Emma have both seen it," said Knox. "We don't need a repeat of the whole restaurant disaster."

"In my defence, that was your idea," stated Sam.

"Not *all* my idea—" said Knox, looking at Andrew.

"It was a bad group project," admitted Andrew.

"I can't believe Priya is leaving tomorrow," said Sam, placing his head in his hands. "And then you and Isla leave next week."

The truck zoomed back to Liam, who picked up and inexplicably smashed it against the counter with a loud growl. He zoomed it back to Sam with more force, and it bounced off Sam's distracted hand and smashed to the floor. Liam yelled, ending the melancholy they had fallen into.

"I'm sorry, buddy," said Sam gently, picking up the dump truck and sending it back to Liam.

"I'll go get the burgers," said Andrew.

9:53pm

"What are we doing?" asked Emma as Isla led them across the Esplanade Riel bridge, spanning the Red River.

"A ritual," Isla said, coming to a stop at the centre of the bridge.

"Oh god." Priya rolled her eyes.

Isla pulled a pocketknife out of her bag.

"A knife? Really, Isla?" asked Emma.

 Priya and Emma, as long as the sun and moon shall endure. Now you guys repeat."

"I solemnly swear to be faithful to my bosom friends, Priya and Isla, as long as the sun and moon shall endure," said Emma. Halfway through, tears started streaming down her face, causing Isla to tear up.

"You guys are ridiculous," said Priya.

"Your turn," said Emma.

Priya shook her head.

"*Say it,*" demanded Isla, laughing through her tears.

"Fine! I solemnly swear to be faithful to my bosom friends, Isla and Emma, as long as the sun—" Priya paused. She wiped her face quickly. "Fuck."

"—and moon shall endure," finished Isla, still laughing and crying. The three of them collapsed into a hug.

"What am I going to do without you guys?" Emma wiped her eyes. "It's weird to think that we're all going to make new friends and live lives apart from each other."

Priya was quiet. She didn't like very many people and wasn't looking forward to meeting new people.

Aug 3, early the next morning.

Sam had almost given up when the door opened and a dishevelled Priya stood in front of him, her arms crossed over her chest. "I haven't had coffee yet."

Sam kicked himself for not bringing coffee; he could've been a hero.

"I came to say good-bye," he stammered.

Priya stepped out into the warming morning air. "My parents will be here soon, and Knox and Andy are on their way."

"I know. I wanted to talk, just the two of us."

They stared at each other for a moment in silence.

"Nice beard," said Priya. He looked older, more distinguished. "It suits you."

Sam rubbed his chin. "It started out of laziness, but it's grown on me."

He smiled at his pun. Priya smirked, which relaxed into a smile.

"I brought you something." Sam handed her a gift bag.

Priya pulled out a stuffed tiger — the one she had picked out the day of the ultrasound.

"I tried to get rid of it, but I couldn't. It belongs to you. You are the tiger, Priya. Wild, free, focused, brilliant." He paused, not knowing how much more he should say. "I'm grateful I got to be a part of your life, even for a short time."

Priya held the tiger tight in her hands as he spoke. The grief that she had shoved down for weeks started to rise, and tears threatened at the edge of her eyes. She allowed him to pull her into his chest and to wrap his arms around her.

"Why are you like this? So sweet and thoughtful," she whispered. "It would be a lot easier if you hated me."

"I could never hate you," he said quietly. "We don't have to be love or hate; we can be friends."

"Friends," she repeated, pulling away as she heard a truck approach. "They're here. This means you'll have to help load the truck."

"Obviously," he said, turning to greet Hardeep and Jasminder.

They had the truck and the brown hatchback filled before ten. Priya said her final goodbyes to her friends and climbed into the car. The air was cranked high, Bluetooth speaker played music at top volume and a little stuffed tiger sat as her only passenger.

Saskatoon awaited. Onward.

62.

August 7. 23C°.

After so many difficult goodbyes, Isla spent the first forty-five minutes of their trip staring out the window, silent tears flowing down her face. Her sadness turned to exhaustion, and she curled her legs up under herself and fell asleep with her head against the window.

Knox drove in the quiet, the sun behind him, slowly rising higher in the sky as they headed west. The back seat and trunk were full of boxes and bags, as many as they could cram in. Their remaining possessions were left with Isla's parents to ship later.

They had a full two days of driving ahead of them before they were to meet Graham, Max and Violet at the cabin for a little vacation.

Before the start of everything new.

This was not how he had expected to leave. He didn't expect to feel like a different person, or that he would have a person to accompany him back to Vancouver. Today he enjoyed the expansive sky; the emptiness of it didn't seem as empty anymore. He saw the potential there: space to breathe, move, and grow. He looked forward to getting back to the mountains, but he worried that Isla would find them claustrophobic. She assured him she would go to the beach when she needed to see the sky.

He patted his pocket. He'd let her sleep a little longer.

Isla woke slowly, her neck cricked and her foot asleep. She unfolded herself into a proper seated position and asked, "where are we?"

"We just crossed into Saskatchewan," Knox replied. "Did you have a good sleep?"

"Yeah." She shook the doziness from her brain, taking a sip from the travel mug next to her. "Only eleven more hours."

The road opened to a long straight section; the fields of ripening grain waved in the breeze. Knox used his long legs to steer, and reached for Isla's left hand with his right. He held it for a while as she looked out the window at the farmyard in the distance.

What kind of family lived there? she wondered.

With his left hand he slipped a ring on her fourth finger, keeping it covered with his right. He asked, "You do want to marry me, right?"

Isla tried to pull her hand away, desperate to finally see the elusive ring. But he held on tight, still flying down the highway.

"You have to answer first," he teased.

"*Yes!*" she shouted, trying to wrestle her hand free.

"Great!" he said, grinning and holding on tight.

"Are you kidding me, Harrison? Let me see it!"

Knox laughed and lifted her hand to his mouth, giving it an exaggerated kiss as she groaned impatiently.

"I have to tell you a story about the ring, first," he said. "It's my mom's. But it's not her wedding ring — Violet gets that one. I think this one suits you better, anyway. It's her twenty-first anniversary ring."

"Twenty-first anniversary?"

"My Dad bought her a vacuum for their twentieth anniversary. He swore that it was what she wanted. It was *not*. So, she saved money by pilfering cash out of his wallet until she had enough to order a ring. She had it custom made. Then, when it was ready, she just started wearing it and waited for him to notice. He didn't. It took weeks! One day at supper, she noticed the sunshine in the window; all through supper she angled the ring so it would shine in his eyes.

Iris!

Darling?

Your ring is blinding me.

That reminds me, I wanted to thank you for the early anniversary gift.

"Dad was speechless; it was so out of character for her. She was naturally agreeable and accommodating. He learned his lesson, though. I think she got jewelry every year after that. I thought a piece of jewelry created out of a spirit of independence and rebellion would be a good fit for the beginning of our life together."

With that he let go of her hand.

And the ring, it was beautiful.

Acknowledgments

Thank you to the FriesenPress team, for help with editing and publishing.

Thank you to Alexa Dirks (Begonia) and the New Lightweights for permission to use their song lyric as my title. The full lyric is "there are thirty ways to make a scene, it seems twenty is all I got, so play on" It has inspired this story from the beginning. It is from the song 'play on' on the album What Keeps Us Together.

Thank you to Heather G, Elyssa, and Heather H for being my first readers and for encouraging (and fixing) this story even though the spelling and typos were horrendous.

Thank you to Jaswinder Singh for his thoughts and insights into the more traditional Sikh characters.

Thank you to Raveet Dev for her thoughts and insights into the more modern Sikh characters (and thanks for the Gen Z approval, I didn't realise how important that was to me until you said it!).

Love to my family: will we ever have a conversation not about politics, or religion? Love to my in-laws: who have always accepted me no matter how loud, weird, and awkward I am.

Laura, Karla, Heather G, Luanne, Christina, Heather H: I solemnly swear to be faithful to you my bosom friends, as long as the sun and moon shall endure. This book wouldn't have been written with out your love and friendship. (Sheldon, Brad, Wes, Tom, Casey and Matt, thanks for putting up with us.)

R, D, And Z, I love you, you crack me up, and can we play uno tonight?

Ben, you are the banks to my river, and still give me butterflies.

Printed in Canada